Now, toge ... pping short stories fr ... wrote the classic *A* ...

* *Conditionally Human*, in which a space-age "dog-catcher" learns a sobering lesson.

* *Blood Bank*, in which a space commander becomes an outcast after he destroys a medical-supply ship.

* *Dark Benediction*, in which a plague which turns skin brown is the next stage of evolution . . .

Also by Walter M. Miller Jr.

A CANTICAL FOR LEIBOWITZ
THE DARFSTELLER AND OTHER STORIES

and published by Corgi Books

CONDITIONALLY HUMAN AND OTHER STORIES

WALTER M. MILLER JR.

CORGI BOOKS
A DIVISION OF TRANSWORLD PUBLISHERS LTD

CONDITIONALLY HUMAN AND OTHER STORIES
A CORGI BOOK 0 552 11991 1

First publication in Great Britain

PRINTING HISTORY
Corgi edition published 1982

This book is set in 9½ pt. Times Roman

Corgi Books are published by Transworld Publishers Ltd.,
Century House, 61–63 Uxbridge Road,
Ealing, London, W5 5SA

Printed in Great Britain by
Hunt Barnard Printing Ltd., Aylesbury, Bucks

CONTENTS

CONDITIONALLY HUMAN

He knew there was no use hanging around after breakfast, but he could not bear leaving her like this. He put on his coat in the kitchen, stood uncertainly in the doorway, and twisted his hat in his hands. His wife still sat at the table, fingered the handle of an empty cup, stared fixedly out the window at the kennels behind the house, and pointedly ignored his small coughings and scrapings. He watched the set of her jaw for a moment, then cleared his throat.

'Anne?'

'What?'

'I can't stand seeing you like this.'

'Then go away.'

'Can't I do anything—?'

'I've told you what to do.'

Her voice was a monotone, full of hurt. He could neither endure the hurt nor remove it. He gingerly crossed the room to stand behind her, hoping she'd look up at him and let her face go soft, maybe even cry a little. But she kept gazing out the window in accusing silence. He chuckled suddenly and touched her silk-clad shoulder. The shoulder shivered away. Her dark hair quivered as she shuddered, and her arms were suddenly locked tightly about her breasts as if she were cold. He pulled back his hand; his big pliant face went slack. He gulped forlornly.

'Honeymoon's over, huh?'

'Ha!'

He backed a step away, paused again. 'Hey, baby, you knew before you married me,' he reminded her.

'I did not.'

'You knew I was District Inspector for the F. B. A. You knew I had charge of a pound.'

'I didn't know you *killed* them,' she snapped, whirling.

'I don't have to kill many,' he offered.

'That's like saying you don't kill them very dead.'

'Look, honey, they're only animals.'

'*Intelligent* animals!'

'Intelligent as a human imbecile, maybe.'

'A baby is an imbecile. Would you kill a baby? Of course you would! You do! That's what they are: babies. I hate you.'

He withered, groped desperately for a new approach. 'Look, "intelligence" is a word applicable only to humans. It's the name of a human function, and . . .'

'And that makes *them* human!' she finished. 'Murderer!'

'Baby!'

'Don't call me baby! Call them baby!'

He made a miserable noise in his throat, backed a few steps toward the door, and beat down his better judgment against speaking again. 'Anne, honey, look! Think of the good things about the job. Sure, everything has its ugly angle. But just think: we get this house rent-free; I've got my own district with no local boss to hound us; I make my own hours; you'll meet lots of people that stop in at the pound. It's a fine job, honey!'

Her face was a mask again. She sipped her coffee and seemed to be listening. He blundered hopefully on.

'And what can I do about it? I can't help my Placement Aptitude score. They say Bio-Authority is where I belong, and it's to Bio I have to go. Oh, sure, I don't *have* to work where they send me. You can always join the General Work Pool, but that's all the law allows, and GWP'ers don't have families. So I go where Placement Aptitude says I'm needed.'

'You've got aptitudes for killing kids?'

He groaned and closed his eyes. 'They gave me the job because I like kids. And because I have a biology degree, and a knack for being neighborly, maybe—with plain people. And because I'm not really brainy enough to be a scientists' scientist. Just a technician. Understand? And destroying the unclaimed animals is the smallest part of it. Honey, before the evolvotron, before anybody ever heard of Anthropos Incorporated, people used to have municipal officials for such things. Dogcatchers, I think they called them. Didn't have the Dog-R series then, of course—not mutants. But that's all it is. I'm just an up-to-date dogcatcher.'

Ice-green eyes turned slowly to meet his gaze. Her face by window-light seemed delicately cut from dusty marble. A corner of her mouth twitched contempt. Then she looked out the window toward the kennels again.

He backed to the door, plucked nervously at a splinter on the woodwork, watched her hopefully for a moment.

'Work to do. Got to go.'

'Do you need to be kissed?' Sweetly contemptuous.

He ripped the splinter loose. 'See you tonight.'

The front door slammed. She sat listening to his footsteps on the porch and down the walk. Then the kennel truck's starter grumbled, and its turbines whined to life. She choked back a sob and started after him, but by the time she got to the porch, the truck was already backed into the street. It lurched suddenly away with angry acceleration toward the highway that lay to the east. She stood blinking in the red morning sunlight, shoulders slumped. Things were wrong with the world.

A bell rang somewhere, rang again. She started slightly, shook herself, went to answer the telephone. A carefully enunciated voice that sounded chubby and professional called for Inspector Norris. She told it disconsolately that he was gone.

'Gone? Oh, you mean to work. I thought for a moment you meant . . . heh heh. Can this be the new Mrs. Norris?' The voice was hearty, greasy. She muttered affirmatively.

'Ah, yes. Norris told me. Ah, this is Doctor Georges, my dear. I have a rather urgent matter to talk over with your husband, but perhaps I can talk to you.'

'You can probably get him on the highway. There's a phone in the truck.' What sort of urgent matters, she wondered, did doctors discuss with dogcatchers.

'I'm afraid not, my dear. The inspector doesn't switch on his phone until office hours. I know him well.'

'Can't you wait?'

'It's really an emergency, Mrs. Norris. I need an animal from the pound—a Chimp K-48-3, preferably a five-year-old.'

'I know nothing about the kennels,' she said rather stiffly. 'You'll have to talk to him.'

'Now see here, Mrs. Norris, this is an emergency, and I have to have . . .'

'Why don't you just do whatever you would have done if I hadn't answered the phone?' she said, and quietly hung up.

It began ringing again. She glanced back at it with a twinge of guilt. Emergency? What sort of emergency would require a chimp K-48? 'Butchery,' she muttered vaguely, and let the phone ring. She was not not *not* going to get involved in his work. I'll leave him first, she told herself.

The truck whirred slowly along the suburban street that wound among nestled groups of pastel plastic cottages set approximately two to an acre on the lightly wooded land. With its population fixed by law at half a billion, the continent was one sprawling suburb, dotted with community centers, between the dense belts and blots of industrial development. There was no open country, had been none since the days of his grandparents. This was relative wilderness; he liked it, but there was still no place to be alone.

He approached an intersection. A small animal sat on the curb, wrapped in its own busy tail. The crown of its oversized head was bald, but its body was covered with gray-blue fur. A pink tongue licked daintily at small forepaws that were equipped with prehensile thumbs. It eyed the truck morosely as Norris drew to a halt and smiled down at it from the cab.

'Hi, kitten. What's *your* name?'

The Cat-Q-5 stared at him indifferently for a moment. *'Kiyi Rorry,'* it wailed at last.

'Kitty Rorry. That's a fine name. Where do you live, Rorry?'

The Cat-Q-5 ignored him.

'Whose child are you, Rorry? Will you tell me that?'

Rorry regarded him disgustedly. Norris glanced around. There were no houses near the intersection, and he feared the animal might be lost. It blinked at him sleepily, bored, then resumed its paw bath. He repeated the question.

'Mama kiyi, kiyi Mama,' it finally reported.

'That's right, Mama's kitty. But where is Mama? Suppose she ran away?'

The Cat-Q-5 looked startled. It stuttered briefly. Its fur crept erect. It glanced both ways along the street, shot suddenly away at a fast scamper along the sidewalk. Norris followed it in the truck for two blocks, until it darted onto a porch and began wailing through the screen. 'Mama no run ray! Mama no run ray!'

He chuckled and drove on. A couple who had failed to satisfy the genetic requirements for legal childbearing could become quite attached to a Cat-Q-5, but the cats were safer, emotionally safer, than any of the quasi-human models such as the Chimp-K, or neutroid. The death of a neutroid struck some families as hard as might the death of a child; most couples at least managed to endure the loss of a Cat-Q or Dog-F without formal mourning or quasi-religious rites. A genetic-C couple were permitted to own one neutroid, or two nonanthropic models whose daily food requirements would not exceed eight hundred calories. Many psychologists seemed to regard neutroids as dynamite, recommended pets with a lower love-demand potential.

What about Anne? Norris lost his vestigial smile. His own card was stamped 'genetic-C.' They had agreed to a childless marriage. Anne loved kids. But he had agreed to it. He had been thinking about the kennel animals: how she might help with them, direct her maternal feelings toward them, divert her basic need . . . But now, the hostility.

What if she wanted a pseudoparty, a neutroid for herself?

An invitation of a pseudoparty had come in yesterday's mail. He fumbled in his pocket for the battered card:

You are cordially invited
to attend the pseudoparturition
and ensuing cocktail hour
to celebrate the arrival of
HONEY BLOSSOM
Cherished event to occur on
Twelveweek's Sixday of 2063 at
19:30 hours
Reception Room, Rockabye Hours Clinic
R.s.v.p. Mr. & Mrs. John Hanley Slade

The invitation had come late, the party would be tonight. He had meant to call Slade today and say that he and Anne would probably drop in for cocktails, but would be unable to get there in time for the delivery. But now that she had reacted so sharply to the less pleasant aspects of his job, perhaps he had better keep her away from sentimental occasions involving neutroids.

Glancing at the card again reminded him to stop at Sherman III Community Center for the mail. He turned onto the shopping street that paralleled the great highway and drove past several blocks of commercial buildings that served the surrounding suburbs. At the down-ramp he gave the attendant a four-bit bill and sent the truck down to be parked under the street, then went to the message office. When he dropped his code-disk into the slot, the feedway under his box number chattered out a yard of paper tape. He scanned it slowly end to end—note from Aunt Maye, bill from Synthamilk Products, letter from Anne's mother. The only item of importance was the memo from the chief: a troublesome tidbit, but he had expected it:

Attention All District Inspectors: Subject? Deviant Neutroid. You will immediately initiate systematic and thorough survey of all animals bearing serial numbers in the Bermuda K-99 series for birth dates during 26th through 32nd weeks of year 2062, in re Delmont Negligency Case. Seize animals in this category, impound, run applicable sections of normalcy tests. Observe signs of endocrinal deviation and nonstandard response patterns. Delmont confessed to passing only one nonstandard model, but suspect others. He disclaims memory of deviant's serial number. Possible ruse to stop investigation after first animal found, if more than one.
If allowed to reach age-set or adulthood, such a deviant could be dangerous to its owner or to others. Hold all seized K-99s who exhibit the slightest departure from standard. Forward to Central Lab. Return standard units to owners. Accomplish within seven days.

C. Franklin.

'Seven days,' he remarked irritably, wadded the tape in his pocket, stalked out to get the truck.

The district covered two hundred square miles. With a replacement quota of seventy-five neutroids a week, the district would probably have picked up about forty K-99s from the Bermuda factory influx during the six-week period last year. Could he round them all up in a week? It seemed doubtful. And there were only eleven empty cages in the kennel. The other forty-nine were occupied by the previous inspector's unclaimed inventory, awaiting destruction. The crematorium behind the kennels appeared slated for a busy week. Anne, Anne.

He was halfway to Wylo City when the radiophone buzzed on the dash. He pulled into the slow lane and answered quickly, hoping for his wife's voice. Instead, there was a polite professional purr.

'Inspector Norris?'

Norris made a sour mouth. 'Yes, Georges?'

'Are you extremely busy at the moment?'

'What rich bitch is your problem now, Doctor?'

'Now Norris!'

'Busy. Extremely busy.'

'One of my patients, a Mrs. Sarah Glubbes, called a while ago and said her baby was sick.'

'So?'

'She has no baby. I'm getting absent-minded: I forgot she's genetic-C until I got there.'

'Let me guess. It turned out to be a neutroid.'

'That's right.'

'Why tell me?'

'It's dying. Eighteenth order virus. Naturally, I can't get it admitted to a hospital.'

'Ever hear of vets?'

'You don't understand. She insists it's her baby, believes it's her own. How can I send it to a vet?'

'That's your worry. Is she an old patient of yours?'

'Why, yes, I've known Sarah since—'

'Since you presided at her pseudopart?'

'How did you know?'

'Just a guess. If you put her through pseudopart, then you deserve all the trouble you get.'

'I take it you're an abolitionist.'

'Skip it. What did you want from me?'

'A replacement neutroid. From the kennel.'

'Baloney. You couldn't fool her. If she's blind, she'd still know her own animal.'

'I'll have to take the chance. Listen, Norris, it's pathetic. She knows the disease can be cured—in humans—with hospitalization and expensive treatment that I can't get for a neutroid. No vet could get the drug either. Scarce. It's pathetic.'

'I'm crying all over the steering wheel.'

The doctor paused. 'Sorry, Norris, I thought you were human.'

'Not to the extent of doing half-legal favors that won't be appreciated for some rich neurotic dame and a doc who practices pseudopart.'

'One correction,' Georges said stiffly. 'Sarah's not rich. She's a middle-aged widow and couldn't pay for treatment if she could get it. But thanks anyway, Norris.'

'Hold it,' he grunted. 'What's the chimp's series?'

'It's a K-48, a five-year-old with a three-year age-set.'

Norris thought for a moment. It was a dirty deal, and it wouldn't work.

'I think I've got one in the kennel that's fairly close,' he offered doubtfully.

‘Good, good, I’ll have Fred go over and—’

‘Wait, now. This one’ll be spooky, won’t know her, and the serial number will be different.’

‘I know, I know,’ Georges sighed. ‘But it seems worth a try. An attack of V-18 can cause mild amnesia in humans; that might explain why it won’t know her. About the serial number—’

‘Don’t try changing it,’ Norris growled.

‘How about obliterating—’

‘Don’t, and I’ll check on it a couple of weeks from now to make damn sure you don’t. That’s a felony, Georges.’

‘All right, all right, I’ll just have to take the chance that she won’t notice it. When can I pick it up?’

‘Call my wife in fifteen minutes. I’ll speak to her first.’

‘Uh, yes . . . Mrs. Norris. Uh, very well, thanks, Inspector.’ Georges hung up quickly.

Norris lit a cigarette, steeled himself, called Anne. Her voice was dull, depressed, but no longer angry.

‘All right, Terry,’ she said tonelessly. ‘I’ll go out to the kennel and get the one in cage thirty-one, and give it to Georges when he comes.’

‘Thanks, babe.’

He heard her mutter, ‘And then I’ll go take a bath,’ just before the circuit clicked off.

He flipped off the auto-driver, took control of the truck, slipped into the fast lane and drove furiously toward Wylo City and the district wholesale offices of Anthropos Incorporated to begin tracing down the suspected Bermuda K-99s in accordance with Franklin’s memo. He would have to check through all incoming model files for the six-week period, go over the present inventory, then run down the Bermuda serial numbers in a mountain of invoices covering a thirty-week period, find the pet shops and retail dealers that had taken the doubtful models, and finally survey the retail dealers to trace the models to their present owners. With cooperation from wholesaler and dealers, he might get it down to the retail level by mid-afternoon, but getting the models away from their owners would be the nasty part of the job. He was feeling pretty nasty himself, he decided. The spat with Anne, the distasteful thoughts associated with Slade’s pseudoparty, the gnawing remorse about collaborating with Dr. Georges in a doubtful maneuver to pacify one Sarah Glubbes, a grim week’s work ahead, plus his usual charge of suppressed resentment toward Chief Franklin—it all added up to a mood that could turn either black or vicious, depending on circumstance.

If some doting Mama gave him trouble about impounding her darling tail-wagger, he was, he decided, in the right kind of mood to get a warrant and turn the job over to the sheriff.

The gasping neutroid lay on the examining table under the glaring light. The torso quivered and twitched as muscles contracted spasmodically, but the short legs were already limp and paralyzed, allowing the chubby man in the white coat to lift them easily by the ankles and retrieve the rectal thermometer. The neutroid wheezed and chattered plaintively as the nurse drew the blanket across its small body again.

'A hundred and nine,' grunted the chubby man, his voice muffled by the gauze mask. His eyes probed the nurse's eyes for a moment. He jerked his head toward the door. 'She still out there?'

The nurse nodded.

The doctor stared absently at the thermometer stem for a moment, looked up again, spoke quietly. 'Get a hypo—necrofine.'

She turned toward the sterilizer, paused briefly. 'Three c.c.s?' she asked.

'Twelve,' he corrected.

Her eyes locked with his for several seconds; then she nodded and went to the sterilizer.

'May I leave first?' she asked tonelessly while filling the syringe.

'Certainly.'

'What'll I say to Mrs. Glubbes?' She crossed to the table again and handed him the hypo.

'Nothing. Use the back way. Go tell Fred to run over to the kennels and pick up the substitute. I've called Mrs. Norris. Oh yeah, and tell Fred to stop in here first. I'll have something for him to take out.'

The nurse glanced down at the squirming, whimpering newt, shivered slightly, and left the room. When the door closed, Georges bent over the table with the hypo. When the door opened again, Georges looked up to see his son looking in.

'Take this along,' he grunted, and handed Fred the bundle wrapped in newspapers.

'What'll I do with it?' the youth asked.

'Chuck it in Norris's incinerator.'

Fred glanced at the empty examining table and nodded indifferently. 'Can Miss Laskell come back now?' he asked in going.

'Tell her yeah. And hurry with that other newt.'

'Sure, Pop. See you later.'

The nurse looked in uncertainly before entering.

'Get cleaned up,' he told her. 'And go sit with Mrs. Glubbes.'

'What'll I say?'

'The "baby" will recover. She can take it home late this afternoon if she gets some rest first.'

'What're you going to do—about the substitute?'

'Give it a shot to put it to sleep, give her some codeine to feed it.'

'Why?'

'So it'll be too groggy for a few days to even notice her, so it'll get addicted and attached to her because she gives it the codeine.'

'The serial number?'

'I'll put the tattooed foot in a cast. V-18 paralysis—you know.'

'Smart,' she muttered, but there was no approval in her voice.

When she had changed clothes in the anteroom, she unlocked the door to the office, but paused before passing on into the reception room. The door was ajar, and she gazed through the crack at the woman who sat on the sofa.

Sarah Glubbes was gray and gaunt and rigid as stone. She sat with her hands clenched in her lap, her wide empty eyes—dull blue spots on yellowed marble orbs—staring ceilingward while the colorless lips of a knife-slash mouth moved tautly in earnest prayer. The nurse's throat felt tight. She rubbed it for a moment. After all, the thing was only an animal.

She straightened her shoulders, put on a cheerful smile, and marched on into the reception room. The yellowed orbs snapped demandingly toward her.

'Everything's *all* right, Mrs. Glubbes,' she began.

'Finished,' Norris grunted at three o'clock that afternoon.

'Thirty-six K-99s,' murmured the Anthropos file-clerk, gazing over Norris's shoulder at the clip-board with the list of doubtful newts and the dealers to whom they had been sent. 'Lots of owners may be hard to locate.'

'Yeah. Thanks, Andy, and you too Mabel.'

The girl smiled and handed him a slip of paper. 'Here's a list of owners for thirteen of them. I called the two local shops for you. Most of them live here close.'

He glanced at the names, felt tension gathering in his stomach. It wasn't going to be easy. What could he say to them?

Howdy, ma'am, excuse me, but I've come to take your little boy away to jail. . . . Oh, yes ma'am, he'll have a place to stay —in a little steel cage with a forkful of straw, and he'll get vitaminized mush every day. What's that? His sleepy-time stories and his pink honey-crumbles? Sorry, ma'am, your little boy is only a mutated chimpanzee, you know, and not really human at all.

'That'll go over great,' he grumbled, staring absently at the window.

'Beg pardon, sir?' answered the clerk.

'Nothing, Andy, nothing.' He thanked them again and strode out into the late afternoon sunlight. Still a couple of hours working time left, and plenty of things to do. Checking with the other retail dealers would be the least unpleasant task, but there was no use saving the worst until last. He glanced at the list Mabel had given him, checked it for the nearest address, then squared his shoulders and headed for the kennel truck.

Anne met him at the door when he came home at six. He stood on the porch for a moment, smiling at her weakly. The smile was not returned.

'Doctor Georges' boy came,' she told him. 'He signed for the—'

She stopped to stare at him, then opened the screen, reached up quickly to brush light fingertips over his cheek.

'*Terry!* Those welts! What happened—get scratched by a Cat-Q?'

'No, by a human-F,' he grumbled, and stepped past her into the hall; Anne followed, eyeing him curiously while he reached for the phone and dialed.

'Who're you calling?' she asked.

'Society's watchdog,' he answered as the receiver buzzed in his ear.

'Your eye, Terry—it's all puffy. Will it turn black?'

'Maybe.'

'Did the human-F do that too?'

'Uh-uh. Human-M—name of Pete Klusky . . .'

The phone craked at him suddenly. *'This is the record-voice of Sheriff Yates. I'll be out from five to seven. If it's urgent, call your constable.*'

He hung up briefly, then irritably dialed the locator service.

'*Mnemonic register, trail calls, and official locations,*' grated a mechanical voice. '*Your business, please.*'

'This is T. Norris, Sherman-9-4566-78B, Official rating B, Priority B, code XT-88-U-Bio. Get Sheriff Yates for me.'

'*Nature of the call?*'

'Offish biz.'

'*I shall record the call.*'

He waited. The robot found Yates on the first probability-trial attempt—in the local poolhall.

'I'm getting to hate that infernal gadget,' Yates snapped. 'Acts like it's got me psyched. Whattaya want, Norris?'

'Cooperation. I'm mailing you three letters charging three Wylo citizens with resisting a federal official—namely me—and charging one of them with assault. I tried to pick up their neutroids for a pound inspection, and—'

Yates bellowed lusty laughter in his ear.

'Not funny,' he growled. 'I've got to get those neutroids. It's connected with the Delmont case.'

Yates stopped laughing. 'Oh? Well . . . I'll take care of it.'

'Rush order, Sheriff. Can you get the warrants tonight and pick up the animals in the morning?'

'Easy on those warrants, boy. Judge Charleman can't be bothered just any time. I can get the newts to you by noon, I guess, provided we don't have to get a helicopter posse to chase down the mothers.'

'Well, okay. But listen—I want the charges dropped if they cooperate with you. And don't shake the warrants at them unless you have to. Just get those newts, that's all I want.'

'Okay, boy. Give me the dope.'

Norris read him the names and addresses of the three unwilling owners, and a precise account of what happened in each case. As soon as he hung up, Anne muttered 'Sit still,' perched on his knees, and began stroking chilly ointment across his burning cheek. He watched her cool eyes flicker from his cheek to his own eyes and down again. She was no longer angry, but only gloomy and withdrawn from him. He touched her arm. She seemed not to notice it.

'Hard day, Terry?'

'Slightly. I picked up nine newts out of thirteen, anyhow. They're in the truck now.'

'Good thing you didn't get them all. There are only twelve empty cages.'

'Twelve? Oh, Georges picked one up, didn't he?'

'And sent a package,' she said, eyeing him soberly.

'Package? Where is it?'

'In the crematorium. The boy took it back there.'

He swallowed a tight spot in his throat, said nothing.

'Oh, and darling—Mrs. Slade called. Why didn't you tell me we're going out tonight?'

'Going out?' It sounded a little weak.

'Well, she said she hadn't heard from you. I couldn't very well say no, so I told her *I'd* be there, at least.'

'You—?'

'Oh, I didn't say about you, Terry. I said you'd like to go, but you might have to work. I'll go alone if you don't want to.'

He stared at her with a puzzled frown. '*You* want to go to the pseudoparty?'

'Not particularly. But I've never been to one. I'm just curious.'

He nodded, slowly, felt grim inside. She finished with the ointment, patted his cheek, managed a cheerful smile.

'Come on, Terry. Let's go unload your nine neutroids.'

He stared at her dumbly.

'Let's forget about this morning, Terry.'

He nodded. She averted her face suddenly, and her lips quivered. 'I—I know you've got a job that's got to be—' She swallowed hard and turned away. 'See you out in the kennels,' she choked gaily, then hurried down the hall toward the door. Norris scratched his chin unhappily as he watched her go.

After a moment, he dialed the mnemonic register again. 'Keep a line on this number,' he ordered after identifying himself. 'If Yates or Franklin calls, ring continuously until I can get in to answer. Otherwise, just memorize the call.'

'Instructions acknowledged,' answered the circuitry.

He went out to the kennels to help Anne unload the neutroids.

A sprawling concrete barn housed the cages, and the barn was sectioned into three large rooms, one housing the fragile, humanoid chimpanzee-mutants, and another for the lesser breeds such as Cat-Qs, Dog-Fs, dwarf bears, and foot-high lambs that never matured into sheep. The third room contained a small gas chamber, with a conveyor belt leading from it to the crematorium. He usually kept the third room locked, but he noticed in passing that it was open. Evidently Anne had found the keys in order to let Fred Georges dump his package.

A Noah's Ark chorus greeted him as he passed through the animal room, to be replaced by the mindless chatter of the doll-like neutroids as soon as he entered the air conditioned neutroid section. Dozens of blazing blond heads began dancing about their cages. Their bodies thwacked against the wire mesh as they leaped about their compartments with monkey grace, in recognition of their feeder and keeper.

Their human appearance was broken only by two distinct features: short beaver-like tails decorated with fluffy curls of fur, and an erect thatch of scalp hair that grew up into a bright candle-flame. Otherwise, they appeared completely human, with baby-pink skin, quick little smiles, and cherubic faces. They were sexually neuter and never grew beyond a predetermined age-set which varied for each series. Age-sets were available from one to ten years, human equivalent. Once a neutroid reached its age-set, it remained at this stage of retarded development until death.

'They must be getting to know you pretty well,' Anne said as she came from behind a section of cages. 'A big loud welcome for Pappa, huh?'

He frowned slightly as he glanced around the gloomy room and sniffed the animal odors. 'That's funny. They don't usually get this excited.'

She grinned. 'Big confession: it started when *I* came in.'

He shot her a quick suspicious glance, then walked slowly along a row of cages, peering inside. He stopped suddenly beside a three-year-old K-76 to stare.

'Apple cores!'

He turned slowly to face his wife, trying to swallow a sudden spurt of anger.

'Well?' he demanded.

Anne reddened. 'I felt sorry for them, eating that goo from the mechanical feeders. So I drove down to Sherman III and bought six dozen cooking apples.'

'That was a mistake.'

She frowned irritably. 'We can afford it.'

'That's not the point. There's a reason for mechanical feedings.'

'Oh? What is it?'

He hesitated, knowing she wouldn't like the answer. But she was already stiffening.

'Let me guess,' she said coldly. 'If you feed them yourself they get to love you. Right?'

'Uh, yeah. They even attach some affection to me because they know that right after I come in, the feeders get turned on.'

'I see. And if they love you, you might get queasy about running them through Room 3's line, eh?'

'That's about the size of it,' he admitted.

'Okay, Terry, I feed them apples, you run your production line,' she announced firmly. 'I can't see anything contradictory about that, can you?'

Her eyes told him that he had damn well better see something contradictory about it, whether he admitted it or not.

'Planning to get real chummy with them, are you?' he inquired stiffly.

'Planning to dispose of any soon?' she countered.

'Honeymoon's off again, eh?'

She shook her head slowly, came toward him a little, 'I hope not, Terry—I hope not.' She stopped again. They watched each other doubtfully amid the chatter of the neutroids.

After a time, he turned and walked to the truck, pulled out the snare pole and began fishing for the squealing, squeaking doll-things that bounded about like frightened monkeys in the truck's wire mesh cage. They were one-family pets, always frightened of strangers, and these in the truck remembered him only as the villain who had dragged them away from Mama into a terrifying world of whirling scenery and roaring traffic.

They worked for a time without talking; then Anne asked casually: 'What's the Delmont case, Terry?'

'Huh? What makes you ask?'

'I heard you mention it on the phone. Anything to do with a black eye and a scratched face?'

He nodded sourly. 'Indirectly. It's a long story. Well—you know about the evolvotron.'

'Only that Anthropos Incorporated uses it to induce mutation.'

'It's sort of a sub-atomic surgical instrument—for doing "plastic surgery" to reproductive cells— Here! Grab this chimp! Get him by the leg.'

'Oops! Got him. . . . Go ahead, Terry.'

'Using an evolvotron on the gene-structure of an ovum is like playing microscopic billiards—with protons and deuterons and alpha particles for cue balls. The operator takes the living ovum, mounts it in the device, gets a tremendously magnified image of it with the slow-neutrino shadowscope, compares the image with a gene-map, starts gouging out sub-molecular tidbits with single-particle shots. He juggles them around, hammers chunks in where nothing was before, plugs up gaps, makes new gaps. Catch?'

She looked thoughtful, nodded. 'Catch. And the Lord Man made neutroid from the slime of an ape,' she murmured.

'Heh? Here, catch this critter! Snare's choking him!'

'Okay—come to Mama. . . . Well, go on, tell me about Delmont.'

'Delmont was a green evolvotron operator. Takes years of training, months of practice.'

'Practice?'

'It's an art more than a science. Speed's the thing. You've got to perform the whole operation from start to finish in a few seconds. Ovum dies if you take too long.'

'About Delmont—'

'Got through training and practice tryouts okay. Good rating, in fact. But he was just one of those people that blow up when rehearsals stop and the act begins. He spoiled over a hundred ova the first week. That's to be expected. One success out of ten tries is a good average. But he didn't get any successes.'

'Why didn't they fire him?'

'Threatened to. Guess he got hysterical. Anyhow, he reported one success the next day. It was faked. The ovum had a couple of flaws—something wrong in the nervous system's determinants, and in the endocrinal set-up. Not a standard neutroid ovum. He passed it on to the incubators to get a credit, knowing it wouldn't be caught until after birth.'

'It wasn't caught at all?'

'Heh. He was afraid it might *not* be caught. So he suppressed the testosterone flow to its incubator so that it *would* be—later on.'

'Why that?'

'All the neutroids are potential females, you know. But male hormone is pumped to the foetus as it develops. Keeps female sexuality from developing, results in a neuter. He decided that the inspectors would surely catch a female, and that would be blamed on a malfunction of the incubator, not on him.'

'So?'

Norris shrugged. 'So inspectors are human. So maybe a guy came on the job with a hangover and missed a trick or two. Besides, they all *look* female. Anyhow, she didn't get caught.'

'How did they ever find out Delmont did it?'

'He got caught last month—trying it again. Confessed to doing it once before. No telling how many times he *really* did it.'

Norris held up the final kicking, squealing, tassel-haired doll from the back of the kennel truck. He grinned down at Anne.

'Now take this little yeep, for instance. Might be a potential she. Might also be a potential murderer. *All* these kiddos from the truck came from the machines in the section where Delmont worked last year when he passed that fake. Can't have nonstandard models on the loose. Can't have sexed models either—then they'd breed, get out of hand. The evolvotron could be shut down any time it became necessary, and when that generation of mutants died off . . .' He shrugged.

Anne caught the struggling baby-creature in her arms. It struggled and tried to bite, but subsided a little when she disentangled it from the snare.

'Kkr-r-reeee!' it cooed nervously. 'Kree. Kkr-r-reee!'

'You tell him you're no murderer,' she purred to it.

He watched disapprovingly while she fondled it. One code he had accepted: steer clear of emotional attachment. It was eight months old and looked like a child of two years—a year short of its age-set. And it was designed to be as affectionate as a human child.

'Put it in the cage, Anne,' he said quietly.

She looked up and shook her head.

'It belongs to somebody else. Suppose it transfers its fixation to you? You'd be robbing its owners. They can't love many people at once.'

She snorted, but installed the thing in its cage.

'Anne—' Norris hesitated, knowing that it was a bad time to approach the subject, but thinking about Slade's pseudoparty tonight, and wondering why she had accepted.

'What, Terry?'

He leaned on the snare pole and watched her. 'Do you want one of them for yourself? I can sign an unclaimed one over to you. Wouldn't cost anything.'

She stared at him evenly for a moment, glanced down at her feet, paced slowly to the window to stand hugging her arms and looking out into the twilight.

'With a pseudoparty, Terry?'

He swallowed a lump of anxiety, found his voice. 'Whatever you want.'

'I hear the phone ringing in the house.'

He waited.

'It stopped,' she said after a moment.

'Well, babe?'

'Whatever I want, Terry?' She turned slowly to lean back against a patch of gray light and look at him.

He nodded. 'Whatever you want.'

'I want your child.'

He stiffened with hurt, stared at her open-mouthed.

'I want your child.'

He thrust his hand slowly in his hip pocket.

'Oh, don't reach for your social security card. I don't care if it's got "genetic triple-Z" on it. I want your child.'

'Uncle Federal says "no," babe.'

'To hell with Uncle Federal! They can't send a human through your Room 3! Not yet, anyhow! If it's born, the world's stuck with it!'

'And the parents are forcibly separated, reduced to common-labor status. Remember?'

She stamped her foot and whirled to the window again. 'Damn the whole hellish world!' she snarled.

Norris sighed heavily. He was sorry she felt that way. She was probably right in feeling that way, but he was still sorry. Righteous anger, frustrated, was no less searing a psychic acid than the unrighteous sort, nor did a stomach pause to weigh the moral worth of the wrath that drenched it before giving birth to an ulcer.

'Hey, babe, if we're going to the Slade affair—'

She nodded grimly and turned to walk with him toward the house. At least it was better having her direct her anger at the world rather than at him, he thought.

The expectant mother played three games of badminton before sundown, then went inside to shower and dress before the guests arrived. Her face was wreathed in a merry smile as she trotted downstairs in a fresh smock, her neck still pink from the hot water, her wake fragrant with faint perfume. There was no apparent need for the smock, nor was there any pregnant caution in the way she threw her arms around John's neck and kicked up her heels behind her.

'Darling,' she chirped. 'There'll be plenty of milk. I never believed in bottle-feeding. Isn't it wonderful?'

'Great. The injections are working, I guess.'

She looked around. 'It's a lovely resort hotel. I'm glad you didn't pick Angel's Haven.'

'So am I,' he grunted. 'We'll have the reception room all to ourselves tonight.'

'What time is it?'

'Seven ten. Oh, the doc called to say he'd be a few minutes late. He was busy all day with a sick baby.'

She licked her lips and glanced aside uneasily. 'Class A couple?'

'No, doll. Class C—and a widow.'

'Oh.' She brightened and watched his face teasingly. 'Will you pace and chain-smoke while I'm in delivery?'

He snorted amusement. 'Hey, it's not as if you were really . . .' He stopped amid a fit of coughing.

'Not as if I were really what?'

'Now look, I didn't mean . . .'

'Not as if I were really what?' she demanded, eyes beginning to brim.

'Listen, darling, I'll pace and I'll chain-smoke.'

A nurse came clicking across the floor. 'Mrs. Slade, it's time for your first injection. Doctor Georges just called. Will you come with me, please?'

'Not as if I what, John?' she insisted, ignoring the nurse.

He lit a cigarette from the butt of the last and looked around nervously. 'She'll be all right?' he asked the nurse.

'Mrs. Slade, will you please . . .'

'All right, nurse, I'm coming.' She tossed her husband a hurt glance, walked away dabbing at her eyes.

'Expectant dames are always cranky,' sympathized an attendant who sat on a bench nearby. 'Take it easy. She won't be so touchy after it comes.'

John Hanley Slade shot an irritable glare at the eavesdropper, saw a friendly comedian-face grinning at him, returned the grin uneasily, and went over to sit down.

'Your first?'

John Hanley nodded, stroked nervously at his thin hair.

'I see 'em come, I see 'em go. It's always the same.'

'Whattaya mean?' John grunted.

'Same expressions, same worries, same attitudes, same conversation, same questions. The guy always makes some remark about how it's not *really* having a baby, and the dame always gets sore. Happens every time.'

'It's all pretty routine for you, eh?' he muttered stiffly.

The attendant nodded. He watched the expectant father for several seconds, then grunted: 'Go ahead, ask me.'

'Ask you what?'

'If I think all this is silly. They always do.'

John stared at the attendant irritably. 'Well—?'

'Do I think it's silly? No, I don't.'

'Fine. That's settled, then.'

'No, I don't think it's silly, because for a dame it ain't satisfying if she plunks down the dough, buys a newt, and lets it go at that. There's something missing between bedroom and baby.'

'That so?'

John's sarcastic tone was apparently lost on the man. 'It's so,' he announced. 'Physiological change—that's what's missing. For a newt to really take the place of a baby, the mother's got to go through the whole build-up. Doc gives her injections, she craves pickles and mangoes. More injections for morning sickness. More injections, she gets chubby. And finally shots to bring mild labor and false delivery. So then she gets the newt, and everything's right with the world.'

'Mmmph.'

'Ask me something else,' the attendant offered.

John looked around helplessly, spied an elderly woman near the entrance. She had just entered, and stood looking around as if lost or confused. He did not recognize her, but he got up quickly.

'Excuse me, chum. Probably one of my guests.'

'Sure, sure. I gotta get on the job anyhow.'

The woman turned to stare at him as he crossed the floor to meet her. Perhaps one of Mary's friends, he thought. There were at least a dozen people coming that he hadn't met. But his welcoming smile faded slightly as he approached her. She wore a shabby dress, her hair was disheveled in a gray tangle, her match-stick legs were without makeup, and there were fierce red lines around her eyelids. She stared at him with wide wild eyes —dull orbs of dirty marble with tiny blue patches for pupils. And her mouth was a thin slash between gaunt leathery cheeks.

'Are—are you here for the party?' he asked doubtfully.

She seemed not to hear him, but continued to stare at or through him. Her mouth made words out of a quivering hiss of a voice. 'I'm looking for *him*.'

'Who?'

'The doctor.'

He decided from her voice that she had laryngitis. 'Doctor Georges? He'll be here soon, but he'll be busy tonight. Couldn't you consult another physician?'

The woman fumbled in her bag and brought out a small parcel to display. 'I want to give him this,' she hissed.

'I could—'

'I want to give it to him myself,' she interrupted.

Two guests that he recognized came through the entrance. He glanced toward them nervously, returned their grins, glanced indecisively back at the haggard woman.

'I'll wait,' she croaked, turned her back, and marched to the nearest chair where she perched like a sick crow, eyes glued to the door.

John Hanley Slade felt suddenly chilly. He shrugged it off and went to greet the Willinghams, who were the first arrivals.

Anne Norris, with her husband in tow, zig-zagged her way through a throng of chattering guests toward the hostess, who now occupied a wheel chair near the entrance to the delivery room. They were a few minutes late, but the party had not yet actually begun.

'Why don't you go join the father's sweating circle?' Anne called over her shoulder. 'The men are all over with John.'

Norris glanced at the group that had gathered under a cloud of cigar smoke over by the portable bar. John Slade stood at the focus of it and looked persecuted.

'Job's counselors,' Terry grunted.

A hand reached out from a nearby conversation-group and caught his arm. 'Norris,' coughed a gruff voice.

He glanced around. 'Oh—Chief Franklin. Hello!'

Anne released his hand and said, 'See you later,' then wound her way out of sight in the milling herd.

Franklin separated himself from the small congregation and glanced down coolly at his district inspector. He was a tall man, with shoulders hunched up close to his head, long spindly legs, a face that was exceedingly wide across the cheekbones but narrow at the jaw. Black eyes gazed from under heavy brows, and his unruly black hair was badly cut. His family tree had a few Cherokee Indians among its branches, Norris had heard, and they were frequently on the warpath.

Franklin gulped his drink casually and handed the glass to a passing attendant. 'Thought you'd be working tonight, Norris,' he said.

'I got trapped into coming, Chief,' he replied amiably.

'How're you doing with the Delmont pickup?'

'Nearly finished with record-tracing. I took a break today and picked up nine of them.'

'Mmmph. I *wondered* why you plastipainted that right eye.' Franklin rolled back his head and laughed loudly toward the ceiling. 'Newt's mama tossed the crockery at you, did she?'

'Her husband,' he corrected a little stiffly.

'Well—get them in a hurry, Norris. If the newt's owner knows it's a deviant, he might hear we're after something and hide it somewhere. I want them rounded up quickly.'

'Expect to find the one?'

Franklin nodded grimly. 'It's somewhere in this part of the country—or *was*. It narrows down to about six or eight districts. Yours has a good chance of being it. If I had my way, we'd destroy every Bermuda K-99 that came out during that period. That way, we'd be sure—in case Delmont faked more than one.'

'Be pretty tough on dames like Mary,' Norris reminded him, glancing toward Mrs. Slade.

'Yeah, yeah, five hundred Rachels blubbering for their children, and all on my neck. I'd almost rather let the deviant get away than have to put up with the screaming mommies.'

'The burdens of office, Chief. Bear up under the brickbats. Herod did.'

Franklin glowered at him suspiciously, noticed Norris's bland expression, muttered 'eh heh heh,' and glanced around the room.

'Who's presiding over the whelping tonight?' Norris asked.

'Local doctor. Georges. You ought to know him.'

Terry's eyebrows went up. He nodded.

'He's already here. Saw him come in the doctor's entrance a few minutes ago. He's probably getting ready. Well, Norris . . . if you'll excuse me . . .'

Norris wandered toward the bar. He had been to several pseudoparties before. There was nothing to it, really. After the guests had gathered, the medics rolled the mother into delivery, and everyone paced restlessly and talked in hushed voices while she re-enacted the age-old drama of Birth—in a way that was only mildly uncomfortable and did nothing to aggravate the population problem. Then, when they rolled her out again —fatigued and emotionally spent—the nurse brought out a newly purchased neutroid, only a few days out of the incubator, and presented it to the mother. When the oohs and aahs were finished, the mother went home with her child to rest, and the father whooped it up with the guests. Norris hoped to get away early. He had things to do before dawn.

'Who's that hag by the door?' a guest grunted in his ear.

Norris glanced incuriously at the thin-lipped woman who sat stiffly with her hands in her lap, not gazing at the guests but looking through and beyond them. He shook his head and moved on to shake hands with his host.

'Glad you came, Norris!' Slade said with a grin, then leaned closer. 'Your presence could be embarrassing at a time like this, though.'

'How's that?'

'You should have brought your net and snare pole, Norris,' said a man at Slade's elbow. 'Then when they bring the baby out, go charging across the room yelling: "That's it! That's the one I'm after!" '

The men laughed heartily. Norris grinned weakly and started away.

'Hey, Slade,' a voice called. 'They're coming after Mary.'

Norris stood aside to let John hurry toward his wife. Most of the crowd stopped milling about to watch Dr. Georges, a nurse and an attendant coming from a rear door to take charge of Mary.

'Stop! Stop right there!'

The voice came from near the front entrance. It was a choked and hoarse gasp of sound, not loud, but somehow penetrating enough to command the room. Norris glanced aside during the sudden lull to see the thin-lipped woman threading her way through the crowd, and the crowd folded back to clear a way. The farther she walked, the quieter the room became, and Norris suddenly realized that somehow the center of the room was almost clear of people so that he could see Mary and John and the medics standing near the delivery room door. They had turned to stare at the intruder. Georges' mouth fell open slightly. He spoke in a low voice, but the room was suddenly silent enough so that Norris could hear.

'Why, Sarah—what're you doing here?'

The woman stopped six feet away from him. She pulled out a small parcel and reached it toward him. 'This is for you,' she croaked.

When Georges did not advance to take it, she threw it at his feet. 'Open it!' she commanded.

Norris expected him to snort and tell the attendants to toss the nutty old dame out. Instead, he stooped, very slowly, keeping his eyes on the woman, and picked up the bundle.

'Unwrap it!' she hissed when he paused.

His hands fumbled with it, but his eyes never left her face. The package came open. Georges glanced down. He dropped it quickly to the floor.

'An amputated—'

Chubby mouth gaping, he stared at the gaunt woman.

'My Primrose had a black cowlick in her tail!'

The doctor swallowed and continued to stare.

'Where is my Primrose?'

The woman had her hand in her purse. The doctor retreated a step.

'Where is my baby?'

'Really, Sarah, there was nothing to do but—'

Her hand brought a heavy automatic out of the purse. It wavered and moved uncertainly, too weighty for her scrawny wrist and arm. The room was suddenly a scramble and a babble.

'You killed my baby!'

'The first shot ricocheted from the ceiling and shattered a window,' said the television announcer. 'The second shot went into the wall. The third shot struck Doctor Georges in the back of the head as he ran toward the delivery room door. He died instantly. Mrs. Glubbes fled from the room before any of the guests could stop her, and a dragnet is now combing . . .'

Norris shuddered and looked away from the television screen that revealed the present state of the reception room where they had been not more than two hours ago. He turned off the set, nervously lit a cigarette, and glanced at Anne who sat staring at nothing at the other end of the sofa.

'How do you feel?' he murmured.

She looked at him dumbly, shook her head. Norris got up, paced to the magazine rack, thumbed idly through its contents, glanced back at her nervously, walked to the window, stood smoking and staring toward the street for a time, moved to the piano, glanced back at her nervously again, tried to play a few bars of *Beethoven's Fifth* with one finger, hit a foul note after the opening ta-ta-ta-taaaahh, grunted a curse, banged a crashing discord with his fist, and leaned forward with a sigh to press his forehead against the music rack and close his eyes.

'Don't blame yourself, Terry,' she said softly.

'If I hadn't let him have that impounded newt, it wouldn't have happened.'

She thought that over briefly. 'And if my maternal grandfather hadn't lied to his wife back in 2013, I would never have been born.'

'Why not?'

'Because if he'd told her the truth, she'd have up and left him, and Mother wouldn't have been born.'

'Oh. Nevertheless—'

'Nevertheless nothing!' She shook herself out of the blue mood. 'You come here, Terry Norris!'

He came, and there was comfort in holding her. She was prepared to blame the world all right, but he was in the world, and a part of it, and so was she. And there was no sharing of guilt, but only the whole weight of it on the shoulders of each of them. He thought of the Delmont case, and the way Franklin talked casually of slaughtering five hundred K-99s just to be sure, and how he continued to hate Franklin's guts for no apparent reason. Franklin was not a pleasant fellow, to be sure, but he had done nothing to Norris personally. He wondered if he hated what Franklin represented, but directed the hate at Franklin's person because he, Norris, represented it *too*. Franklin, however, liked the world as he found it, and was glad to help keep it that way.

If I think something's wrong with the setup, but keep on being a part of it, then the wrongness is not part mine, he thought, it's *all* mine, because I bought it.

'It's hard to decide,' he murmured.

'What's that, Terry?'

'Whether it's all wrong, dead wrong—or whether it's the best that can be done under the circumstances.'

'Whatever are you talking about?'

He shook himself and yawned. 'About going to bed,' he grunted.

They went to bed at midnight. At one o'clock, he became certain she was asleep. He lay in darkness for a time, listening to her even breathing. Then he sat up and eased himself out of bed. There was work to be done. He tiptoed quietly out of the bedroom, carrying his shoes and his trousers. He dressed in the kitchen by the glow of a cigarette ember and stole quietly out into the chilly night. A half-moon hung low in a misty sky, and the wind was sharp out of the north. He walked quietly toward the kennels. There were only three empty cages. He needed twenty-seven to accommodate the doubtful K-99s that were to be picked up during the next few days. There was work to be done.

He went into the neutroid room and flicked a switch. A few sleepy chatters greeted the light.

One at a time he awoke twenty-four of the older creatures and carried them to a large glass-walled compartment. These were the longtime residents; they knew him well, and they came willingly, snuggling sleepily against his chest. He whistled tunelessly while he worked, began carrying them by the tails, two in each hand, to speed the chore.

When he had gotten them in the glass chamber, he sealed the door and turned on the gas. Then he switched off the lights, locked up for the night again, and walked back toward the house through the crisp grass. The conveyor belt from the chamber to the crematorium would finish the job unaided.

Norris felt suddenly ill. He sank down on the back steps and laid his head on his arms across his knees. His eyes burned, but thought of tears made him sicker. When the low *chug* of the crematorium's igniter coughed quietly from the kennels, he staggered hurriedly away from the steps to retch.

She was waiting for him in the bedroom. She sat on the windowseat, her small figure silhouetted against the paleness of the moonlit yard.

She was staring silently out at the dull red tongue of exhaust gas from the crematorium chimney when he tiptoed down the hall and paused in the doorway. She looked around. Dead silence between them, then:

'Out for a walk, eh, Terry?'

A resumption of the dead silence. He backed quietly away without speaking. He went to the parlor and lay down on the couch.

After a time, he heard her puttering around in the kitchen, and saw a light. A little later, he opened his eyes to see her dark shadow over him, surrounded by an aura of negligee. She sat down on the edge of the couch and offered him a glass.

'Drink it. Make your stomach rest easy.'

'Alcoholic?'

'Yeah.'

He tasted it: milk, egg yolk, honey, and rum.

'No arsenic?'

She shook her head. He drank it quickly, lay back with a grunt, took her hand. They were silent for a time.

'I—I guess every new wife thinks her husband's flawless, for awhile,' she murmured absently. 'Silly, how it's such a shock to find out the obvious: that he's not much different from other bull humans of the tribe.'

Norris stiffened, rolled his face away from her. After a moment her hand crept out to touch his cheek. Her fingertips traced a soft line up and along his temple.

'It's all right, Terry,' she whispered.

He kept his face averted. Her fingers stroked for a moment more, as if she were feeling something new and different in the familiar texture of his hair. Then she arose and padded quietly back to the bedroom.

Norris lay awake until dawn, knowing that it would never be all right Terry, nor all right World—never, as long as the prohibiting, the creating, the killing, the mockery, the falsification of birth, death, and life continued.

Dawn inherited the night mist, gathered it into clouds, and made a gloomy gray morning of it.

Anne was still asleep when he left for work. He backed out the kennel truck, meaning to get the rest of the Bermuda K-99s as quickly as possible so that he could begin running the normalcy tests and get the whole thing over with. The night's guilt was still with him as he drove away, a sticky dew that refused to depart with morning. Why should he have to kill the things? Why couldn't Franklin arrange for a central slaughter house for destroying neutroids that had been deserted, or whose owners could not be located, or that found themselves unclaimed for any other reason? But Franklin would purple at the notion. It was only a routine part of the job. Why shouldn't it be routine? Why were neutroids manufactured anyhow? Obviously, because they were disposable—an important feature which human babies unfortunately lacked. When the market became glutted with humans, the merchandise could not be dumped in the sea.

Anthropos' mutant pets fulfilled a basic biological need of Man—of all life, for that matter—the need to have young, or a reasonable facsimile, and care for them. Neutroids kept humanity satisfied with the restricted birth rate, and if it were not satisfied, it would breed itself into famine, epidemic, and possible extinction. With the population held constant at five billions, the Federation could insure a decent living standard for everyone. And as long as birth must be restricted, why not restrict it logically and limit it to genetic desirables?

Why not? Norris felt no answer, but he was acutely aware of the 'genetic-C' on his social security card.

The world was a better place, wasn't it? Great strides since the last century. Science had made life easier to live and harder to lose. The populace thoughtlessly responded by pouring forth a flood of babies and doddering old codgers to clutter the earth and make things tougher again by eating and not producing; but again science increased the individual's chances to survive and augmented his motives for doing so—and again the populace responded with fecundity and long white beards, making more trouble for science again. So it had continued until it became obvious that progress wasn't headed toward 'The Good Life' but toward more lives to continue the same old meager life as always. What could be done? Impede science? Unthinkable! Chuck the old codgers into the sea? Advance the retirement age to ninety and work them to death? The old codgers still had the suffrage, and plenty of time to go to the polls.

The unborn, however, were not permitted to vote.

Man's technology had created little for the individual. Man used his technology to lengthen his life and sweeten it, but something had to be subtracted somewhere. The lives of the unborn were added onto the years of the aged. A son of Terry Norris might easily live till 110, but he would have damn little chance of being born to do it.

Neutroids filled the cradles. Neutroids never ate much, nor grew up to eat more or be on the unemployment roles. Neutroids could be bashed with a shovel and buried in the back yard when hard times came. Neutroids could satisfy a woman's longing for something small and lovable, but they never got in the economic way.

It was no good thinking about it, he decided. It was a Way Of Doing Things, and most people accepted it, and if it sometimes yielded heartache and horrors such as had occurred at Slade's pseudoparty, it was still an Accepted Way, and he couldn't change it, even if he knew what to do about it. He was already adjusted to the world-as-it-was, a world that loved the artificial mutants as children, looked the other way when crematorium flames licked in the night. He had been brought up in such a world, and it was only when emotion conflicted with the grim necessity of his job that he thought to question the world. And Anne? Eventually, he supposed, she would have her pseudo-party, cuddle a neutroid, forget about romantic notions like having a kid of her own.

At noon he brought home another dozen K-99s and installed them in the cages. Two reluctant mothers had put up a howl, but he departed without protest and left seizure of animals to the local authorities. Yates had already delivered the three from yesterday.

'What, no more scratches, bruises, broken bones?' Anne asked at lunch.

He smiled mechanically. 'If Mama puts up a squawk, I go. Quietly.'

'Learned your lesson yesterday?'

'Mmm! One dame pulled a fast one on me, though. I think. Told her what I wanted. She started moaning, but she let me in. I got her newt, started out with it. She wanted a receipt. So, I took the newt's serial number off the check list, made out the receipt. She took one look and squealed, "That's not Chichi's number!" and grabbed for her tail-wagger. I looked at its foot-tattoo. Sure enough—wrong number. Had to leave it. A K-99 all right, but not even from Bermuda Plant.'

'I thought they were all registered.'

'They are, babe. Wires get crossed sometimes. I told her she had the wrong newt, and she started boiling. Got the sales receipt and showed it to me. Number checked with the newt's. Something's fouled up somewhere.'

'Where'd she get it?'

'O'Reilley's pet shop—over in Sherman II. Right place, wrong serial number.'

'Anything to worry about, Terry?'

'Well, I've got to track down that doubtful Bermuda model.'

'Oh.'

'And—well—' He frowned out the window at the kennels. 'Ever think what'd happen if somebody started a black market in neutroids?'

They finished the meal in silence. Apparently there was going to be no further mention of last night's mass disposal, nor any rehash of the nightmare at Slade's party. He was thankful.

The afternoon's work yielded seven more Bermuda neutroids for the pound. Except for the missing newt that was involved in the confusion of serial numbers, the rest of them would have to be collected by Yates or his deputies, armed with warrants. The groans and the tears of the owners left him in a gloomy mood, but the pick-up phase of the operation was nearly finished. The normalcy tests, however, would consume the rest of the week and leave little time for sleeping and eating. If Delmont's falsification proved extensive, it might be necessary to deliver several of the animals to Central Lab for dissection and complete analysis, thus bringing the murderous wrath of the owners upon his head. He had a hunch about why bio-inspectors were frequently shifted from one territory to another.

On the way home, he stopped in Sherman II to check with the dealer about the confusion of serial numbers. Sherman II was the largest of the Sherman communities, covering fifty blocks of commercial buildings. He parked in the outskirts and took a sidewalk escalator toward O'Reilley's address. He had spoken to O'Reilley on the phone, but had not yet visited the dealer's shop.

It lay on a dingy side street that was reminiscent of centuries past, a street of small bars and bowling alleys and cigar stores. There was even a shop with three gold balls above the entrance, but the place was now an antique store. A light mist was falling when he stepped off the escalator and stood in front of the pet shop. A sign hung out over the sidewalk, announcing:

J. 'DOGGY' O'REILLEY
PETS FOR SALE
DUMB BLONDES AND GOLDFISH
MUTANTS FOR THE CHILDLESS
BUY A BUNDLE OF JOY

He frowned at the sign for a moment, then wandered through the entrance into a warm and gloomy shop, wrinkling his nose at the strong musk of animal odors. O'Reilley's was no shining example of cleanliness.

Somewhere a puppy was yapping, and a parrot croaked the lyrics of *A Chimp To Call My Own*—theme song of a soap opera about a lady evolvotron operator, Norris recalled.

He paused briefly by a tank of silk-draped goldfish. The shop had a customer. An elderly lady haggled with the wizened manager over the price of a half-grown second-hand Dog-F. She shook her last dog's death certificate under his nose and demanded a guarantee of the dog's alleged F-5 intelligence. The old man offered to swear on a Bible that the dog was more knowledgeable than some humans, but he demurred when asked to swear by his ledger.

The dog was lamenting, 'Don' sell me, Dada, don' sell me,' and punctuating the pleas with mournful train-whistle howls.

Norris smiled quietly. The nonhuman pets were brighter than the neutroids. A K-108 could speak a dozen words, but a K-99 never got farther than 'mama,' 'papa,' and 'cookie.' Anthropos feared making quasihumans too intelligent, lest sentimentalists proclaim them really human.

He wandered on toward the rear of the building, pausing briefly by the cash register to inspect O'Reilley's license which hung in a dusty frame on the wall behind the counter: 'James Fallon O'Reilley . . . authorized dealer in mutant animals . . . all nonpredatory mammals including Chimpanzee-K series . . . license expires 15w 3d 2063y. . . .'

Expiration date approaching, he noticed, but otherwise okay. He headed for a bank of neutroid cages along the opposite wall, but O'Reilley minced across the floor to meet him. The elderly lady was leaving. O'Reilley's face wore a v-shaped smirk on a loose-skinned face, and his bald head bobbled professionally.

'And a good afternoon to ye, sir. What'll it be this foine drizzlin' afternoon? A dwarf kangaroo perhaps, or a—' He paused to adjust his spectacles as Norris flashed a badge and presented his card. O'Reilley's smile waned. 'Inspector Norris is it,' he muttered at the card, then looked up. 'What'd they do with the last 'un, flay him alive?'

'My predecessor was transferred to the Montreal area.'

'And *I* thought that I spoke to him only yesterday!'

'On the phone? That was me, O'Reilley. About the rundown on the K-99 sales.'

'I gave it to you properly, did I not?' the oldster demanded.

'You gave it to me. Maybe properly.'

O'Reilley seemed to puff up slightly and glower. 'Meaning?'

'There's a mix-up in serial numbers on one of them. May not be your mistake.'

'No mistakes, no mistakes.'

'Okay, we'll see.' Norris glanced at his list. 'Let's check this number again—K-99-LJZ-351.'

'It's nearly closing time,' the oldster protested. 'Come back some other day, Norris.'

'Sorry, this one's rush. It'll only take a minute. Where's your book?'

The oldster began to quiver angrily. 'Are you suggestin', sir, that I falsely—'

'No,' he growled, 'I'm suggesting that there was a mistake. Maybe *my* mistake, maybe yours, maybe Anthropos', maybe the owner's. I've got to find out, that's all. Let's have the book.'

'What kind of a mistake? I gave you the owner's name!'

'She has a different newt.'

'Can I help it if she traded with somebody?'

'She didn't. She bought it here. I saw the receipt.' Norris was beginning to become impatient, tried to suppress it.

'Then she traded with one of my other customers!' O'Reilley insisted.

Norris snorted irritably. 'You got two customers named Adelia Schultz? Come on, pop, let's look at the duplicate receipt. *Now*.'

'Doubt if it's still around,' O'Reilley grumbled, refusing to budge.

Norris suddenly erupted. He turned away angrily and began pacing briskly around the shop, looking under cages, inspecting fixtures, probing into feeding troughs with a pencil, looking into feed bags, examining a Dog-F's wiry coat.

'Here there! What do you think you're doing?' the owner demanded.

Norris began barking off check-points in a loud voice. 'Dirty cat-cage . . . inadequate ventilation . . . food trough not clean . . . no water in the newt cages . . . .'

'I water them twice a day!' O'Reilley raged.

'. . . mouldy rabbit-meal . . . no signs of disinfectant . . . What kind of disease-trap are you running here?'

He came back to face O'Reilley who stood trembling with rage and cursing him with his eyes.

'Not to mention that sign outside,' Norris added casually. ' "Dumb blondes"—they outlawed that one the year Kleyton got sent up for using hormones on K-108s, trying to grow himself a harem. Well?'

'Doubt if it's still around,' O'Reilley repeated.

'Look, pop!' Norris snapped. 'You're required to keep sales receipts until they're microfilmed. There hasn't been a micro-filming for over a year . . .'

'Get out of my shop!'

'If I go, you won't *have* a shop after tomorrow.'

'Are you threatening me?'

'Yeah.'

For a moment, Norris thought the old man would attack him. But O'Reilley spat a sudden curse, scurried toward the counter, grabbed a fat book from beneath the cash register, then hurried away toward the stairs at the rear of the shop.

'Hey, pop! Where you going?'

'Get me glasses!'

'You're wearing your glasses!' Norris started after him.

'New ones. Can't see through them.' O'Reilley bounded upstairs.

'Leave the book *here* and *I'll* check it!'

Norris stopped with his foot on the bottom step. O'Reilley slammed the door at the head of the stairs, locked it behind him. Grumbling suspiciously, the inspector went back to the counter to wait.

Five minutes passed. The door opened. O'Reilley came downstairs, looking less angry but decidedly nervous. He slammed the book on the counter, riffled its pages, found a place, muttered, 'Here it is, see for yourself,' and held it at a difficult angle.

'Give it here.'

O'Reilley reluctantly released it, began babbling about bureaucracy and tin-horn inspectors who acted like dictators and inspection codes that prescribed and circumscribed and prohibited. Norris ignored him and stared at the duplicate receipt.

'Adelia Schultz . . . received Chimpanzee-K-99-LJZ-351 on . . .'

It was the number on the list from Anthropos. It was the number of the animal he wanted for normalcy tests. But it was not the number of Mrs. Schultz's neutroid, nor was it the number written on Mrs. Schultz's copy of *this very same invoice*.

O'Reilley was still babbling at him. Norris held the book up to his eye, took aim at the bright doorway across the surface of the page. O'Reilley stopped babbling.

'Rub marks,' the inspector grunted. 'Scrape marks on the paper.'

O'Reilley's breathing sounded asthmatic. Norris lowered the book.

'Nice erasure job—for a carbon copy. Do it while you were upstairs?'

O'Reilley said nothing. Norris took a scrap of paper, folded his handkerchief over the point of his pocketknife blade, used the point to clean out the eraser dust from between the receipts, emptied the dust on the paper, folded it and put it in his pocket.

'Evidence.'

O'Reilley said nothing.

Norris tore out the erased receipt, pocketed it, put on his hat and started for the door.

'See you in court, O'Reilley.'

'Wait!'

He turned. 'Okay—I'm waiting.'

'Let's go sit down first,' the deflated oldster muttered weakly.

'Sure.'

They walked up the flight of stairs and entered a dingy parlor. He glanced around, sniffed at the smell of cabbage boiling and sweaty bedclothing. An orange-haired neutroid lay sleeping on a dirty rug in the corner. Norris stared down at it curiously. O'Reilley made a whining sound and slumped into a chair, his breath coming in little whiffs that suggested inward sobbing. Norris gazed at him expressionlessly for a moment, then went to kneel beside the newt.

'K-99-LJZ-351,' he read aloud, peering at the sole of the tattooed foot. The newt stirred in its sleep at the sound of a strange voice. When Norris looked at O'Reilley again, the old man was staring at his feet, his forehead supported by a leathery old hand that shielded his eyes.

'Lots of good explanations, O'Reilley?'

'Ye've seen what ye've seen; now do what ye must. I'll say nothing to ye.'

'Look, O'Reilley, the newt is what I'm after. So I found it. I don't know what else I've found, but juggling serial numbers is a serious offense. If you've got a story, you better tell it. Otherwise, you'll be telling it behind bars. I'm willing to listen here and now. You'd better grab the chance.'

O'Reilley sighed, looked at the sleeping newt in the corner. 'What'll ye do with her?'

'The newt? Take her in.'

O'Reilley sat in gloomy silence while he thought things over. 'We were class-B, me and the missus,' he mumbled suddenly, 'allowed a child of our own if we could have 'um. Fancy that, eh? Ugly old coot like me—class-B.'

'So?'

'The government said we could have a child, but Nature said we couldn't.'

'Tough.'

'But since we were class-B, we weren't entitled to own a newt. See?'

'Yeah. Where's your wife?'

'With the saints, let's hope.'

Norris wondered what sort of a sob-story this was getting to be. The oldster went on quietly, all the while staring at the sleeping figure in the corner.

'Couldn't have a kid, couldn't own a newt either—so we

opened the pet shop. It wasn't like havin' yer own, though. Missus always blubbered when I sold a newt she'd got to feeling like a mother to. Never swiped one, though—not till Peony came long. Last year this Bermuda shipment come in, and I sold most of 'em pretty quick, but Peony here was puny. People afraid she'd not last long. Couldn't sell her. Kept her around so long thet we both loved her. Missus died last year. "Don't let anybody take Peony," she kept saying afore she passed on. I promised I wouldn't. So I switched 'em around and moved her up here.'

'That's all?'

O'Reilley hesitated, then nodded.

'Ever done this before?'

O'Reilley shook his head.

There was a long silence while Norris stared at the child-thing. 'Your license could be revoked,' he said absently.

'I know.'

He ground his fist thoughtfully in his palm, thought it over some more. If O'Reilley told the truth, he couldn't live with himself if he reported the old man . . . unless it wasn't the whole truth.

'I want to take your books home with me tonight.'

'Help yourself.'

'I'm going to make a complete check, investigate you from stem to stern.'

He watched O'Reilley closely. The oldster was unaffected. He seemed concerned—grief-stricken—only by the thought of losing the neutroid.

'If plucking a newt out of stock to keep you company was the only thing you did, O'Reilley, I won't report you.'

O'Reilley was not consoled. He continued to gaze hungrily at the little being on the rug.

'And if the newt turns out not to be a deviant,' he added gently, 'I'll send it back. We'll have to attach a correction to that invoice, of course, and you'll just have to take your chances about somebody wanting to buy it, but . . .' he paused. O'Reilley was staring at him strangely.

'And if she *is* a deviant, Mr. Norris?'

He started to reply, hesitated.

'*Is* she, O'Reilley?'

The oldster said nothing. His face tightened slowly. His shoulders shook slightly, and his squinted eyes were brimming. He choked.

'I see.'

O'Reilley shook himself, produced a red bandanna, dabbed at his eyes, blew his nose loudly, regathered his composure.

'How do you know she's deviant?'

O'Reilley gave him a bitter glance, chuckled hoarsely, shuffled across the room and sat on the floor beside the sleeping newt. He patted a small bare shoulder.

'Peony? . . . Peony-girl . . . wake up, me child, wake up.'

Its fluffy tail twitched for a moment. It sat up, rubbed its eyes, and yawned. There was a lazy casualness about its movements that caused Norris to lean closer to stare. Neutroids usually moved in bounces and jerks and scrambles. This one stretched, arched its back, and smiled—like a two-year-old with soft brown eyes. It glanced at Norris. The eyes went wider for a moment, then it studiously ignored him.

'Shall I play bouncey, Daddy?' it piped.

Norris sucked in a long slow breath and sat frozen.

'No need to, Peony.' O'Reilley glanced at the inspector. 'Bouncey's a game we play for visitors,' he explained. 'Making believe we're a neutroid.'

The inspector could find nothing to say.

Peony licked her lips. 'Wanna glass of water, Daddy.'

O'Reilley nodded and hobbled away to the kitchen, leaving the man and the neutroid to stare at each other in silence. She was quite a deviant. Even a fully age-set K-108 could not have spoken the two sentences that he had heard, and Peony was still a long way from age-set and a K-99 at that.

O'Reilley came back with the water. She drank it greedily, holding the glass herself while she peered up at the old man.

'Daddy's eyes all wet,' she observed.

O'Reilley began trembling again. 'Never mind, child. You go get your coat.'

'Whyyyy?'

'You're going for a ride with Mr. Norris.'

She whirled to stare hostilely at the stunned visitor.

'I don't *want* to!'

The old man choked out a sob and flung himself down to seize her in his arms and hug her against his chest. He tearfully uttered a spasmodic babble of reassurances that would have frightened even a human child.

The deviant neutroid began to cry. Standard neutroids never cried, they whimpered and yeeped. Norris felt weak inside. Slowly, the old man lifted his head to peer at the inspector, blinking away tears. He began loosening Peony from the embrace. Suddenly he put her down and stood up.

'Take her quickly,' he hissed, and strode away to the kitchen. He slammed the door behind him. The latch clicked.

Peony scampered to the door and began beating on it with tiny fists. 'Daddy . . . *Daddy! ! !* Open 'a door!' she wailed.

Norris licked his lips and swallowed a dry place. Still he did not budge from the sofa, his gaze fastened on the child-thing. Disjointed phrases tumbled through his mind . . . what Man hath wrought . . . out of the slime of an ape . . . fat legs and baby fists and a brain to know . . . and the State spoke to Job out of a whirlwind, saying . . .

'Take her!' came a roaring bellow from the kitchen. *'Take her before I lose me wits and kill ye!'*

Norris got unsteadily to his feet and advanced toward the frightened child-thing. He carried her, kicking and squealing, out into the early evening. By the time he turned into his own driveway, she had subsided a little, but she was still crying.

He saw Anne coming down from the porch to meet him. She was staring at the neutroid who sat on the front seat beside him, while seven of its siblings chattered from their cages in the rear of the truck. She said nothing, only stared through the window at the small tear-stained face.

'Home! I want to go home!' it whined.

Norris lifted the newt and handed it to his wife. 'Take it inside. Keep your mouth shut about it. I'll be in as soon as I chuck the others in their cages.'

She seemed not to notice his curtness as she cradled the being in her arms and walked away. The truck lurched on to the kennels.

He thought the whole thing over while he worked. When he was finished, he went back in the house and stopped in the hall to call Chief Franklin. It was the only thing to do: get it over with as quickly as possible. The operator said, 'His office fails to answer. No taped readback. Shall I give you the locator?'

Anne came into the hall and stood glaring at him, her arms clenched across her bosom, one foot tapping the floor angrily. Peony stood behind her, no longer crying, and peering at him curiously around Anne's skirt.

'Are you doing what I think you're doing, Terry?'

He gulped. 'Cancel the call,' he told the operator. 'It'll wait till tomorrow.' He dropped the phone hard and sank down in the straight chair. It was the only thing to do: delay it as long as he could.

'We'd better have a little talk,' she said.

'Maybe we'd better,' he admitted.

They went into the living room. Peony's world had evidently been restricted to the pet shop, and she seemed awed by the clean, neat house, no longer frightened, and curious enough about her surroundings to forget to cry for O'Reilley. She sat in the center of the rug, occasionally twitching her tail as she blinked around at the furniture and the two humans who sat in it.

'The deviant?'

'A deviant.'

'Just what are you going to do?'

He squirmed. 'You know what I'm supposed to do.'

'What you were going to do in the hall?'

'Franklin's bound to find out anyway.'

'How?'

'Do you imagine that Franklin would trust *anybody?*'

'So?'

'So, he's probably already got a list of all serial numbers from the District Anthropos Wholesalers. As a double-check on *us*. And we'd better deliver.'

'I see. That leaves you in a pinch, doesn't it?'

'Not if I do what I'm supposed to.'

'By whose law?'

He tugged nervously at his collar, stared at the child-thing who gazed at him fixedly. 'Heh heh,' he said weakly, waggled a finger at it, held out his hands invitingly. The child-thing inched away nervously.

'Don't evade, Terry.'

'I wanna go home . . . I want Dada.'

'I gotta think. Gotta have time to think.'

'Listen, Terry, you know what calling Franklin would be? It would be M, U, R, D, E, R.'

'She's just a newt.'

'She?'

'Probably. Have to examine her to make sure.'

'Great. Intelligent, capable of reproduction. Just great.'

'Well, what they do with her after I'm finished with the normalcy tests is none of my affair.'

'It's not? *Look* at me, Terry. . . . No, not with that patiently suffering . . . *Terry!*'

He stopped doing it and sat with his head in his hands, staring at the patterns in the rug, working his toes anxiously. 'Think—gotta think.'

'While you're thinking, I'll feed the child,' she said crisply. 'Come on, Peony.'

'How'd you know her name?'

'*She* told me, naturally.'

'Oh.' He sat trying grimly to concentrate, but the house was infused with Anne-ness, and it influenced him. After a while, he got up and went out to the kennels where he could think objectively. But that was wrong too. The kennels were full of Franklin and the system he represented. Finally he went out into the back yard and lay on the cool grass to stare up at the twilight sky. The problem shaped up quite formidably. Either he turned her over to Franklin to be studied and ultimately destroyed, or he didn't. If he didn't, he was guilty of Delmont's crime. Either he lost Anne and maybe something of himself, or his job and maybe his freedom.

A big silence filled the house during dinner. Only Peony spoke, demanding at irregular intervals to be taken home. Each time the child-thing spoke, Anne looked at him, and each time she looked at him, her eyes said 'See?'—until finally he slammed down his fork and marched out to the porch to sulk in the gloom. He heard their voices faintly from the kitchen.

'You've got a good appetite, Peony.'

'I like Dada's cooking better.'

'Well, maybe mine'll do for awhile.'

'I wanna go home.'

'I know—but I think your dada wants you to stay with us for awhile.'

'I don't want to.'

'Why don't you like it here?'

'I want Dada.'

'Well maybe we can call him on the phone, eh?'

'Phone?'

'After you get some sleep.'

The child-thing whimpered, began to cry. He heard Anne walking with it, murmuring softly. When he had heard as much as he could take, he trotted down the steps and went for a long walk in the night, stalking slowly along cracked sidewalks beneath overhanging trees, past houses and scattered lights of the suburbs. Suburbs hadn't changed much in a century, only grown more extensive. Some things underwent drastic revision with the passing years, other things—like walking sticks and garden hoes and carving knives and telephones and bicycles —stayed pretty much as they were. Why bother the established system?

He eyed the lighted windows through the hedges as he wandered past. Fluorescent lights, not much different from those of a century ago. But once they had been campfires, the fires of shivering hunters in the forest, when man was young and the world was sparsely planted with his seed. Now the world was choked with his riotous growth, glittering with his lights and his flashing signs, full of the sound of his engines and the roar of his rockets. He had inherited it and filled it—filled it too full, perhaps.

There was no escaping from the past. The last century had glutted the Earth with its children and grandchildren, had strained the Earth's capacity to feed, and the limit had been reached. It had to be guarded. There was no escape into space, either. Man's rockets had touched two planets, but they were sorry worlds, and even if he made them better, Earth could beget children—if allowed—faster than ships could haul them away. The only choice: increase the death rate, or decrease the birth rate—or, as a dismal third possibility—do nothing, and let Nature wield the scythe as she had once done in India and China. But letting-Nature-do-it was not in the nature of Man, for he could always do it better. If his choice robbed his wife of a biological need, then he would build her a disposable baby to pacify her. He would give it a tail and only half a mind, so that she would not confuse it with her own occasional children.

Peony, however, was a grim mistake. The mistake had to be quickly corrected before anyone noticed.

What was he, Norris, going to do about it, if anything? Defy the world? Outwit the world? The world was made in the shape of Franklin, and it snickered at him out of the shadows. He turned and walked back home.

Anne was rocking on the porch with Peony in her arms when he came up the sidewalk. The small creature dozed fitfully, muttered in its sleep.

'How old is she, Terry?' Anne asked.

'About nine months, or about two years, depending on what you mean.'

'Born nine months ago?'

'Mmm. But two years by the development scale, human equivalent. Newts would be fully mature at nine or ten, if they didn't stop at an age-set. Fast maturation.'

'But she's brighter than most two-year-olds.'

'Maybe.'

'You've heard her talk.'

'You can't make degree-comparisons between two species, Anne. Not easily anyhow. "Bright"—signifying I.Q.—by what yardstick?'

'Bright—signifying on-the-ball—by my yardstick. And if you turn her over to Franklin, I'll leave you.'

'Car coming,' he grunted tonelessly. 'Get in the house. It's slowing down.'

Anne slipped out of her chair and hurried inside. Norris lingered only a moment, then followed. The headlights paused in front of a house down the block, then inched ahead. He watched from deep in the hall.

'Shall I take her out to the kennels right quick?' Anne called tensely.

'Stick where you are,' he muttered, and a moment later regretted it. The headlights stopped in front. The beam of a powerful flashlight played over the porch, found the house number, winked out. The driver cut the engine. Norris strode to the living room.

'Play bouncey!' he growled to Peony.

'Don't want to,' she grumbled back.

'There's a man coming, and you'd better play bouncey if you ever want to see your Dada again!' he hissed.

Peony yeeped and backed away from him, whimpering.

'Terry! What're you talking about! You should be ashamed!'

'Shut up. . . . Peony, play bouncey.'

Peony chattered and leaped to the back of the sofa with monkeylike grace.

'She's frightened! She's acting like a common newt!'

'That's bouncey,' he grunted. 'That's good.'

The car door slammed. Norris went to put on the porch light and watch the visitor come up the steps—a husky, bald gentleman in a black suit and Roman collar. He blinked and shook his head. Clergyman? The fellow must have the wrong house.

'Good evening.'

'Uh—yeah.'

'I'm Father Mulreany. Norris residence?' The priest had a slight brogue; it stirred a vague hunch in Norris' mind, but failed to clear it.

'I'm Norris. What's up?'

'Uh, well, one of my parishioners—I think you've met him—'

'Countryman of yours?'

'Mmm.'

'O'Reilley?'

'Yes.'

'What'd he do, hang himself?'

'Nothing that bad. May I come in?'

'I doubt it. What do you want?'

'Information.'

'Personal or official?'

The priest paused, studied Norris' silhouette through the screen. He seemed not taken aback by the inspector's brusqueness, perhaps accepting it as normal in an era that had little regard for the cloth.

'O'Reilley's in bad shape, Inspector,' Mulreany said quietly. 'I don't know whether to call a doctor, a psychiatrist, or a cop.'

Norris stiffened. 'A cop?' He hesitated, feeling a vague hostility, and a less vague suspicion. He opened the screen, let the priest in, led him to the living room. Anne muttered half-politely, excused herself, snatched Peony, and headed for the rear of the house. The priest's eyes followed the neutroid intently.

'So O'Reilley did something?'

'Mmm.'

'What's it to you?'

Mulreany frowned. 'In addition to things you wouldn't understand—he was my sister's husband.'

Norris waved him into a chair. 'Okay, so—?'

'He called me tonight. He was loaded. Just a senseless babble, but I knew something was wrong. So I went over to the shop.' Mulreany stopped to light a cigarette and frown at the floor. He looked up suddenly. 'You see him today?'

Norris could think of no reason not to admit it. He nodded irritably.

Mulreany leaned forward curiously. 'Was he sober?'

'Yeah.'

'Sane?'

'How should I know?'

'Did he impress you as the sort of man who would suddenly decide to take a joint of pipe and a meat cleaver and mass-slaughter about sixty helpless animals?'

Norris felt slightly dazed. He sank back, shaking his head and blinking. There was a long silence. Mulreany was watching him carefully.

'I can't help you,' Norris muttered. 'I've got nothing to say.'

'Look, Inspector, forget this will you?' He touched his collar.

Norris shook his head, managed a sour smile. 'I can't help you.'

'All right,' Mulreany sighed, starting to his feet. 'I'm just trying to find out if what he says . . .'

'Men talking about Dada?' came a piping voice from the kitchen.

Mulreany shot a quick glance toward it. '. . . is true,' he finished softly.

There was a sudden hush. He could hear Anne whispering in the kitchen, saw her steal a glance through the door.

'So it *is* true,' Mulreany murmured.

Face frozen, Norris came to his feet. 'Anne,' he called in a bitter voice. 'Bouncey's off.'

She came in carrying Peony and looking murderous. 'Why did you ask him in?' she demanded in a hiss.

Mulreany stared at the small creature. Anne stared at the priest.

'It's poison to you isn't it!' she snapped, then held Peony up toward him. 'Here! Look at your enemy. Offends your humano-centrism, doesn't she?'

'Not at all,' he said rather wistfully.

'You condemn them.'

He shook his head. 'Not *them*. Only what they're used for by society.' He looked at Norris, a bit puzzled. 'I'd better leave.'

'Maybe not. Better spill it. What do you want?'

'I told you. O'Reilley went berserk, made a butcher shop out of his place. When I got there, he was babbling about a talking neutroid—"his baby"—said you took it to the pound to destroy it. Threatened to kill you. I got a friend to stay with him, came over to see if I could find out what it's all about.'

'The newt's a deviant. You've heard of the Delmont case?'

'Rumors.'

'She's it.'

'I see.' Mulreany looked glum, grim, gloomy. 'Nothing more I need to know I guess. Well—'

Norris grabbed his arm as he turned. 'Sit a spell,' he grunted ominously.

The priest looked puzzled, let himself be guided back to the chair. Norris stood looking down at him.

'What's the matter with Dada?' Peony chirped. 'I wanna go see Dada.'

'Well?' Norris growled. 'What about her?'
'I don't understand.'
'You people are down on Anthropos, aren't you?'
Mulreany kept patience with an effort. 'To make nitroglycerine for curing heart trouble is good, to make it for blowing open safes is bad. The stuff itself is morally neutral. The same goes for mutant animals. As pets, okay; as replacements for humans, no.'
'Yeah, but you'd just as soon see them dead, eh?'
Mulreany hesitated. 'I admit a personal dislike for them.'
'This one?'
'What about her?'
'Better dead, eh?'
'I didn't say that.'
'You couldn't admit she might be human?'
'Don't know her that well. Human? How do you mean—biologically? Obviously not. Theologically? Why should *you* care?'
'I'm interested in your particular attitude, buster.'
Mulreany gazed at him, gathering a glower. 'I'm a little doubtful about my status here,' he growled. 'I came for information; the roles got switched somewhere. Okay, Norris, but I'm sick of neopagan innocents like you. Now sit down, or show me the door.'
Norris sat down slowly.
The priest watched the small neutroid for a moment before speaking. 'She's alive, performs the function of living, is evidently aware. Life—a kind of functioning. A specific life—an invariant kind of functioning—with sameness-of-self about it. Invariance of functioning—a principle. Self, soul, call it what you like. Whatever's alive has it.' He paused to watch Norris doubtfully.
Norris nodded curtly. 'Go on.'
'Doesn't have to be anything immortal about it. Not unless she were known to be human. Or intelligent.'
'You heard her,' Anne snapped.
'I've heard metal boxes speak with great wisdom,' Mulreany said sourly. 'And if I were a Hottentot, a vocalizing computer would . . .'
'Skip the analogies. Go on.'
'What's intelligence? A function of Man, immortal. What's Man? An intelligent immortal creature, capable of choice.'
'Quit talking in circles.'

'That's the point. I can't—not where Peony's concerned. What do you want to know? If I think she's equal to Man? Give me all the intelligence test results, and all the data you can get—I still couldn't decide.'

'Whattaya need? Mystic writings in the sky?'

'Precisely.'

'I feel a bush being beat about,' Anne said suddenly. 'Is this guy going to make things tough, or isn't he?'

Mulreany looked puzzled again.

'To the point, then,' Norris said. 'Would you applaud if she gets the gasser?'

'Hardly.'

'If you had to decide for yourself—'

'What? Whether to destroy her or not?' Mulreany snorted irritably. 'Not if there was the least doubt in my mind about her. She's a shadow in the brush. Maybe it's ten to one that the shadow's a bear and not a man—but on the one chance, don't shoot, son, don't shoot.'

'You think the authorities have the right to kill her, maybe?' Anne asked.

'Who, him?' Mulreany jerked his head toward Norris.

'Well *say* him.'

'I'd have to think about it. But I don't think so.'

'Why? The government made her. Why can't it unmake her?'

'Made her? *Did* it now?'

'Delmont did,' Norris corrected.

'*Did* he now?' said Mulreany.

'Why not?' Anne snorted.

'I, the state, am Big Fertility,' Norris said sourly; then baiting Mulreany: 'Thou shalt accept no phallus but the evolvotron.'

Mulreany reddened, slapped his knee, and chortled. The Norrises exchanged puzzled glances.

'I feel an affinity,' Anne murmured suspiciously.

Norris came slowly to his feet. 'If you talk to anybody about Peony, you may be responsible for her death.'

'I don't quite see—'

'You don't need to.'

Mulreany shrugged.

'Tell O'Reilley the same.'

Mulreany nodded. 'You've got my word.'

'Your which?'

'Sorry, I forgot. Ancient usage. I won't mention Peony. I'll see that O'Reilley doesn't.'

Norris led him to the door. The priest was obviously suppressing large quantities of curiosity, but contained it well. On the steps, he paused to look back, wearing a curious smirk.

'It just occurred to me—if the child is "human" in the broad sense, she's rather superior to you and me.'

'Why?'

'Hasn't picked an apple yet.'

Norris shrugged slightly.

'And Inspector—if Delmont made her—ask yourself: Just what was it that he "made"?' He nodded quickly. 'Good night.'

'What do you make of him?' Anne hissed nervously.

'Backworldsman. Can't say.'

'Fool, why'd you bring him in?'

'I'm no good at conspiracies.'

'Then you *will* do it?'

'What?'

'Hide her, or something.'

He stared at her doubtfully. 'The only thing I can hope to do is falsify the test reports and send her back to O'Reilley as a standard model.'

'That's better than nothing.'

'And then spend the rest of our days waiting for it to be uncovered,' he added grimly.

'You've got to, Terry.'

Maybe, he thought, maybe.

If he gave her back to O'Reilley, there was a good chance she'd be discovered when the auditor came to microfilm the records and check inventory. He certainly couldn't keep her himself—not with other bio agents wandering in and out every few days. She could not be hidden.

He sat down for a smoke and watched Anne tiptoe to the sofa with the sleeping Peony. It would be easy to obey the law, turn her over to Franklin, and tell Anne that he had done something else with her, something like . . .

He shuddered and chopped the thought off short. She glanced at him curiously.

'I don't like the way you're looking at me,' she muttered.

'You imagine things.'

'Uh-uh. Listen to me, Terry, if you let that baby . . .'

'I'm sick of your ifs!' he barked. 'If I hear another goddam threat of your leaving *if*, then to hell with it, you can leave any time!'

'Terry!'

She stared, puzzled, in his direction for a moment, then slowly wandered out, still puzzling. He sank lower in the chair, brooding. Then it hit him. It wasn't Anne that worried him; it was a piece of himself. It was a piece of himself that threatened to go, and if he let Peony be packed off to Central Lab, it *would* go, and thereafter he would not be able to stomach anything, even himself.

The morning news from the Scriber was carefully folded beside his plate when he came to the table for breakfast. It was so deliberately folded that he bothered to notice the advertisement in the center of the displayed portion.

'You lay this out for my benefit?' he asked.

'Not particularly,' she said casually.

He read it with a suspicious frown:

BIOLOGISTS WANTED
by
ANTHROPOS INCORPORATED
for
Evolvotron Operators
Incubator Tenders
Nursery Supervisors
Laboratory Personnel
in
NEW ATLANTA PLANT
Call or write
Personnel Manager
ANTHROPOS INCORPORATED
Atlanta, Ga.
Note: Secure Labor Dept.
release from present job
before applying.

'What's this supposed to mean to me?' he demanded.

'Nothing in particular. Why? Does it mean something to you?'

He brushed the paper aside and decided to ignore the subtlety, if any. She picked it up, glanced at it as if she had not seen it before. 'New jobs, new places to live,' she murmured.

After breakfast, he went down to police headquarters to sign a statement concerning the motive in Doctor Georges' murder.

Sarah Glubbes had been stashed away in a psychopathic ward, according to Chief Miler, and would probably stay awhile.

'Funny thing, Norris,' the cop said. 'What people won't do over a newt! You know, it's a wonder you don't get your head blown off. I don't covet your job.'

'Good.' He signed the paper and glanced at Miler coolly.

'Must take an iron gut, huh, Norris?'

'Sure. Just a matter of adaptation.'

'Guess so.' Miler patted his paunch and yawned. 'How you coming on this Delmont business? Picked up any deviants yet?'

Norris pitched the fountain pen on the desk, splattering ink. 'What made you ask that?' he said stiffly.

'Nothing *made* me. I did it myself. Touchy today?'

'Maybe.'

Miler shrugged. 'Something made you jump when I said "deviants." '

'Nothing made me. I—'

'Ya, ya, sure, but—'

'Save it for a suspect, Fat.' He stalked out of the office, leaving Miler tapping his pencil and gazing curiously after him. A phone rang somewhere behind him. He hurried on—angry with himself for jumpiness and for indecisiveness. He had to make a choice, and make it soon. It was the lack of a choice that left him jumpy, susceptible to a jolt from either side.

'Norris . . . Hey, Norris . . .'

Miler's voice. He whirled to see the cop trotting down the steps behind him, his pudgy face glistening in the morning sun.

'Your wife's on the phone, Norris. Says it's urgent.'

When he got back to the office, he heard the faint, 'Hello, *hello!*' coming from the receiver on the desk, caught it up quickly.

'Anne? What's wrong?'

Her voice was low and strained beneath a cheerful overnote. 'Nothing's wrong, darling. We have a visitor. Come right home. Chief Franklin's here.'

It knocked the breath out of him. He felt himself going white. He glanced at Chief Miler, sitting calmly nearby.

'Can you tell me about it now?' he asked her.

'Not very well. Please hurry home. He wants to talk to you about the K-99s.'

'Have the two of them met?'

'Yes, they have.' She paused, as if waiting for him to speak, then said, 'Oh, *that!* Bouncey, honey—remember bouncey?'

'Good, I'll be right home.' He hung up and started out.

'Troubles?' the chief called after him.

'Just a sick newt, if it's any of your business,' he called back.

Franklin's helicopter was parked in the empty lot next door when Norris drove up in front of the house. The departmental chief heard the truck and came out on the porch to watch his agent walk up the path. His bulky body was loosely draped in gray tweeds, and his hawk face was a dark, solemn mask. He greeted Norris with a slow, almost sarcastic mood.

'I see you don't read your mail. If you'd looked at it, you'd have known I was coming. I wrote you yesterday.'

'Sorry Chief, I didn't have a chance to stop by the message office this morning.'

Franklin grunted. 'Then you don't know why I'm here?'

'No, sir.'

'Let's sit out on the porch,' Franklin said, and perched his bony frame on the railing. 'We've got to get busy on these Bermuda K-99s, Norris. How many have you got?'

'Thirty-four, I think.'

'I counted thirty-five.'

'Maybe you're right. I—I'm not sure.'

'Found any deviants yet?'

'Uh—I haven't run any tests yet, sir.'

Franklin's voice went sharp. 'Do you need a test to know when a neutroid is talking a blue streak?'

'What do you mean?'

'Just this. We've found at least a dozen of Delmont's units that have mental ages that correspond to their physical age. What's more, they're functioning females, and they have normal pituitaries. Know what that means?'

'They won't take an age-set then,' Norris said. 'They'll grow to adulthood.'

'And have children.'

Norris frowned. 'How can they have children? There aren't any males.'

'No? Guess what we found in one of Delmont's incubators.'

'Not a—'

'Yeah. And it's probably not the first. This business about padding his quota is baloney! Hell, man, he was going to start his own black market! He finally admitted it, after twenty hours' questioning without a letup. He was going to raise them, Norris. He was stealing them right out of the incubators before an inspector ever saw them. The K-99s—the numbered ones—are just the ones he couldn't get back. Lord knows how many males he's got hidden away someplace!'

'What're you going to do?'

'Do! What do you *think* we'll do? Smash the whole scheme, that's what! Find the deviants and kill them. We've got enough now for lab work.'

Norris felt sick. He looked away. 'I suppose you'll want me to handle the destruction, then.'

Franklin gave him a suspicious glance. 'Yes, but why do you ask? You *have* found one, haven't you?'

'Yes, sir,' he admitted.

A moan came from the doorway. Norris looked up to see his wife's white face staring at him in horror, just before she turned and fled into the house. Franklin's bony head lifted.

'I see,' he said. 'We have a fixation on our deviant. Very well, Norris, I'll take care of it myself. Where is it?'

'In the house, sir. My wife's bedroom.'

'Get it.'

Norris went glumly in the house. The bedroom door was locked.

'Honey,' he called softly. There was no answer. He knocked gently.

A key turned in the lock, and his wife stood facing him. Her eyes were weeping ice.

'Stay back!' she said. He could see Peony behind her, sitting in the center of the floor and looking mystified.

Then he saw his own service revolver in her trembling hand.

'Honey, look—it's *me.*'

She shook her head. 'No, it's not you. It's a man that wants to kill a little girl. Stay back.'

'You'd shoot, wouldn't you?' he asked softly.

'Try to come in and find out,' she invited.

'Let me have Peony.'

She laughed, her eyes bright with hate. 'I wonder where Terry went. I guess he died. Or adapted. I guess I'm a widow now. Stay back, mister, or I'll kill you.'

Norris smiled. 'Okay, I'll stay back. But the gun isn't loaded.'

She tried to slam the door; he caught it with his foot. She struck at him with the pistol, but he dragged it out of her hand. He pushed her aside and held her against the wall while she clawed at his arm.

'Stop it!' he said. 'Nothing will happen to Peony, I promise you!' He glanced back at the child-thing, who had begun to cry.

Anne subsided a little, staring at him angrily.

'There's no other way out, honey. Just trust me. She'll be all right.'

Breathing quickly, Anne stood aside and watched him. 'Okay, Terry. But if you're lying—tell me, is it murder to kill a man to protect a child?'

Norris lifted Peony in his arms. Her wailing ceased, but her tail switched nervously.

'In whose law book?' he asked his wife. 'I was wondering the same thing.' Norris started toward the door. 'By the way—find my instruments while I'm outside, will you?'

'The dissecting instruments?' she gasped. 'If you intend—'

'Let's call them surgical instruments, shall we? And get them sterilized.'

He went on outside, carrying the child. Franklin was waiting for him in the kennel doorway.

'Was that Mrs. Norris I heard screaming?'

Norris nodded. 'Let's get this over with. I don't stomach it so well.' He let his eyes rest unhappily on the top of Peony's head.

Franklin grinned at her and took a bit of candy out of his pocket. She refused it and snuggled closer to Norris.

'When can I go home?' she piped. 'I want Dada.'

Franklin straightened, watching her with amusement. 'You're going home in a few minutes, little newt. Just a few minutes.'

They went into the kennels together, and Franklin headed straight for the third room. He seemed to be enjoying the situation. Norris, hating him silently, stopped at a workbench and pulled on a pair of gloves. Then he called after Franklin.

'Chief, since you're in there, check the outlet pressure while I turn on the main line, will you?'

Franklin nodded assent. He stood outside the gas chamber, watching the dials on the door. Norris could see his back while he twisted the main-line valve.

'Pressure's up!' Franklin called.

'Okay. Leave the hatch ajar so it won't lock, and crack the intake valves. Read it again.'

'Got a mask for me?'

Norris laughed. 'If you're scared, there's one on the shelf. But just open the hatch, take a reading, and close it. There's no danger.'

Franklin frowned at him and cracked the intakes. Norris quietly closed the main valve again.

'Drops to zero!' Franklin called.

'Leave it open, then. Smell anything?'

'No. I'm turning it off, Norris.' He twisted the intakes.

Simultaneously, Norris opened the main line.

'Pressure's up again!'

Norris dropped his wrench and walked back to the chamber, leaving Peony perched on the workbench.

'Trouble with the intakes,' he said gruffly. 'It's happened before. Mind getting your hands dirty with me, Chief?'

Franklin frowned irritably. 'Let's hurry this up, Norris. I've got five territories to visit.'

'Okay, but we'd better put on our masks.' He climbed a metal ladder to the top of the chamber, leaned over to inspect the intakes. On his way down, he shouldered a light-bulb over the door, shattering it. Franklin cursed and stepped back, brushing glass fragments from his head and shoulders.

'Good thing the light was off,' he snapped.

Norris handed him the gas mask and put on his own. 'The main switch is off,' he said. He opened the intakes again. This time the dials fell to normal open-line pressure. 'Well, look —it's okay,' he called through the mask. 'You sure it was zero before?'

'Of course I'm sure!' came the muffled reply.

'Leave it on for a minute. We'll see. I'll go get the newt. Don't let the door close, sir. It'll start the automatics and we can't get it open for half an hour.'

'I know, Norris. Hurry up.'

Norris left him standing just outside the chamber, propping the door open with his foot. A faint wind was coming through the opening. It should reach an explosive mixture quickly with the hatch ajar.

He stepped into the next room, waited a moment, and jerked the switch. The roar was deafening as the exposed tungsten filament flared and detonated the escaping anesthetic vapor. Norris went to cut off the main line. Peony was crying plaintively. He moved to the door and glanced at the smouldering remains of Franklin.

Feeling no emotion whatever, Norris left the kennels, carrying the sobbing child under one arm. His wife stared at him without understanding.

'Here, hold Peony while I call the police,' he said.

'Police? What's happened?'

He dialed quickly. 'Chief Miler? This is Norris. Get over here quick. My gas chamber exploded—killed Chief Agent Franklin. Man, it's awful! Hurry!'

He hung up and went back to the kennels. He selected a normal Bermuda K-99 and coldly killed it with a wrench. 'You'll serve for a deviant,' he said, and left it lying in the middle of the floor.

Then he went back to the house, mixed a sleeping capsule in a glass of water, and forced Peony to drink it.

'So she'll be out when the cops come,' he explained to Anne.

She stamped her foot. 'Will you tell me what's happened?'

'You heard me on the phone. Franklin accidentally died. That's all you have to know.'

He carried Peony out and locked her in a cage. She was too sleepy to protest, and she was dozing when the police came.

Chief Miler strode about the three rooms like a man looking for a burglar at midnight. He nudged the body of the neutroid with his foot. 'What's this, Norris?'

'The deviant we were about to destroy. I finished her with a wrench.'

'I thought you said there weren't any deviants.'

'As far as the public's concerned, there aren't. I couldn't see that it was any of your business. It still isn't.'

'I see. It may become my business, though. How'd the blast happen?'

Norris told him the story up to the point of the detonation. 'The light over the door was loose. Kept flickering on and off. Franklin reached up to tighten it. Must have been a little gas in the socket. Soon as he touched it—wham!'

'Why was the door open with the gas on?'

'I told you—we were checking the intakes. If you close the door, it starts the automatics. Then you can't get it open till the cycle's finished.'

'Where were you?'

'I'd gone to cut off the gas again.'

'Okay, stay in the house until we're finished out here.'

When Norris went back in the house, his wife's white face turned slowly toward him.

She sat stiffly by the living room window, looking sick. Her voice was quietly frightened.

'Terry, I'm sorry about everything.'

'Skip it.'

'What did you do?'

He grinned sourly. 'I adapted to an era. Did you find the instruments?'

She nodded. 'What are they for?'

'To cut off a tail and a skin-tattooed foot. Go to the store and buy some brown hair-dye and a pair of boy's trousers, age two. Peony's going to get a crew cut. From now on, she's Mike.'

'We're class-C, Terry! We can't pass her off as our own.'

'We're class-A, honey. I'm going to forge a heredity certificate.'

Anne put her face in her hands and rocked slowly to and fro.

'Don't feel bad, baby. It was Franklin or a little girl. And from now on, it's society or the Norrises.'

'What'll we do?'

'Go to Atlanta and work for Anthropos. I'll take up where Delmont left off.'

'Terry!'

'Peony will need a husband. They may find all of Delmont's males. I'll *make* her one. Then we'll see if a pair of Chimp-Ks can do better than their makers.'

Wearily, he stretched out on the sofa.

'What about the priest? Suppose he tells about Peony. Suppose he guesses about Franklin and tells the police?'

'The police,' he said, 'would then smell a motive. They'd figure it out and I'd be finished. We'll wait and see. Let's don't talk; I'm tired. We'll just wait for Miler to come in.'

She began rubbing his temples gently, and he smiled.

'So we wait,' she said. 'Shall I read to you, Terry?'

'That would be pleasant,' he murmured, closing his eyes.

She slipped away, but returned quickly. He heard the rustle of dry pages and smelled musty leather. Then her voice came, speaking old words softly. And he thought of the small child-thing lying peacefully in her cage while angry men stalked about her. A small life with a mind; she came into the world as quietly as a thief, a burglar in the crowded house of Man.

'I will send my fear before thee, and I will destroy the peoples before whom thou shalt come, sending hornets to drive out the Hevite and the Canaanite and the Hethite before thou enterest the land. Little by little, I will drive them out before thee, till thou be increased, and dost possess the land. Then shalt thou be to me a new people, and I to thee a God . . .'

And on the quiet afternoon in May, while he waited for the

police to finish puzzling in the kennels, it seemed to Terrell Norris that an end to scheming and pushing and arrogance was not too far ahead. It should be a pretty good world then.

He hoped Man could fit into it somehow.

BLOOD BANK

The colonel's secretary heard clomping footsteps in the corridor and looked up from her typing. The footsteps stopped in the doorway. A pair of jet-black eyes bored through her once, then looked away. A tall, thin joker in a space commander's uniform stalked into the reception room, sat in the corner, and folded his hands stiffly in his lap. The secretary arched her plucked brows. It had been six months since a visitor had done that—walked in without saying boo to the girl behind the rail.

'You have an appointment, sir?' she asked with a professional smile.

The man nodded curtly but said nothing. His eyes flickered toward her briefly, then returned to the wall. She tried to decide whether he was angry or in pain. The black eyes burned with cold fire. She checked the list of appointments. Her smile disappeared, to be replaced by a tight-lipped expression of scorn.

'You're Space Commander Eli Roki?' she asked in an icy tone.

Again the curt nod. She gazed at him steadily for several seconds. 'Colonel Beth will see you in a few minutes.' Then her typewriter began clattering with sharp sounds of hate.

The man sat quietly, motionlessly. The colonel passed through the reception room once and gave him a brief nod. Two majors came in from the corridor and entered the colonel's office without looking at him. A few moments later, the intercom crackled, 'Send Roki in, Dela. Bring your pad and come with him.'

The girl looked at Roki, but he was already on his feet, striding toward the door. Evidently he came from an unchivalrous planet; he opened the door without looking at her and let her catch in when it started to slam.

Chubby, elderly Colonel Beth sat waiting behind his desk, flanked by the pair of majors. Roki's bearing as he approached and saluted was that of the professional soldier, trained from birth for the military.

'Sit down, Roki.'

The tall space commander sat at attention and waited, his face expressionless, his eyes coolly upon the colonel's forehead. Beth shuffled some papers on his desk, then spoke slowly.

'Before we begin, I want you to understand something, commander.'

'Yes, sir.'

'You are not being tried. This is not a court-martial. There are no charges against you. Is that clear?'

'Yes, sir.'

The colonel's pale eyes managed to look at Roki's face without showing any contempt. 'This investigation is for the record, and for the public. The incident has already been investigated, as you know. But the people are aroused, and we have to make a show of some kind.'

'I understand, sir.'

'Then let's begin. Dela, take notes, please.' The colonel glanced at the papers before him. 'Space Commander Roki, will you please tell us in your own words what happened during patrol flight Sixty-one on fourday sixmonth, year eighty-seven?'

There was a brief silence. The girl was staring at the back of Roki's neck as if she longed to attack it with a hatchet. Roki's thin face was a waxen mask as he framed his words. His voice came calm as a bell and clear.

'The flight was a random patrol. We blasted off Jod VII at thirteen hours, Universal Patrol Time, switched on the high-C drive, and penetrated to the ten-thousandth level of the C'th component. We re-entered the continuum on the outer patrol radius at thirty-six degrees theta and two-hundred degrees psi. My navigator threw the dice to select a random course. We were to proceed to a point on the same co-ordinate shell at thirty theta and one-fifty psi. We began—'

The colonel interrupted. 'Were you aware at the time that your course would intersect that of the mercy ship?'

The girl looked up again. Roki failed to wince at the question. 'I was aware of it, sir.'

'Go on.'

'We proceeded along the randomly selected course until the

warp detectors warned us of a ship. When we came in range, I told the engineer to jockey into a parallel course and to lock the automatics to *keep* us parallel. When that was accomplished, I called the unknown freighter with the standard challenge.'

'You saw its insignia?'

'Yes, sir. The yellow mercy star.'

'Go on. Did they answer your challenge?'

'Yes, sir. The reply, decoded, was: Mercy liner Sol-G-6, departure Sol III, destination Jod VI, cargo emergency surgi-bank supplies, Cluster Request A-4-J.'

Beth nodded and watched Roki with clinical curiosity. 'You knew about the Jod VI disaster? That twenty thousand casualties were waiting in Suspendfreeze lockers for those supplies?'

'Yes, sir. I'm sorry they died.'

'Go on with your account.'

'I ordered the navigator to throw the dice again, to determine whether or not the freighter should be boarded for random cargo inspection. He threw a twelve, the yes-number. I called the freighter again, ordered the outer locks opened. It failed to answer, or respond in any way.'

'One moment. You explained the reason for boarding? Sol is on the outer rim of the galaxy. It doesn't belong to any cluster system. Primitive place—or regressed. They wouldn't understand our ways.'

'I allowed for that, sir,' continued the cold-faced Roki. 'I explained the situation, even read them extracts of our patrol regs. They failed to acknowledge. I thought perhaps they were out of contact, so I had the message repeated to them by blinker. I know they got it, because the blinker-operator acknowledged the message. Evidently carried it to his superiors. Apparently they told him to ignore us, because when we blinked again, he failed to acknowledge. I then attempted to pull alongside and attach to their hull by magnetic grapples.'

'They resisted?'

'Yes, sir. They tried to break away by driving to a higher C-level. Our warp was already at six-thousand C's. The mass-components of our star cluster at that level were just a collapsing gas cloud. Of course, with our automatic trackers, they just dragged us with them, stalled, and plunged the other way. They pulled us down to the quarter-C level; most of the galaxy was at the red-dwarf stage. I suppose they realized then that they couldn't get away from us like that. They came back to a sensible warp and continued on their previous course.'

'And you did what?'

'We warned them by every means of communication at our disposal, read them the standard warning.'

'They acknowledge?'

'Once, sir. They came back to say: This is an emergency shipment. We have orders not to stop. We are continuing on course, and will report you to authority upon arrival.' Roki paused, eyeing the colonel doubtfully. 'May I make a personal observation, sir?'

Beth nodded tolerantly. 'Go ahead.'

'They wasted more time dodging about in the C'th component than they would have lost if they had allowed us to board them. I regarded this behavior as highly suspicious.'

'Did it occur to you that it might be due to some peculiarity in Sol III's culture? Some stubbornness, or resentment of authority?'

'Yes, sir.'

'Did you ask opinions of your crew?'

A slight frown creased Roki's high forehead. 'No, sir.'

'Why not?'

'Regulation does not require it, sir. My personal reason—the cultural peculiarities of my planet.'

The barb struck home. Colonel Beth knew the military culture of Roki's world—Coph IV. Military rank was inherited. On his own planet, Roki was a nobleman and an officer of the war-college. He had been taught to rely upon his own decisions and to expect crisp, quick obedience. The colonel frowned at his desk.

'Let's put it this way: Did you *know* the opinions of the crew?'

'Yes, sir. They thought that we should abandon the pursuit and allow the freighter to continue. I was forced to confine two of them to the brig for insubordination and attempted mutiny.' He stopped and glanced at one of the majors. 'All due apologies to you, sir.'

The major flushed. He ranked Roki, but he had been with the patrol as an observer, and despite his higher rank, he was subject to the ship commander's authority while in space. He had also been tossed in the brig. Now he glared at the Cophian space commander without speaking.

'All right, commander, when they refused to halt, what did you do?'

'I withdrew to a safe range and fired a warning charge ahead of them. It exploded in full view of their scopes, dead ahead. They ignored the warning and tried to flee again.'

'Go on.'

Roki's shoulders lifted in the suggestion of a shrug. 'In accordance with Article Thirty of the Code, I shot them out of space.'

The girl made a choking sound. 'And over ten thousand people died on Jod VI because you—'

'That will do, Dela!' snapped Colonel Beth.

There was a long silence. Roki waited calmly for further questioning. He seemed unaware of the girl's outburst. The colonel's voice came again with a forced softness.

'You examined the debris of the destroyed vessel?'

'Yes, sir.'

'What did you find?'

'Fragments of quick-frozen bone, blood plasma, various bodily organs and tissues in cultured or frozen form, prepared for surgical use in transplanting operations; in other words, a complete stock of surgibank supplies, as was anticipated. We gathered up samples, but we had no facilities for preserving what was left.'

The colonel drummed his fingers. 'You said "anticipated." Then you knew full well the nature of the cargo, and you did not suspect contraband material of any kind?'

Roki paused. 'I suspected contraband, colonel,' he said quietly.

Beth lifted his eyebrows in surprise. 'You didn't say that before.'

'I was never asked.'

'Why didn't you say it anyway?'

'I had no proof.'

'Ah, yes,' murmured the colonel. 'The culture of Coph IV again. Very well, but in examining the debris, you found no evidence of contraband?' The colonel's distasteful expression told the room that he knew the answer, but only wanted it on the record.

But Roki paused a long time. Finally, he said, 'No evidence, sir.'

'Why do you hesitate?'

'Because I still suspect an illegality—without proof, I'm afraid.'

This time, the colonel's personal feelings betrayed him in a snort of disgust. He shuffled his papers for a long time, then looked at the major who had accompanied the patrol. 'Will you confirm Roki's testimony, major? Is it essentially truthful, as far as you know?'

The embarrassed officer glared at Roki in undisguised hatred. 'For the record, sir—I think the commander behaved disgracefully and insensibly. The results of the stoppage of vitally needed supplies prove—'

'I didn't ask for a moral judgment!' Beth snapped. 'I asked you to confirm what he has said here. Were the incidents as he described them?'

The major swallowed hard. 'Yes, sir.'

The colonel nodded. 'Very well. I'll ask your opinions, gentlemen. Was there an infraction of regulations? Did Commander Roki behave as required by Space Code, or did he not? Yes or no, please. Major Tuli?'

'No direct infraction, sir, but—'

'No *buts!* Major Go'an?'

'Uh—no infraction, sir.'

'I find myself in agreement.' The colonel spoke directly at Dela's note pad. 'The ultimate results of the incident were disastrous, indeed. And, Roki's action was unfortunate, ill-advised, and not as the Sixty Star Patrol would approve. Laws, codes, regulations are made for men, not men for regulations. Roki observed the letter of the law, but was perhaps forgetful of its spirit. However, no charge can be found against him. This investigating body recommends that he be temporarily grounded without prejudice, and given thorough physical and mental examinations before being returned to duty. That brings us to an end, gentlemen. Dela, you may go.'

With another glare at the haughty Cophian, the girl stalked out of the room. Beth leaned back in his chair, while the majors saluted and excused themselves. His eyes kept Roki locked in his chair. When they were alone, Beth said:

'You have anything to say to me off the record?'

Roki nodded. 'I can submit my resignation from the patrol through your office, can't I, sir?'

Beth smiled coldly. 'I thought you'd do that, Roki.' He opened a desk drawer and brought out a single sheet of paper. 'I took the liberty of having it prepared for your signature. Don't misunderstand. I'm not urging you to resign, but we're prepared to accept it if you choose to do so. If you don't like this standard form, you may prepare your own.'

The jet-eyed commander took the paper quickly and slashed his name quickly across the bottom. 'Is this effective immediately, sir?'

'In this case, we can make it so.'

'Thank you, sir.'

'Don't regard it as a favor.' The colonel witnessed the signature.

The Cophian could not be stung. 'May I go now?'

Beth looked up, noticing with amusement that Roki—now a civilian—had suddenly dropped the 'sir.' And his eyes were no longer cold. They were angry, hurt, despairing.

'What makes you Cophians tick anyway?' he murmured thoughtfully.

Roki stood up. 'I don't care to discuss it with you, colonel. I'll be going now.'

'Wait, Roki.' Beth frowned ominously to cover whatever he felt.

'I'm waiting.'

'Up until this incident, I liked you, Roki. In fact, I told the general that you were the most promising young officer in my force.'

'Kind of you,' he replied tonelessly.

'And you could have been sitting at this desk, in a few years. You hoped to, I believe.'

A curt nod, and a quick glance at Beth's shoulder insignia.

'You chose your career, and now you don't have it. I know what it means to you.'

A tightening of the Cophian's jaw told the colonel that he wanted no sympathy, but Beth continued.

'Since this is the oldest, most established, most static planet in the Cluster, you're out of a job in a place where there's no work.'

'That's none of your business, colonel,' Roki said quietly.

'According to my culture's ethics it *is* my business,' he bellowed. 'Of course you Cophians think differently. But we're not quite so cold. Now you listen: I'm prepared to help you a little, although you're probably too pig-headed to accept. God knows, you don't deserve it anyway.'

'Go on.'

'I'm prepared to have a patrol ship take you to any planet in the galaxy. Name it, and we'll take you there.' He paused. 'All right, go ahead and refuse. Then get out.'

Roki's thin face twitched for a moment. Then he nodded. 'I'll accept. Take me to Sol III.'

The colonel got his breath again slowly. He reddened and chewed his lip. 'I did say galaxy, didn't I? I meant . . . well . . . you know we can't send a military ship outside the Sixty-Star Cluster.'

Roki waited impassively, his dark eyes measuring the colonel.

'Why do you want to go *there?*'

'Personal reasons.'

'Connected with the mercy ship incident?'

'The investigation is over.'

Beth pounded his desk. 'It's crazy, man! Nobody's been to Sol for a thousand years. No reason to go. Sloppy, decadent place. I never suspected *they'd* answer Jod VI's plea for surgibank supplies!'

'Why not? They were *selling* them.'

'Of course. But I doubted that Sol still had ships, especially C-drive ships. Only contribution Sol ever made to the galaxy was to spawn the race of Man—if you believe that story. It's way out of contact with any interstellar nation. I just don't get it.'

'Then you restrict your offer, colonel?' Roki's eyes mocked him.

Beth sighed. 'No, no—I *said* it. I'll do it. But I can't send a patrol ship that far. I'll have to pay your way on a private vessel. We can find some excuse—exploration maybe.'

Roki's eyes flickered sardonically. 'Why not send a diplomatic delegation—to apologize to Sol for the blasting of their mercy ship.'

'Uk! With YOU aboard?'

'Certainly. They won't know me.'

Beth just stared at Roki as if he were of a strange species.

'You'll do it?' urged Roki.

'I'll think it over. I'll see that you get there, if you insist on going. Now get out of here. I've had enough of you, Roki.'

The Cophian was not offended. He turned on his heel and left the office. The girl looked up from her filing cabinets as he came out. She darted ahead of him and blocked the doorway with her small tense body. Her face was a white mask of disgust, and she spoke between her teeth.

'How does it feel to murder ten thousand people and get away with it?' she hissed.

Roki looked at her face more closely and saw the racial characteristics of Jod VI—the slightly oversized irises of her yellow-brown eyes, the thin nose with flaring nostrils, the pointed jaw. Evidently some of her relatives had died in the disaster and she held him personally responsible. He had destroyed the help that was on its way to casualties.

'How does it feel?' she demanded, her voice going higher, and her hands clenching into weapons.

'Would you step aside please, Miss?'

A quick hand slashed out to rake his cheek with sharp nails. Pain seared his face. He did not move. Two bright stripes of blood appeared from his eye to the corner of his mouth. A drop trickled to the point of his chin and splattered down upon the girl's shoe.

'On my planet,' he said, in a not unkindly tone, 'when a woman insists on behaving like an animal, we assist her—by having her flogged naked in the public square. I see personal dignity is not so highly prized here. You do not regard it as a crime to behave like an alley cat?'

Her breath gushed out of her in a sound of rage, and she tore at the wounds again. Then, when he did nothing but look at her coldly, she fled.

Eli Roki, born to the nobility of Coph, dedicated to the service of the Sixty-Star Cluster, suddenly found himself something of an outcast. As he strode down the corridor away from Beth's office, he seemed to be walking into a thickening fog of desolation. He had no home now; for he had abdicated his hereditary rights on Coph in order to accept a commission with the SSC Patrol. That, too, was gone; and with it his career.

He had known from the moment he pressed the firing stud to blast the mercy freighter that unless the freighter proved to be a smuggler, his career would be forfeit. He was still morally certain that he had made no mistake. Had the freighter been carrying any other cargo, he would have been disciplined for *not* blasting it. And, if they had had nothing to hide, they would have stopped for inspection. Somewhere among Sol's planets lay the answer to the question—'What else was aboard besides the cargo of mercy?'

Roki shivered and stiffened his shoulders as he rode homeward in a heliocab. If the answer to the question were 'Nothing,' then according to the code of his planet, there was only one course left to follow. 'The Sword of Apology' it was called.

He waited in his quarters for the colonel to fulfill his promise. On the following day, Beth called.

'I've found a Dalethian ship, Roki. Privately owned. Pilot's willing to fly you out of the Cluster. It's going as an observation mission—gather data on the Sol System. The commissioners vetoed the idea of sending a diplomatic delegation until we try to contact Solarians by high-C radio.'

'When do I leave?'

'Be at the spaceport tonight. And good luck, son. I'm sorry all this happened, and I hope—'

'Yeah, thanks.'

'Well—'

'Well?'

The colonel grunted and hung up. Ex-Commander Roki gathered up his uniforms and went looking for a pawn shop. 'Hock 'em, or sell 'em?' asked a bald man behind the counter. Then he peered more closely at Roki's face, and paused to glance at a picture on the front page of the paper. 'Oh,' he grunted, 'you. You wanta sell 'em.' With a slight sneer, he pulled two bills from his pocket and slapped them on the counter with a contemptuous take-it-or-leave-it stare. The clothing was worth at least twice as much. Roki took it after a moment's hesitation. The money just matched the price tag on a sleek, snub-nosed Multin automatic that lay in the display case.

'And three hundred rounds of ammunition,' he said quietly as he pocketed the weapon.

The dealer sniffed. 'It only takes one shot, bud—for what *you* need to do.'

Roki thanked him for the advice and took his three hundred rounds.

He arrived at the spaceport before his pilot, and went out to inspect the small Dalethian freighter that would bear him to the rim of the galaxy. His face clouded as he saw the pitted hull and the glaze of fusion around the lips of the jet tubes. Some of the ground personnel had left a Geiger hanging on the stern, to warn wanderers to keep away. Its dial indicator was fluttering in the red. He carried it into the ship. The needle dropped to a safe reading in the control cabin, but there were dangerous spots in the reactor room. Angrily he went to look over the controls.

His irritation grew. The ship—aptly named the *Idiot*—was of ancient vintage, without the standard warning systems or safety devices, and with no armament other than its ion guns. The fifth dial of its position-indicator was calibrated only to one hundred thousand C's, and was redlined at ninety thousand. A modern service-ship, on the other hand, could have penetrated to a segment of five-space where light's velocity was constant at one hundred fifty thousand C's and could reach Sol in two months. The *Idiot* would need five or six, if it could make the trip at all. Roki doubted it. Under normal circumstances, he would hesitate to use the vessel even within the volume of the Sixty-Star Cluster.

He thought of protesting to Beth, but realized that the colonel had fulfilled his promise, and would do nothing more. Grumbling, he stowed his gear in the cargo hold, and settled down in the control room to doze in wait for the pilot.

A sharp whack across the soles of his boots brought him painfully awake. 'Get your feet off the controls!' snapped an angry voice.

Roki winced and blinked at a narrow frowning face with a cigar clenched in its teeth. 'And get out of that chair!' the face growled around its cigar.

His feet stung with pain. He hissed a snarl and bounded to his feet; grabbing a handful of the intruder's shirt-front, he aimed a punch at the cigar—then stayed the fist in midair. Something felt wrong about the shirt. Aghast, he realized there was a woman inside it. He let go and reddened. 'I . . . I thought you were the pilot.'

She eyed him contemptuously as she tucked in her shirt. 'I am, Doc.' She tossed her hat on the navigation desk, revealing a close-cropped head of dark hair. She removed the cigar from her face, neatly pinched out the fire, and filed the butt in the pocket of her dungarees for a rainy day. She had a nice mouth, with the cigar gone, but it was tight with anger.

'Stay out of my seat,' she told him crisply, 'and out of my hair. Let's get that straight before we start.'

'This . . . this is *your* tub?' he gasped.

She stalked to a panel and began punching settings into the courser. 'That's right. I'm Daleth Shipping Incorporated. Any comments?'

'You expect this wreck to make it to Sol?' he growled.

She snapped him a sharp, green-eyed glance. 'Well listen to the free ride! Make your complaints to the colonel, fellow. I don't expect anything, except my pay. I'm willing to chance it. Why shouldn't you?'

'The existence of a fool is not necessarily a proof of the existence of two fools,' he said sourly.

'If you don't like it, go elsewhere.' She straightened and swept him with a clinical glance. 'But as I understand it, *you* can't be too particular.'

He frowned. 'Are you planning to make *that* your business?'

'*Uh*-uh! You're nothing to me, fellow. I don't care *who* I haul, as long as it's legal. Now do you want a ride, or don't you?'

He nodded curtly and stalked back to find quarters. 'Stay outa my cabin,' she bellowed after him.

Roki grunted disgustedly. The pilot was typical of Daleth civilization. It was still a rough, uncouth planet with a thinly scattered population, a wild frontier, and growing pains. The girl was the product of a wildly expanding tough-fisted culture with little respect for authority. It occurred to him immediately that she might be thinking of selling him to the Solarian officials—as the man who blasted the mercy ship.

'Prepare to lift,' came the voice of the intercom. 'Two minutes before blast-off.'

Roki suppressed an urge to scramble out of the ship and call the whole thing off. The rockets belched, coughed, and then hissed faintly, idling in wait for a command. Roki stretched out on his bunk, for some of these older ships were rather rough on blast-off. The hiss became a thunder, and the *Idiot* moved skyward—first slowly, then with a spurt of speed. When it cleared the atmosphere, there was a sudden lurch as it shed the now empty booster burners. There was a moment of dead silence, as the ship hovered without power. Then the faint shriek of the ion streams came to his ears—as the ion drive became useful in the vacuum of space. He glanced out the port to watch the faint streak of luminescence focus into a slender needle of high-speed particles, pushing the *Idiot* ever higher in a rush of acceleration.

He punched the intercom button. 'Not bad, for a Dalethian,' he called admiringly.

'Keep your opinions to yourself,' growled Daleth Incorporated.

The penetration to higher C-levels came without subjective sensation. Roki knew it was happening when the purr from the reactor room went deep-throated and when the cabin lights went dimmer. He stared calmly out the port, for the phenomenon of penetration never ceased to thrill him.

The transition to high-C began as a blue-shift in the starlight. Distant, dull-red stars came slowly brighter, whiter—until they burned like myriad welding arcs in the black vault. They were not identical with the stars of the home continuum, but rather, projections of the same star-masses at higher C-levels of five-space, where the velocity of light was gradually increasing as the *Idiot* climbed higher in the C-component.

At last he had to close the port, for the starlight was becoming unbearable as its wave-length moved into the ultra-violet and the X-ray bands. He watched on a fluorescent viewing screen. The projective star-masses were flaring into supernovae, and the changing continuums seemed to be collapsing toward the ship in the blue-shift of the cosmos. As the radiant energy increased, the cabin became warmer, and the pilot set up a partial radiation screen.

At last the penetration stopped. Roki punched the intercom again. 'What level are we on, Daleth?'

'Ninety thousand,' she replied curtly.

Roki made a wry mouth. She had pushed it up to the red line without a blink. It was O.K.—if the radiation screens held out. If they failed to hold it, the ship would be blistered into a drifting dust cloud.

'Want me to navigate for you?' he called.

'I'm capable of handling my own ship,' she barked.

'I'm aware of that. But I have nothing else to do. You might as well put me to work.'

She paused, then softened a little. 'O.K., come on forward.'

She swung around in her chair as he entered the cabin, and for the first time he noticed that, despite the close-cropped hair and the dungarees and the cigar-smoking, she was quite a handsome girl—handsome, proud, and highly capable. Daleth, the frontier planet, bred a healthy if somewhat unscrupulous species.

'The C-maps are in that case,' she said, jerking her thumb toward a filing cabinet. 'Work out a course for maximum radiant thrust.'

Roki frowned. 'Why not a least-time course?'

She shook her head. 'My reactors aren't too efficient. We need all the boost we can get from external energy. Otherwise we'll have to dive back down for fuel.'

Worse and worse!—Roki thought as he dragged out the C-maps. Flying this boat to Sol would have been a feat of daring two centuries ago. Now, in an age of finer ships, it was a feat of idiocy.

Half an hour later, he handed her a course plan that would allow the *Idiot* to derive about half of its thrust from the variations in radiation pressure from the roaring inferno of the high-level cosmos. She looked it over without change of expression, then glanced at him curiously, after noting the time.

'You're pretty quick,' she said.

'Thank you.'

'You're hardly stupid. Why did you pull such a stupid boner?'

Roki stiffened. 'I thought you planned to regard that as none of your business.'

She shrugged and began punching course-settings into the courser. 'Sorry, I forgot.'

Still angry, he said, 'I don't regard it as a boner. I'd do it again.'

She shrugged again and pretended a lack of interest.

'Space-smuggling could be the death of the galaxy,' he went on. 'That's been proven. A billion people once died on Tau II because somebody smuggled in a load of non-Tauian animals —for house pets. I did only what history has proven best.'

'I'm trying to mind my own business,' she growled, eyeing him sourly.

Roki fell silent and watched her reshape the radiation screen to catch a maximum of force from the flare of energy that blazed behind them. Roki was not sure that he wanted her to mind her own business. They would have to bear each other's presence for several months, and it would be nice to know how things stood.

'So you think it was a stupid boner,' he continued at last. 'So does everyone else. It hasn't been very pleasant.'

She snorted scornfully as she worked. 'Where I come from, we don't condemn fools. We don't need to. They just don't live very long, not on Daleth.'

'And I am a fool, by your code?'

'How should I know? If you live to a ripe old age and get what you want, you probably aren't a fool.'

And *that,* thought Roki, was the Dalethian golden rule. If the universe lets you live, then you're doing all right. And there was truth in it, perhaps. Man was born with only one right—the right to a chance at proving his fitness. And that right was the foundation of every culture, even though most civilized worlds tried to define 'fitness' in terms of cultural values. Where life was rough, it was rated in terms of survival.

'I really don't mind talking about it,' he said with some embarrassment. 'I have nothing to hide.'

'That's nice.'

'Do you have a name—other than your firm name?'

'As far as you're concerned, I'm Daleth Incorporated.' She gave him a suspicious look that lingered a while and became contemplative. 'There's only one thing I'm curious about—why are you going to Sol?'

He smiled wryly. 'If I told a Dalethian that, she would indeed think me a fool.'

Slowly the girl nodded. 'I see. I know of Cophian ethics. If an officer's blunder results in someone's death, he either proves that it was not a blunder or he cuts his throat—ceremonially, I believe. Will you do that?'

Roki shrugged. He had been away from Coph a long time. He didn't know.

'A stupid custom,' she said.

'It manages to drain off the fools, doesn't it? It's better than having society try them and execute them forcibly for their crimes. On Coph, a man doesn't need to be afraid of society. He needs only to be afraid of his own weakness. Society's function is to protect individuals against unfortunate accidents, but not against their own blunders. And when a man blunders, Coph simply excludes him from the protectorate. As an outcast, he sacrifices himself. It's not too bad a system.'

'You can have it.'

'Dalethian?'

'Yeah?'

'You have no personal anger against what I did?'

She frowned at him contemptuously. 'Uh-uh! I judge no one. I judge no one unless I'm personally involved. Why are you worried about what others think?'

'In our more highly developed society,' he said stiffly, 'a man inevitably grows a set of thinking-habits called "conscience."'

'Oh—yeah.' Her dull tone indicated a complete lack of interest.

Again Roki wondered if she would think of making a quick bit of cash by informing Solarian officials of his identity. He began a mental search for a plan to avoid such possible treachery.

They ate and slept by the ship's clock. On the tenth day, Roki noticed a deviation in the readings of the radiation-screen instruments. The shape of the screen shell was gradually trying to drift toward minimum torsion, and assume a spherical shape. He pointed it out to Daleth, and she quickly made the necessary readjustments. But the output of the reactors crept a notch higher as a result of the added drain. Roki wore an apprehensive frown as the flight progressed.

Two days later, the screen began creeping again. Once more the additional power was applied. And the reactor output needle hung in the yellow band of warning. The field-generators were groaning and shivering with threatening overload. Roki worked furiously to locate the trouble, and at last he found it. He returned to the control cabin in a cold fury.

'Did you have this ship pre-flighted before blast-off?' he demanded.

Her mouth fluttered with amusement as she watched his anger. 'Certainly, commander.'

He flushed at the worthless title. 'May I see the papers?'

For a moment she hesitated, then fumbled in her pocket and displayed a folded pink paper.

'Pink!' he roared. 'You had no business taking off!'

Haughtily, she read him the first line of the pre-flight report. '"Base personnel disclaim any responsibility for accidents resulting from flight of Daleth Ship—" It doesn't say I can't take off.'

'I'll see you banned from space!' he growled.

She gave him a look that reminded him of his current status. It was a tolerant, amused stare. 'What's wrong, commander?'

'The synchronizers are out, that's all,' he fumed. 'Screen's getting farther and farther from resonance.'

'So?'

'So the overload'll get worse, and the screen'll break down. You'll have to drop back down out of the C-component and get it repaired.'

She shook her head. 'We'll chance it like it is. I've always wanted to find out how much overload the reactor'll take.'

Roki choked. There wasn't a chance of making it. 'Are you a graduate space engineer?' he asked.

'No.'

'Then you'd better take one's advice.'

'Yours?'

'Yes.'

'No! We're going on.'

'Suppose I refuse to let you?'

She whirled quickly, eyes flashing. 'I'm in command of my

ship. I'm also armed. I suggest you return to your quarters, passenger.'

Roki sized up the situation, measured the determination in the girl's eyes, and decided that there was only one thing to do. He shrugged and looked away, as if admitting her authority. She glared at him for a moment, but did not press her demand that he leave the control room. As soon as she glanced back at the instruments, Roki padded his rough knuckles with a handkerchief, selected a target at the back of her short crop of dark hair, and removed her objections with a short chopping blow to the head. 'Sorry, friend,' he murmured as he lifted her limp body out of the seat.

He carried her to her quarters and placed her on the bunk. After removing a small needle gun from her pocket, he left a box of headache tablets in easy reach, locked her inside, and went back to the controls. His fist was numb, and he felt like a heel, but there was no use arguing with a Dalethian. Clubbing her to sleep was the only way to avoid bloodier mayhem in which she might have emerged the victor—until the screen gave way.

The power-indication was threateningly high as Roki activated the C-drive and began piloting the ship downward through the fifth component. But with proper adjustments, he made the process analogous to freefall, and the power reading fell off slowly. A glance at the C-maps told him that the *Idiot* would emerge far beyond the limits of Sixty-Star Cluster. When it re-entered the continuum, it would be in the general volume of space controlled by another interstellar organization called The Viggern Federation. He knew little of its culture, but certainly it should have facilities for repairing a set of screen-synchronizers. He looked up its capitol planet, and began jetting toward it while the ship drifted downward in C. As he reached lower energy-levels, he cut out the screen altogether and went to look in on Daleth Incorporated who had made no sound for two hours.

He was surprised to see her awake and sitting up on the bunk. She gave him a cold and deadly stare, but displayed no rage. 'I should've known better than to turn my back on you.'

'Sorry. You were going to—'

'Save it. Where are we?'

'Coming in on Tragor III.'

'I'll have you jailed on Tragor III, then.'

He nodded. 'You *could* do that, but then you might have trouble collecting my fare from Beth.'

'That's all right.'

'Suit yourself. I'd rather be jailed on your trumped-up charges than be a wisp of gas at ninety-thousand C's.'

'Trumped up?'

'Sure, the pink pre-flight. Any court will say that whatever happened was your own fault. You lose your authority if you fly pink, unless your crew signs a release.'

'You a lawyer?'

'I've had a few courses in space law. But if you don't believe me, check with the Interfed Service on Tragor III.'

'I will. Now how about opening the door. I want out.'

'Behave?'

She paused, then: 'My promise wouldn't mean anything, Roki. I don't share your system of ethics.'

He watched her cool green eyes for a moment, then chuckled. 'In a sense you *do*—or you wouldn't have said *that*.' He unlocked the cabin and released her, not trusting her, but realizing that the synchronizers were so bad by now that she couldn't attempt to go on without repairs. She could have no motive for turning on him—except anger perhaps.

'My gun?' she said.

Again Roki hesitated. Then, smiling faintly, he handed it to her. She took the weapon, sniffed scornfully, and cocked it.

'Turn around, fool!' she barked.

Roki folded his arms across his chest, and remained facing her. 'Go to the devil,' he said quietly.

Her fingers whitened on the trigger. Still the Cophian failed to flinch, lose his smile, or move. Daleth Incorporated arched her eyebrows, uncocked the pistol, and returned it to her belt. Then she patted his cheek and chuckled nastily. 'Just watch yourself, commander. I don't like you.'

And he noticed, as she turned away, that she had a bump on her head to prove it. He wondered how much the bump would cost him before it was over. Treachery on Sol, perhaps.

The pilot called Tragor III and received instructions to set an orbital course to await inspection. All foreign ships were boarded before being permitted to land. A few hours later, a small patrol ship winged close and grappled to the hull. Roki went to manipulate the locks.

A captain and two assistants came through. The inspector was a young man with glasses and oversized ears. His eyebrows were ridiculously bushy and extended down on each side to his cheekbones. The ears were also filled with yellow brush. Roki recognized the peculiarities as local evolutionary tendencies; for they were shared also by the assistants. Tragor III evidently had an exceedingly dusty atmosphere.

The captain nodded a greeting and requested the ship's flight papers. He glanced at the pink pre-flight, clucked to himself, and read every word in the dispatcher's forms. 'Observation flight? To Sol?' He addressed himself to Roki, using the interstellar Esperanto.

The girl answered. 'That's right. Let's get this over with.'

The captain gave her a searing, head-to toe glance. 'Are you the ship's owner, woman?'

Daleth Incorporated contained her anger with an effort. 'I am.'

The captain told her what a Tragorian thought of it by turning aside from her, and continuing to address Roki as if he were ship's skipper. 'Please leave the ship while we fumigate and inspect. Wohr will make you comfortable in the patrol vessel. You will have to submit to physical examination—a contagion precaution.'

Roki nodded, and they started out after the assistant. As they entered the corridor, he grinned at Daleth, and received a savage kick in the shin for his trouble.

'Oops, sorry!' she muttered.

'Oh—one moment, sir,' the captain called after them. 'May I speak to you a moment—'

They both stopped and turned.

'Privately,' the captain added.

The girl marched angrily on. Roki stepped back in the cabin and nodded.

'You are a well-traveled man, E Roki?' the bushy-browed man asked politely.

'Space has been my business.'

'Then you need no warning about local customs.' The captain bowed.

'I know enough to respect them and conform to them,' Roki assured him. 'That's a general rule. But I'm not familiar with Tragor III. Is there anything special I should know before we start out?'

'Your woman, E Roki. You might do well to inform her that she will have to wear a veil, speak to no man, and be escorted upon the streets at all times. Otherwise, she will be wise to remain on the ship, in her quarters.'

Roki suppressed a grin. 'I shall try to insure her good behavior.'

The captain looked defensive. 'You regard our customs as primitive?'

'Every society to its own tastes, captain. The wisdom of one society would be folly for another. Who is qualified to judge? Only the universe, which passes the judgment of survival on all peoples.'

'Thank you. You are a wise traveler. I might explain that our purdah is the result of an evolutionary peculiarity. You will see for yourself, however.'

'I can't *guarantee* my companion's behavior,' Roki said before he went to join Daleth. 'But I'll try my best to influence her.'

Roki was grinning broadly as he went to the patrol vessel to wait. One thing was certain: the girl would have a rough time on Tragor if she tried to have him jailed for mutiny.

Her face reddened to forge-heat as he relayed the captain's warning.

'I shall do nothing of the sort,' she said stiffly.

Roki shrugged. 'You know enough to respect local customs.'

'Not when they're personally humiliating!' She curled up on a padded seat in the visitor's room and began to pout. He decided to drop the subject.

Repairing the synchronizers promised to be a week-long job, according to the Tragorian inspector who accompanied the *Idiot* upon landing. 'Our replacements are standardized, of course—within our own system. But parts for SSC ships aren't carried in stock. The synchronizers will have to be specially tailored.'

'Any chance of rushing the job?'

'A week *is* rushing it.'

'All right, we'll have to wait.' Roki nudged the controls a bit, guiding the ship toward the landing site pointed out by the captain. Daleth was in her cabin, alone, to save herself embarrassment.

'May I ask a question about your mission, E Roki—or is it confidential in nature?'

Roki paused to think before answering. He would have to lie, of course, but he had to make it safe. Suddenly he chuckled. 'I forgot for a moment that you weren't with Sixty-Star Cluster. So I'll tell you the truth. This is supposed to be an observation mission, officially—but actually, our superior sent us to buy him a holdful of a certain scarce commodity.'

The captain grinned. Graft and corruption were apparently not entirely foreign to Tragor III. But then his grin faded into thoughtfulness. 'On Sol's planets?'

Roki nodded.

'This scarce commodity—if I'm not too curious—is it surgibank supplies?'

Roki felt his face twitch with surprise. But he recovered from his shock in an instant. 'Perhaps,' he said calmly. He wanted to grab the man by the shoulders and shout a thousand questions, but he said nothing else.

The official squirmed in his seat for a time. 'Does your federation buy many mercy cargoes from Sol?'

Roki glanced at him curiously. The captain was brimming with ill-concealed curiosity. Why?

'Occasionally, yes.'

The captain chewed his lip for a moment. 'Tell me,' he blurted, 'will the Solarian ships stop for your patrol inspections?'

Roki hesitated for a long time. Then he said, 'I suppose that you and I could get together and share what we know about Sol without revealing any secrets of our own governments. Frankly, I, too, am curious about Sol.'

The official, whose name was WeJan, was eager to accept. He scrawled a peculiar series of lines on a scrap of paper and gave it to Roki. 'Show this to a heliocab driver. He will take you to my apartment. Would dinner be convenient?'

Roki said that it would.

The girl remained in her quarters when they landed. Roki knocked at the door, but she was either stubborn or asleep. He left the ship and stood for a moment on the ramp, staring at the hazy violet sky. Fine grit sifted against his face and stung his eyes.

'You will be provided goggles, suitable clothing, and an interpreter to accompany you during your stay,' said WeJan as they started toward a low building.

But Roki was scarcely listening as he stared across the ramp. A thousand yards away was a yellow-starred mercy ship, bearing Solar markings. The most peculiar thing about it was the ring of guards that surrounded it. They apparently belonged to the ship, for their uniforms were different from those of the base personnel.

WeJan saw him looking. 'Strange creatures, aren't they?' he whispered confidentially.

Roki had decided that in the long run he could gain more information by pretending to know more than he did. So he nodded wisely and said nothing. The mercy ship was too far away for him to decide whether the guards were human. He could make out only that they were bipeds. 'Sometimes one meets strange ones all right. Do you know the Quinjori—from the other side of the galaxy?'

'No—no, I believe not, E Roki. Quinjori?'

'Yes. A very curious folk. Very curious indeed.' He smiled to himself and fell silent. Perhaps, before his visit was over, he could trade fictions about the fictitious Quinjori for facts about the Solarians.

Roki met his interpreter in the spaceport offices, donned the loose garb of Tragor, and went to quibble with repair service. Still he could not shorten the promised-time on the new synchros. They were obviously stuck for a week on Tragor. He thought of trying to approach the Solarian ship, but decided that it would be better to avoid suspicion.

Accompanied by the bandy-legged interpreter, whose mannerisms were those of a dog who had received too many beatings, Roki set out for Polarin, the Tragorian capital, a few miles away. His companion was a small middle-aged man with a piping voice and flaring ears; Roki decided that his real job was to watch his alien charge for suspicious activities, for the little man was no expert linguist. He spoke two or three of the tongues used in the Sixty-Star Cluster, but not fluently. The Cophian decided to rely on the Esperanto of space, and let the interpreter translate it into native Tragorian wherever necessary.

'How would E Roki care to amuse himself?' the little man asked. 'A drink? A pretty girl? A museum?'

Roki chuckled. 'What do most of your visitors do while they're here?' He wondered quietly what, in particular, the *Solarian* visitors did. But it might not be safe to ask.

'Uh—that would depend on nationality, sir,' murmured Pok. 'The true-human foreigners often like to visit the Wanderer, an establishment which caters to their business. The evolved-human and the nonhuman visitors like to frequent The Court of Kings—a rather, uh, peculiar place.' He looked at Roki, doubtfully, as if wondering about his biological status.

'Which is most expensive?' he asked, although he really didn't care. Because of the phony 'observation mission papers,' he could make Colonel Beth foot the bill.

'The Court of Kings is rather high,' Pok said. 'But so is the Wanderer.'

'Such impartiality deserves a return. We will visit them both, E Pok. If it suits you.'

'I am your servant, E Roki.'

How to identify a Solarian without asking?—Roki wondered as they sat sipping a sticky, yeasty drink in the lounge of the Wanderer. The dimly lighted room was filled with men of all races—pygmies, giants, black, red, and brown. All appeared human, or nearly so. There were a few women among the crewmen, and most of them removed their borrowed veils while in the tolerant sanctuary of the Wanderer. The Tragorian staff kept stealing furtive glances at these out-system females, and the Cophian wondered about their covetousness.

'Why do you keep watching the strange women, E Pok?' he asked the interpreter a few minutes later.

The small man sighed. 'Evidently you have not yet seen Tragorian women.'

Roki had seen a few heavily draped figures on the street outside, clinging tightly to the arms of men, but there hadn't been much to look at. Still, Pok's hint was enough to give him an idea.

'You don't mean Tragor III is one of those places where evolution has pushed the sexes further apart?'

'I do,' Pok said sadly. 'The feminine I.Q. is seldom higher than sixty, the height is seldom taller than your jacket pocket, and the weight is usually greater than your own. As one traveler put it: "short, dumpy, and dumb". Hence, the Purdah.'

'Because you don't like looking at them?'

'Not at all. Theirs is our standard of beauty. The Purdah is because they are frequently too stupid to remember which man is their husband.'

'Sorry I asked.'

'Not at all,' said Pok, whose tongue was being loosened by the yeasty brew. 'It is our tragedy. We can bear it.'

'Well, you've got it better than some planets. On Jevah, for instance, the men evolved into sluggish spidery little fellows, and the women are big husky brawlers.'

'Ah yes. But Sol is the most peculiar of all, is it not?' said Pok.

'How do you mean?' Roki carefully controlled his voice and tried to look bored.

'Why, the Vamir, of course.'

Because of the fact that Pok's eyes failed to move toward any particular part of the room, Roki concluded that there were no Solarians in the place. 'Shall we visit the Court of Kings now, E Pok?' he suggested.

The small man was obviously not anxious to go. He murmured about ugly brutes, lingered over his drink, and gazed wistfully at a big dusky Sanbe woman. 'Do you suppose she would notice me if I spoke to her?' the small interpreter asked.

'Probably. So would her five husbands. Let's go.'

Pok sighed mournfully and came with him.

The Court of Kings catered to a peculiar clientele indeed; but not a one, so far as Roki could see, was completely inhuman. There seemed to be at least one common denominator to all intelligent life: it was bipedal and bimanual. Four legs was the most practical number for any animal on any planet, and it seemed that nature had nothing else to work with. When she decided to give intelligence to a species, she taught him to stand on his hind legs, freeing his forefeet to become tools of his intellect. And she usually taught him by making him use his hands to climb. As a Cophian biologist had said, 'Life first tries to climb a tree to get to the stars. When it fails, it comes down and invents the high-C drive.'

Again, Roki looked around for something that might be a Solarian. He saw several familiar species, some horned, some tailed, scaled, or heavily furred. Some stumbled and drooped as if Tragorian gravity weighted them down. Others bounced about as if floating free in space. One small creature, the native of a planet with an eight-hour rotational period, curled up on the table and fell asleep. Roki guessed that ninety per cent of the customers were of human ancestry, for at one time during the history of the galaxy, Man had sprung forth like a sudden blossom to inherit most of space. Some said they came from Sol III, but there was no positive evidence.

As if echoing his thoughts, Pok suddenly grunted, 'I will never believe we are descended from those surly creatures.'

Roki looked up quickly, wondering if the small interpreter was telepathic. But Pok was sneering toward the doorway. The

Cophian followed his tipsy gaze and saw a man enter. The man was distinguished only by his height and by the fact that he appeared more human, in the classical sense, than most of the other customers. He wore a uniform—maroon jacket and gray trousers—and it matched the ones Roki had seen from a distance at the spaceport.

So this was a Solarian. He stared hard, trying to take in much at once. The man wore a short beard, but there seemed to be something peculiar about the jaw. It was—predatory, perhaps. The skull was massive, but plump and rounded like a baby's, and covered with sparse yellow fur. The eyes were quick and sharp, and seemed almost to leap about the room. He was at least seven feet tall, and there was a look of savagery about him that caused the Cophian to tense, as if sensing an adversary.

'What is it you don't like about them?' he asked, without taking his eyes from the Solarian.

'Their sharp ears for one thing,' whispered Pok as the Solarian whirled to stare toward their table. 'Their nasty tempers for another.'

'Ah? Rage reactions show biologic weakness,' said the Cophian in a mild tone, but as loud as the first time.

The Solarian, who had been waiting for a seat at the bar, turned and stalked straight toward them. Pok whimpered. Roki stared at him cooly. The Solarian loomed over them and glared from one to the other. He seemed to decide that Pok was properly cowed, and he turned his fierce eyes on the ex-patrolman.

'Would you like to discuss biology, manthing?' he growled like distant thunder. His speaking exposed his teeth—huge white chisels of heavy ivory. They were not regressed toward the fanged stage, but they suggested, together with the massive jaw, that nature might be working toward an efficient bone-crusher.

Roki swirled his drink thoughtfully. 'I don't know you, Bristleface,' he murmured. 'But if your biology bothers you, I'd be glad to discuss it with you.'

He watched carefully for the reaction. The Solarian went gray-purple. His eyes danced with fire, and his slit mouth quivered as if to bare the strong teeth. Just as he seemed about to explode, the anger faded—or rather, settled in upon itself to brood. 'This is beneath me,' the eyes seemed to be saying. Then he laughed cordially.

'My apologies. I thought to share a table with you.'

'Help yourself.'

The Solarian paused. 'Where are you from, manthing?'

Roki also paused. They might have heard that a Cophian commander blasted one of their ships. Still he didn't care to be caught in a lie. 'Sixty-Star Cluster,' he grunted.

'Which sun?' The Solarian's voice suggested that he was accustomed to being answered instantly.

Roki glowered at him. 'Information for information, fellow. And I don't talk to people who stand over me.' He pointedly turned to Pok. 'As we were saying—'

'I am of Sol,' growled the big one.

'Fair enough. I am of Coph.'

The giant's brows lifted slightly. 'Ah, yes.' He inspected Roki curiously and sat down. The chair creaked a warning. 'Perhaps that explains it.'

'Explains what?' Roki frowned ominously. He disliked overbearing men, and his hackles were rising. There was something about this fellow—

'I understand that Cophians are given to a certain ruthlessness.'

Roki pretended to ponder the statement while he eyed the big man coldly. 'True, perhaps. It would be dangerous for you to go to Coph, I think. You would probably be killed rather quickly.'

The angry color reappeared, but the man smiled politely. 'A nation of duelists, I believe, military in character, highly disciplined. Yes? They sometimes serve in the Sixty-Star Forces, eh?'

The words left no doubt in Roki's mind that the Solarian knew who had blasted their ship and why. But he doubted that the man had guessed his identity.

'I know less of your world, Solarian.'

'Such ignorance is common. We are regarded as the galactic rurals, so to speak. We are too far from your dense star cluster.' He paused. 'You knew us once. We planted you here. And I feel sure you will know us again.' He smiled to himself, finished his drink, and arose. 'May we meet again, Cophian.'

Roki nodded and watched the giant stride away. Pok was breathing asthmatically and picking nervously at his nails. He let out a sigh of relief with the Solarian's departure.

Roki offered the frightened interpreter a stiff drink, and then another. After two more, Pok swayed dizzily, then fell asleep across the table. Roki left him there. If Pok were an informer, it would be better to keep him out of the meeting with the patrol officer, Captain WeJan.

He hailed a cab and gave the driver the scrap of paper. A few minutes later, he arrived before a small building in the suburbs. WeJan's name was on the door—written in the space-tongue—but the officer was not at home. Frowning, he tried the door; locked. Then, glancing back toward the street, he caught a glimpse of a man standing in the shadows. It was a Solarian.

Slowly, Roki walked across the street. 'Got a match, Bristle-face?' he grunted.

In the light of triple-moons, he saw the giant figure swell with rage. The man looked quickly up and down the street. No one was watching. He emitted a low animal-growl, exposing the brutal teeth. His arms shot out to grasp the Cophian's shoulders, dragging him close. Roki gripped the Multin automatic in his pocket and struggled to slip free. The Solarian jerked him up toward the bared teeth.

His throat about to be crushed, Roki pulled the trigger. There was a dull *chug*. The Solarian looked surprised. He released Roki and felt of his chest. There was no visible wound. Then, within his chest, the incendiary needle flared to incandescent heat. The Solarian sat down in the street. He breathed a frying sound. He crumpled. Roki left hastily before the needle burned its way out of the body.

He hadn't meant to kill the man, and it had been in self-defense, but he might have a hard time proving it. He hurried along back alleys toward the spaceport. If only they could leave Tragor immediately!

What had happened to WeJan? Bribed, beaten, or frightened away. Then the Solarians *did* know who he was and where he was going. There were half a dozen men around the spaceport who knew—and the information would be easy to buy. Pok had known that he was to meet with WeJan, and the Solarian had evidently been sent to watch the captain's quarters. It wasn't going to be easy now—getting to Sol III and landing.

What manner of creatures were these, he wondered. Men who supplied mercy cargoes to the galactic nations—as if charity were the theme and purpose of their culture—yet who seemed as arrogant as the warriors of some primitive culture whose central value was brutal power? What did they really want here? The Solarian had called him 'manthing' as if he regarded the Cophian as a member of some lesser species.

The Solarians were definitely different. Roki could see it.

Their heads were plump and soft like a baby's, hinting of some new evolutionary trend—a brain that could continue growing, perhaps. But the jaws, the teeth, the quick tempers, and the hypersensitive ears—what sort of animal developed such traits? There was only one answer: a nocturnal predator with the instincts of a lion. 'You shall get to know us again,' the man had said.

It spelled politico-galactic ambitions. And it hinted at something else—something that made the Cophian shiver, and shy away from dark shadows as he hurried shipward.

Daleth Incorporated was either asleep or out. He checked at the ship, then went to the Administration Building to inquire about her. The clerk seemed embarrassed.

'Uh . . . E Roki, she departed from the port about five.'

'You've heard nothing of her since?'

'Well . . . there was a call from the police agency, I understand.' He looked apologetic. 'I assure you I had nothing to do with the matter.'

'Police! What . . . what's wrong, man?'

'I hear she went unescorted and unveiled. The police are holding her.'

'How long will they keep her?'

'Until some gentleman signs for her custody.'

'You mean I have to sign for her?'

'Yes, sir.'

Roki smiled thoughtfully. 'Tell me, young man—are Tragorian jails particularly uncomfortable?'

'I wouldn't know, personally,' the clerk said stiffly. 'I understand they conform to the intergalactic "Code of Humanity" however.'

'Good enough,' Roki grunted. 'I'll leave her there till we're ready to go.'

'Not a bad idea,' murmured the clerk, who had evidently encountered the cigar-chewing lady from Daleth.

Roki was not amused by the reversal of positions, but it seemed as good a place as any to leave her for safe-keeping. If the Solarians became interested in him, they might also notice his pilot.

He spent the following day watching the Sol ship, and waiting fatalistically for the police to come and question him about the Solarian's death. But the police failed to come. A check with the news agencies revealed that the man's body had not even been found. Roki was puzzled. He had left the giant lying in plain sight where he had fallen. At noon, the Solarian crew came bearing several lead cases slung from the centers of carrying poles. They wore metal gauntlets and handled the cases cautiously. Roki knew they contained radioactive materials. So that was what they purchased with their surgibank supplies—nuclear fuels.

Toward nightfall, they loaded two large crates aboard. He noted the shape of the crates, and decided that one of them contained the body of the man he had killed. Why didn't they want the police to know? Was it possible that they wanted him free to follow them?

The Sol-ship blasted-off during the night. He was surprised to find it gone, and himself still unmolested by morning. Wandering around the spaceport, he saw WeJan, but the man had developed a sudden lapse of memory. He failed to recognize the Cophian visitor. With the Solarians gone, Roki grew bolder in his questioning.

'How often do the Solarians visit you?' he inquired of a desk clerk at Administration.

'Whenever a hospital places an order, sir. Not often. Every six months perhaps.'

'That's all the traffic they have with Tragor?'

'Yes, sir. This is our only interstellar port.'

'Do the supplies pass through your government channels?'

The clerk looked around nervously. 'Uh, no sir. They refuse to deal through our government. They contact their customers directly. The government lets them because the supplies are badly needed.'

Roki stabbed out bluntly. 'What do you think of the Solarians?'

The clerk looked blank for a moment, then chuckled. 'I don't know, myself. But if you want a low opinion, ask at the spaceport cafe.'

'Why? Do they cause trouble there?'

'No, sir. They bring their own lunches, so to speak. They eat and sleep aboard ship, and won't spend a thin galak around town.'

Roki turned away and went back to the *Idiot*. Somewhere in his mind, an idea was refusing to let itself be believed. A mercy ship visited Tragor every six months. Roki had seen the scattered, ruined cargo of such a ship, and he had estimated it at about four thousand pints of blood, six thousand pounds of frozen bone, and seven thousand pounds of various replaceable organs and tissues. That tonnage in itself was not so startling, but if Sol III supplied an equal amount twice annually to even a third of the twenty-eight thousand civilized worlds in the galaxy, a numbing question arose: where did they get their raw material? Surgibank supplies were normally obtained by contributions from accident victims who lived long enough to voluntarily contribute their undamaged organs to a good cause.

Charitable organizations tried to secure pledges from men in dangerous jobs, donating their bodies to the planet's surgibank in the event of death. But no man felt easy about signing over his kidneys or his liver to the bank, and such recruiters were less popular than hangmen or life insurance agents. Mercy supplies were quite understandably scarce.

The grim question lingered in Roki's mind: where did the Sol III traders find between three and five million healthy accident victims annually? Perhaps they made the accidents themselves, accidents very similar to those occurring at the end of the chute in the slaughterhouse. He shook his head, refusing to believe it. No planet's population, however terrorized by its rulers, could endure such a thing without generating a sociological explosion that would make the world quiver in its orbit. There was a limit to the endurance of tyranny.

He spent the rest of the week asking innocent questions here and there about the city. He learned nearly nothing. The Solarians came bearing their peculiar cargo, sold it quickly at a good price, purchased fissionable materials, and blasted-off without a civil word to anyone. Most men seemed nervous in their presence, perhaps because of their bulk and their native arrogance.

When the base personnel finished installing the synchronizers, he decided the time had come to secure Daleth Incorporated from the local jail. Sometimes he had chided himself for leaving her there after the Solarians had blasted-off, but it seemed to be the best place to keep the willful wench out of trouble. Belatedly, as he rode toward the police station, he wondered what sort of mayhem she would attempt to commit on his person for leaving her to fume in a cell. His smile was rueful as he marched in to pay her fine. The man behind the desk frowned sharply.

'Who did you say?' he grunted.

'The foreign woman from the Dalethian Ship.'

The officer studied his records. 'Ah, yes—Talewa Walkeka the name?'

Roki realized he didn't know her name. She was still Daleth Incorporated. 'From the Daleth Ship,' he insisted.

'Yes. Talewa Walkeka—she was released into the custody of Eli Roki on twoday of last spaceweek.'

'That's imposs—' Roki choked and whitened. 'I am Eli Roki. Was the man a Solarian?'

'I don't recall.'

'*Why don't you?* Didn't you ask him for identification?'

'Stop bellowing, please,' said the official coldly. 'And get your fists off my desk.'

The Cophian closed his eyes and tried to control himself. 'Who is responsible for this?'

The officer failed to answer.

'*You* are responsible!'

'I cannot look out for all the problems of all the foreigners who—'

'Stop! You have let her die.'

'She is only a female.'

Roki straightened. 'Meet me at any secluded place of your choice and I will kill you with any weapon of your choice.'

The official eyed him coldly, then turned to call over his shoulder. 'Sergeant, escort this barbarian to his ship and see that he remains aboard for the rest of his visit.'

The Cophian went peacefully, realizing that violence would gain him nothing but the iron hospitality of a cell. Besides, he had only himself to blame for leaving her there. It was obvious to him now—the contents of the second crate the Solarians had carried aboard consisted of Talewa Walkeka, lately of Daleth and high-C. Undoubtedly they had taken her alive. Undoubtedly she was additional bait to bring him on to Sol. Why did they want him to come? *I'll oblige them and find out for myself*, he thought.

The ship was ready. The bill would be sent back to Beth. He signed the papers, and blasted off as soon as possible. The lonely old freighter crept upward into the fifth component like a struggling old vulture, too ancient to leave its sunny lair. But the synchros were working perfectly, and the screen held its shape when the ascent ceased just below red-line level. He chose an evasive course toward Sol and began gathering velocity.

Then he fed a message into the coder, to be broadcast back

toward the Sixty-Star Cluster: *Pilot abducted by Solarians; evidence secured to indicate that Solarian mercy-merchandise is obtained through genocide*. He recorded the coded message on tape and let it feed continuously into the transmitters, knowing that the carrier made him a perfect target for homing devices, if anyone chose to silence him.

And he knew it was a rather poor bluff. The message might or might not be picked up. A listening ship would have to be at the same C-level to catch the signal. Few ships, save the old freighters, lingered long at ninety-thousand C's. But if the Solarians let him live long enough, the message would eventually be picked up—but not necessarily believed. The most he could hope for was to arouse curiosity about Sol. No one would care much about the girl's abduction, or about his own death. Interstellar federations never tried to protect their citizens beyond the limits of their own volume of space. It would be an impossible task.

Unless the Solarians were looking for him however, they themselves would probably not intercept the call. Their ships would be on higher C. And since they knew he was coming, they had no reason to search for him. At his present velocity and energy-level, he was four months from Sol. The mercy ship on a higher level, would probably reach Sol within three weeks. He was a sparrow chasing a smug hawk.

But now there was more at stake than pride or reputation. He had set out to clear himself of a bad name, but now his name mattered little. If what he suspected were true, then Sol III was a potential threat to every world in the galaxy. Again he remembered the Solarian's form of address—'manthing'—as if a new race had arisen to inherit the places of their ancestors. If so, the new race had a right to bid for survival. And the old race called Man had a right to crush it if he could. Such was the dialectic of life.

Four months in the solitary confinement of a spaceship was enough to unnerve any man, however well-conditioned to it. He paced restlessly in his cell, from quarters to control to reactor room, reading everything that was aboard to read and devouring it several times. Sometimes he stopped to stare in Daleth's doorway. Her gear was still in the compartment, gathering dust. A pair of boots in the corner, a box of Dalethia cigars on the shelf.

'Maybe she has a book or two,' he said once, and entered. He opened the closet and chuckled at the rough masculine clothing that hung there. But among the coarse fabrics was a wisp of pale green silk. He parted the dungarees to stare at the frail feminine frock, nestled toward the end and half-hidden like a suppressed desire. For a moment he saw her in it, strolling along the cool avenues of a Cophian city. But quickly he let the dungarees fall back, slammed the door, and stalked outside, feeling ashamed. He never entered again.

The loneliness was overpowering. After three months, he shut off the transmitters and listened on the space-frequencies for the sound of a human voice. There was nothing except the occasional twittering of a coded message. Some of them came from the direction of Sol.

Why were they letting him come without interference? Why had they allowed him to transmit the message freely? Perhaps they wanted him as a man who knew a great deal about the military and economic resources of the Sixty-Star Cluster, information they would need if they had high ambitions in space. And perhaps the message no longer mattered, if they had already acquired enough nuclear materials for their plans.

After a logical analysis of the situation, he hit upon a better answer. Their ships didn't have the warp-locking devices that permitted one ship to slip into a parallel C with an enemy and stay with that enemy while it maneuvered in the fifth component. The Solarians had proven that deficiency when the 'mercy ship' had tried to escape him by evasive coursing. If their own ships were equipped with the warp lockers, they would have known better than to try. They wanted such equipment. Perhaps they thought that the *Idiot* possessed it, or that he could furnish them with enough information to let them build it.

After several days of correlating such facts as he already knew, Roki cut on his transmitters, fanned the beam down to a narrow pencil, and directed it toward Sol. 'Blind Stab from Cluster-Ship *Idiot,*' he called. 'Any Sol Ship from *Idiot*. I have information to sell in exchange for the person of Talewa Walkeka. Acknowledge, please.'

He repeated the message several times, and expected to wait a few days for an answer. But the reply came within three hours, indicating that a ship had been hovering just ahead of him, beyond the range of his own out-moded detectors.

'Cluster-Ship from Sol Seven,' crackled the loudspeaker. 'Do you wish to land on our planet? If so, please prepare to be boarded. One of our pilots will take you in. You are approaching our outer patrol zone. If you refuse to be boarded, you will have to turn back. Noncooperative vessels are destroyed upon attempting to land. Over.'

There was a note of amusement in the voice. They knew he wouldn't turn back. They had a hostage. They were inviting him to surrender but phrasing the invitation politely.

Roki hesitated. Why had the man said—'destroyed upon attempting to land?' After a moment's thought, he realized that it was because they could not destroy a ship while maneuvering in the fifth component. They could not even stay in the same continuum with it, unless they had the warp-locking devices. A vague plan began forming in his mind.

'I agree conditionally. Do you have Talewa Walkeka aboard? If so, prove it by asking her to answer the following request in her own voice: "List the garments contained in the closet of her quarters aboard this ship." If this is accomplished satisfactorily, then I'll tentatively assume intentions are not hostile. Let me remind you, however, that while we are grappled together, I can rip half your hull off by hitting my C-drive—unless you're equipped with warp-locking devices.'

That should do it, he thought. With such a warning, they would make certain that they had him aboard their own ship as a captive before they made any other move. And he would do his best to make it easy for them. Two or three hours would pass before he could expect an answer, so he began work immediately, preparing to use every means at his disposal to make a booby trap of the *Idiot,* and to set the trap so that only his continued well-being would keep it from springing.

The *Idiot*'s stock of spare parts was strictly limited, as he had discovered previously. There were a few spare selsyns, replacement units for the calculator and courser, radio and radar parts, control-mechanisms for the reactors, and an assortment of spare instruments and detectors. He augmented this stock by ruthlessly tearing into the calculator and taking what he needed.

He was hard at work when the answer came from the Sol ship. It was Daleth's voice, crisp and angry, saying, 'Six pairs of dungarees, a jacket, a robe, and a silk frock. Drop dead, Roki.'

The Solarian operator took over. 'Expect a meeting in six hours. In view of your threat, we must ask that you stand in the outer lock with the hatch open, so that we may see you as we grapple together. Please acknowledge willingness to cooperate.'

*

Roki grinned. They wanted to make certain that he was nowhere near the controls. He gave them a grumbling acknowledgment and returned to his work, tearing into the electronic control-circuits, the radio equipment, the reaction-rate limiters, and the controls of the C-drive. He wove a network of inter-dependency throughout the ship, running linking-circuits from the air-lock mechanisms to the reactors, and from the communication equipment to the C-drive. Gradually the ship became useless as a means of transportation. The jets were silent. He set time clocks to activate some of the apparatus, and keyed other equipment by relays set to trip upon the occurrence of various events.

It was not a difficult task, nor a long one. He added nothing really new. For example, it was easy to remove the wires from the air lock indicator lamp and feed their signal into a relay section removed from the calculator, a section which would send a control pulse to the reactors if the air locks were opened twice. The control pulse, if it came, would push the units past the red line. The relay sections were like single-task robots, set to obey the command: 'If *this* happens, then push *that* switch.'

When he was finished, the six hours were nearly gone. Pacing restlessly, he waited for them to come. Then, noticing a sudden flutter on the instruments, he glanced out to see the dark hulk slipping through his radiation screen. It came to a stop a short distance away.

Roki started the timers he had set, then donned a pressure suit. Carrying a circuit diagram of the changes he had wrought, he went to stand in the outer lock. He held open the outer hatch. The beam of a searchlight stabbed out to hold him while the Sol Ship eased closer. He could see another suited figure in its lock, calling guidance to the pilot. Roki glanced up at his own grapples; they were already energized and waiting for something to which they could cling.

The ships came together with a rocking jerk as both sets of grapples caught and clung. Roki swung himself across a gravityless space, then stood facing the burly figure of the Solarian. The man pushed him into the next lock and stepped after him.

'Search him for weapons,' growled a harsh voice as Roki removed his helmet. 'And get the boarding party through the locks.'

'If you do that, you'll blow both ships to hell,' the Cophian commented quietly. 'The hatches are rigged to throw the reactors past red line.'

The commander, a sharp-eyed oldster with a massive bald skull, gave him a cold stare that slowly became a sneer. 'Very well, we can cut through the hull.'

Roki nodded. 'You can, but don't let any pressure escape. The throttles are also keyed to the pressure gauge.'

The commander reddened slightly. 'Is there anything else?'

'Several things.' Roki handed him the circuit diagram. 'Have your engineer study this. Until he gets the idea, anything you do may be dangerous, like trying to pull away from my grapples. I assure you we're either permanently grappled together, or permanently dead.'

The Solarian was apparently his own engineer. He stared at the schematic while another relieved Roki of his weapon. There were four of them in the cabin. Three were armed and watching him carefully. He knew by their expressions that they considered him to be of a lesser species. And he watched them communicate silently among themselves by a soundless language of facial twitches and peculiar nods. Once the commander looked up to ask a question.

'When will this timer activate this network?'

Roki glanced at his watch. 'In about ten minutes. If the transmitter's periodic signals aren't answered in the correct code, the signals serve to activate C-drive.'

'I see that,' he snapped. He glanced at a burly assistant. 'Take him out. Skin him—from the feet up. He'll give you the code.'

'I'll give it to you now,' Roki offered calmly.

The commander showed faint surprise. 'Do so then.'

'The Cophian multiplication tables is the code. My transmitter will send a pair of Cophian numbers every two minutes. If you fail to supply the product within one second, a relay starts the C-drive. Since you can't guarantee an exactly simultaneous thrust, there should be quite a crash.'

'Very well, give us your Cophian number symbols.'

'Gladly. But they won't help you.'

'Why not?'

'Our numbers are to the base eighteen instead of base ten. You couldn't react quickly enough unless you've been using them since childhood.'

The Solarian's lips pulled back from his heavy teeth and his jaw muscles began twitching. Roki looked at his watch.

'You have seven minutes to get your transmitter set up, with me at the key. We'll talk while I keep us intact.'

The commander hesitated, then nodded to one of the guards who promptly left the room.

'Very well, manthing, we will set it up temporarily.' He paused to smile arrogantly. 'You have much to learn about our race. But you have little time in which to learn it.'

'What do you mean?'

'Just this. This transmitter—and the whole apparatus—will be shut down after a certain period of time.'

Roki stiffened. 'Just how do you propose to do it?'

'Fool! By waiting until the signals stop. You obviously must have set a time limit on it. I would guess a few hours at the most.'

It was true, but he had hoped to avoid mentioning it. The power to the control circuits would be interrupted after four hours, and the booby trap would be deactivated. For if he hadn't achieved his goal by then, he meant to neglect a signal during the last half-hour and let the C-ward lurch tear them apart. He nodded slowly.

'You're quite right. You have four hours in which to surrender your ship into my control. Maybe. I'll send the signals until I decide you don't mean to co-operate. Then—' He shrugged.

The Solarian gave a command to his aides. They departed in different directions. Roki guessed that they had been sent to check for some way to enter the *Idiot* that would not energize a booby circuit.

His host waved him through a doorway, and he found himself in their control room. A glance told him that their science still fell short of the most modern cultures. They had the earmarks of a new race, and yet Sol's civilization was supposedly the oldest in the galaxy.

'There are the transmitters,' the commander barked. 'Say what you have to say, and we shall see who is best at waiting.'

Roki sat down, fingered the key, and watched his adversary closely. The commander fell into a seat opposite him and gazed coolly through narrowed lids. He wore a fixed smile of amusement. 'Your name is Eli Roki, I believe. I am Space Commander Hulgruv.'

A blare of sound suddenly came from the receiver. Hulgruv frowned and lowered the volume. The sound came forth as a steady musical tone. He questioned the Cophian with his eyes.

'When the tone ceases, the signals will begin.'

'I see.'

'I warn you, I may get bored rather quickly. I'll keep the signals going only until I think you've had time to assure yourselves that this is not a bluff I am trying to put over on you.'

'I'm sure it's not. It's merely an inconvenience.'

'You know little of my home planet then.'

'I know a little.'

'Then you've heard of the "Sword of Apology." '

'How does that—' Hulgruv paused and lost his smirk for an instant. 'I see. If you blunder, your code demands that you die anyway. So you think you wouldn't hesitate to neglect a signal.'

'Try me.'

'It may not be necessary. Tell me, why did you space them two minutes apart? Why not one signal every hour?'

'You can answer that.'

'Ah yes. You think the short period insures you against any painful method of persuasion, eh?'

'Uh-huh. And it gives me a chance to decide frequently whether it's worth it.'

'What is it you want, Cophian? Suppose we give you the girl and release you.'

'She is a mere incidental,' he growled, fearful of choking on the words. 'The price is surrender.'

Hulgruv laughed heartily. It was obvious he had other plans. 'Why do you deem us your enemy?'

'You heard the accusation I beamed back to my Cluster.'

'Certainly. We ignored it, directly. Indirectly we made a fool of you by launching another, uh, mercy ship to your system. The cargo was labeled as to source, and the ship made a point of meeting one of your patrol vessels. It stopped for inspection. You're less popular at home than ever.' He grinned. 'I suggest you return to Sol with us. Help us develop the warp locks.'

Roki hesitated. 'You say the ship *stopped for inspection?*'

'Certainly.'

'Wasn't it inconvenient? Changing your diet, leaving your "livestock" at home—so our people wouldn't know you for what you really are.'

Hulgruv stiffened slightly, then nodded. 'Good guess.'

'Cannibal!'

'Not at all. I am not a man.'

They stared fixedly at one another. The Cophian felt the clammy cloak of hate creeping about him. The tone from the speaker suddenly stopped. A moment of dead silence. Roki leaned back in his chair.

'I'm not going to answer the first signal.'

The commander glanced through the doorway and jerked his head. A moment later, Talewa Walkeka stepped proudly into the room, escorted by a burly guard. She gave him an icy glance and said nothing.

'Daleth—'

She made a noise like an angry cat and sat where the guard pushed her. They waited. The first signal suddenly screeched from the receiver: two series of short bleats of three different notes.

Involuntarily his hand leaped to the key. He bleated back the answering signal.

Daleth wore a puzzled frown. 'Ilgen times ufneg is hork-segan,' she muttered in translation.

A slow grin spread across Hulgruv's heavy face. He turned to look at the girl. 'You're trained in the Cophian number system?'

'Don't answer that!' Roki bellowed.

'She *has* answered it, manthing. Are you aware of what your friend is doing, female?'

She shook her head. Hulgruv told her briefly. She frowned at Roki, shook her head, and stared impassively at the floor. Apparently she was either drugged or had learned nothing about the Solarians to convince her that they were enemies of the galaxy.

'Tell me, Daleth. Have they been feeding you well?'

She hissed at him again. 'Are you crazy—'

Hulgruv chuckled. 'He is trying to tell you that we are cannibals. Do you believe it?'

Fright appeared in her face for an instant, then disbelief. She stared at the commander, saw no guilt in his expression. She looked scorn at Roki.

'Listen, Daleth! That's why they wouldn't stop. Human livestock aboard. One look in their holds and we would have known, seen through their guise of mercy, recognized them as self-styled supermen, guessed their plans for galactic conquest. They breed their human cattle on their home planet and make a business of selling the parts. Their first weapon is infiltration into our confidence. They knew that if we gained an insight into their bloodthirsty culture, we would crush them.'

'You're insane, Roki!' she snapped.

'No! Why else would they refuse to stop? Technical secrets?

Baloney! Their technology is still inferior to ours. They carried a cargo of hate, our hate, riding with them unrecognized. They couldn't afford to reveal it.'

Hulgruv laughed uproariously. The girl shook her head slowly at Roki, as if pitying him.

'It's true, I tell you! I guessed, sure. But it was pretty obvious they were taking their surgibank supplies by murder. And they contend they're not men. They guard their ships so closely, live around them while in port. And he admitted it to me.'

The second signal came. Roki answered it, then began ignoring the girl. She didn't believe him. Hulgruv appeared amused. He hummed the signals over to himself—*without mistake*.

'You're using polytonal code for challenge, monotonal for reply. That makes it harder to learn.'

The Cophian caught his breath. He glanced at the Solarian's huge, bald braincase. 'You hope to learn some three or four hundred sounds—and sound-combinations within the time I allow you?'

'We'll see.'

Some note of contempt in Hulgruv's voice gave Roki warning.

'I shorten my ultimatum to one hour! Decide by then. Surrender, or I stop answering. Learn it, if you can.'

'He can, Roki,' muttered Daleth. 'They can memorize a whole page at a glance.'

Roki keyed another answer. 'I'll cut it off if he tries it.'

The commander was enduring the tension of the stalemate superbly. 'Ask yourself, Cophian,' he grunted with a smile, 'what would you gain by destroying the ship—and yourself? We are not important. If we're destroyed, our planet loses another gnat in space, nothing more. Do you imagine we are incapable of self-sacrifice?'

Roki found no answer. He set his jaw in silence and answered the signals as they came. He hoped the bluff would win, but now he saw that Hulgruv would let him destroy the ship. And—if the situation were reversed, Roki knew that he would do the same. He had mistakenly refused to concede honor to an enemy. The commander seemed to sense his quiet dismay, and he leaned forward to speak softly.

'We are a new race, Roki—grown out of man. We have abilities of which you know nothing. It's useless to fight us.

Ultimately, your people will pass away. Or become stagnant. Already it has happened to man on Earth.'

'Then—there *are two* races on Earth.'

'Yes, of course. Did apes pass away when man appeared? The new does not replace the old. It adds to it, builds above it. The old species is the root of the new tree.'

'Feeding it,' the Cophian grunted bitterly.

He noticed that Talewa was becoming disturbed. Her eyes fluttered from one to the other of them.

'That was inevitable, manthing. There are no other animal foodstuffs on Earth. Man exhausted his planet, overpopulated it, drove lesser species into extinction. He spent the world's resources getting your ancestors to the denser star-clusters. He saw his own approaching stagnation on Earth. And, since Sol is near the rim of the galaxy, with no close star-neighbors, he realized he could never achieve a mass-exodus into space. He didn't have the C-drive in its present form. The best he could do was a field-cancellation drive.'

'But that's the heart of the C-drive.'

'True. But he was too stupid to realize what he had. He penetrated the fifth component and failed to realize what he had done. His ships went up to five-hundred C's or so, spent a few hours there by the ship's clock, and came down to find several years had passed on Earth. They never got around that time-lag.'

'But that's hardly more than a problem in five-space navigation!'

'True again. But they still thought of it in terms of field-cancellation. They didn't realize they'd actually left the four-space continuum. They failed to see the blue-shift as anything more than a field-phenomenon. Even in high-C, you measure light's velocity as the same constant—because your measuring instruments have changed proportionally. It's different, relative to the home continuum, but you can't know it except by pure reasoning. They never found out.

'Using what they had, they saw that they could send a few of their numbers to the denser star-clusters, if they wanted to wait twenty thousand years for them to arrive. Of course, only a few years would pass aboard ship. They knew they could do it, but they procrastinated. Society was egalitarian at the time. Who would go? And why should the planet's industry exhaust itself to launch a handful of ships that no one would ever see again? Who wanted to make a twenty thousand year investment that would impoverish the world? Sol's atomic resources were never plentiful.'

'How did it come about then?'

'Through a small group of men who didn't *care* about the cost. They seized power during a "population rebellion"—when the sterilizers were fighting the euthanasiasts and the do-nothings. The small clique came into power by the fantastic promise of draining off the population-surplus into space. Enough of the stupid believed it to furnish them with a strong backing. They clamped censorship on the news agencies and imprisoned everyone who said it couldn't be done. They put the planet to work building ships. Their fanatic personal philosophy was: "We are giving the galaxy to Man. What does it matter if he perishes on Earth?" They put about twelve hundred ships into space before their slave-structure collapsed. Man never developed another technology on Sol III. He was sick of it.'

'And *your* people?'

Hulgruv smiled. 'A natural outgrowth of the situation. If a planet were glutted with rabbits who ate all the grass, a species of rabbits who learned to exploit other rabbits would have the best chance for survival. We are predators, Cophian. Nature raised us up to be a check on your race.'

'You pompous fool!' Roki snapped. 'Predators are specialists. What abilities do you have—besides the ability to prey on man?'

'I'll show you in a few minutes,' the commander muttered darkly.

Daleth had lost color slowly as she listened to the Solarian's roundabout admission of Roki's charge. She suddenly moaned and slumped in a sick heap. Hulgruv spoke to the guard in the soundless facial language. The guard carried her away quickly.

'If you were an advanced species, Hulgruv—you would not have let yourself be tricked so easily, by me. And a highly intelligent race would discover the warp locks for themselves.'

Hulgruv flushed. 'We underestimated you, manthing. It was a natural mistake. Your race has sunk to the level of cattle on earth. As for the warp locks, we know their principles. We have experimental models. But we could short-circuit needless research by using your design. We are a new race, new to space. Naturally we cannot do in a few years what you needed centuries to accomplish.'

'You'll have to look for help elsewhere. In ten minutes, I'm quitting the key—unless you change your mind.'

Hulgruv shrugged. While Roki answered the signals, he

listened for sounds of activity throughout the ship. He heard nothing except the occasional clump of boots, the brief mutter of a voice in the corridor, the intermittent rattling of small tools. There seemed to be no excitement or anxiety. The Solarians conducted themselves with quiet self-assurance.

'Is your crew aware of what is happening?'

'Certainly.'

As the deadline approached, his fingers grew nervous on the key. He steeled himself, and waited, clutching at each second as it marched past. What good would it do to sacrifice Daleth and himself? He would succeed only in destroying one ship and one crew. But it was a good trade—two pawns for several knights and a rook. And, when the Solarians began their march across space, there would be many such sacrifices.

For the last time, he answered a signal, then leaned back to stare at Hulgruv. 'Two minutes, Solarian. There's still time to change your mind.'

Hulgruv only smiled. Roki shrugged and stood up. A pistol flashed into the commander's hand, warning him back. Roki laughed contemptuously.

'Afraid I'll try to take your last two minutes away?'

He strolled away from the table toward the door.

'Stop!' Hulgruv barked.

'Why? I want to see the girl.'

'Very touching. But she's busy at the moment.'

'What?' He turned slowly, and glanced at his watch. 'You don't seem to realize that in fifty seconds—'

'We'll see. Stay where you are.'

The Cophian felt a sudden coldness in his face. Could they have found a flaw in his net of death?—a way to circumvent the sudden application of the *Idiot*'s C-drive, with its consequent ruinous stresses to both ships? Or had they truly memorized the Cophian symbols to a one second reaction time?

He shrugged agreeably and moved in the general direction of the transmitter tuning units. There was one way to test the possibility. He stopped several feet away and turned to face Hulgruv's suspicious eyes. 'You are braver than I thought,' he growled.

The admission had the desired effect. Hulgruv tossed his head and laughed arrogantly. There was an instant of relaxation. The heavy automatic wavered slightly. Roki backed against the transmitters and cut the power switch. The hum died.

'Ten seconds, Hulgruv! Toss me your weapon. Shoot and you shatter the set. Wait and the tubes get cold. *Toss it!*'

Hulgruv bellowed, and raised the weapon to fire. Roki grinned. The gun quivered. Then with a choking sound, the Solarian threw it to him. 'Get it on!' he howled. *'Get it on!'*

As Roki tripped the switch again, the signals were already chirping in the loud-speaker. He darted aside, out of view from the corridor. Footsteps were already racing toward the control room.

The signals stopped. Then the bleat of an answer! Another key had been set up in the adjoining room! With Daleth answering the challenges?

The pistol exploded in his hand as the first crewman came racing through the doorway. The others backed out of sight into the corridor as the projectile-weapon knocked their comrade back in a bleeding sprawl. Hulgruv made a dash for the door. Roki cut him down with a shot at the knee.

'The next one takes the transmitter,' he bellowed. 'Stay back.'

Hulgruv roared a command. 'Take him! If you can't, let the trap spring!'

Roki stooped over him and brought the pistol butt crashing against his skull, meaning only to silence him. It was a mistake; he had forgotten about the structure of the Solarian skull. He put his foot on Hulgruv's neck and jerked. The butt came free with a wet *cluck*. He raced to the doorway and pressed himself against the wall to listen. The crewmen were apparently having a parley at the far end of the corridor. He waited for the next signal.

When it came, he dropped to the floor—to furnish an unexpected sort of target—and snaked into view. He shot twice at three figures a dozen yards away. The answering fire did something to the side of his face, blurring his vision. Another shot sprayed him with flakes from the deck. One crewman was down. The others backed through a door at the end of the corridor. They slammed it and a pressure seal tightened with a rubbery sound.

Roki climbed to his feet and slipped toward a doorway from which he heard the click of the auxiliary key. He felt certain someone was there besides Daleth. But when he risked a quick glance around the corner, he saw only the girl. She sat at a small desk, her hand frozen to the key, her eyes staring dazedly at nothing. He started to speak, then realized what was wrong.

Hypnosis! Or a hypnotic drug. She sensed nothing but the key beneath her fingers, waiting for the next challenge.

The door was only half-open. He could see no one, but there had been another man; of that he was certain. Thoughtfully he took aim at the plastic door panel and fired. A gun skidded toward Daleth's desk. A heavy body sprawled across the floor.

The girl started. The dull daze left her face, to be replaced with wide-eyed shock. She clasped her hands to her cheeks and whimpered. A challenge bleated from the radio.

'Answer!' he bellowed.

Her hand shot to the key and just in time. But she seemed about to faint.

'Stay on it!' he barked, and dashed back to the control room. The crewmen had locked themselves aft of the bulkhead, and had started the ventilator fans. Roki heard their whine, then caught the faint odor of gas. His eyes were burning and he sneezed spasmodically.

"Surrender immediately, manthing!' blared the intercom.

Roki looked around, then darted toward the controls. He threw a damping voltage on the drive tubes, defocused the ion streams, and threw the reactors to full emission. The random shower of high-speed particles would spray toward the focusing coils, scatter like deflected buckshot, and loose a blast of hard X-radiation as they peppered the walls of the reaction chambers. Within a few seconds, if the walls failed to melt, the crewmen back of the bulkhead should recognize the possibility of being quickly fried by the radiant inferno.

The tear gas was choking him. From the next compartment, he could hear Daleth coughing and moaning. How could she hear the signals for her own weeping? He tried to watch the corridor and the reaction-chamber temperature at the same time. The needle crept toward the danger-point. An explosion could result, if the walls failed to melt.

Suddenly the voice of the intercom again: 'Shut it off, you fool! You'll destroy the ship.'

He said nothing, but waited in tense silence, watching the other end of the corridor. Suddenly the ventilator fans died. Then the bulkhead door opened a crack, and paused.

'Throw out your weapon first!' he barked.

A gun fell through the crack and to the floor. A Solarian slipped through, sneezed, and rubbed his eyes.

'Turn around and back down the corridor.'

The crewman obeyed slowly. Roki stood a few feet behind

him, using him for a shield while the others emerged. The fight was gone out of them. It was strange, he thought; they were willing to risk the danger of the *Idiot*'s C-drive, but they couldn't stand being locked up with a runaway reactor. They could see death coming then. He throttled back the reactors, and prodded the men toward the storage rooms. There was only one door that suggested a lockup. He halted the prisoners in the hallway and tried the bolt.

'Not in there, manthing!' growled one of the Solarians.

'Why not?'

'There are—'

A muffled wail from within the compartment interrupted the explanation. It was the cry of a child. His hand trembled on the bolt.

'They are wild, and we are weaponless,' pleaded the Solarian.

'How many are in there?'

'Four adults, three children.'

Roki paused. 'There's nowhere else to put you. One of you —*you* there—go inside, and we'll see what happens.'

The man shook his head stubbornly in refusal. Roki repeated the order. Again the man refused. The predator, unarmed, was afraid of its prey. The Cophian aimed low and calmly shot him through the leg.

'Throw him inside,' he ordered tonelessly.

With ill-concealed fright for their own safety, the other two lifted their screaming comrade. Roki swung open the door and caught a brief glimpse of several human shadows in the gloom. Then the Solarian was thrown through the doorway and the bolt snapped closed.

At first there was silence, then a bull-roar from some angry throat. Stamping feet—then the Solarian's shriek—and a body was being dashed against the inside walls while several savage voices roared approval. The two remaining crewmen stood in stunned silence.

'Doesn't work so well, does it?' Roki murmured with ruthless unconcern.

After a brief search, he found a closet to lock them in, and went to relieve Daleth at the key. When the last signal came, at the end of the four hours, she was asleep from exhaustion. And curled up on the floor, she looked less like a tough little frontier urchin than a frightened bedraggled kitten. He grinned at her for a moment, then went back to inspect the damage to the briefly overloaded reactors. It was not as bad as it might have been. He worked for two hours, replacing fused focusing sections. The jets would carry them home.

The *Idiot* was left drifting in space to await the coming of a repair ship. And Daleth was not anxious to fly it back alone. Roki set the Solarian vessel on a course with a variable C-level, so that no Sol ship could track them without warp lockers. As far as Roki was concerned the job was done. He had a shipful of evidence and two live Solarians who could be forced to confirm it.

'What will they do about it?' Daleth asked as the captured ship jetted them back toward the Sixty-Star Cluster.

'Crush the Solarian race immediately.'

'I thought we were supposed to keep hands-off nonhuman races?'

'We are, unless they try to exploit human beings. That is automatically an act of war. But I imagine an ultimatum will bring a surrender. They can't fight without warp lockers.'

'What will happen on Earth when they do surrender?'

Roki turned to grin. 'Go ask the human Earthers. Climb in their cage.'

She shuddered, and murmured, 'Some day—they'll be a civilized race again, won't they?'

He sobered, and stared thoughtfully at the star-lanced cosmos. 'Theirs is the past, Daleth. Theirs is the glory of having founded the race of man. They sent us into space. They gave the galaxy to man—in the beginning. We would do well to let them alone.'

He watched her for a moment. She had lost cockiness, temporarily.

'Stop grinning at me like that!' she snapped.

Roki went to feed the Solarian captives: canned cabbage.

DARK BENEDICTION

Always fearful of being set upon during the night, Paul slept uneasily despite his weariness from the long trek southward. When dawn broke, he rolled out of his blankets and found himself still stiff with fatigue. He kicked dirt over the remains of the campfire and breakfasted on a tough forequarter of cold boiled rabbit which he washed down with a swallow of earthy-tasting ditch-water. Then he buckled the cartridge belt about his waist, leaped the ditch, and climbed the embankment to the trafficless four-lane highway whose pavement was scattered with blown leaves and unsightly debris dropped by a long-departed throng of refugees whose only wish had been to escape from one another. Paul, with characteristic independence, had decided to go where the crowds had been the thickest—to the cities—on the theory that they would now be deserted, and therefore noncontagious.

The fog lay heavy over the silent land, and for a moment he paused groping for cognizance of direction. Then he saw the stalled car on the opposite shoulder of the road—a late model convertible, but rusted, flat-tired, with last year's license plates, and most certainly out of fuel. It obviously had been deserted by its owner during the exodus, and he trusted in its northward heading as he would have trusted the reading of a compass. He turned right and moved south on the empty highway. Somewhere just ahead in the gray vapor lay the outskirts of Houston. He had seen the high skyline before the setting of yesterday's sun, and knew that his journey would soon be drawing to a close.

Occasionally he passed a deserted cottage or a burned-out roadside tavern, but he did not pause to scrounge for food. The exodus would have stripped such buildings clean. Pickings should be better in the heart of the metropolitan area, he thought —where the hysteria had swept humanity away quickly.

Suddenly Paul froze on the highway, listening to the fog. Footsteps in the distance—footsteps and a voice singing an absent-minded ditty to itself. No other sounds penetrated the sepulchral silence which once had growled with the life of a great city. Anxiety caught him with clammy hands. An old man's voice it was, crackling and tuneless. Paul groped for his holster and brought out the revolver he had taken from a deserted police station.

'Stop where you are, dermie!' he bellowed at the fog. 'I'm armed.'

The footsteps and the singing stopped. Paul strained his eyes to penetrate the swirling mist-shroud. After a moment, the oldster answered: 'Sure foggy, ain't it, sonny? Can't see ya. Better come a little closer. I ain't no dermie.'

Loathing choked in Paul's throat. 'The hell you're not. Nobody else'd be crazy enough to sing. Get off the road! I'm going south, and if I see you I'll shoot. Now move!'

'Sure, sonny. I'll move. But I'm no dermie. I was just singing to keep myself company. I'm past caring about the plague. I'm heading north, where there's people, and if some dermie hears me a'singing . . . why, I'll tell him t'come jine in. What's the good o' being healthy if yer alone?'

While the old man spoke, Paul heard his sloshing across the ditch and climbing through the brush. Doubt assailed him. Maybe the old crank wasn't a dermie. An ordinary plague victim would have whimpered and pleaded for satisfaction of his strange craving—the laying-on of hands, the feel of healthy skin beneath moist gray palms. Nevertheless, Paul meant to take no chances with the oldster.

'Stay back in the brush while I walk past!' he called.

'Okay, sonny. You go right by. I ain't gonna touch you. You aiming to scrounge in Houston?'

Paul began to advance. 'Yeah, I figure people got out so fast that they must have left plenty of canned goods and stuff behind.'

'Mmmm, there's a mite here and there,' said the cracked voice in a tone that implied understatement. 'Course, now, you ain't the first to figure that way, y'know.'

Paul slacked his pace, frowning. 'You mean . . . a lot of people are coming back?'

'Mmmm, no—not a lot. But you'll bump into people every

day or two. Ain't my kind o' folks. Rough characters, mostly —don't take chances, either. They'll shoot first, then look to see if you was a dermie. Don't never come busting out of a doorway without taking a peek at the street first. And if two people come around a corner in opposite directions, somebody's gonna die. The few that's there is trigger happy. Just thought I'd warn ya.'

'Thanks.'

'D'mention it. Been good t'hear a body's voice again, tho I can't see ye.'

Paul moved on until he was fifty paces past the voice. Then he stopped and turned. 'Okay, you can get back on the road now. Start walking north. Scuff your feet until you're out of earshot.'

'Taking no chanccs, are ye?' said the old man as he waded the ditch. 'All right, sonny.' The sound of his footsteps hesitated on the pavement. 'A word of advice—your best scrounging'll be around the warehouses. Most of the stores are picked clean. Good luck!'

Paul stood listening to the shuffling feet recede northward. When they became inaudible, he turned to continue his journey. The meeting had depressed him, reminded him of the animal-level to which he and others like him had sunk. The oldster was obviously healthy; but Paul had been chased by three dermies in as many days. And the thought of being trapped by a band of them in the fog left him unnerved. Once he had seen a pair of the grinning, maddened compulsives seize a screaming young child while each of them took turns caressing the youngster's arms and face with the gray and slippery hands that spelled certain contraction of the disease—if disease it was. The dark pall of neuroderm was unlike any illness that Earth had ever seen.

The victim became the eager ally of the sickness that gripped him. Caught in its demoniac madness, the stricken human searched hungrily for healthy comrades, then set upon them with no other purpose than to paw at the clean skin and praise the virtues of the blind compulsion that drove him to do so. One touch, and infection was insured. It was as if a third of humanity had become night-prowling maniacs, lurking in the shadows to seize the unwary, working in bands to trap the unarmed wanderer. And two-thirds of humanity found itself fleeing in horror from the mania, seeking the frigid northern climates where, according to rumor, the disease was less infectious. The normal functioning of civilization had been dropped like a hot potato within six months after the first alarm. When the man at the next lathe might be hiding gray discolorations beneath his shirt, industrial society was no place for humanity.

Rumor connected the onslaught of the plague with an unpredicted swarm of meteorites which had brightened the sky one October evening two weeks before the first case was discovered. The first case was, in fact, a machinist who had found one of the celestial cannon balls, handled it, weighed it, estimated its volume by fluid-displacement, then cut into it on his lathe because its low density suggested that it might be hollow. He claimed to have found a pocket of frozen jelly, still rigid from deep space, although the outershell had been heated white-hot by atmospheric friction. He said he let the jelly thaw, then fed it to his cat because it had an unpleasant fishy odor. Shortly thereafter, the cat disappeared.

Other meteorites had been discovered and similarly treated by university staffs before there was any reason to blame them for the plague. Paul, who had been an engineering student at Texas U at the time of the incident, had heard it said that the missiles were purposefully manufactured by parties unknown, that the jelly contained micro-organisms which under the microscope suggested a cross between a sperm-cell (because of a similar tail) and a Pucini Corpuscle (because of a marked resemblance to nerve tissue in subcellular detail).

When the meteorites were connected with the new and mushrooming disease, some people started a panic by theorizing that the meteor-swarm was a pre-invasion artillery attack by some space-horde lurking beyond telescope range, and waiting for their biological bombardment to wreck civilization before they moved in upon Earth. The government had immediately labeled all investigations 'top-secret,' and Paul had heard no news since the initial speculations. Indeed, the government might have explained the whole thing and proclaimed it to the country for all he knew. One thing was certain: the country had not heard. It no longer possessed channels of communication.

Paul thought that if any such invaders were coming, they would have already arrived—months ago. Civilization was not truly wrecked; it had simply been discarded during the crazed flight of the individual away from the herd. Industry lay idle and unmanned, but still intact. Man was fleeing from Man. Fear had destroyed the integration of his society, and had left him powerless before any hypothetical invaders. Earth was ripe for plucking, but it remained unplucked and withering. Paul, therefore, discarded the invasion hypothesis, and searched for nothing new to replace it. He accepted the fact of his own existence in the midst of chaos, and sought to protect that existence as best he could. It proved to be a full-time job, with no spare time for theorizing.

Life was a rabbit scurrying over a hill. Life was a warm blanket, and a secluded sleeping place. Life was ditchwater, and an unbloated can of corned beef, and a suit of clothing looted from a deserted cottage. Life, above all else, was an avoidance of other human beings. For no dermie had the grace to cry 'unclean!' to the unsuspecting. If the dermie's discolorations were still in the concealable stage, then concealed they would be, while the lost creature deliberately sought to infect his wife, his children, his friends—whoever would not protest an idle touch of the hand. When the grayness touched the face and the backs of the hands, the creature became a feverish night wanderer, subject to strange hallucinations and delusions and desires.

The fog began to part toward midmorning as Paul drove deeper into the outskirts of Houston. The highway was becoming a commercial subcenter, lined with businesses and small shops. The sidewalks were showered with broken glass from windows kicked in by looters. Paul kept to the center of the deserted street, listening and watching cautiously for signs of life. The distant barking of a dog was the only sound in the once-growling metropolis. A flight of sparrows winged down the street, then darted in through a broken window to an inside nesting place.

He searched a small grocery store, looking for a snack, but the shelves were bare. The thoroughfare had served as a main avenue of escape, and the fugitives had looted it thoroughly to obtain provisions. He turned onto a side street, then after several blocks turned again to parallel the highway, moving through an old residential section. Many houses had been left open, but few had been looted. He entered one old frame mansion and found a can of tomatoes in the kitchen. He opened it and sipped the tender delicacy from the container, while curiosity sent him prowling through the rooms.

He wandered up the first flight of stairs, then halted with one foot on the landing. A body lay sprawled across the second flight —the body of a young man, dead quite a while. A well-rusted pistol had fallen from his hand. Paul dropped the tomatoes and bolted for the street. Suicide was a common recourse, when a man learned that he had been touched.

After two blocks, Paul stopped running. He sat panting on a fire hydrant and chided himself for being overly cautious. The man had been dead for months; and infection was achieved only through contact. Nevertheless, his scalp was still tingling. When he had rested briefly, he continued his plodding course toward the heart of the city. Toward noon, he saw another human being.

The man was standing on the loading dock of a warehouse, apparently enjoying the sunlight that came with the dissolving of the fog. He was slowly and solemnly spooning the contents of a can into a red-lipped mouth while his beard bobbled with appreciative chewing. Suddenly he saw Paul who had stopped in the center of the street with his hand on the butt of his pistol. The man backed away, tossed the can aside, and sprinted the length of the platform. He bounded off the end, snatched a bicycle away from the wall, and pedalled quickly out of sight while he bleated shrill blasts on a police whistle clenched between his teeth.

Paul trotted to the corner, but the man had made another turn. His whistle continued bleating. A signal? A dermie summons to a touching orgy? Paul stood still while he tried to overcome an urge to break into panicked flight. After a minute, the clamor ceased; but the silence was ominous.

If a party of cyclists moved in, he could not escape on foot. He darted toward the nearest warehouse, seeking a place to hide. Inside, he climbed a stack of boxes to a horizontal girder, kicked the stack to topple it, and stretched out belly-down on the steel eye-beam to command a clear shot at the entrances. He lay for an hour, waiting quietly for searchers. None came. At last he slid down a vertical support and returned to the loading platform. The street was empty and silent. With weapon ready, he continued his journey. He passed the next intersection without mishap.

Halfway up the block, a calm voice drawled a command from behind him: 'Drop the gun, dermie. Get your hands behind your head.'

He halted, motionless. No plague victim would hurl the dermie-charge at another. He dropped the pistol and turned slowly. Three men with drawn revolvers were clambering from the back of a stalled truck. They were all bearded, wore blue jeans, blue neckerchiefs, and green woolen shirts. He suddenly recalled that the man on the loading platform had been similarly dressed. A uniform?

'Turn around again!' barked the speaker.

Paul turned, realizing that the men were probably some sort of self-appointed quarantine patrol. Two ropes suddenly skidded out from behind and came to a stop near his feet on the pavement —a pair of lariat loops.

'One foot in each loop, dermie!' the speaker snapped.

When Paul obeyed, the ropes were jerked taut about his ankles, and two of the men trotted out to the sides, stood thirty feet apart, and pulled his legs out into a wide straddle. He quickly saw that any movement would cost him his balance.

'Strip to the skin.'

'I'm no dermie,' Paul protested as he unbuttoned his shirt.

'We'll see for ourselves, Joe,' grunted the leader as he moved around to the front. 'Get the top off first. If your chest's okay, we'll let your feet go.'

When Paul had undressed, the leader walked around him slowly, making him spread his fingers and display the soles of his feet. He stood shivering and angry in the chilly winter air while the men satisfied themselves that he wore no gray patches of neuroderm.

'You're all right, I guess,' the speaker admitted; then as Paul stooped to recover his clothing, the man growled, 'Not those! Jim, get him a probie outfit.'

Paul caught a bundle of clean clothing, tossed to him from the back of the truck. There were jeans, a woolen shirt, and a kerchief, but the shirt and kerchief were red. He shot an inquiring glance at the leader, while he climbed into the welcome change.

'All newcomers are on two weeks probation,' the man explained. 'If you decide to stay in Houston, you'll get another exam next time the uniform code changes. Then you can join our outfit, if you don't show up with the plague. In fact, you'll have to join if you stay.'

'What is the outfit?' Paul asked suspiciously.

'It just started. Schoolteacher name of Georgelle organized it. We aim to keep dermies out. There's about six hundred of us now. We guard the downtown area, but soon as there's enough of us we'll move out to take in more territory. Set up road blocks and all that. You're welcome, soon as we're sure you're clean . . . and can take orders.'

'Whose orders?'

'Georgelle's. We got no room for goof-offs, and no time for argument. Anybody don't like the setup, he's welcome to get out. Jim here'll give you a leaflet on the rules. Better read it before you go anywhere. If you don't, you might make a wrong move. Make a wrong move, and you catch a bullet.'

The man called Jim interrupted, 'Reckon you better call off the other patrols, Digger?' he said respectfully to the leader.

Digger nodded curtly and turned to blow three short blasts and a long with his whistle. An answering short-long-short came from several blocks away. Other posts followed suit. Paul realized that he had been surrounded by a ring of similar ambushes.

'Jim, take him to the nearest water barrel, and see that he shaves,' Digger ordered, then: 'What's your name, probie? Also your job, if you had one.'

'Paul Harris Oberlin. I was a mechanical engineering student when the plague struck. Part-time garage mechanic while I was in school.'

Digger nodded and jotted down the information on a scratch-pad. 'Good, I'll turn your name in to the registrar. Georgelle says to watch for college men. You might get a good assignment, later. Report to the Esperson Building on the seventeenth. That's inspection day. If you don't show up, we'll come looking for you. All loose probies'll get shot. Now Jim here's gonna see to it that you shave. Don't shave again until your two-weeker. That way, we can estimate how long you been in town—by looking at your beard. We got other ways that you don't need to know about. Georgelle's got a system worked out for everything, so don't try any tricks.'

'Tell me, what do you do with dermies?'

Digger grinned at his men. 'You'll find out, probie.'

Paul was led to a rain barrel, given a basin, razor, and soap. He scraped his face clean while Jim sat at a safe distance, munching a quid of tobacco and watching the operation with tired boredom. The other men had gone.

'May I have my pistol back?'

'Uh-uh! Read the rules. No weapons for probies.'

'Suppose I bump into a dermie?'

'Find yourself a whistle and toot a bunch of short blasts. Then run like hell. We'll take care of the dermies. Read the rules.'

'Can I scrounge wherever I want to?'

'Probies have their own assigned areas. There's a map in the rules.'

'Who wrote the rules, anyhow?'

'Jeezis!' the guard grunted disgustedly. 'Read 'em and find out.'

When Paul finished shaving, Jim stood up, stretched, then bounded off the platform and picked up his bicycle.

'Where do I go from here?' Paul called.

The man gave him a contemptuous snort, mounted the bike, and pedalled leisurely away. Paul gathered that he was to read the rules. He sat down beside the rain barrel and began studying the mimeographed leaflet.

Everything was cut and dried. As a probie, he was confined to an area six blocks square near the heart of the city. Once he entered it, a blue mark would be stamped on his forehead. At the two-week inspection, the indelible brand would be removed with a special solution. If a branded probie were caught outside his area, he would be forcibly escorted from the city. He was warned against attempting to impersonate permanent personnel, because a system of codes and passwords would ensnare him. One full page of the leaflet was devoted to propaganda. Houston was to become a 'Bulwark of health in a stricken world, and the leader of a glorious recovery.' The paper was signed by Dr. Georgelle, who had given himself the title of Director.

The pamphlet left Paul with a vague uneasiness. The uniforms —they reminded him of neighborhood boys' gangs in the slums, wearing special sweaters and uttering secret passwords, whipping intruders and amputating the tails of stray cats in darkened garages. And, in another way, it made him think of frustrated little people, gathering at night in brown shirts around a bonfire to sing the *Horst Wessel Leid* and listen to grandiose oratory about glorious destinies. *Their* stray cats had been an unfavored race.

Of course, the dermies were not merely harmless alley prowlers. They were a real menace. And maybe Georgelle's methods were the only ones effective.

While Paul sat with the pamphlet on the platform, he had been gazing absently at the stalled truck from which the men had emerged. Suddenly it broke upon his consciousness that it was a diesel. He bounded off the platform, and went to check its fuel tank, which had been left uncapped.

He knew that it was useless to search for gasoline, but diesel fuel was another matter. The exodus had drained all existing supplies of high octane fuel for the escaping motorcade, but the evacuation had been too hasty and too fear-crazed to worry with out-of-the-ordinary methods. He sniffed the tank. It smelled faintly of gasoline. Some unknowing fugitive had evidently filled it with ordinary fuel, which had later evaporated. But if the cylinders had not been damaged by the trial, the truck might be useful. He checked the engine briefly, and decided that it had not been tried at all. The starting battery had been removed.

He walked across the street and looked back at the warehouse. It bore the sign of a trucking firm. He walked around the block, eyeing the streets cautiously for other patrolmen. There was a fueling platform on the opposite side of the block. A fresh splash of oil on the concrete told him that Georgelle's crew was using the fuel for some purpose—possibly for heating or cooking. He entered the building and found a repair shop, with several dismantled engines lying about. There was a rack of batteries in the corner, but a screwdriver placed across the terminals brought only a weak spark.

The chargers, of course, drew power from the city's electric service, which was dead. After giving the problem some thought, Paul connected five of the batteries in series, then placed a sixth across the total voltage, so that it would collect the charge that the others lost. Then he went to carry buckets of fuel from the pumps to the truck. When the tank was filled, he hoisted each end of the truck with a roll-under jack and inflated the tires with a hand-pump. It was a long and laborious job.

Twilight was gathering by the time he was ready to try it. Several times during the afternoon, he had been forced to hide from cyclists who wandered past, lest they send him on to the probie area and use the truck for their own purposes. Evidently they had long since decided that automotive transportation was a thing of the past.

A series of short whistle-blasts came to his ears just as he was climbing into the cab. The signals were several blocks away, but some of the answering bleats were closer. Evidently another newcomer, he thought. Most new arrivals from the north would pass through the same area on their way downtown. He entered the cab, closed the door softly, and ducked low behind the dashboard as three cyclists raced across the intersection just ahead.

Paul settled down to wait for the all-clear. It came after about ten minutes. Apparently the newcomer had tried to run instead of hiding. When the cyclists returned, they were moving leisurely, and laughing among themselves. After they had passed the intersection, Paul stole quietly out of the cab and moved along the wall to the corner, to assure himself that all the patrolmen had gone. But the sound of shrill pleading came to his ears.

At the end of the building, he clung close to the wall and risked a glance around the corner. A block away, the nude figure of a girl was struggling between taut ropes held by green-shirted guards. She was a pretty girl, with a tousled mop of chestnut hair and clean white limbs—clean except for her forearms, which appeared dipped in dark stain. Then he saw the dark irregular splotch across her flank, like a splash of ink not quite washed clean. She was a dermie.

Paul ducked close to the ground so that his face was hidden by a clump of grass at the corner. A man—the leader of the group—had left the girl, and was advancing up the street toward Paul, who prepared to roll under the building out of sight. But in the middle of the block, the man stopped. He lifted a manhole cover in the pavement, then went back for the girl's clothing, which he dragged at the end of a fishing pole with a wire hook at its tip. He dropped the clothing, one piece at a time into the manhole. A cloud of white dust arose from it, and the man stepped back to avoid the dust. Quicklime, Paul guessed.

Then the leader cupped his hands to his mouth and called back to the others. 'Okay, drag her on up here!' He drew his revolver and waited while they tugged the struggling girl toward the manhole.

Paul felt suddenly ill. He had seen dermies shot in self-defense by fugitives from their deathly gray hands, but here was cold and efficient elimination. Here was Dachau and Buchenwald and the nameless camps of Siberia. He turned and bolted for the truck.

The sound of its engine starting brought a halt to the disposal of the pest-girl. The leader appeared at the intersection and stared uncertainly at the truck, as Paul nosed it away from the building. He fidgeted with his revolver doubtfully, and called something over his shoulder to the others. Then he began walking out into the street and signaling for the truck to stop. Paul let it crawl slowly ahead, and leaned out the window to eye the man questioningly.

'How the hell you get that started?' the leader called excitedly. He was still holding the pistol, but it dangled almost unnoticed in his hand. Paul suddenly fed fuel to the diesel and swerved sharply toward the surprised guardsman.

The leader yelped and dived for safety, but the fender caught his hips, spun him off balance, and smashed him down against the pavement. As the truck thundered around the corner toward the girl and her captors, he glanced in the mirror to see the hurt man weakly trying to crawl out of the street. Paul was certain that he was not mortally wounded.

As the truck lumbered on, the girl threw herself prone before it, since the ropes prevented any escape. Paul swerved erratically, sending the girl's captors scurrying for the alley. Then he aimed the wheels to straddle her body. She glanced up, screamed, then hugged the pavement as the behemoth thundered overhead. A bullet ploughed a furrow across the hood. Paul ducked low in the seat and jammed the brake pedal down, as soon as he thought she was clear.

There were several shots, but apparently they were shooting at the girl. Paul counted three seconds, then gunned the engine again. If she hadn't climbed aboard, it was just tough luck, he thought grimly. He shouldn't have tried to save her anyway. But continued shooting told him that she had managed to get inside. The trailer was heaped with clothing, and he trusted the mound of material to halt the barrage of bullets. He heard the explosion of a blowout as he swung around the next corner, and the trailer lurched dangerously. It swayed from side to side as he gathered speed down the wide and trafficless avenue. But the truck had double wheels, and soon the dangerous lurching ceased.

He roared on through the metropolitan area, staying on the same street and gathering speed. An occasional scrounger or cyclist stopped to stare, but they seemed too surprised to act. And they could not have known what had transpired a few blocks away.

Paul could not stop to see if he had a passenger, or if she was still alive. She was more dangerous than the gunmen. Any gratitude she might feel toward her rescuer would be quickly buried beneath her craving to spread the disease. He wished fervently that he had let the patrolmen kill her. Now he was faced with the problem of getting rid of her. He noticed, however, that mirrors were mounted on both sides of the cab. If he stopped the truck, and if she climbed out, he could see, and move away again before she had a chance to approach him. But he decided to wait until they were out of the city.

Soon he saw a highway marker, then a sign that said 'Galveston—58 miles.' He bore ahead, thinking that perhaps the island-city would provide good scrounging, without the regimentation of Doctor Georgelle's efficient system with its plans for 'glorious recovery.'

Twenty miles beyond the city limits, he stopped the truck, let the engine idle, and waited for his passenger to climb out. He locked the doors and laid a jack-handle across the seat as an added precaution. Nothing happened. He rolled down the window and shouted toward the rear.

'All passengers off the bus! Last stop! Everybody out!'

Still the girl did not appear. Then he heard something—a light tap from the trailer, and a murmur . . . or a moan. She was there all right. He called again, but she made no response. It was nearly dark outside.

At last he seized the jack-handle, opened the door, and stepped out of the cab. Wary of a trick, he skirted wide around the trailer and approached it from the rear. One door was closed, while the other swung free. He stopped a few yards away and peered inside. At first he saw nothing.

'Get out, but keep away or I'll kill you.'

Then he saw her move. She was sitting on the floor, leaning back against a heap of clothing, a dozen feet from the entrance. He stepped forward cautiously and flung open the other door. She turned her head to look at him peculiarly, but said nothing. He could see that she had donned some of the clothing, but one trouser-leg was rolled up, and she had tied a rag tightly about her ankle.

'Are you hurt?'

She nodded. 'Bullet . . .' She rolled her head dizzily and moaned.

Paul went back to the cab to search for a first aid kit. He found one, together with a flashlight and spare batteries in the glove compartment. He made certain that the cells were not corroded and that the light would burn feebly. Then he returned to the trailer, chiding himself for a prize fool. A sensible human would haul the dermie out at the end of a towing chain and leave her sitting by the side of the road.

'If you try to touch me, I'll brain you!' he warned, as he clambered into the trailer.

She looked up again. 'Would you feel . . . like enjoying anything . . . if you were bleeding like this?' she muttered weakly. The flashlight beam caught the glitter of pain in her eyes, and accentuated the pallor of her small face. She was a pretty girl—scarcely older than twenty—but Paul was in no mood to appreciate pretty women, especially dermies.

'So that's how you think of it, eh? Enjoying yourself!'

She said nothing. She dropped her forehead against her knee and rolled it slowly.

'Where are you hit? Just the foot?'

'Ankle . . .'

'All right, take the rag off. Let's see.'

'The wound's in back.'

'All right, lie down on your stomach, and keep your hands under your head.'

She stretched out weakly, and he shone the light over her leg, to make certain its skin was clear of neuroderm. Then he looked at the ankle, and said nothing for a time. The bullet had missed the joint, but had neatly severed the Achilles' tendon just above the heel.

'You're a plucky kid,' he grunted, wondering how she had endured the self-torture of getting the shoe off and clothing herself.

'It was cold back here—without clothes,' she muttered.

Paul opened the first aid packet and found an envelope of sulfa powder. Without touching her, he emptied it into the wound, which was beginning to bleed again. There was nothing else he could do. The tendon had pulled apart and would require surgical stitching to bring it together until it could heal. Such attention was out of the question.

She broke the silence. 'I . . . I'm going to be crippled, aren't I?'

'Oh, not crippled,' he heard himself telling her. 'If we can get you to a doctor, anyway. Tendons can be sutured with wire. He'll probably put your foot in a cast, and you might get a stiff ankle from it.'

She lay breathing quietly, denying his hopeful words by her silence.

'Here!' he said. 'Here's a gauze pad and some tape. Can you manage it yourself?'

She started to sit up. He placed the first aid pack beside her, and backed to the door. She fumbled in the kit, and whimpered while she taped the pad in place.

'There's a tourniquet in there, too. Use it if the bleeding's worse.'

She looked up to watch his silhouette against the darkening sky. 'Thanks . . . thanks a lot, mister. I'm grateful. I promise not to touch you. Not if you don't want me to.'

Shivering, he moved back to the cab. Why did they always get that insane idea that they were doing their victims a favor by giving them the neural plague? *Not if you don't want me to*. He shuddered as he drove away. She felt that way now, while the pain robbed her of the craving, but later—unless he got rid of her quickly—she would come to feel that she owed it to him—as a favor. The disease perpetuated itself by arousing such strange delusions in its bearer. The micro-organisms' methods of survival were indeed highly specialized. Paul felt certain that such animalicules had not evolved on Earth.

A light gleamed here and there along the Alvin-Galveston highway—oil lamps, shining from lonely cottages whose occupants had not felt the pressing urgency of the crowded city. But he had no doubt that to approach one of the farmhouses would bring a rifle bullet as a welcome. Where could he find help for the girl? No one would touch her but another dermie. Perhaps he could unhitch the trailer and leave her in downtown Galveston, with a sign hung on the back—'Wounded dermie inside.' The plague victims would care for their own—if they found her.

He chided himself again for worrying about her. Saving her life didn't make him responsible for her . . . did it? After all, if she lived, and the leg healed, she would only prowl in search of healthy victims again. She would never be rid of the disease, nor would she ever die of it—so far as anyone knew. The death rate was high among dermies, but the cause was usually a bullet.

Paul passed a fork in the highway and knew that the bridge was just ahead. Beyond the channel lay Galveston Island, once brightly lit and laughing in its role as seaside resort—now immersed in darkness. The wind whipped at the truck from the southwest as the road led up onto the wide causeway. A faint glow in the east spoke of a moon about to rise. He saw the wide structure of the drawbridge just ahead.

Suddenly he clutched at the wheel, smashed furiously down on the brake, and tugged the emergency back. The tires howled ahead on the smooth concrete, and the force threw him forward over the wheel. Dusty water swirled far below where the upward folding gates of the drawbridge had once been. He skidded to a stop ten feet from the end. When he climbed out, the girl was calling weakly from the trailer, but he walked to the edge and looked over. Someone had done a job with dynamite.

Why, he wondered. To keep islanders on the island, or to keep mainlanders off? Had another Doctor Georgelle started his own small nation in Galveston? It seemed more likely that the lower island dwellers had done the demolition.

He looked back at the truck. An experienced truckster might

be able to swing it around all right, but Paul was doubtful. Nevertheless, he climbed back in the cab and tried it. Half an hour later he was hopelessly jammed, with the trailer twisted aside and the cab wedged near the sheer drop to the water. He gave it up and went back to inspect his infected cargo.

She was asleep, but moaning faintly. He prodded her awake with the jack-handle. 'Can you crawl, kid? If you can, come back to the door.'

She nodded, and began dragging herself toward the flashlight. She clenched her lip between her teeth to keep from whimpering, but her breath came as a voiced murmur . . . *nnnng* . . . *nnnng* . . .

She sagged weakly when she reached the entrance, and for a moment he thought she had fainted. Then she looked up. 'What next, skipper?' she panted.

'I . . . I don't know. Can you let yourself down to the pavement?'

She glanced over the edge and shook her head. 'With a rope, maybe. There's one back there someplace. If you're scared of me, I'll try to crawl and get it.'

'Hands to yourself?' he asked suspiciously; then he thanked the darkness for hiding the heat of shame that crawled to his face.

'I won't . . .'

He scrambled into the trailer quickly and brought back the rope. 'I'll climb up on top and let it down in front of you. Grab hold and let yourself down.'

A few minutes later she was sitting on the concrete causeway looking at the wrecked draw. 'Oh!' she muttered as he scrambled down from atop the trailer. 'I thought you just wanted to dump me here. We're stuck, huh?'

'Yeah! We might swim it, but doubt if you could make it.'

'I'd try . . .' She paused, cocking her head slightly. 'There's a boat moored under the bridge. Right over there.'

'What makes you think so?'

'Water lapping against wood. Listen.' Then she shook her head. 'I forgot. You're not hyper.'

'I'm not what?' Paul listened. The water sounds seemed homogeneous.

'Hyperacute. Sharp senses. You know, it's one of the symptoms.'

He nodded, remembering vaguely that he'd heard something

to that effect—but he'd chalked it up as hallucinatory phenomenon. He walked to the rail and shone his light toward the water. The boat was there—tugging its rope taut from the mooring as the tide swirled about it. The bottom was still fairly dry, indicating that a recent rower had crossed from the island to the mainland.

'Think you can hold onto the rope if I let you down?' he called.

She gave him a quick glance, then picked up the end she had previously touched and tied a loop about her waist. She began crawling toward the rail. Paul fought down a crazy urge to pick her up and carry her; plague be damned. But he had already left himself dangerously open to contagion. Still, he felt the drumming charges of conscience . . . *depart from me, ye accursed, for I was sick and you visited me not . . .*

He turned quickly away, and began knotting the end of the rope about the rail. He reminded himself that any sane person would desert her at once, and swim on to safety. Yet, he could not. In the oversized clothing she looked like a child, hurt and helpless. Paul knew the demanding arrogance that could possess the wounded—*help me, you've got to help me, you damn merciless bastard! . . . No, don't touch me there, damn you!* Too many times, he had heard the sick curse the physician, and the injured curse the rescuer. Blind aggression, trying to strike back at pain.

But the girl made no complaint except the involuntary hurt sounds. She asked nothing, and accepted his aid with a wide-eyed gratitude that left him weak. He thought that it would be easier to leave her if she would only beg or plead, or demand.

'Can you start me swinging a little?' she called as he lowered her toward the water.

Paul's eyes probed the darkness below, trying to sort the shadows, to make certain which was the boat. He used both hands to feed out the rope, and the light laid on the rail only seemed to blind him. She began swinging herself pendulum-wise somewhere beneath him.

'When I say "ready," let me go!' she shrilled.

'You're not going to drop!'

'Have to! Boat's out further. Got to swing for it. I can't swim, really.'

'But you'll hurt your—'

'Ready!'

Paul still clung to the rope. 'I'll let you down into the water and you can hang onto the rope. I'll dive, and then pull you into the boat.'

'Uh-uh! You'd have to touch me. You don't want that, do you! Just a second now . . . one more swing . . . ready!'

He let the rope go. With a clatter and a thud, she hit the boat. Three sharp cries of pain clawed at him. Then—muffled sobbing.

'Are you all right?'

Sobs. She seemed not to hear him.

'Jeezis!' He sprinted for the brink of the drawbridge and dived out over the deep channel. How far . . . down . . . down. . . . Icy water stung his body with sharp whips, then opened to embrace him. He fought to the surface and swam toward the dark shadow of the boat. The sobbing had subsided. He grasped the prow and hauled himself dripping from the channel. She was lying curled in the bottom of the boat.

'Kid . . . you all right, kid?'

'Sorry . . . I'm such a baby,' she gasped, and dragged herself back to the stern.

Paul found a paddle, but no oars. He cast off and began digging water toward the other side, but the tide tugged them relentlessly away from the bridge. He gave it up and paddled toward the distant shore. 'You know anything about Galveston?' he called—mostly to reassure himself that she was not approaching him in the darkness with the death-gray hands.

'I used to come here for the summer, I know a little about it.'

Paul urged her to talk while he plowed toward the island. Her name was Willie, and she insisted that it was for Willow, not for Wilhelmina. She came from Dallas, and claimed she was a salesman's daughter who was done in by a traveling farmer. The farmer, she explained, was just a wandering dermie who had caught her napping by the roadside. He had stroked her arms until she awoke, then had run away, howling with glee.

'That was three weeks ago,' she said. 'If I'd had a gun, I'd have dropped him. Of course, I know better now.'

Paul shuddered and paddled on. 'Why did you head south?'

'I was coming here.'

'Here? To Galveston?'

'Uh-huh. I heard someone say that a lot of nuns were coming to the island. I thought maybe they'd take me in.'

The moon was high over the lightless city, and the tide had swept the small boat far east from the bridge by the time Paul's paddle dug into the mud beneath the shallow water. He bounded out and dragged the boat through thin marsh grass onto the shore. Fifty yards away, a ramshackle fishing cottage lay sleeping in the moonlight.

'Stay here, Willie,' he grunted. 'I'll find a couple of boards or something for crutches.'

He rummaged about through a shed behind the cottage and brought back a wheelbarrow. Moaning and laughing at once, she struggled into it, and he wheeled her to the house, humming a verse of *Rickshaw Boy*.

'You're a funny guy, Paul. I'm sorry . . .' She jiggled her tousled head in the moonlight, as if she disapproved of her own words.

Paul tried the cottage door, kicked it open, then walked the wheelbarrow up three steps and into a musty room. He struck a match, found an oil lamp with a little kerosene, and lit it. Willie caught her breath.

He looked around. 'Company,' he grunted.

The company sat in a fragile rocker with a shawl about her shoulders and a shotgun between her knees. She had been dead at least a month. The charge of buckshot had sieved the ceiling and spattered it with bits of gray hair and brown blood.

'Stay here,' he told the girl tonelessly. 'I'll try to get a dermie somewhere—one who knows how to sew a tendon. Got any ideas?'

She was staring with a sick face at the old woman. 'Here? With—'

'She won't bother you,' he said as he gently disentangled the gun from the corpse. He moved to a cupboard and found a box of shells behind an orange teapot. 'I may not be back, but I'll send somebody.'

She buried her face in her plague-stained hands, and he stood for a moment watching her shoulders shiver. 'Don't worry . . . I will send somebody.' He stepped to the porcelain sink and pocketed a wafer-thin sliver of dry soap.

'What's that for?' she muttered, looking up again.

He thought of a lie, then checked it. 'To wash you off of me,' he said truthfully. 'I might have got too close. Soap won't do much good, but I'll feel better.' He looked at the corpse coolly. 'Didn't do her much good. Buckshot's the best antiseptic all right.'

Willie moaned as he went out the door. He heard her crying as he walked down to the waterfront. She was still crying when he waded back to shore, after a thorough scrubbing. He was sorry he'd spoken cruelly, but it was such a damned relief to get rid of her . . .

With the shotgun cradled on his arm, he began putting distance between himself and the sobbing. But the sound worried his ears, even after he realized that he was no longer hearing her.

He strode a short distance inland past scattered fishing shanties, then took the highway toward the city whose outskirts he was entering. It would be at least an hour's trek to the end of the island where he would be most likely to encounter someone with medical training. The hospitals were down there, the medical school, the most likely place for any charitable nuns—if Willie's rumor were true. Paul meant to capture a dermie doctor or nurse and force the amorous-handed maniac at gunpoint to go to Willie's aid. Then he would be done with her. When she stopped hurting, she would start craving—and he had no doubt that he would be the object of her manual affections.

The bay was wind-chopped in the moonglow, no longer glittering from the lights along 61st Street. The oleanders along Broadway were choked up with weeds. Cats or rabbits rustled in the tousled growth that had been a carefully tended parkway.

Paul wondered why the plague had chosen Man, and not the lower animals. It was true that an occasional dog or cow was seen with the plague, but the focus was upon humanity. And the craving to spread the disease was Man-directed, even in animals. It was as if the neural entity deliberately sought out the species with the most complex nervous system. Was its onslaught really connected with the meteorite swarm? Paul believed that it was.

In the first place, the meteorites had not been predicted. They were not a part of the regular cosmic bombardment. And then there was the strange report that they were *manufactured* projectiles, teeming with frozen microorganisms which came alive upon thawing. In these days of tumult and confusion, however, it was hard. Nevertheless Paul believed it. Neuroderm had no first cousins among Earth diseases.

What manner of beings, then, had sent such a curse? Potential invaders? If so, they were slow in coming. One thing was generally agreed upon by the scientists: the missiles had not been 'sent' from another solar planet. Their direction upon entering the atmosphere was wrong. They could conceivably have been fired from an interplanetary launching ship, but their velocity was about equal to the theoretical velocity which a body would obtain in falling sunward from the near-infinite distance. This seemed to hint the projectiles had come from another star.

Paul was startled suddenly by the flare of a match from the shadow of a building. He stopped dead still in the street. A man was leaning against the wall to light a cigarette. He flicked the match out, and Paul watched the cigarette-glow make an arc as the man waved at him.

'Nice night, isn't it?' said the voice from the darkness.

Paul stood exposed in the moonlight, carrying the shotgun at the ready. The voice sounded like that of an adolescent, not fully changed to its adult timbre. If the youth wasn't a dermie, why wasn't he afraid that Paul might be one? And if he was a dermie, why wasn't he advancing in the hope that Paul might be as yet untouched?

'I said, "Nice night, isn't it?" Whatcha carrying the gun for? Been shooting rabbits?'

Paul moved a little closer and fumbled for his flashlight. Then he threw its beam on the slouching figure in the shadows. He saw a young man, perhaps sixteen, reclining against the wall. He saw the pearl-gray face that characterized the final and permanent stage of neuroderm! He stood frozen to the spot a dozen feet away from the youth, who blinked perplexedly into the light. The kid was assuming automatically that he was another dermie! Paul tried to keep him blinded while he played along with the fallacy.

'Yeah, it's a nice night. You got any idea where I can find a doctor?'

The boy frowned. 'Doctor? You mean you don't know?'

'Know what? I'm new here.'

'New? Oh . . .' the boy's nostrils began twitching slightly, as if he were sniffing at the night air. 'Well, most of the priests down at Saint Mary's were missionaries. They're all doctors. Why? You sick?'

'No, there's a girl . . . But never mind. How do I get there? And are any of them dermies?'

The boy's eyes wandered peculiarly, and his mouth fell open, as if he had been asked why a circle wasn't square. 'You are new, aren't you? They're all dermies, if you want to call them that. Wh—' Again the nostrils were flaring. He flicked the cigarette away suddenly and inhaled a slow draught of the breeze. 'I . . . I smell a non-hyper,' he muttered.

Paul started to back away. His scalp bristled a warning. The boy advanced a step toward him. A slow beam of anticipation began to glow in his face. He bared his teeth in a wide grin of pleasure.

'You're not a hyper yet,' he hissed, moving forward. 'I've never had a chance to touch a nonhyper . . .'

'Stay back, or I'll kill you!'

The lad giggled and came on, talking to himself. 'The padre says it's wrong, but . . . you smell so . . . so . . . ugh . . .' He flung himself forward with a low throaty cry.

Paul sidestepped the charge and brought the gun barrel down across the boy's head. The dermie sprawled howling in the street. Paul pushed the gun close to his face, but the youth started up again. Paul jabbed viciously with the barrel, and felt it strike and tear. 'I don't want to have to blow your head off—'

The boy howled and fell back. He crouched panting on his hands and knees, head hung low, watching a dark puddle of blood gather on the pavement from a deep gash across his cheek. 'Whatcha wanta do that for?' he whimpered. 'I wasn't gonna hurt you.' His tone was that of a wronged and rejected suitor.

'Now, where's Saint Mary's? Is that one of the hospitals? How do I get there?' Paul had backed to a safe distance and was covering the youth with the gun.

'Straight down Broadway . . . to the Boulevard . . . you'll see it down that neighborhood. About the fourth street, I think.' The boy looked up, and Paul saw the extent of the gash. It was deep and ragged, and the kid was crying.

'Get up! You're going to lead me there.'

Pain had blanketed the call of the craving. The boy struggled to his feet, pressed a handkerchief against the wound, and with an angry glance at Paul, he set out down the road. Paul followed ten yards behind.

'If you take me through any dermie traps, I'll kill you.'

'There aren't any traps,' the youth mumbled.

Paul snorted unbelief, but did not repeat the warning. 'What made you think I was another dermie?' he snapped.

'Because there's no nonhypers in Galveston. This is a hyper colony. A nonhyper used to drift in occasionally, but the priests had the bridge dynamited. The nonhypers upset the colony. As long as there aren't any around to smell, nobody causes any trouble. During the day, there's a guard out on the causeway, and if any hypers come looking for a place to stay, the guard ferries them across. If nonhypers come, he tells them about the colony, and they go away.'

Paul groaned. He had stumbled into a rat's nest. Was there no refuge from the gray curse? Now he would have to move on. It seemed a hopeless quest. Maybe the old man he met on his way to Houston had arrived at the only possible hope for peace: submission to the plague. But the thought sickened him somehow. He would have to find some barren island, find a healthy mate, and go to live a savage existence apart from all traces of civilization.

'Didn't the guard stop you at the bridge?' the boy asked. 'He never came back today. He must be still out there.'

Paul grunted 'no' in a tone that warned against idle conversation. He guessed what had happened. The dermie guard had probably spotted some healthy wanderers; and instead of warning them away, he rowed across the drawbridge and set out to chase them. His body probably lay along the highway somewhere, if the hypothetical wanderers were armed.

When they reached 23rd Street, a few blocks from the heart of the city, Paul hissed at the boy to stop. He heard someone laugh. Footsteps were wandering along the sidewalk, overhung by trees. He whispered to the boy to take refuge behind a hedge. They crouched in the shadows several yards apart while the voices drew nearer.

'Brother James has a nice tenor,' someone said softly. 'But he sings his Latin with a western drawl. It sounds . . . well . . . peculiar, to say the least. Brother John is a stickler for pronunciation. He won't let Fra James solo. Says it gives a burlesque effect to the choir. Says it makes the sisters giggle.'

The other man chuckled quietly and started to reply. But his voice broke off suddenly. The footsteps stopped a dozen feet from Paul's hiding place. Paul, peering through the hedge, saw a pair of brown-robed monks standing on the sidewalk. They were looking around suspiciously.

'Brother Thomas, do you smell—'

'Aye, I smell it.'

Paul changed his position slightly, so as to keep the gun pointed toward the pair of plague-stricken monastics. They stood in embarrassed silence, peering into the darkness, and shuffling their feet uneasily. One of them suddenly pinched his nose between thumb and forefinger. His companion followed suit.

'Blessed be God,' quavered one.

'Blessed be His Holy Name,' answered the other.

'Blessed be Jesus Christ, true God and true Man.'

'Blessed be . . .'

Gathering their robes high about their shins, the two monks turned and scurried away, muttering the Litany of the Divine Praises as they went. Paul stood up and stared after them in amazement. The sight of dermies running from a potential victim was almost beyond belief. He questioned his young guide. Still holding the handkerchief against his bleeding face, the boy hung his head.

'Bishop made a ruling against touching nonhypers,' he explained miserably. 'Says it's a sin, unless the nonhyper submits of his own free will. Says even then it's wrong, except in the ordinary ways that people come in contact with each other. Calls it fleshly desire, and all that.'

'Then why did you try to do it?'

'I ain't so religious.'

'Well, sonny, you better get religious until we come to the hospital. Now, let's go.'

They marched on down Broadway encountering no other pedestrians. Twenty minutes later, they were standing in the shadows before a hulking brick building, some of whose windows were yellow with lamplight. Moonlight bathed the statue of a woman standing on a ledge over the entrance, indicating to Paul that this was the hospital.

'All right, boy. You go in and send out a dermie doctor. Tell him somebody wants to see him, but if you say I'm not a dermie, I'll come in and kill you. Now move. And don't come back. Stay to get your face fixed.'

The youth stumbled toward the entrance. Paul sat in the shadow of a tree, where he could see twenty yards in all directions and guard himself against approach. Soon a black-clad priest came out of the emergency entrance, stopped on the sidewalk, and glanced around.

'Over here!' Paul hissed from across the street.

The priest advanced uncertainly. In the center of the road he stopped again, and held his nose. 'Y-you're a nonhyper,' he said, almost accusingly.

'That's right, and I've got a gun, so don't try anything.'

'What's wrong? Are you sick? The lad said—'

'There's a dermie girl down the island. She's been shot. Tendon behind her heel is cut clean through. You're going to help her.'

'Of course, but . . .' The priest paused. 'You? A nonhyper? Helping a so-called dermie?' His voice went high with amazement.

'So I'm a sucker!' Paul barked. 'Now get what you need, and come on.'

'The Lord bless you,' the priest mumbled in embarrassment as he hurried away.

'Don't sic any of your maniacs on me!' Paul called after him. 'I'm armed.'

'I'll have to bring a surgeon,' the cleric said over his shoulder.

Five minutes later, Paul heard the muffled grunt of a starter. Then an engine coughed to life. Startled, he scurried away from the tree and sought safety in a clump of shrubs. An ambulance backed out of the driveway and into the street. It parked at the curb by the tree, engine running. A pallid face glanced out curiously toward the shadows. 'Where are you?' it called, but it was not the priest's voice.

Paul stood up and advanced a few steps.

'We'll have to wait on Father Mendelhaus,' the driver called. 'He'll be a few minutes.'

'You a dermie?'

'Of course. But don't worry. I've plugged my nose and I'm wearing rubber gloves. I can't smell you. The sight of a nonhyper arouses some craving, of course. But it can be overcome with a little will power. I won't infect you, although I don't understand why you nonhypers fight so hard. You're bound to catch it sooner or later. And the world can't get back to normal until everybody has it.'

Paul avoided the startling thought. 'You the surgeon?'

'Uh, yes. Father Williamson's the name. I'm not really a specialist, but I did some surgery in Korea. How's the girl's condition? Suffering shock?'

'I wouldn't know.'

They fell silent until Father Mendelhaus returned. He came across the street carrying a bag in one hand and a brown bottle in the other. He held the bottle by the neck with a pair of tongs and Paul could see the exterior of the bottle steaming slightly as the priest passed through the beam of the ambulance's headlights. He placed the flask on the curb without touching it, then spoke to the man in the shadows.

'Would you step behind the hedge and disrobe, young man? Then rub yourself thoroughly with this oil.'

'I doubt it,' Paul snapped. 'What is it?'

'Don't worry, it's been in the sterilizer. That's what took me so long. It may be a little hot for you, however. It's only an antiseptic and deodorant. It'll kill your odor, and it'll also give you some protection against picking up stray micro-organisms.'

After a few moments of anxious hesitation, Paul decided to trust the priest. He carried the hot flask into the brush, undressed, and bathed himself with the warm aromatic oil. Then he slipped back into his clothes and reapproached the ambulance.

'Ride in back,' Mendelhaus told him. 'And you won't be infected. No one's been in there for several weeks, and as you probably know, the micro-organisms die after a few hours exposure. They have to be transmitted from skin to skin, or else an object has to be handled very soon after a hyper has touched it.'

Paul warily climbed inside. Mendelhaus opened a slide and spoke through it from the front seat. 'You'll have to show us the way.'

'Straight out Broadway. Say, where did you get the gasoline for this wagon?'

The priest paused. 'That has been something of a secret. Oh well . . . I'll tell you. There's a tanker out in the harbor. The people left town too quickly to think of it. Automobiles are scarcer than fuel in Galveston. Up north, you find them stalled everywhere. But since Galveston didn't have any through-traffic, there were no cars running out of gas. The ones we have are the ones that were left in the repair shop. Something wrong with them. And we don't have any mechanics to fix them.'

Paul neglected to mention that he was qualified for the job. The priest might get ideas. He fell into gloomy silence as the ambulance turned onto Broadway and headed down-island. He watched the backs of the priests' heads, silhouetted against the headlighted pavement. They seemed not at all concerned about their disease. Mendelhaus was a slender man, with a blond crew cut and rather bushy eyebrows. He had a thin, aristocratic face —now plague-gray—but jovial enough. It might be the face of an ascetic, but for the quick blue eyes that seemed full of lively interest rather than inward-turning mysticism. Williamson, on the other hand, was a rather plain man, with a stolid tweedy look, despite his black cassock.

'What do you think of our plan here?' asked Father Mendelhaus.

'What plan?' Paul grunted.

'Oh, didn't the boy tell you? We're trying to make the island a refuge for hypers who are willing to sublimate their craving and turn their attentions toward reconstruction. We're also trying to make an objective study of this neural condition. We have some good scientific minds, too—Doctor Relmone of Fordham, Father Seyes of Notre Dame, two biologists from Boston College. . . .'

'Dermies trying to cure the plague?' Paul gasped.

Mendelhaus laughed merrily. 'I didn't say cure it, son. I said "study it." '

'Why?'

'To learn how to live with it, of course. It's been pointed out by our philosophers that things become evil only through human misuse. Morphine, for instance, is a product of the Creator; it is therefore good when properly used for relief of pain. When mistreated by an addict, it becomes a monster. We bear this in mind as we study neuroderm.'

Paul snorted contemptuously. 'Leprosy is evil, I suppose, because Man mistreated bacteria?'

The priest laughed again. 'You've got me there. I'm no philosopher. But you can't compare neuroderm with leprosy.'

Paul shuddered. 'The hell I can't! It's worse.'

'Ah? Suppose you tell me what makes it worse? List the symptoms for me.'

Paul hesitated, listing them mentally. They were: discoloration of the skin, low fever, hallucinations, and the insane craving to infect others. They seemed bad enough, so he listed them orally. 'Of course, people don't die of it,' he added. 'But which is worse, insanity or death?'

The priest turned to smile back at him through the porthole. 'Would you call me insane? It's true that victims have frequently lost their minds. But that's not a direct result of neuroderm. Tell me, how would you feel if everyone screamed and ran when they saw you coming, or hunted you down like a criminal? How long would your sanity last?'

Paul said nothing. Perhaps the anathema was a contributing factor. . . .

'Unless you were of very sound mind to begin with, you probably couldn't endure it.'

'But the craving . . . and the hallucinations . . .'

'True,' murmured the priest thoughtfully. 'The hallucinations. Tell me something else, if all the world was blind save one man, wouldn't the world be inclined to call that man's sight a hallucination? And the man with eyes might even come to agree with the world.'

Again Paul was silent. There was no arguing with Mendelhaus, who probably suffered the strange delusions and thought them real.

'And the craving,' the priest went on. 'It's true that the craving can be a rather unpleasant symptom. It's the condition's way of perpetuating itself. Although we're not certain how it works, it seems able to stimulate erotic sensations in the hands. We do know the micro-organisms get to the brain, but we're not yet sure what they do there.'

'What facts have you discovered?' Paul asked cautiously.

Mendelhaus grinned at him. 'Tut! I'm not going to tell you, because I don't want to be called a "crazy dermie." You wouldn't believe me, you see.'

Paul glanced outside and saw that they were approaching the vicinity of the fishing cottage. He pointed out the lamplit window to the driver, and the ambulance turned onto a side road. Soon they were parked behind the shanty. The priests scrambled out and carried the stretcher toward the light, while Paul skulked to a safer distance and sat down in the grass to watch. When Willie was safe in the vehicle, he meant to walk back to the bridge, swim across the gap, and return to the mainland.

Soon Mendelhaus came out and walked toward him with a solemn stride, although Pau' was sitting quietly in the deepest shadow—invisible, he had thought. He arose quickly as the priest approached. Anxiety tightened his throat. 'Is she . . . is Willie . . . ?'

'She's irrational,' Mendelhaus murmured sadly. 'Almost . . . less than sane. Some of it may be due to high fever, but . . .'

'Yes?'

'She tried to kill herself. With a knife. Said something about buckshot being the best way, or something . . .'

'Jeezis! Jeezis!' Paul sank weakly in the grass and covered his face with his hands.

'Blessed be His Holy Name,' murmured the priest by way of turning the oath aside. 'She didn't hurt herself badly, though. Wrist's cut a little. She was too weak to do a real job of it. Father Will's giving her a hypo and a tetanus shot and some sulfa. We're out of penicillin.'

He stopped speaking and watched Paul's wretchedness for a moment. 'You love the girl, don't you?'

Paul stiffened. 'Are you crazy? Love a little tramp dermie? Jeezis . . .'

'Blessed be—'

'Listen! Will she be all right? I'm getting out of here!' He climbed unsteadily to his feet.

'I don't know, son. Infection's the real threat, and shock. If we'd got to her sooner, she'd have been safer. And if she was in the ultimate stage of neuroderm, it would help.

'Why?'

'Oh, various reasons. You'll learn, someday. But listen, you look exhausted. Why don't you come back to the hospital with us? The third floor is entirely vacant. There's no danger of infection up there, and we keep a sterile room ready just in case we get a nonhyper case. You can lock the door inside, if you want to, but it wouldn't be necessary. Nuns are on the floor below. Our male staff lives in the basement. There aren't any laymen in the building. I'll guarantee that you won't be bothered.'

'No, I've got to go,' he growled, then softened his voice: 'I appreciate it though, Father.'

'Whatever you wish. I'm sorry, though. You might be able to provide yourself with some kind of transportation if you waited.'

'Uh-uh! I don't mind telling you, your island makes me jumpy.'

'Why?'

Paul glanced at the priest's gray hands. 'Well . . . you still feel the craving, don't you?'

Mendelhaus touched his nose. 'Cotton plugs, with a little camphor. I can't smell you.' He hesitated. 'No, I won't lie to you. The urge to touch is still there to some extent.'

'And in a moment of weakness, somebody might—'

The priest straightened his shoulders. His eyes went chilly. 'I have taken certain vows, young man. Sometimes when I see a beautiful woman, I feel desire. When I see a man eating a thick steak on a fast-day, I feel envy and hunger. When I sec a doctor earning large fees, I chafe under the vow of poverty. But by denying desire's demands, one learns to make desire useful in other ways. Sublimation, some call it. A priest can use it and do more useful work thereby. I am a priest.'

He nodded curtly, turned on his heel and strode away. Halfway to the cottage, he paused. 'She's calling for someone named Paul. Know who it might be? Family perhaps?'

Paul stood speechless. The priest shrugged and continued toward the lighted doorway.

'Father, wait . . .'

'Yes?'

'I—I am a little tired. The room . . . I mean, will you show me where to get transportation tomorrow?'

'Certainly.'

Before midnight, the party had returned to the hospital. Paul lay on a comfortable mattress for the first time in weeks, sleepless, and staring at the moonlight on the sill. Somewhere downstairs, Willie was lying unconscious in an operating room, while the surgeon tried to repair the torn tendon. Paul had ridden back with them in the ambulance, sitting a few feet from the stretcher, avoiding her sometimes wandering arms, and listening to her delirious moaning.

Now he felt his skin crawling with belated hypochondria. What a fool he had been—touching the rope, the boat, the wheelbarrow, riding in the ambulance. There were a thousand ways he could have picked up a few stray micro-organisms lingering from a dermie's touch. And now, he lay here in this nest of disease. . . .

But strange—it was the most peaceful, the sanest place he'd seen in months. The religious orders simply accepted the plague —with masochistic complacency perhaps—but calmly. A cross, or a penance, or something. But no, they seemed to accept it almost gladly. Nothing peculiar about that. All dermies went wild-eyed with happiness about the 'lovely desire' they possessed. The priests weren't wild-eyed.

Neither was normal man equipped with socially-shaped sexual desire. Sublimation?

'Peace,' he muttered, and went to sleep.

A knocking at the door awoke him at dawn. He grunted at it disgustedly and sat up in bed. The door, which he had forgotten to lock, swung open. A chubby nun with a breakfast tray started into the room. She saw his face, then stopped. She closed her eyes, wrinkled her nose, and framed a silent prayer with her lips. Then she backed slowly out.

'I'm sorry, sir!' she quavered through the door. 'I—I knew there was a patient in here, but I didn't know . . . you weren't a hyper. Forgive me.'

He heard her scurrying away down the hall. Somehow, he began to feel safe. But wasn't that exactly what they wanted him to feel! He realized suddenly that he was trapped. He had left the shotgun in the emergency room. What was he—guest or captive? Months of fleeing from the gray terror had left him suspicious.

Soon he would find out. He arose and began dressing. Before he finished, Mendelhaus came. He did not enter, but stood in the hallway beyond the door. He smiled a faint greeting, and said, 'So you're Paul?'

He felt heat rising in his face. 'She's awake, then?' he asked gruffly.

The priest nodded. 'Want to see her?'

'No, I've got to be going.'

'It would do her good.'

He coughed angrily. Why did the black-cassocked dermie have to put it that way? 'Well it wouldn't do me any good!' he snarled. 'I've been around too many gray-leather hides already!'

Mendelhaus shrugged, but his eyes bore a hint of contempt. 'As you wish. You may leave by the outside stairway—to avoid disturbing the sisters.'

'To avoid being touched, you mean!'

'No one will touch you.'

Paul finished dressing in silence. The reversal of attitudes disturbed him. He resented the seeming 'tolerance' that was being extended him. It was like asylum inmates being 'tolerant' of the psychiatrist.

'I'm ready!' he growled.

Mendelhaus led him down the corridor and out onto a sunlit balcony. They descended a stone stairway while the priest talked over his shoulder.

'She's still not fully rational, and there's some fever. It wouldn't be anything to worry about two years ago, but now we're out of most of the latest drugs. If sulfa won't hold the infection, we'll have to amputate, of course. We should know in two or three days.'

He paused and looked back at Paul, who had stopped on the stairway. 'Coming?'

'Where is she?' Paul asked weakly. 'I'll see her.'

The priest frowned. 'You don't have to, son. I'm sorry if I implied any obligation on your part. Really, you've done enough. I gather that you saved her life. Very few nonhypers would do a thing like that. I—'

'Where is she?' he snapped angrily.

The priest nodded. 'Downstairs. Come on.'

As they re-entered the building on the ground floor, the priest cupped his hands to his mouth and called out, 'Nonhyper coming! Plug your noses, or get out of the way! Avoid circumstances of temptation!'

When they moved along the corridor, it was Paul who felt like the leper. Mendelhaus led him into the third room.

Willie saw him enter and hid her gray hands beneath the sheet. She smiled faintly, tried to sit up, and failed. Williamson and a nun-nurse who had both been standing by the bedside turned to leave the room. Mendelhaus followed them out and closed the door.

There was a long, painful pause. Willie tried to grin. He shuffled his feet.

'They've got me in a cast,' she said conversationally.

'You'll be all right,' he said hastily. 'It won't be long before you'll be up. Galveston's a good place for you. They're all dermies here.'

She clenched her eyes tightly shut. 'God! God! I hope I never hear that word again. After last night . . . that old woman in the rocking chair . . . I stayed there all alone . . . and the wind'd start the chair rocking. Ooh!' She looked at him with abnormally bright eyes. 'I'd rather die than touch anybody now . . . after seeing that. Somebody touched her, didn't they, Paul? That's why she did it, wasn't it?'

He squirmed and backed toward the door. 'Willie . . . I'm sorry for what I said. I mean—'

'Don't worry, Paul! I wouldn't touch you now.' She clenched her hands and brought them up before her face, to stare at them with glittering hate. 'I loathe myself!' she hissed.

What was it Mendelhaus had said, about the dermie going insane because of being an outcast rather than because of the plague? But she wouldn't be an outcast here. Only among nonhypers, like himself . . .

'Get well quick, Willie,' he muttered, then hurriedly slipped out into the corridor. She called his name twice, then fell silent.

'That was quick,' murmured Mendelhaus, glancing at his pale face.

'Where can I get a car?'

The priest rubbed his chin. 'I was just speaking to Brother Matthew about that. Uh . . . how would you like to have a small yacht instead?'

Paul caught his breath. A yacht would mean access to the seas, and to an island. A yacht was the perfect solution. He stammered gratefully.

'Good,' said Mendelhaus. 'There's a small craft in dry dock

down at the basin. It was apparently left there because there weren't any dock crews around to get her afloat again. I took the liberty of asking Brother Matthew to find some men and get her in the water.'

'Dermies?'

'Of course. The boat will be fumigated, but it isn't really necessary. The infection dies out in a few hours. It'll take a while, of course, to get the boat ready. Tomorrow . . . next day, maybe. Bottom's cracked; it'll need some patching.'

Paul's smile weakened. More delay. Two more days of living in the gray shadow. Was the priest really to be trusted? Why should he even provide the boat? The jaws of an invisible trap, slowly closing.

Mendelhaus saw his doubt. 'If you'd rather leave now, you're free to do so. We're really not going to as much trouble as it might seem. There are several yachts at the dock; Brother Matthew's been preparing to clean one or two up for our own use. And we might as well let you have one. They've been deserted by their owners. And . . . well . . . you helped the girl when nobody else would have done so. Consider the boat as our way of returning the favor, eh?'

A yacht. The open sea. A semitropical island, uninhabited, on the brink of the Caribbean. And a woman, of course—chosen from among the many who would be willing to share such an escape. Peculiarly, he glanced at Willie's door. It was too bad about her. But she'd get along okay. The yacht . . . if he were only certain of Mendelhaus' intentions . . .

The priest began frowning at Paul's hesitation. 'Well?'

'I don't want to put you to any trouble. . . .'

'Nonsense! You're still afraid of us! Very well, come with me. There's someone I want you to see.' Mendelhaus turned and started down the corridor.

Paul lingered. 'Who . . . what—'

'Come on!' the priest snapped impatiently.

Reluctantly, Paul followed him to the stairway. They descended to a gloomy basement and entered a smelly laboratory through a double-door. Electric illumination startled him; then he heard the sound of a gasoline engine and knew that the power was generated locally.

'Germicidal lamps,' murmured the priest, following his ceilingward gaze. 'Some of them are. Don't worry about touching things. It's sterile in here.'

'But it's not sterile for your convenience,' growled an

invisible voice. 'And it won't be sterile at all if you don't stay out! Beat it, preacher!'

Paul looked for the source of the voice, and saw a small, short-necked man bending his shaggy gray head over a microscope at the other end of the lab. He had spoken without glancing up at his visitors.

'This is Doctor Seevers, of Princeton, son,' said the priest, unruffled by the scientist's ire. 'Claims he's an atheist, but personally I think he's a puritan. Doctor, this is the young man I was telling you about. Will you tell him what you know about neuroderm?'

Seevers jotted something on a pad, but kept his eye to the instrument. 'Why don't we just give it to him, and let him find out for himself?' the scientist grumbled sadistically.

'Don't frighten him, you heretic! I brought him here to be illuminated.'

'Illuminate him yourself. I'm busy. And stop calling me names. I'm not an atheist; I'm a biochemist.'

'Yesterday you were a biophysicist. Now, entertain my young man.' Mendelhaus blocked the doorway with his body. Paul, with his jaw clenched angrily, had turned to leave.

'That's all I can do, preacher,' Seevers grunted. 'Entertain him. I know nothing. Absolutely nothing. I have some observed data. I have noticed some correlations. I have seen things happen. I have traced the patterns of the happenings and found some probable common denominators. And that is all! I admit it. Why don't you preachers admit it in your racket?'

'Seevers, as you can see, is inordinately proud of his humility—if that's not a paradox,' the priest said to Paul.

'Now, Doctor, this young man—'

Seevers heaved a resigned sigh. His voice went sour-sweet. 'All right, sit down, young man. I'll entertain you as soon as I get through counting free nerve-endings in this piece of skin.'

Mendelhaus winked at his guest. 'Seevers calls it masochism when we observe a fast-day or do penance. And there he sits, ripping off patches of his own hide to look at through his peeping glass. Masochism—heh!'

'Get out, preacher!' the scientist bellowed.

Mendelhaus laughed mockingly, nodded Paul toward a chair, and left the lab. Paul sat uneasily watching the back of Seevers' lab jacket.

'Nice bunch of people really—these black-frocked ya-hoos,'

Seevers murmured conversationally. 'If they'd just stop trying to convert me.'

'Doctor Seevers, maybe I'd better—'

'Quiet! You bother me. And sit still, I can't stand to have people running in and out of here. You're in; now stay in.'

Paul fell silent. He was uncertain whether or not Seevers was a dermie. The small man's lab jacket bunched up to hide the back of his neck, and the sleeves covered his arms. His hands were rubber-gloved, and a knot of white cord behind his head told Paul that he was wearing a gauze mask. His ears were bright pink, but their color was meaningless; it took several months for the gray coloring to seep to all areas of the skin. But Paul guessed he was a dermie—and wearing the gloves and mask to keep his equipment sterile.

He glanced idly around the large room. There were several glass cages of rats against the wall. They seemed airtight, with ducts for forced ventilation. About half the rats were afflicted with neuroderm in its various stages. A few wore shaved patches of skin where the disease had been freshly and forcibly inflicted. Paul caught the fleeting impression that several of the animals were staring at him fixedly. He shuddered and looked away.

He glanced casually at the usual maze of laboratory glassware, then turned his attention to a pair of hemispheres, suspended like a trophy on the wall. He recognized them as the twin halves of one of the meteorites, with the small jelly-pocket in the center. Beyond it hung a large picture frame containing several typewritten sheets. Another frame held four pictures of bearded scientists from another century, obviously clipped from magazine or textbook. There was nothing spectacular about the lab. It smelled of clean dust and sour things. Just a small respectable workshop.

Seevers' chair creaked suddenly. 'It checks,' he said to himself. 'It checks again. Forty per cent increase.' He threw down the stub pencil and whirled suddenly. Paul saw a pudgy round face with glittering eyes. A dark splotch of neuroderm had crept up from the chin to split his mouth and cover one cheek and an eye, giving him the appearance of a black and white bulldog with a mixed color muzzle.

'It checks,' he barked at Paul, then smirked contentedly.

'What checks?'

The scientist rolled up a sleeve to display a patch of adhesive tape on a portion of his arm which had been discolored by the disease. 'Here,' he grunted. 'Two weeks ago this area was normal. I took a centimeter of skin from right next to this one, and counted the nerve endings. Since that time, the derm's crept down over the area. I took another square centimeter today, and recounted. Forty per cent increase.'

Paul frowned with disbelief. It was generally known that neuroderm had a sensitizing effect, but new nerve endings . . . No. He didn't believe it.

'Third time I've checked it,' Seevers said happily. 'One place ran up to sixty-five per cent. Heh! Smart little bugs, aren't they? Inventing new somesthetic receptors that way!'

Paul swallowed with difficulty. 'What did you say?' he gasped.

Seevers inspected him serenely. 'So you're a nonhyper, are you? Yes, indeed, I can smell that you are. Vile, really. Can't understand why sensible hypers would want to paw you. But then, I've insured myself against such foolishness.'

He said it so casually that Paul blinked before he caught the full impact of it. 'Y-y-you've done what?'

'What I said. When I first caught it, I simply sat down with a velvet-tipped stylus and located the spots of my hands that gave rise to pleasurable sensations. Then I burned them out with an electric needle. There aren't many of them, really—one or two points per square centimeter.' He tugged off his gloves and exhibited pock-marked palms to prove it. 'I didn't want to be bothered with such silly urges. Waste of time, chasing nonhypers—for me it is. I never learned what it's like, so I've never missed it.' He turned his hands over and stared at them. 'Stubborn little critters keep growing new ones, and I keep burning them out.'

Paul leaped to his feet. 'Are you trying to tell me that the plague causes new nerve cells to grow?'

Seevers looked up coldly. 'Ah, yes. You came here to be illoooominated, as the padre put it. If you wish to be de-idiotized, please stop shouting. Otherwise, I'll ask you to leave.'

Paul, who had felt like leaving a moment ago, now subsided quickly. 'I'm sorry,' he snapped, then softened his tone to repeat: 'I'm sorry.'

Seevers took a deep breath, stretched his short meaty arms in an unexpected yawn, then relaxed and grinned. 'Sit down, sit down, m'boy. I'll tell you what you want to know, if you really want to know anything. Do you?'

'Of course!'

'You don't! You just want to know how you—whatever your

name is—will be affected by events. You don't care about understanding for its own sake. Few people do. That's why we're in this mess. The padre now, he cares about understanding events—but not for their own sake. He cares, but for his flock's sake and for his God's sake—which is, I must admit, a better attitude than that of the common herd, whose only interest is in their own safety. But if people would just want to understand events for the understanding's sake, we wouldn't be in such a pickle.'

Paul watched the professor's bright eyes and took the lecture quietly.

'And so, before I illuminate you, I want to make an impossible request.'

'Yes, sir.'

'I ask you to be completely objective,' Seevers continued, rubbing the bridge of his nose and covering his eyes with his hand. 'I want you to forget you ever heard of neuroderm while you listen to me. Rid yourself of all preconceptions, especially those connected with fear. Pretend these are purely hypothetical events that I'm going to discuss.' He took his hands down from his eyes and grinned sheepishly. 'It always embarrasses me to ask for that kind of cooperation when I know damn well I'll never get it.'

'I'll try to be objective, sir.'

'Bah!' Seevers slid down to sit on his spine, and hooked the base of his skull over the back of the chair. He blinked thoughtfully at the ceiling for a moment, then folded his hands across his small paunch and closed his eyes.

When he spoke again, he was speaking to himself: 'Assume a planet, somewhat earthlike, but not quite. It has carboniferous life forms, but not human. Warm blooded, probably, and semi-intelligent. And the planet has something else—it has an overabundance of parasite forms. Actually, the various types of parasites are the dominant species. The warm blooded animals are the parasites' vegetables, so to speak. Now, during two billion years, say, of survival contests between parasite species, some parasites are quite likely to develop some curious methods of adaption. Methods of insuring the food supply—animals, who must have been taking a beating.'

Seevers glanced down from the ceiling. 'Tell me, youngster, what major activity did Man invent to secure his vegetable food supply?'

'Agriculture?'

'Certainly. Man is a parasite, as far as vegetables are

concerned. But he learned to eat his cake and have it, too. He learned to perpetuate the species he was devouring. A very remarkable idea, if you stop to think about it. Very!'

'I don't see—'

'Hush! Now, let's suppose that one species of microparasites on our hypothetical planet learned, through long evolutionary processes, to stimulate regrowth in the animal tissue they devoured. Through exuding controlled amounts of growth hormone, I think. Quite an advancement, eh?'

Paul had begun leaning forward tensely.

'But it's only the first step. It let the host live longer, although not pleasantly, I imagine. The growth control would be clumsy at first. But soon, all parasite-species either learned to do it, or died out. Then came the contest for the best kind of control. The parasites who kept their hosts in the best physical condition naturally did a better job of survival—since the parasite-ascendancy had cut down on the food supply, just as Man wastes his own resources. And since animals were contending among themselves for a place in the sun, it was to the parasite's advantage to help insure the survival of his host-species—through growth control.'

Seevers winked solemnly. 'Now begins the downfall of the parasites—their decadence. They concentrated all their efforts along the lines of . . . uh . . . scientific farming, you might say. They began growing various sorts of defense and attack weapons for their hosts—weird bio-devices, perhaps. Horns, swords, fangs, stingers, poison throwers—we can only guess. But eventually, one group of parasites hit upon—what?'

Paul, who was beginning to stir uneasily, could only stammer. Where was Seevers getting all this?

'Say it!' the scientist demanded.

'The . . . nervous system?'

'That's right. You don't need to whisper it. The nervous system. It was probably an unsuccessful parasite at first, because nerve tissue grows slowly. And it's a long stretch of evolution between a microspecies which could stimulate nerve growth and one which could direct and utilize that growth for the host's advantage—and for its own. But at last, after a long struggle, our little species gets there. It begins sharpening the host's senses, building up complex senses from aggregates of old style receptors, and increasing the host's intelligence within limits.'

Seevers grinned mischievously. 'Comes a planetary shake-up of the first magnitude. Such parasites would naturally pick the host species with the highest intelligence to begin with. With the extra boost, this brainy animal quickly beats down its own enemies, and consequently the enemies of its microbenefactor. It puts itself in much the same position that Man's in on Earth —lord it over the beasts, divine right to run the place, and all that. Now understand—it's the animal who's become intelligent, not the parasites. The parasites are operating on complex instinct patterns, like a hive of bees. They're wonderful neurological engineers—like bees are good structural engineers; blind instinct, accumulated through evolution.'

He paused to light a cigarette. 'If you feel ill, young man, there's drinking water in that bottle. You look ill.'

'I'm all right!'

'Well, to continue: The intelligent animal became master of his planet. Threats to his existence were overcome—unless he was a threat to himself, like we are. But now, the parasites had found a safe home. No new threats to force readaption. They sat back and sighed and became stagnant—as unchanging as horseshoe crabs or amoeba or other Earth ancients. They kept right on working in their neurological beehives, and now they became cultivated by the animal, who recognized their benefactors. They didn't know it, but they were no longer the dominant species. They had insured their survival by leaning on their animal prop, who now took care of them with god-like charity —and selfishness. The parasites had achieved biological heaven. They kept on working, but they stopped fighting. The host was their welfare state, you might say. End of a sequence.'

He blew a long breath of smoke and leaned forward to watch Paul, with casual amusement. Paul suddenly realized that he was sitting on the edge of his chair and gaping. He forced a relaxation.

'Wild guesswork,' he breathed uncertainly.

'Some of it's guesswork,' Seevers admitted. 'But none of it's wild. There is supporting evidence. It's in the form of a message.'

'Message?'

'Sure. Come, I'll show you.' Seevers arose and moved toward the wall. He stopped before the two hemispheres. 'On second thought, you better show yourself. Take down that sliced meteorite, will you? It's sterile.'

Paul crossed the room, climbed unsteadily upon a bench, and brought down the globular meteorite. It was the first time he had examined one of the things, and he inspected it curiously. It was a near-perfect sphere, about eight inches in diameter, with a four-inch hollow in the center. The globe was made up of several concentric shells, tightly fitted, each apparently of a different metal. It was not seemingly heavier than aluminum, although the outer shell was obviously of tough steel.

'Set it face down,' Seevers told him. 'Both halves. Give it a quick little twist. The shells will come apart. Take out the center shell—the hard, thin one between the soft protecting shells.'

'How do you know their purposes?' Paul growled as he followed instructions. The shells came apart easily.

'Envelopes are to protect messages,' snorted Seevers.

Paul sorted out the hemispheres, and found two mirror-polished shells of paper-thin tough metal. They bore no inscription, either inside or out. He gave Seevers a puzzled frown.

'Handle them carefully while they're out of the protectors. They're already a little blurred . . .'

'I don't see any message.'

'There's a small bottle of iron filings in that drawer by your knee. Sift them carefully over the outside of the shells. That powder isn't fine enough, really, but it's the best I could do. Felger had some better stuff up at Princeton, before we all got out. This business wasn't my discovery, incidentally.'

Baffled, Paul found the iron filings and dusted the mirror-shells with the powder. Delicate patterns appeared—latitudinal circles, etched in iron dust and laced here and there with diagonal lines. He gasped. It looked like the map of a planet.

'I know what you're thinking,' Seevers said. 'That's what we thought too, at first. Then Felger came up with this very fine dust. Fine as they are, those lines are rows of pictograph symbols. You can make them out vaguely with a good reading glass, even with this coarse stuff. It's magnetic printing—like two-dimensional wire-recording. Evidently, the animals that printed it had either very powerful eyes, or a magnetic sense.'

'Anyone understand it?'

'Princeton staff was working on it when the world went crazy. They figured out enough to guess at what I've just told you. They found five different shell-messages among a dozen or so spheres. One of them was a sort of a key. A symbol equated to a diagram of a carbon atom. Another symbol equated to a pi in binary numbers. Things like that—about five hundred symbols, in fact. Some we couldn't figure. Then they defined other symbols by what amounted to blank-filling quizzes. Things like —"A star is . . ." and there would be the unknown symbol.

We would try to decide whether it meant "hot," "white," "huge," and so forth.'

'And you managed it?'

'In part. The ruthless way in which the missiles were opened destroyed some of the clarity. The senders were guilty of their own brand of anthropomorphism. They projected their own psychology on us. They expected us to open the things shell by shell, cautiously, and figure out the text before we went further. Heh! What happens? Some machinist grabs one, shakes it, weighs it, sticks it on a lathe, and—brrrrrr! Our curiosity is still rather apelike. Stick our arm in a gopher hole to see if there's a rattlesnake inside.'

There was a long silence while Paul stood peering over the patterns on the shell. 'Why haven't people heard about this?' he asked quietly.

'Heard about it!' Seevers roared. 'And how do you propose to tell them about it?'

Paul shook his head. It was easy to forget that Man had scurried away from his presses and his boardcasting stations and his railroads, leaving his mechanical creatures to sleep in their own rust while he fled like a bee-stung bear before the strange terror.

'What, exactly, do the patterns say, Doctor?'

'I've told you some of it—the evolutionary origin of the neuroderm parasites. We also pieced together their reasons for launching the missiles across space—several thousand years ago. Their sun was about to flare, into a supernova. They worked out a theoretical space-drive, but they couldn't fuel it —needed some element that was scarce in their system. They could get to their outer planet, but that wouldn't help much. So they just cultured up a batch of their parasite-benefactors, rolled them into these balls, and fired them like charges of buckshot at various stars. Interception-course, naturally. They meant to miss just a little, so that the projectiles would swing into long elliptical orbits around the suns—close enough in to intersect the radiational "life-belt" and eventually cross paths with planets whose orbits were near-circular. Looks like they hit us on the first pass.'

'You mean they weren't aiming at Earth in particular?'

'Evidently not. They couldn't know we were here. Not at a range like that. Hundreds of light-years. They just took a chance on several stars. Shipping off their pets was sort of a last ditch stand against extinction—symbolic, to be sure—but a noble gesture, as far as they were concerned. A giving away of part of their souls. Like a man writing his will and leaving his last worldly possession to some unknown species beyond the stars. Imagine them standing there—watching the projectiles being fired out toward deep space. There goes their inheritance, to an unknown heir, or perhaps to no one. The little creatures that brought them up from beasthood.'

Seevers paused, staring up at the sunlight beyond the high basement window. He was talking to himself again, quietly: 'You can see them turn away and silently go back . . . to wait for their collapsing sun to reach the critical point, the detonating point. They've left their last mark—a dark and uncertain benediction to the cosmos.'

'You're a fool, Seevers,' Paul grunted suddenly.

Seevers whirled, whitening. His hand darted out forgetfully toward the young man's arm, but he drew it back as Paul sidestepped.

'You actually regard this thing as desirable, don't you?' Paul asked. 'You can't see that you're under its effect. Why does it affect people that way? And you say I can't be objective.'

The professor smiled coldly. 'I didn't say it's desirable. I was simply pointing out that the beings who sent it saw it as desirable. They were making some unwarranted assumptions.'

'Maybe they just didn't care.'

'Of course they cared. Their fallacy was that we would open it as they would have done—cautiously. Perhaps they couldn't see how a creature could be both brash and intelligent. They meant for us to read the warning on the shells before we went further.'

'Warning . . . ?'

Seevers smiled bitterly. 'Yes, warning. There was one group of oversized symbols on all the spheres. See that pattern on the top ring? It says, in effect—"Finder-creatures, you who destroy your own people—if you do this thing, then destroy this container without penetrating deeper. If you are self-destroyers, then the contents will only help to destroy you."'

There was a frigid silence.

'But somebody would have opened one anyway,' Paul protested.

Seevers turned his bitter smile on the window. 'You couldn't be more right. The senders just didn't foresee our monkey-minded species. If they saw Man digging out the nuggets, braying over them, chortling over them, cracking them like walnuts, then turning tail to run howling for the forests—well, they'd think twice before they fired another round of their celestial buckshot.'

'Doctor Seevers, what do you think will happen now? To the world, I mean?'

Seevers shrugged. 'I saw a baby born yesterday—to a woman down the island. It was fully covered with neuroderm at birth. It has some new sensory equipment—small pores in the fingertips, with taste buds and olfactory cells in them. Also a nodule above each eye sensitive to infrared.'

Paul groaned.

'It's not the first case. Those things are happening to adults, too, but you have to have the condition for quite a while. Brother Thomas has the finger pores already. Hasn't learned to use them yet, of course. He gets sensations from them, but the receptors aren't connected to olfactory and taste centers of the brain. They're still linked with the somesthetic interpretive centers. He can touch various substances and get different perceptive combinations of heat, pain, cold, pressure, and so forth. He says vinegar feels ice-cold, quinine sharp-hot, cologne warm-velvet-prickly, and . . . he blushes when he touches a musky perfume.'

Paul laughed, and the hollow sound startled him.

'It may be several generations before we know all that will happen,' Seevers went on. 'I've examined sections of rat brain and found the micro-organisms. They may be working at rerouting these new receptors to proper brain areas. Our grandchildren—if Man's still on Earth by then—can perhaps taste analyze substances by touch, qualitatively determine the contents of a test tube by sticking a finger in it. See a warm radiator in a dark room—by infrared. Perhaps there'll be some ultraviolet sensitization. My rats are sensitive to it.'

Paul went to the rat cages and stared in at three gray-pelted animals that seemed larger than the others. They retreated against the back wall and watched him warily. They began squeaking and exchanging glances among themselves.

'Those are third-generation hypers,' Seevers told him. 'They've developed a simple language. Not intelligent by human standards, but crafty. They've learned to use their sensory equipment. They know when I mean to feed them, and when I mean to take one out to kill and dissect. A slight change in my emotional odor, I imagine. Learning's a big hurdle, youngster. A hyper with finger pores gets sensations from them, but it takes a long time to attach meaning to the various sensations—through learning. A baby gets visual sensations from his untrained eyes —but the sensation is utterly without significance until he associates milk with white, mother with a face shape, and so forth.'

'What will happen to the brain?' Paul breathed.

'Not too much, I imagine. I haven't observed much happening. The rats show an increase in intelligence, but not in brain size. The intellectual boost apparently comes from an ability to perceive things in terms of more senses. Ideas, concepts, precepts—are made of memory collections of past sensory experiences. An apple is red, fruity-smelling, sweet-acid flavored—that's your sensory idea of an apple. A blind man without a tongue couldn't form such a complete idea. A hyper, on the other hand, could add some new adjectives that you couldn't understand. The fully-developed hyper—I'm not one yet—has more sensory tools with which to grasp ideas. When he learns to use them, he'll be mentally more efficient. But there's apparently a hitch.

'The parasite's instinctive goal is to insure the host's survival. That's the substance of the warning. If Man has the capacity to work together, then the parasites will help him shape his environment. If Man intends to keep fighting with his fellows, the parasite will help him do a better job of that, too. Help him destroy himself more efficiently.'

'Men have worked together—'

'In small tribes,' Seevers interrupted. 'Yes, we have group spirit. Ape-tribe spirit, not race spirit.'

Paul moved restlessly toward the door. Seevers had turned to watch him with a cool smirk.

'Well, you're illuminated, youngster. Now what do you intend to do?'

Paul shook his head to scatter the confusion of ideas. 'What can anyone do? Except run. To an island, perhaps.'

Seevers hoisted a cynical eyebrow. 'Intend taking the condition with you? Or will you try to stay nonhyper?'

'Take . . . are you crazy? I mean to stay healthy!'

'That's what I thought. If you were objective about this, you'd give yourself the condition and get it over with. I did. You remind me of a monkey running away from a hypodermic needle. The hypo has serum health-insurance in it, but the needle looks sharp. The monkey chatters with fright.'

Paul stalked angrily to the door, then paused. 'There's a girl upstairs, a dermie. Would you—'

'Tell her all this? I always brief new hypers. It's one of my duties around this ecclesiastical leper ranch. She's on the verge of insanity, I suppose. They all are, before they get rid of the idea that they're damned souls. What's she to you?'

Paul strode out into the corridor without answering. He felt physically ill. He hated Seevers' smug bulldog face with a violence that was unfamiliar to him. The man had given the plague to himself! So he said. But was it true? Was any of it true? To claim that the hallucinations were new sensory phenomena, to pose the plague as possibly desirable—Seevers had no patent on those ideas. Every dermie made such claims; it was a symptom. Seevers had simply invented clever rationalizations to support his delusions, and Paul had been nearly taken in. Seevers was clever. *Do you mean to take the condition with you when you go?* Wasn't that just another way of suggesting, 'Why don't you allow me to touch you?' Paul was shivering as he returned to the third floor room to recoat himself with the pungent oil. Why not leave now? he thought.

But he spent the day wandering along the waterfront, stopping briefly at the docks to watch a crew of monks scrambling over the scaffolding that surrounded the hulls of two small sea-going vessels. The monks were caulking split seams and trotting along the platforms with buckets of tar and paint. Upon inquiry, Paul learned which of the vessels was intended for his own use. And he put aside all thoughts of immediate departure.

She was a fifty-footer, a slender craft with a weighted fin-keel that would cut too deep for bay navigation. Paul guessed that the colony wanted only a flat-bottomed vessel for hauling passengers and cargo across from the mainland. They would have little use for the trim seaster with the lines of a baby destroyer. Upon closer examination, he guessed that it had been a police boat, or Coast Guard craft. There was a gun-mounting on the forward deck, minus the gun. She was built for speed, and powered by diesels, and she could be provisioned for a nice long cruise.

Paul went to scrounge among the warehouses and locate a stock of supplies. He met an occasional monk or nun, but the gray-skinned monastics seemed only desirous of avoiding him. The dermie desire was keyed principally by smell, and the deodorant oil helped preserve him from their affections. Once he was approached by a wild-eyed layman who startled him amidst a heap of warehouse crates. The dermie was almost upon him before Paul heard the footfall. Caught without an escape route, and assailed by startled terror, he shattered the man's arm with a shotgun blast, then fled from the warehouse to escape the dermie's screams.

Choking with shame, he found a dermie monk and sent him to care for the wounded creature. Paul had shot at other plague victims when there was no escape, but never with intent to kill. The man's life had been spared only by hasty aim.

'It was self-defense,' he reminded himself.

But defense against what? Against the inevitable?

He hurried back to the hospital and found Mendelhaus outside the small chapel. 'I better not wait for your boat,' he told the priest. 'I just shot one of your people. I better leave before it happens again.'

Mendelhaus' thin lips tightened. 'You shot—'

'Didn't kill him,' Paul explained hastily. 'Broke his arm. One of the brothers is bringing him over. I'm sorry, Father, but he jumped me.'

The priest glanced aside silently, apparently wrestling against anger. 'I'm glad you told me,' he said quietly. 'I suppose you couldn't help it. But why did you leave the hospital? You're safe here. The yacht will be provisioned for you. I suggest you remain in your room until it's ready. I won't vouch for your safety any farther than the building.' There was a tone of command in his voice, and Paul nodded slowly. He started away.

'The young lady's been asking for you,' the priest called after him.

Paul stopped. 'How is she?'

'Over the crisis, I think. Infection's down. Nervous condition not so good. Deep depression. Sometimes she goes a little hysterical.' He paused, then lowered his voice. 'You're at the focus of it, young man. Sometimes she gets the idea that she touched you, and then sometimes she raves about how she wouldn't do it.'

Paul whirled angrily, forming a protest, but the priest continued: 'Seevers talked to her, and then a psychologist—one of our sisters. It seemed to help some. She's asleep now. I don't know how much of Seevers' talk she understood, however. She's dazed—combined effects of pain, shock, infection, guilt feelings, fright, hysteria—and some other things. Morphine doesn't make her mind any clearer. Neither does the fact that she thinks you're avoiding her.'

'It's the plague I'm avoiding!' Paul snapped. 'Not her.'

Mendelhaus chuckled mirthlessly. 'You're talking to me, aren't you?' He turned and entered the chapel through a swinging door. As the door fanned back and forth, Paul caught a glimpse of a candlelit altar and a stark wooden crucifix, and a sea of monk-robes flowing over the pews, waiting for the celebrant priest to enter the sanctuary and begin the Sacrifice of the Mass. He realized vaguely that it was Sunday.

Paul wandered back to the main corridor and found himself drifting toward Willie's room. The door was ajar, and he stopped short lest she see him. But after a moment he inched forward until he caught a glimpse of her dark mass of hair unfurled across the pillow. One of the sisters had combed it for her, and it spread in dark waves, gleaming in the candlelight. She was still asleep. The candle startled him for an instant —suggesting a deathbed and the sacrament of the dying. But a dog-eared magazine lay beneath it; someone had been reading to her.

He stood in the doorway, watching the slow rise of her breathing. Fresh, young, shapely—even in the crude cotton gown they had given her, even beneath the blue-white pallor of her skin—soon to become gray as a cloudy sky in a wintery twilight. Her lips moved slightly, and he backed a step away. They paused, parted moistly, showing thin white teeth. Her delicately carved face was thrown back slightly on the pillow. There was a sudden tightening of her jaw.

A weirdly pitched voice floated unexpectedly from down the hall, echoing the semisinging of Gregorian chant: *'Asperges me, Domine, hyssopo, et mundabor . . .'* The priest was beginning Mass.

As the sound came, the girl's hands clenched into rigid fists beneath the sheet. Her eyes flared open to stare wildly at the ceiling. Clutching the bedclothes, she pressed the fists up against her face and cried out: 'No! Noooo! God, I won't!'

Paul backed out of sight and pressed himself against the wall. A knot of desolation tightened in his stomach. He looked around nervously. A nun, hearing the outcry, came scurrying down the hall, murmuring anxiously to herself. A plump mother hen in a dozen yards of starched white cloth. She gave him a quick challenging glance and waddled inside.

'Child, my child, what's wrong! Nightmares again?'

He heard Willie breathe a nervous moan of relief. Then her voice, weakly— 'They . . . they made me . . . touch . . . Ooo, God! I want to cut off my hands!'

Paul fled, leaving the nun's sympathetic reassurance to fade into a murmur behind him.

He spent the rest of the day and the night in his room. On the following day, Mendelhaus came with word that the boat was not yet ready. They needed to finish caulking and stock it with provisions. But the priest assured him that it should be afloat within twenty-four hours. Paul could not bring himself to ask about the girl.

A monk brought his food—unopened cans, still steaming from the sterilizer, and on a covered tray. The monk wore gloves and mask, and he had oiled his own skin. There were moments when Paul felt as if he were the diseased and contagious patient from whom the others protected themselves. Like Omar, he thought, wondering—'which is the Potter, pray, and which the Pot?'

Was Man, as Seevers implied, a terrorized ape-tribe fleeing illogically from the gray hands that only wanted to offer a blessing? How narrow was the line dividing blessing from curse, god from demon! The parasites came in a devil's mask, the mask of disease. 'Diseases have often killed me,' said Man. 'All disease is therefore evil.' But was that necessarily true? Fire had often killed Man's club-bearing ancestors, but later came to serve him. Even diseases had been used to good advantage —artificially induced typhoid and malaria to fight venereal infections.

But the gray skin . . . taste buds in the fingertips . . . alien micro-organisms tampering with the nerves and the brain. Such concepts caused his scalp to bristle. Man—made over to suit the tastes of a bunch of supposedly beneficent parasites—was he still Man, or something else? Little bacteriological farmers imbedded in the skin, raising a crop of nerve cells—eat one, plant two, sow an olfactor in a new field, reshuffle the feeder-fibers to the brain.

Monday brought a cold rain and stiff wind from the Gulf. He watched the water swirling through littered gutters in the street. Sitting in the window, he watched the gloom and waited, praying that the storm would not delay his departure. Mendelhaus smiled politely, through his doorway once. 'Willie's ankle seems healing nicely,' he said. 'Swelling's gone down so much we had to change casts. If only she would—'

'Thanks for the free report, Padre,' Paul growled irritably.

The priest shrugged and went away.

It was still raining when the sky darkened with evening. The monastic dock-crew had certainly been unable to finish. Tomorrow . . . perhaps.

After nightfall, he lit a candle and lay awake watching its unflickering yellow tongue until drowsiness lolled his head aside. He snuffed it out and went to bed.

Dreams assailed him, tormented him, stroked him with dark hands while he lay back, submitting freely. Small hands, soft, cool, tender—touching his forehead and his cheeks, while a voice whispered caresses.

He awoke suddenly to blackness. The feel of the dream-hands was still on his face. What had aroused him? A sound in the hall, a creaking hinge? The darkness was impenetrable. The rain had stopped—perhaps its cessation had disturbed him. He felt curiously tense as he lay listening to the humid, musty corridors. A . . . faint . . . rustle . . . and . . .

Breathing! The sound of soft breathing was in the room with him!

He let out a hoarse shriek that shattered the unearthly silence. A high-pitched scream of fright answered him! From a few feet away in the room. He groped toward it and fumbled against a bare wall. He roared curses, and tried to find first matches, then the shotgun. At last he found the gun, aimed at nothing across the room, and jerked the trigger. The explosion deafened him. The window shattered, and a sift of plaster rustled to the floor.

The brief flash had illuminated the room. It was empty. He stood frozen. Had he imagined it all? But no, the visitor's startled scream had been real enough.

A cool draft fanned his face. The door was open. Had he forgotten to lock it again? A tumult of sound was beginning to arise from the lower floors. His shot had aroused the sleepers. But there was a closer sound—sobbing in the corridor, and an irregular creaking noise.

At last he found a match and rushed to the door. But the tiny flame revealed nothing within its limited aura. He heard a doorknob rattle in the distance; his visitor was escaping via the outside stairway. He thought of pursuit and vengeance. But instead, he rushed to the washbasin and began scrubbing himself thoroughly with harsh brown soap. Had his visitor touched him —or had the hands been only dream-stuff? He was frightened and sickened.

Voices were filling the corridor. The light of several candles was advancing toward his doorway. He turned to see monks' faces peering anxiously inside. Father Mendelhaus shouldered his way through the others, glanced at the window, the wall, then at Paul.

'What—'

'Safety, eh?' Paul hissed. 'Well, I had a prowler! A woman! I think I've been touched.'

The priest turned and spoke to a monk. 'Go to the stairway and call for the Mother Superior. Ask her to make an immediate inspection of the sisters' quarters. If any nuns have been out of their rooms—'

A shrill voice called from down the hallway: 'Father, Father! The girl with the injured ankle! She's not in her bed! She's gone!'

'Willie!' Paul gasped.

A small nun with a candle scurried up and panted to recover her breath for a moment. 'She's gone, Father. I was on night duty. I heard the shot, and I went to see if it disturbed her. She wasn't there!'

The priest grumbled incredulously. 'How could she get out? She can't walk with that cast.'

'Crutches, Father. We told her she could get up in a few days. While she was still irrational, she kept saying they were going to amputate her leg. We brought the crutches in to prove she'd be up soon. It's my fault, Father. I should have—'

'Never mind! Search the building for her.'

Paul dried his wet skin and faced the priest angrily. 'What can I do to disinfect myself?' he demanded.

Mendelhaus called out into the hallway where a crowd had gathered. 'Someone please get Doctor Seevers.'

'I'm here, preacher,' grunted the scientist. The monastics parted ranks to make way for his short chubby body. He grinned amusedly at Paul. 'So, you decided to make your home here after all, eh?'

Paul croaked an insult at him. 'Have you got any effective—'

'Disinfectants? Afraid not. Nitric acid will do the trick on one or two local spots. Where were you touched?'

'I don't know. I was asleep.'

Seevers' grin widened. 'Well, you can't take a bath in nitric acid. We'll try something else, but I doubt if it'll work for a direct touch.'

'That oil—'

'Uh-uh! That'll do for exposure-weakened parasites you might pick up by handling an object that's been touched. But with skin to skin contact, the bugs're pretty stout little rascals. Come on downstairs, though, we'll make a pass at it.'

Paul followed him quickly down the corridor. Behind him, a soft voice was murmuring: 'I just can't understand why nonhypers are so . . .' Mendelhaus said something to Seevers, blotting out the voice. Paul chafed at the thought that they might consider him cowardly.

But with the herds fleeing northward, cowardice was the social norm. And after a year's flight, Paul had accepted the norm as the only possible way to fight.

Seevers was emptying chemicals into a tub of water in the basement when a monk hurried in to tug at Mendelhaus' sleeve. 'Father, the sisters report that the girl's not in the building.'

'What? Well, she can't be far! Search the grounds. If she's not there, try the adjoining blocks.'

Paul stopped unbuttoning his shirt. Willie had said some mournful things about what she would rather do than submit to the craving. And her startled scream when he had cried out in the darkness—the scream of someone suddenly awakening to reality—from a dazeworld.

The monk left the room. Seevers sloshed more chemicals into the tub. Paul could hear the wind whipping about the basement windows and the growl of an angry surf not so far away. Paul rebuttoned his shirt.

'Which way's the ocean?' he asked suddenly. He backed toward the door.

'No, you fool!' roared Seevers. 'You're not going to—*get him,* preacher!'

Paul sidestepped as the priest grabbed for him. He darted outside and began running for the stairs. Mendelhaus bellowed for him to stop.

'Not me!' Paul called back angrily. 'Willie!'

Moments later, he was racing across the sodden lawn and into the street. He stopped on the corner to get his bearings. The wind brought the sound of the surf with it. He began running east and calling her name into the night.

The rain had ceased, but the pavement was wet and water gurgled in the gutters. Occasionally the moon peered through the thinning veil of clouds, but its light failed to furnish a view of the street ahead. After a minute's running, he found himself standing on the seawall. The breakers thundered a stone's throw across the sand. For a moment they became visible under the coy moon, then vanished again in blackness. He had not seen her.

'Willie!'

Only the breakers' growl responded. And a glimmer of phosphorescence from the waves.

'Willie!' He slipped down from the seawall and began feeling along the jagged rocks that lay beneath it. She could not have gotten down without falling. Then he remembered a rickety flight of steps just to the north, and he trotted quickly toward it.

The moon came out suddenly. He saw her, and stopped. She was sitting motionless on the bottom step, holding her face in her hands. The crutches were stacked neatly against the handrail. Ten yards across the sand slope lay the hungry, devouring surf. Paul approached her slowly. The moon went out again. His feet sucked at the rainsoaked sand.

He stopped by the handrail, peering at her motionless shadow. 'Willie?'

A low moan, then a long silence. 'I did it, Paul,' she muttered miserably. 'It was like a dream at first, but then . . . you shouted . . . and . . .'

He crouched in front of her, sitting on his heels. Then he took her wrists firmly and tugged her hands from her face.

'Don't . . .'

He pulled her close and kissed her. Her mouth was frightened. Then he lifted her—being cautious of the now-sodden cast. He climbed the steps and started back to the hospital. Willie, dazed and weary and still uncomprehending, fell asleep in his arms. Her hair blew about his face in the wind. It smelled warm and alive. He wondered what sensation it would produce to the finger-pore receptors. 'Wait and see,' he said to himself.

The priest met him with a growing grin when he brought her into the candlelit corridor. 'Shall we forget the boat, son?'

Paul paused. 'No . . . I'd like to borrow it anyway.'

Mendelhaus looked puzzled.

Seevers snorted at him: 'Preacher, don't you know any reasons for traveling besides running away?'

Paul carried her back to her room. He meant to have a long talk when she awoke. About an island—until the world sobered up.

DUMB WAITER

He came riding a battered bicycle down the bullet-scarred highway that wound among the hills, and he whistled a tortuous flight of the blues. Hot August sunlight glistened on his forehead and sparkled in the droplets that collected in his week's growth of blond beard. He wore faded khaki trousers and a ragged shirt, but his clothing was no shabbier than that of the other occasional travelers on the road. His eyes were half-closed against the glare of the road, and his head swayed listlessly to the rhythm of the melancholy song. Distant artillery was rumbling gloomily, and there were black flecks of smoke in the northern sky. The young cyclist watched with only casual interest.

The bombers came out of the east. The ram-jet fighters thundered upward from the outskirts of the city. They charged, spitting steel teeth and coughing rockets at the bombers. The sky snarled and slashed at itself. The bombers came on in waves, occasionally loosing an earthward trail of black smoke. The bombers leveled and opened their bays. The bays yawned down at the city. The bombers aimed. Releases clicked. No bombs fell. The bombers closed their bays and turned away to go home. The fighters followed them for a time, then returned to land. The big guns fell silent. And the sky began cleaning away the dusky smoke.

The young cyclist rode on toward the city, still whistling the blues. An occasional pedestrian had stopped to watch the battle.

'You'd think they'd learn someday,' growled a chubby man at the side of the road. 'You'd think they'd know they didn't drop anything. Don't they realize they're out of bombs?'

'They're only machines, Edward,' said a plump lady who stood beside him. 'How can they know?'

'Well, they're supposed to *think*. They're supposed to be able to learn.'

The voices faded as he left them behind. Some of the wanderers who had been walking toward the city now turned around and walked the other way. Urbanophiles looked at the city and became urbanophobes. Occasionally a wanderer who had gone all the way to the outskirts came trudging back. Occasionally a phobe stopped a phile and they talked. Usually the phile became a phobe and they both walked away together. As the young man moved on, the traffic became almost non-existent. Several travelers warned him back, but he continued stubbornly. He had come a long way. He meant to return to the city. Permanently.

He met an old lady on top of a hill. She sat in an antique chair in the center of the highway, staring north. The chair was light and fragile, of handcarved cherrywood. A knitting bag lay in the road beside her. She was muttering softly to herself: 'Crazy machines! War's over. Crazy machines! Can't quit fightin'. Somebody oughta—'

He cleared his throat softly as he pushed his bicycle up beside her. She looked at him sharply with haggard eyes, set in a seamy mask.

'Hi!' he called, grinning at her.

She studied him irritably for a moment. 'Who're you, boy?'

'Name's Mitch Laskell, Grandmaw. Hop on behind. I'll give you a ride.'

'Hm-m-! I'm going t'other way. You will too, if y'got any sense.'

Mitch shook his head firmly. 'I've been going the other way too long. I'm going back, to stay.'

'To the city? Haw! You're crazier than them machines.'

His face fell thoughtful. He kicked at the bike pedal and stared at the ground. 'You're right, Grandmaw.'

'Right?'

'Machines—they aren't crazy. It's just people.'

'Go on!' she snorted. She popped her false teeth back in her mouth and chomped them in place. She hooked withered hands on her knees and pulled herself wearily erect. She hoisted the antique chair lightly to her shoulder and shuffled slowly away toward the south.

Mitch watched her, and marveled on the tenacity of life. Then he resumed his northward journey along the trash-littered road where motor vehicles no longer moved. But the gusts of wind brought faint traffic noises from the direction of the city, and he smiled. The sound was like music, a deep-throated whisper of the city's song.

There was a man watching his approach from the next hill. He sat on an apple crate by the side of the road, and a shotgun lay casually across his knees. He was a big, red-faced man, wearing a sweat-soaked undershirt, and his eyes were narrowed to slits in the sun. He peered fixedly at the approaching cyclist, then came slowly to his feet and stood as if blocking the way.

'Hi, fellow,' he grunted.

Mitch stopped and gave him a friendly nod while he mopped his face with a kerchief. But he eyed the shotgun suspiciously.

'If this is a stick-up—'

The big man laughed. 'Naw, no heist. Just want to talk to you a minute. I'm Frank Ferris.' He offered a burly paw.

'Mitch Laskell.'

They shook hands gingerly and studied each other.

'Why you heading north, Laskell?'

'Going to the city.'

'The planes are still fighting. You know that?'

'Yeah. I know they've run out of bombs, too.'

'You know the city's still making the Geigers click?'

Mitch frowned irritably. 'What *is* this? There can't be much radioactivity left. It's been three years since they scattered the dust. I'm not corn-fed, Ferris. The half-life of that dust is five months. It should be less than one per cent—'

The big man chuckled, 'O.K., you win. But the city's not safe anyhow. The central computer's still at work.'

'So what?'

'Ever think what would happen to a city if every ordinance was kept in force after the people cleared out?'

Mitch hesitated, then nodded. 'I see. Thanks for the warning.' He started away.

Frank Ferris caught the handlebars in a big hand. 'Hold on!' he snapped. 'I ain't finished talking.'

The smaller man glanced at the shotgun and swallowed his anger. 'Maybe your audience isn't interested, Buster,' he said with quiet contempt.

'You will be. Just simmer down and listen!'

'I don't hear anything.'

Ferris glowered at him. 'I'm recruitin' for the Sugarton crowd, Laskell. We need good men.'

'Count me out. I'm a wreck.'

'Cut the cute stuff boy! This is serious. We've got two dozen men now. We need twice that many. When we get them, we'll go into the city and dynamite the computer installations. Then we can start cleaning it up.'

'Dynamite? *Why?*' Mitch Laskell's face slowly gathered angry color.

'So people can live in it, of course! So we can search for food without having a dozen mechanical cops jump us when we break into a store.'

'How much did Central cost?' Mitch asked stiffly. It was a rhetorical question.

Ferris shook his head irritably. 'What does that matter now? Money's no good anyway. You can't sell Central for junk. Heh heh! Wake up, boy!'

The cyclist swallowed hard. A jaw muscle tightened in his cheek, but his voice came calmly.

'You help build Central, Ferris? You help design her?'

'Wh-why, no! What kind of a question is that?'

'You know anything about her? What makes her work? How she's rigged to control all the subunits? You know that?'

'No, I—'

'You got any idea about how much sweat dripped on the drafting boards before they got her plans drawn? How many engineers slaved over her, and cussed her, and got drunk when their piece of the job was done?'

Ferris was sneering faintly. 'You *know*, huh?'

'Yeah.'

'Well that's all too bad, boy. But she's no good to anybody now. She's a hazard to life and limb. Why you can't go inside the city without—'

'She's a machine, Ferris. An intricate machine. You don't destroy a tool just because you're finished with it for a while.'

They glared at each other in the hot sunlight.

'Listen, boy—people built Central. People got the right to wreck her, too.'

'I don't care about rights,' Mitch snapped. 'I'm talking about what's sensible, sane. But nobody's got the right to be stupid.'

Ferris stiffened. 'Watch your tongue, smart boy.'

'I didn't ask for this conversation.'

Ferris released the handlebars. 'Get off the bicycle,' he grunted ominously.

'Why? You want to settle it the hard way?'

'No. We're requisitioning your bicycle. You can walk from

here on. The Sugarton crowd needs transportation. We need good men, but I guess you ain't one. Start walking.'

Mitch hesitated briefly. Then he shrugged and dismounted on the side away from Ferris. The big man held the shotgun cradled lazily across one forearm. He watched Mitch with a mocking grin.

Mitch grasped the handle bars tightly and suddenly rammed the front wheel between Ferris' legs. The fender made a tearing sound. The shotgun exploded skyward as the big man fell back. He sat down screaming and doubling over. The gun clattered in the road. He groped for it with a frenzied hand. Mitch kicked him in the face, and a tooth slashed at his toe through the boot leather. Ferris fell aside, his mouth spitting blood and white fragments.

Mitch retrieved the shotgun and helped himself to a dozen shells from the other's pockets then mounted the bicycle and pedaled away. When he had gone half a mile, a rifle slug spanged off the pavement beside him. Looking back, he saw three tiny figures standing beside Ferris in the distance. The 'Sugarton crowd' had come to take care of their own, no doubt. He pedaled hard to get out of range, but they wasted no more ammunition.

He realized uneasily that he might meet them again, if they came to the city intending to sabotagc Central. And Ferris wouldn't miss a chance to kill him, if the chance came. Mitch didn't believe he was really hurt, but he was badly humiliated. And for some time to come, he would dream of pleasant ways to murder Mitch Laskell.

Mitch no longer whistled as he rode along the deserted highway toward the sun-drenched skyline in the distance. To a man born and bred to the tune of mechanical thunder, amid vistas of concrete and steel, the skyline looked good—looked good even with several of the buildings twisted into ugly wreckage. It had been dusted in the radiological attack, but not badly bombed. Its defenses had been more than adequately provided for—which was understandable, since it was the capital, and the legislators had appropriated freely.

It seemed unreasonable to him that Central was still working. Why hadn't some group of engineers made their way into the main power vaults to kill the circuits temporarily? Then he remembered that the vaults were self-defending, and that there were probably very few technicians left who knew how to handle the job. Technicians had a way of inhabiting industrial regions, and wars had a way of destroying these regions. Dirt farmers usually had the best survival value.

Mitch had been working with aircraft computers before he became displaced, but a city's Central Service Co-ordinator was a far cry from a robot pilot. Centrals weren't built all at once; they grew over a period of years. At first, small units were set up in power plants and water works to automatically regulate voltages and flows and circuit conditions. Small units replaced switchboards in telephone exchanges. Small computers measured traffic-flow and regulated lights and speed-limits accordingly. Small computers handled bookkeeping where large amounts of money were exchanged. A computer checked books in and out at the library, also assessing the fines. Computers operated the city buses, and eventually drove most of the routine traffic.

That was the way the city's Central Service grew. As more computers were assigned to various tasks, engineers were hired to co-ordinate them, to link them with special circuits and to set up central 'data tanks,' so that a traffic regulator in the north end would be aware of traffic conditions in the main thoroughfares to the south. Then, when the micro-learner relay was invented, the engineers built a central unit to be used in conjunction with the central 'data tanks.' With the learning units in operation, Central was able to perform most of the city's routine tasks without attention from human supervisors.

The system had worked well. Apparently, it was still working well three years after the inhabitants had fled before the chatter of the Geiger counters. In one sense, Ferris had been right: a city whose machines carried on as if nothing had happened—that city might be a dangerous place for a lone wanderer.

But dynamite certainly wasn't the answer, Mitch thought. Most of Man's machinery was already wrecked or lying idle. Humanity had waited a hundred thousand years before deciding to build a technological civilization. If he wrecked this one completely, he might never decide to build another.

Some men thought that a return to the soil was desirable. Some men tried to pin their guilt on the machines, to lay their own stupidity on the head of a mechanical scapegoat and absolve themselves with dynamite. But Mitch Laskell was a man who liked the feel of a wrench and a soldering iron—liked it better than the feel of even the most well-balanced stone ax or wooden plow. And he liked the purr of a pint-sized nuclear engine much better than the braying of a harnessed jackass.

He was willing to kill Frank Ferris or any other man who sought to wreck what little remained. But gloom settled over him as he thought, 'If everybody decides to tear it down, what can *I* do to stop it?' For that matter, would he then be right in trying to stop it.

At sundown he came to the limits of the city, and he stopped just short of the outskirts. Three blocks away a robot cop rolled about in the center of the intersection, rolled on tricycle wheels while he directed the thin trickle of traffic with candy-striped arms and with 'eyes' that changed color like a stop-light. His body was like an oil drum, painted fire-engine red. The head, however, had been cast in a human mold, with a remarkably Irish face and a perpetual predatory smile. A short radar antenna grew from the center of his head, and the radar was his link with Central.

Mitch sat watching him with a nostalgic smile, even though he knew such cops might give him considerable trouble, once he entered the city. The 'Skaters' were incapable of winking at petty violations of ordinance.

As the daylight faded, photronic cells notified Central, and the streetlights winked promptly on. A moment later, a car without a tail light whisked by the policeman's corner. A siren wailed in the policeman's belly. He skated away in hot pursuit, charging like a mechanical bull. The car screeched to a stop. 'O'Reilley' wrote out a ticket and offered it to an empty back seat. When no one took it, the cop fed it into a slot in his belly, memorized the car's license number, and came clattering back to his intersection where the traffic had automatically begun obeying the ordinances governing nonpoliced intersections.

The cars were empty, computer-piloted. Their destinations were the same as when they had driven regular daily routes for human passengers: salesmen calling on regular customers, inspectors making their rounds, taxis prowling their assigned service-areas.

Mitch Laskell stood shivering. The city sounded sleepy but alive. The city moved and grumbled. But as far as he could see down the wide boulevard, no human figure was visible. The city was depopulated. There was a Geiger on a nearby lamp post. It clucked idly through a loudspeaker. But it indicated no danger. The city should be radiologically safe.

But after staring for a long time at the weirdly active streets, Mitch muttered, 'It'll wait for tomorrow.'

He turned onto a side road that led through a residential district just outside the city limits. Central's jurisdiction did not extend here, except for providing water and lights. He meant to spend the night in a deserted house, then enter the city at dawn.

Here and there, a light burned in one of the houses, indicating that he was not alone in his desire to return. But the pavement was scattered with rusty shrapnel, with fragments fallen from the sky battles that still continued. Even by streetlight, he could see that some of the roofs were damaged. Even though the bombers came without bombs, there was still danger from falling debris and from fire. Most former city-dwellers who were still alive preferred to remain in the country.

Once he passed a house from which music floated softly into the street, and he paused to listen. The music was scratchy—a worn record. When the piece was finished, there was a moment of silence, and the player played it again—the last record on the stack, repeating itself. Otherwise, the house was still.

Mitch frowned, sensing some kind of trouble. He wheeled the bicycle toward the curb, meaning to investigate.

'I live there,' said a woman's voice from the shadows.

She had been standing under a tree that overhung the sidewalk, and she came slowly out into the streetlight. She was a dark, slender girl with haunted eyes, and she was holding a baby in her arms.

'Why don't you turn off your record player?' he asked. 'or change to the other side?'

'My husband's in there,' she told him. 'He's listening to it. He's been listening to it for a long time. His name is George. Why don't you go say hello to him?'

Mitch felt vaguely disturbed. There was a peculiar note in the girl's quiet Spanish accent. Still, he wanted to talk to someone who had ventured into the city. He nodded and smiled at the girl.

'I'd like to.'

'You just go on in. I'll stay out here. The baby needs fresh air.'

He thanked her and strolled up on the porch. The record player stopped, tried to change, and played the same piece again. Mitch knocked once. Hearing no answer, he entered and moved along the hallway toward the light in the kitchen. But suddenly he stopped.

The house smelled musty. And it smelled of something else.

Many times he had smelled the syrup-and-stale-fish odor of death. He advanced another step toward the kitchen.

He saw a porcelain-topped table. He saw a hand lying across the table. The hand was bloated, and lying amid brown stains that also covered the forearm and sleeve. The hand had dropped a butcher knife.

Dead several days, he thought—and backed away.

He turned the record player off as he left the house. The girl was standing at the curb gazing down at his bicycle. She glanced at him amiably and spoke.

'I'm glad you turned that record off, George. A man just came by and wanted to know why you played it so often. You must have been asleep.'

Mitch started. He moistened his lips and stared at her wonderingly. 'I'm not—' He fell silent for a moment, then stuttered. 'You haven't been in the house?'

'Yes, but you were asleep in the kitchen. Did the man come talk to you?'

'Look, I'm not—' He choked and said nothing. The dark-eyed baby was eying him suspiciously. He lifted the bicycle and swung a long leg across the saddle.

'George, where are you going?'

'Just for a little ride,' he managed to gasp.

'On the man's bicycle?'

Something was twisting cruelly at his insides. He stared at the girl's wide brown eyes for a moment. And then he said it.

'Sure, it's all right. He's asleep—at the kitchen table.'

Her mouth flickered open, and for an instant sanity threatened to return. She rocked dizzily. Then after a deep breath, she straightened.

'Don't be gone too long, George.'

'I won't! Take good care of the baby.'

He pedaled away on wings of fright. For a time he cursed himself, and then he fell to cursing the husband who had taken an easy road, leaving his wife to stumble along. Mitch wondered if he should have stayed to help her. But there was nothing to be done for her, nothing at least that was in his power to do. Any gesture of help might become an irreparable blunder. At least she still had the child.

A few blocks away he found another house with an intact roof, and he prepared to spend the night. He wheeled the bicycle into the parlor and fumbled for the lights. They came on, revealing a dusty room and furniture with frayed upholstery. He made a brief tour of the house. It had been recently occupied, but there were still unopened cans in the kitchen, and still crumpled sheets on the bed. He ate a cold supper, shaved, and prepared to retire. Tomorrow would be a dangerous day.

Sleep came slowly. Sleep was full of charging ram-jets in flak-scarred skies, full of tormented masses of people that swarmed in exodus from death-sickened cities. Sleep was full of babies wailing, and women crying in choking sobs. Sleep became white arms and soft caresses.

The wailing and sobbing had stopped. It was later. Was he awake? Or still asleep? He was warm, basking in a golden glow, steeped in quiet pleasure. Something—something was there, something that breathed.

'What—!'

'*Sshhh!*' purred a quiet voice. 'Don't say anything.'

Some of the warmth fled before a sudden shiver. He opened his eyes. The room was full of blackness. He shook his head dizzily and stuttered.

'*Sshhh!*' she whispered again.

'What is this?' he gasped. 'How did you get—?'

'Be quiet, George. You'll wake the baby.'

He sank back in utter bewilderment, with winter frosts gathering along his spine.

Night was dreamlike. And dawn came, washing the shadows with grayness. He opened his eyes briefly and went back to sleep. When he opened them again, sunlight was flooding the room..

He sat up. *He was alone*. Of course! It had only been a dream.

He muttered irritably as he dressed. Then he wandered to the kitchen for breakfast.

Warm biscuits waiting in the oven! The table was set! There was a note on his plate. He read it, and slowly flushed.

There's jam in the cupboard, and I hope you like the biscuits. I know he's dead. Now I think I can go on alone. Thanks for the shotgun and the bicycle. Marta.

He bellowed a curse and charged into the parlor. The bike was gone. He darted to the bedroom. The shotgun was gone. He ran shouting to the porch, but the street was empty.

Sparrows fluttered about the eaves. The skyline of the business district lay lonesome in the morning sun. Squirrels were rustling in the branches of the trees. He looked at the weedy lawns where no children played, at the doors askew on their hinges, at a bit of aircraft wreckage jutting from the roof of a fire-gutted home—the rotting porches—the emptiness.

He rubbed his cheek ruefully. It was no world for a young mother and her baby. The baby would fit nicely in the bicycle's basket. The shotgun would offer some protection against the human wolf-packs that prowled everywhere these days.

'Little thief!' he growled half-heartedly.

But when the human animal would no longer steal to protect its offspring, then its prospects for survival would be bleak indeed. He shrugged gloomily and wandered back to the kitchen. He sat down and ate the expensive biscuits—and decided that George couldn't have cut his throat for culinary reasons. Marta was a good cook.

He entered the city on foot and unarmed, later in the morning.

He chose the alleyways, avoiding the thoroughfares, where traffic purred, and where the robot cops enforced the letter of the law. At each corner, he paused to glance in both directions against possible mechanical observers before darting across the open street to the next alley. The Geigers on the lamp posts were clicking faster as he progressed deeper into the city, and twice he paused to inspect the readings of their integrating dials. The radioactivity was not yet dangerous, but it was higher than he had anticipated. Perhaps it had been dusted again after the exodus.

He stopped to prowl through an empty house and an empty garage. He came out with a flashlight, a box of tools, and a crowbar. He had no certain plan, but tools would be needed if he meant to call a temporary halt to Central's activities. It was dangerous to enter any building however; Central would call it burglary, unless the prowler could show legitimate reason for entering. He needed some kind of identification.

After an hour's search through several houses in the residential district, he found a billfold containing a union card and a pass to several restricted buildings in the downtown area. The billfold belonged to a Willie Jesser, an air-conditioning and refrigeration mechanic for the Howard Cooler Company. He pocketed it after a moment's hesitation. It might not be enough to satisfy Central, but for the time being, it would have to do.

By early afternoon he had reached the beginning of the commercial area. Still he had seen no signs of human life. The thinly scattered traffic moved smoothly along the streets, carrying no passengers. Once he saw a group of robot climbers working high on a telephone pole. Some of the telephone cables carried the co-ordinating circuits for the city's network of computers. He detoured several blocks to avoid them, and wandered glumly on. He began to realize that he was wandering aimlessly.

The siren came suddenly from half a block away. Mitch stopped in the center of the street and glanced fearfully toward it. A robot cop was rolling toward him at twenty miles an hour! He broke into a run.

'You will halt, please!' croaked the cop's mechanical voice. 'The pedestrian with the toolbox will please halt!'

Mitch stopped at the curb. Flight was impossible. The skater could whisk along at forty miles an hour if he chose.

The cop's steel wheels screeched to a stop a yard away. The head nodded a polite but jerky greeting. Mitch stared at the creature's eyes, even though he knew the eyes were duds; the cop was seeing him by the heat waves from his bodily warmth, and touching him with a delicate aura of radar.

'You are charged with jay-walking, sir. I must present you with a summons. Your identification, please.'

Mitch nervously produced the billfold and extracted the cards. The cop accepted them in a pair of tweezerlike fingers and instantly memorized the information.

'This is insufficient identification. Have you nothing else?'

'That's all I have with me. What's wrong with it?'

'The pass and the union card expired in 1987.'

Mitch swallowed hard and said nothing. He had been afraid of this. Now he might be picked up for vagrancy.

'I shall consult Central Co-ordinator for instructions,' croaked the cop. 'One moment, please.'

A dynamotor purred softly in the policeman's cylindrical body. Then Mitch heard the faint twittering of computer code as the cop's radio spoke to Central. There was a silence lasting several seconds. Then an answer twittered back. Still the cop said nothing. But he extracted a summons form from a pad, inserted it in a slot in his chassis, and made chomping sounds like a small typesetter. When he pulled the ticket out again, it was neatly printed with a summons for Willie Jesser to appear before Traffic Court on July 29, 1989. The charge was jay-walking.

Mitch accepted it with bewilderment. 'I believe I have a right to ask for an explanation,' he muttered.

The cop nodded crisply. 'Central Service units are required to furnish explanations of decisions when such explanations are demanded.'

'Then why did Central regard my identification as sufficient?'

'Pause for translation of Central's message,' said the cop. He stood for a moment, making burring and clicking sounds. Then: 'Referring to arrest of Willie Jesser by unit Six-Baker. Do not book for investigation. Previous investigations have revealed no identification papers dated later than May 1987 in the possession of any human pedestrian. Data based on one hundred sample cases. Tentative generalization by Central Service: it has become impossible for humans to produce satisfactory identification. Therefore, "satisfactory identification" is temporarily redefined, pending instruction from authorized human legislative agency.'

Mitch nodded thoughtfully. The decision indicated that Central was still capable of 'learning,' of gathering data and making generalizations about it. But the difficulty was still apparent. She was allowed to act on such generalizations only in certain very minor matters. Although she might very well realize the situation in the city, she could do nothing about it without authority from an authorized agency. That agency was a department of the city government, currently nonexistent.

The cop croaked a courteous 'Good day, sir!' and skated smoothly back to his intersection.

Mitch stared at his summons for a moment. The date was still four days away. If he weren't out of the city by then, he might find himself in the lockup, since he had no money to pay a fine.

Reassured now that his borrowed identity gave him a certain amount of safety, he began walking along the sidewalks instead of using the alleys. Still he knew that Central was observing him through a thousand eyes. Counters on every corner were set to record the passage of pedestrian traffic, and to relay the information to Central, thus helping to avoid congestion. But Mitch *was* the pedestrian traffic. And the counters clocked his passage. Since the data was available to the logic units, Central might make some unpleasant deductions about his presence in the city.

Brazenness, he decided, was probably the safest course to steer. He stopped at the next intersection and called to another mechanical cop, requesting directions to City Hall.

But the cop paused before answering, paused to speak with Central, and Mitch suddenly regretted his question. The cop came skating slowly to the curb.

'Six blocks west and four blocks north, sir,' croaked the cop. 'Central requests the following information which you may refuse to furnish if you so desire: As a resident of the city; how is it that you do not know the way to City Hall, Mr. Jesser?'

Mitch whitened and stuttered nervously. 'Why, I've been gone three years. I . . . I had forgotten.'

The cop relayed the information, then nodded. 'Central thanks you. Data has been recorded.'

'Wait,' Mitch muttered, 'is there a direct contact with Central in City Hall?'

'Affirmative.'

'I want to speak to Central. May I use it?'

The computer code twittered briefly. 'Negative. You are not listed among the city's authorized computer personnel. Central suggests you use the Public Information Unit, also in City Hall, ground floor rotunda.'

Grumbling to himself, Mitch wandered away. The P.I.U. was better than nothing, but if he had access to the direct service contact, perhaps to some extent, he could have altered Central's rigid behavior pattern. The P.I.U. however would be well guarded.

A few minutes later he was standing in the center of the main lobby of the city hall. The great building had suffered some damage during an air raid, and one wing was charred by fire. But the rest of it was still alive with the rattle of machinery. A headless servo-secretary came rolling past him, carrying a trayful of pink envelopes. Delinquent utility bills, he guessed. Central would keep sending them out, but of course human authority would be needed to suspend service to the delinquent customers. The servo-secretary deposited the envelopes in a mailbox by the door, then rolled quickly back to its office.

Mitch looked around the gloomy rotunda. There was a desk at the far wall. Recessed in a panel behind the desk were a microphone, a loud-speaker, and the lens of a television camera. A sign hung over the desk, indicating that here was the place to complain about utility bills, garbage disposal service, taxes, and inaccurate weather forecasts. A citizen could also request any information contained in Central Data except information relating to defense or to police records.

*

Mitch crossed the rotunda and sat at the desk facing the panel. A light came on overhead. The speaker crackled for a moment.

'Your name, please?' it asked.

'Willie Jesser.'

'What do you wish from Information Service, please?'

'A direct contact with Central Data.'

'You have a screened contact with Central Data. Unauthorized personnel are not permitted an unrestricted contact, for security reasons. Your contact must be monitored by this unit.'

Mitch shrugged. It was as he had expected. Central Data was listening, and speaking, but the automatics of the P.I.U. would be censoring the exchange.

'All right,' he grumbled. 'Tell me this: Is Central aware that the city has been abandoned? That its population is gone?'

'Screening, screening, screening,' said the unit. 'Question relates to civil defense.'

'Is Central aware that her services are now interfering with human interests?'

There was a brief pause. 'Is this question in the nature of a complaint?'

'Yes,' he grated acidly. 'It's a complaint.'

'About your utility services, Mr. Jesser?'

Mitch spat an angry curse. 'About all services!' he bellowed. 'Central has got to suspend all operations until new ordinances are fed into Data.'

'That will be impossible, sir.'

'Why?'

'There is no authorization from Department of City Services.'

He slapped the desk and groaned. 'There *is* no such department now! There is no city government! The city is abandoned!'

The speaker was silent.

'Well?' he snapped.

'Screening,' said the machine.

'Listen,' he hissed. 'Are you screening what I say, or are you just blocking Central's reply?'

There was a pause. 'Your statements are being recorded in Central Data. Replies to certain questions must be blocked for security reasons.'

'The war is over!'

'Screening.'

'You're trying to maintain a civil status quo that went out of existence three years ago. Can't you use your logic units to correct for present conditions?'

'The degree of self-adjustment permitted to Central Service is limited by ordinance number—'

'Never mind!'

'Is there anything else?'

'Yes! What will you do when fifty men come marching in to dynamite the vaults and destroy Central Data?'

'Destroying city property is punishable by a fine of—'

Mitch cursed softly and listened to the voice reading the applicable ordinance.

'Well, they're planning to do it anyway,' he snapped.

'Conspiracy to destroy city property is punishable by—'

Mitch stood up and walked away in disgust. But he had taken perhaps ten steps when a pair of robot guards came skating out from their wall niches to intercept him.

'One moment, sir,' they croaked in unison.

'Well?'

'Central wishes to question you in connection with the alleged conspiracy to destroy city property. You are free to refuse. However, if you refuse, and if such a conspiracy is shown to exist, you may be charged with complicity. Will you accompany us to Interrogation?'

A step closer to jail, he thought gloomily. But what was there to lose? He grunted assent and accompanied the skaters out the entrance, down an inclined ramp, and past a group of heavily barred windows. They entered the police court, where a booking computer clicked behind its desk. Several servo-secretaries and robot cops were waiting quietly for task assignments.

Mitch stopped suddenly. His escorts waited politely.

'Will you come with us, please?'

He stood staring around at the big room—at the various doorways, one leading to traffic court, and at the iron gate to the cell block.

'I hear a woman crying,' he muttered.

The guards offered no comment.

'Is someone locked in a cell?'

'We are not permitted to answer.'

'Suppose I wanted to go bail,' he snapped. 'I have a right to know.'

'You may ask the booking desk whether a specific individual is being held. But generalized information cannot be released.'

Mitch strode to the booking computer. 'Are you holding a woman in jail?'

'Screening.'

It was only a vague suspicion, but he said, 'A woman named Marta.'

'Full name, please.'

'I don't know it. Can't you tell me?'

'Screening.'

'Listen! I loaned my bicycle to a woman named Marta. If you have the bicycle, I want it!'

'License number, please.'

'A 1987 license—number Six Zebra Five Zero.'

'Check with Lost and Found, please.'

Mitch controlled himself slowly. 'Look—*you* check. I'll wait.'

The computer paused. 'A bicycle with that license number has been impounded. Can you produce proof of ownership?'

'*Of a bicycle?* I knew the number. Isn't that enough?'

'Describe it please?'

Mitch described it wearily. He began to understand Ferris' desire to retire Central permanently and forcibly. At the moment, he longed to convert several subcomputers to scrap metal.

'Then,' said the speaker, 'if vehicle is yours, you may have it by applying for a new license and paying the required fee.'

'Refer that to Central Data,' Mitch groaned.

The booking computer paused to confer with the Coordinator. 'Decision stands, sir.'

'But there aren't any new licenses!' he growled. 'A while ago, Central said—Oh, never mind!'

'That decision applied to identification, sir. This applies to licensing of vehicles. Insufficient data has been gathered to permit generalization.'

'Sure, sure. All right, what do I do to get the girl out of jail?'

There was another conference with the Co-ordinator, then: 'She is being held for investigation. She may not be released for seventy-two hours.'

Mitch dropped the toolbox that he had been carrying since morning. With a savage curse, he rammed the crowbar through a vent in the device's front panel, and slashed it about in the opening. There was a crash of shattering glass and a shower of sparks. Mitch yelped at the electric jolt and lurched away. Steel fingers clutched his wrists.

Five minutes later he was being led through the gate to the cell blocks, charged with maliciously destroying city property; and he cursed himself for a hot-tempered fool. They would hold him until a grand jury convened, which would probably be forever.

The girl's sobbing grew louder as he was led along the iron corridors toward a cell. He passed three cells and glanced inside. The cells were occupied by dead men's bones. *Why?* The rear wall was badly cracked, and bits of loose masonry were scattered on the floor. Had they died of concussion during an attack? Or been gassed to death?

They led him to the fifth cell and unlocked the door. Mitch stared inside and grinned. The rear wall had been partially wrecked by a bomb blast, and there was room to crawl through the opening to the street. The partition that separated the adjoining cell was also damaged, and he caught a glimpse of a white, frightened face peering through the hole. Marta.

He glanced at his captors. They were pushing him gently through the door. Evidently Central's talents did not extend to bricklaying, and she could not judge that the cell was less than escapeproof.

The door clanged shut behind him.

'Marta,' he called.

Her face had disappeared from the opening. There was no answer.

'Marta.'

'Let me alone,' grumbled a muffled voice.

'I'm not angry about the bicycle.'

He walked to the hole and peered through the partition into the next cell. She crouched in a corner, peering at him with frightened, tear-reddened eyes. He glanced at the opening in the rear wall.

'Why haven't you gone outside?' he asked.

She giggled hysterically. 'Why don't you go look down?'

He stepped to the opening and glanced twenty feet down to a concrete sidewalk. He went back to stare at the girl.

'Where's your baby?'

'They took him away,' she whimpered.

Mitch frowned and thought about it for a moment. 'To the city nursery, probably—while you're in jail.'

'They won't take care of him! They'll let him die!'

'Don't scream like that. He'll be all right.'

'Robots don't give milk!'

'No, but there are such things as bottles, you know,' he chuckled.

'Are there?' Her eyes were wide with horror. 'And what will they put in the bottles?'

'Why—' He paused. Central certainly wasn't running any dairy farms.

'Wait'll they bring you a meal,' she said. 'You'll see.'

'Meal?'

'Empty tray,' she hissed. 'Empty tray, empty paper cup, paper fork, clean paper napkin. No food.'

Mitch swallowed hard. Central's logic was sometimes hard to see. The servo-attendants probably went through the motions of ladling stew from an empty pot and drawing coffee from an empty urn. Of course, there weren't any truck farmers to keep the city supplied with produce.

'So that's why . . . the bones . . . in the other cells,' he muttered.

'They'll starve us to death!'

'Don't scream so. We'll get out. All we need is something to climb down on.'

'There isn't any bedding.'

'There's our clothing. We can plait a rope. And if necessary, we can risk a jump.'

She shook her head dully and stared at her hands. 'It's no use. They'd catch us again.'

Mitch sat down to think. There was bound to be a police arsenal somewhere in the building, probably in the basement. The robot cops were always unarmed. But, of course, there had been a human organization for investigation purposes and to assume command in the event of violence. When one of the traffic units faced a threat, it could do nothing but try to handcuff the offender and call for human help. There were arms in the building somewhere, and a well-placed rifle shot could penetrate the thin sheet-steel bodies.

He deplored the thought of destroying any of the city's service machinery, but if it became necessary to wreck a few subunits, it would have to be done. He must somehow get access to the vaults where the central data tanks and the co-ordinators were located—get to them before Ferris' gang came to wreck them completely so that they might be free to pick the city clean.

An hour later, he heard the cell block gate groan open, and he arose quickly. Interrogation, he thought. They were coming to question him about the plot to wreck Central. He paused to make a hasty decision, then scrambled for the narrow opening and clambered through it into the adjoining cell while the skater came rolling down the corridor.

The girl's eyes widened. 'Wh-what are you—'

'Shhh!' he hissed. 'This might work.'

The skater halted before his cell while he crouched against the wall beyond the opening.

'Willie Jesser, please,' the robot croaked.

There was a silence. He heard the door swing open. The robot rolled around inside his cell for a few seconds, repeating his name and brushing rubble aside to make way. If only he failed to look through the opening!

Suddenly a siren growled, and the robot went tearing down the corridor again. Mitch stole a quick glance. The robot had left the door ajar. He dragged the girl to her feet and snapped, 'Let's go.'

They squeezed through the hole and raced out into the corridor. The cell-block gate was closed. The girl moaned weakly. There was no place to hide.

The door bolts were operated from remote boxes, placed in the corridor so as to be beyond the reach of the inmates. Mitch dragged the girl quickly toward another cell, opened the control panel, and threw the bolt. He closed the panel, leaving the bolt open. They slipped quickly inside the new cell, and he pulled the door quietly closed. The girl made a choking sound as she stumbled over the remains of a former inmate.

'Lie down in the corner,' he hissed, 'and keep still. They're coming back in force.'

'What if they notice the bolt is open?'

'Then we're sunk. But they'll be busy down at our end of the hall. Now shut up.'

They rolled under the steel cot and lay scarcely breathing. The robot was returning with others. The faint twitter of computer code echoed through the cell blocks. Then the skaters rushed past, and screeched to a stop before the escapees' cell. He heard them enter. He crawled to the door for a look, then pushed it open and stole outside.

He beckoned the girl to his side and whispered briefly. Then they darted down the corridor on tiptoe toward the investigators. They turned as he raced into view. He seized the bars and jerked the door shut. The bolt snapped in place as Marta tugged at the remote.

Three metal bodies crashed simultaneously against the door,

and rebounded. One of them spun around three times before recovering.

'Release the lock, please.'

Mitch grinned through the bars. 'Why don't you try the hole in the wall?'

The robot who had spun crazily away from the door now turned. He went charging across the cell floor at full acceleration —and sailed out wildly into space.

An ear-splitting crash came from the street. Shattered metal skidded across pavement. A siren wailed, and brakes shrieked. The others went to look—and began twittering.

Then they turned. 'You will surrender, please. We have summoned armed guards to seize you if you resist.'

Mitch laughed and tugged at the whimpering girl.

'Wh-where—?'

'To the gate. Come on.'

They raced swiftly along the corridor. And the gate was opening to admit the 'armed guards.' But, of course, no human bluecoats charged through. The girl muttered frightened bewilderment, and he explained on the run.

'Enforced habit pattern. Central has to do it, even when no guards are available.'

Two repair units were at work on the damaged booking computer as the escapees raced past. The repair units paused, twittered a notation to Central, then continued with their work.

Minutes later they found the arsenal, and the mechanical attendant had set out a pair of .45s for the 'armed guards.' Mitch caught one of them up and fired at the attendant's sheet-metal belly. The robot careened crazily against the wall, emitted a shower of blue sparks, and stood humming while the metal around the hole grew cherry red. There was a dull cough. The machine smoked and fell silent.

Mitch vaulted across the counter and caught a pair of submachine guns from the rack. But the girl backed away, shaking her head.

'I couldn't even use your shotgun,' she panted.

He shrugged and laid it aside. 'Carry as much ammunition as you can, then,' he barked.

Alarm bells were clanging continuously as they raced out of the arsenal, and a loud-speaker was thundering a request for all human personnel to be alert and assist in their capture. Marta was staggering against him as they burst out of the building into the street. He pushed her back against the wall and fired a burst at two skaters who raced toward them down the sidewalk. One crashed into a fire plug; the other went over the curb and fell in the street.

'To the parking lot!' he called over his shoulder.

But the girl had slumped in a heap on the sidewalk. He grumbled a curse and hurried to her side. She was semi-conscious, but her face was white and drawn. She shivered uncontrollably.

'What's wrong?' he snapped.

There was no answer. Fright had dazed her. Her lips moved, seemed to frame a soundless word: 'George.'

Muttering angrily, Mitch stuffed a fifty-round drum of ammunition in his belt, took another between his teeth, and lifted the girl over one shoulder. He turned in time to fire a one-handed burst at another skater. The burst went wide. But the skater stopped. Then the skater ran away.

He gasped, and stared after it. The blare of the loud-speaker was furnishing the answer.

'. . . All human personnel. Central patrol service has reached the limit of permissible subunit expenditure. Responsibility for capture no longer applied without further orders to expend subunits. Please instruct. Commissioner of Police, please instruct. Waiting. Waiting.'

Mitch grinned. Carrying the girl, he stumbled toward a car on the parking lot. He dumped her in the back seat and started in behind her, but a loud-speaker in the front protested.

'Unauthorized personnel. This is Mayor Sarquist's car. Unauthorized personnel. Please use an extra.'

Mitch looked around. There were no extras on the lot. And if there had been one, it would refuse to carry him unless he could identify himself as authorized to use it.

Mayor Sarquist's car began twittering a radio protest to Central. Mitch climbed inside and wrenched loose the cable that fed the antenna. The loud-speaker began barking complaints about sabotage. Mitch found a toolbox under the back seat and removed several of the pilot-computer's panels. He tugged a wire loose, and the speaker ceased complaining. He ripped at another, and a bank of tubes went dead.

He drove away, using a set of dial controls for steering. The girl in the back seat began to recover her wits. She sat up and stared out the window at the thin traffic. The sun was sinking, and the great city was immersing itself in gloom.

'You're worthless!' he growled at Marta. 'The world takes a poke at you, and you jump in your mental coffin and nail the lid shut. How do you expect to take care of your baby?'

She continued to stare gloomily out the window. She said nothing. The car screeched around a corner, narrowly missing a mechanical cop. The cop skated after them for three blocks, siren wailing; then it abandoned the chase.

'You're one of the machine-age's spoiled children,' he fumed. 'Technologists gave you everything you could possibly want. Push a button, and you get it. Instead of taking part in the machine age, you let it wait on you. You spoiled yourself. When the machine age cracks up, you crack up, too. Because you never made yourself its master; you just let yourself be mechanically pampered.'

She seemed not to hear him. He swung around another corner and pulled to the curb. They were in front of a three-storey brick building set in the center of a green-lawned block and surrounded by a high iron fence. The girl stared at it for a moment, and raised her chin slowly from her fist.

'The city orphanage!' she cried suddenly, and bounded outside. She raced across the sidewalk and beat at the iron gate with her fists.

Mitch climbed out calmly and opened it for her. She darted up toward the porch, but a servo-attendant came rolling out to intercept her. Its handcuff-hand was open to grasp her wrist.

'Drop low!' he bellowed at her.

She crouched on the walkway, then rolled quickly aside on the lawn. A burst of machine-gun fire brightened the twilight. The robot spun crazily and stopped, hissing and sputtering. Wrecking a robot could be dangerous. If a bullet struck the tiny nuclear reactor just right, there would be an explosion.

They skirted wide around it and hurried into the building. Somewhere upstairs, a baby was crying. A servo-nurse sat behind a desk in the hall, and she greeted them as if they were guests.

'Good evening, sir and madam. You wish to see one of the children?'

Marta started toward the stairs, but Mitch seized her arm. 'No! Let *me* go up. It won't be pretty.'

But she tore herself free with a snarl and bounded up the steps toward the cry of her child. Mitch shrugged to himself and waited. The robot nurse protested the illegal entry, but did nothing about it.

'Noooo—!'

A horrified shriek from the girl! He glanced up the staircase, knowing what was wrong, but unable to help her. A moment later, he heard her vomiting. He waited.

A few minutes later, she came staggering down the stairway, sobbing and clutching her baby tightly against her. She stared at Mitch with tear-drenched eyes, gave him a wild shake of her head, and babbled hysterically.

'Those cribs! They're full of little bones. Little bones—all over the floor. Little bones—'

'Shut up!' he snapped. 'Be thankful yours is all right. Now let's get out of here.'

After disposing of another robotic interferer, they reached the car, and Mitch drove rapidly toward the outskirts. The girl's sobbing ceased, and she purred a little unsung lullaby to her child, cuddling it as if it had just returned from the dead. Remorse picked dully at Mitch's heart, for having growled at her. Motherwise, she was still a good animal, despite her lack of success in adjusting to the reality of a ruptured world.

'Marta—?'

'What?'

'You're not fit to take care of yourself.'

He said it gently. She only stared at him as he piloted the car.

'You ought to find a big husky gal who wants a baby, and let her take care of it for you.'

'No.'

'It's just a suggestion. None of my business. You want your baby to live, don't you?'

'George promised he'd take care of us. George always took care of us.'

'George killed himself.'

She uttered a little whimper. 'Why did he do it? Why? I went to look for food. I came back, and there he was. Why, *why?'*

'Possibly because he was just like you. What did he do—before the war?'

'Interior decorator. He was good, a real artist.'

'Yeah.'

'Why do you say it *that* way? He *was.*'

'Was he qualified to live in a mechanical culture?'

'I don't know what you mean.'

'I mean—could he control his slice of mechanical civilization, or did it control him?'

'I don't see—'

'Was he a button-pusher and a switch-puller? Or did he care what made the buttons and switches work? Men misuse their tools because they don't understand the principles of the tools. A man who doesn't know how a watch works might try to fix it with a hammer. If the watch is communal property, he's got no right to fool with it. A nontechnologist has no right to take part in a technological civilization. He's a bull in a china shop. That's what happened to our era. Politicians were given powerful tools. They failed to understand the tools. They wrecked our culture with them.'

'You'd have a scientist in the White House?'

'If all men were given a broad technical education, there could be nothing else there, could there?'

'Technocracy—'

'No. Simply a matter of education.'

'People aren't smart enough.'

'You mean they don't *care* enough. Any man above the level of a dullard has enough sense to grasp the principles of physics and basic engineering and mechanics. They just aren't motivated to grasp them. The brain is a tool, not a garbage can for oddments of information! Your baby there—he should learn the principles of logic and semantics before he's ten. He should be taught *how to use* the tool, the brain. We've just begun to learn how to think. If the common man were trained in scientific reasoning methods, we'd solve our problems in a hurry.'

'What has this got to do with us?'

'Everything. Your George folded up because he couldn't control his slice of civilization, and he couldn't live without it. He couldn't fix the broken toy, but he suffered from its loss. And you're in the same fix. I haven't decided yet whether you're crazy or just neurotic.'

She gave him an icy stare. 'Let me know when you figure it out.'

They were leaving the city, driving out through the suburbs again into the night-shrouded residential areas. He drove by streetlight, for the car—accustomed to piloting itself by radar—had no headlights. Mitch thought gloomily that he had stalked into the city without a plan, and had accomplished nothing. He had alerted Central, and had managed to get himself classified as a criminal in the central data tanks. Instead of simplifying his task, he had made things harder for himself.

Whenever they passed a cop at an intersection, the cop retreated to the curb and called Central to inform the Co-ordinator of their position. But no attempt was made to arrest the fugitives. Having reached her limit of subunit expenditures, Central was relying on the nonexistent human police force.

'Mayor Sarquist's house,' the girl muttered suddenly.

'Huh? Where?'

'Just ahead. The big cut-stone house on the right—with part of the roof caved in.'

Mitch twisted a dial in the heart of the pilot-computer, and the car screeched to a stop at the curb. The girl lurched forward.

'You woke the baby,' she complained. 'Why stop here? We're still in the city limits.'

'I don't know,' he murmured, staring thoughtfully at the dark hulk of the two-story mansion set in a nest of oaks. 'Just sort of a hunch.'

There was a long silence while Mitch chewed his lip and frowned at the house.

'I hear a telephone ringing,' she said.

'Central calling Mayor Sarquist. You can't tell. It might have been ringing for three years.'

She was looking out the rear window. 'Mitch—?'

'Huh?'

'There's a cop at the intersection.'

He seemed not to hear her. He opened the door. 'Let's go inside. I want to look around. Bring the gun.'

They strolled slowly up the walkway toward the damaged and deserted house. The wind was breathing in the oaks, and the porch creaked loudly beneath their feet. The door was still locked. Mitch kicked the glass out of a window, and they slipped into an immense living room. He found the light.

'The cop'll hear that noise,' she muttered, glancing at the broken glass.

The noisy clatter of the steelwheeled skater answered her. The cop was coming to investigate. Mitch ignored the sound and began prowling through the house. The phone was still ringing, but he could not answer it without knowing Sarquist's personal identifying code.

The girl called suddenly from the library. 'What's this thing, Mitch?'

'What thing?' he yelled.

'Typewriter keyboard, but no type. Just a bunch of wires and a screen.'

His jaw fell agape. He trotted quickly toward the library.

'A direct channel to the data tanks!' he gasped, staring at the metal wall-panel with its encoders and the keyboard.

'What's it doing here?'

He thought about it briefly. 'Must be . . . I remember: just before the exodus, they gave Sarquist emergency powers in the defense setup. He could requisition whatever was needed for civil defense—draft workers for first aid, traffic direction, and so on. He had the power to draft anybody or anything during an air raid.'

Mitch approached the keyboard slowly. He closed the main power switch, and the tubes came alive. He sat down and typed: *Central from Sarquist; You will completely clear the ordinance section of your data tanks and await revised ordinances. The entire city code is hereby repealed.*

He waited. Nothing happened. There was no acknowledgement. The typed letters had not even appeared on the screen.

'Broken?' asked the girl.

'Maybe,' Mitch grunted. 'Maybe not. I think I know.'

The mechanical cop had lowered his retractable sprockets, climbed the porch steps, and was hammering at the door. 'Mayor Sarquist, please!' he was calling. 'Mayor Sarquist, please!'

'Let him rave,' Mitch grunted, and looked around the library.

There was a mahogany desk, several easy-chairs, a solid wall of books, and a large safe in another wall. The safe—

'Sarquist should have some rather vital papers in there,' he murmured.

'What do you want with papers?' the girl snapped. 'Why don't we get out of the city while we can?'

He glanced at her coldly. 'Like to go the rest of the way alone?'

She opened her mouth, closed it, and frowned. She was holding the tommy gun, and he saw it twitch slightly in her hand, as if reminding him that she didn't *have* to go alone.

He walked to the safe and idly spun the dial. 'Locked,' he muttered. 'It'd take a good charge of T.N.T. . . . or—'

'Or what?'

'Central.' He chuckled dryly. 'Maybe she'll do it for us.'

'Are you crazy?'

'Sure. Go unlock the door. Let the policeman in.'

'No!' she barked.

Mitch snorted impatiently. 'All right then, I'll do it. Pitch me the gun.'

'No!' She pointed it at him and backed away.

'Give me the gun!'

'No!'

She had laid the baby on the sofa where it was now sleeping peacefully. Mitch sat down beside it.

'Trust your aim?'

She caught her breath. Mitch lifted the child gently into his lap.

'Give me the gun.'

'You wouldn't!'

'I'll give the kid back to the cops.'

She whitened, and handed the weapon to him quickly. Mitch saw that the safety was on, laid the baby aside, and stood up.

'Don't look at me like that!' she said nervously.

He walked slowly toward her.

'Don't you dare *touch me!*'

He picked up a ruler from Sarquist's desk, then dived for her. A moment later she was stretched out across his lap, clawing at his legs and shrieking while he applied the ruler resoundingly. Then he dumped her on the rug, caught up the gun, and went to admit the insistent cop.

Man and machine stared at each other across the threshold. The cop radioed a visual image of Mitch to Central, and got an immediate answer.

'Request you surrender immediately, sir.'

'Am I now charged with breaking and entering?' he asked acidly.

'Affirmative.'

'You planning to arrest me?'

Again the cop consulted Central. 'If you will leave the city at once, you will be granted safe passage.'

Mitch lifted his brows. Here was a new twist. Central was doing some interpretation, some slight modification of ordinance. He grinned at the cop and shook his head.

'I locked Mayor Sarquist in the safe,' he stated evenly.

The robot consulted Central. There was a long twittering of computer code. Then it said, 'This is false information.'

'Suit yourself, tin-boy. I don't care whether you believe it or not.'

Again there was a twittering of code. Then: 'Stand aside, please.'

Mitch stepped out of the doorway. The subunit bounced over the threshold with the aid of the four-footed sprockets and clattered hurriedly toward the library. Mitch followed, grinning to himself. Despite Central's limitless 'intelligence,' she was as naive as a child.

He lounged in the doorway to watch the subunit fiddling with the dials of the safe. He motioned the girl down, and she crouched low in a corner. The tumblers clicked. There was a dull snap. The door started to swing.

'Just a minute!' Mitch barked.

The subunit paused and turned. The machine gun exploded, and the brief hail of bullets tore off the robot's antenna. Mitch lowered the gun and grinned. The cop just stood there, unable to contact Central, unable to decide. Mitch crossed the room through the drifting plaster dust and rolled the robot aside. The girl whimpered her relief, and came out of the corner.

The cop was twittering continually as it tried without success to contact the Co-ordinator. Mitch stared at it for a moment, then barked at the girl.

'Go find some tools. Search the garage, attic, basement. I want a screw driver, pliers, soldering iron, solder, whatever you can find.'

She departed silently.

Mitch cleaned out the safe and dumped the heaps of papers, money, and securities on the desk. He began sorting them out. Among the various stacks of irrelevant records, he found a copy of the original specifications for the Central Co-ordinator vaults, dating from the time of installation. He found blue-prints of the city's network of computer circuits, linking the subunits into one. His hands became excited as he shuffled through the stacks. Here was data. Here was substance for reasonable planning.

Heretofore, he had gone off half-cocked, and quite naturally had met with immediate failure. No one ever won a battle by being good, pure, or ethically right, despite Galahad's claims to the contrary. Victories were won by intelligent planning, and Mitch felt ashamed for his previous impulsiveness. To work out a scheme for redirecting Central's efforts would require time.

The girl brought a boxful of assorted small tools. She set them on the floor and sat down to glower at him.

'More cops outside now,' she said. 'Standing and waiting. The place is surrounded.'

He ignored her. Sarquist's identifying code—it had to be here somewhere.

'I tell you, we should get out of here!' she whined.

'Shut up.'

Mitch occasionally plucked a paper from the stack and laid it aside while the girl watched.

'What are those?' she asked.

'Messages he typed into the unit at various times.'

'What good are *they?*'

He showed her one of the slips of yellowed paper. It said: *Unit 67-BJ is retired for repairs*. A number was scrawled in one corner: 5.00326.

'So?'

'That number. It was his identifying code at the time.'

'You mean it's different every day?'

'More likely, it's different every minute. The code is probably based on an equation whose independent variable is *time,* and whose dependent variable is the code number.'

'How silly!'

'Not at all. It's just sort of a combination lock whose combination is continuously changing. All I've got to do is find the equation that describes the change. Then I can get to the Central Co-ordinator.'

She paced restlessly while he continued the search. Half an hour later, he put his head in his hands and gazed despondently at the desk top. The key to the code was not there.

'What's the matter?' she asked.

'Sarquist. I figured he'd have to write it down somewhere. Evidently he memorized it. Or else his secretary did. I didn't figure a politician even had sense enough to substitute numbers in a simple equation.'

The girl walked to the bookshelf and picked out a volume. She brought it to him silently. The title was *Higher Mathematics for Engineers and Physicists*.

'So I was wrong,' he grunted.

'Now what?'

He shuffled the slips of paper idly while he thought about it. 'I've got eleven code numbers here, and the corresponding times when they were good. I might be able to find it empirically.'

'I don't understand.'

'Find an equation that gives the same eleven answers for the same eleven times and use it to predict the code number for now.'

'Will it work?'

He grinned. 'There are an infinite number of equations that would give the same eleven answers for the same eleven substitutions. But it might work, if I assume that the code equation was of a simple form.'

She paced restlessly while he worked at making a graph with time as the abscissa and the code numbers for ordinates. But the points were scattered across the page, and there was no connecting them with any simple sort of curve. 'It almost has to be some kind of repeating function,' he muttered, 'something that Central could check by means of an irregular cam. The normal way for setting a code into a machine is to turn a cam by clock motor, and the height of the cam's rider is the code number for that instant.'

He tried it on polar co-ordinates, hoping to get the shape of such a cam, but the resulting shape was too irregular to be possible, and he had no way of knowing the period of the repeating function.

'That's the craziest clock I ever saw,' the girl murmured.

'What?' He looked up quickly.

'That electric wall clock. Five minutes ahead of the electric clock in the living room. But when we first came, it was twenty minutes ahead.'

'It's stopped, maybe.'

'Look at the second hand.'

The red sweep was running. Mitch stared at it for a moment, then came slowly to his feet and walked to her side. He took the small clock down from its hook and turned it over in his hands. Then he traced the cord to the wall outlet. The plug was held in place by a bracket so that it could not be removed.

The sweep hand moved slowly, it seemed. Silently he removed the screws from the case and stared inside at the works. Then he grunted surprise. 'First clock I ever saw with elliptical gears!'

'What?'

'Look at these two gears in the train. Ellipses, mounted at the foci. That's the story. For a while the clock will run faster than the other one. Then it'll run slower.' He handled it with growing excitement. 'That's *it*, Marta—the key. Central must have another clock just like this one. The amount of lead or lag—in minutes, is probably the code!'

He moved quickly to the direct contact unit. 'Tell me the time on the other clock!'

She hurried into the living room and called back, 'Ten seventeen and forty seconds . . . forty-five . . . fifty—'

The other clock was leading by five minutes and fifteen seconds. He typed 5.250 on the keyboard. Nothing happened.

'You sure that's right?' he called.

'It's now 10:10 . . . fifteen . . . twenty.'

The clock was still slowing down. He tried 5.230, but again nothing happened. The unit refused to respond. He arose with an angry grunt and began prowling around the library. 'There's something else,' he muttered. 'There must be a modifying factor. That clock's too obvious anyway. But what else could they be measuring together except time?'

'Is that another clock on his desk?'

'No, it's a barometer. It doesn't—'

He paused to grin. 'Could be! The barometric pressure-difference from the mean could easily be mechanically added or subtracted from the reading of that wacky clock. Visualize this, inside of Central: The two clock motors mounted on the same shaft, with the distance between their indicator needles as the code number. Except that the distance is modified by having a barometer rigged up to shift one of the clocks one way or the other on its axis when the pressure varies. It's simple enough.'

She shook her head. Mitch took the barometer with him to the unit. The dial was calibrated in atmospheres, and the pressure was now 1.03. Surely, he thought, for simplicity's sake, there would be no other factor involved in the code. This way, Sarquist could have glanced at his watch and the wall clock and the barometer, and could have known the code number with only a little mental arithmetic. The wall time minus the wrist time plus the barometer's reading.

He called to the girl again, and the lag was now a little over four minutes. He typed again. There was a sharp click as the relays worked. The screen came alive, fluttered with momentary phosphorescence, then revealed the numbers in glowing type.

'We've got it!' he yelled at Marta.

She came to sit down on the rug. 'I still don't see what we've got.'

'Watch!' He began typing hurriedly, and the message flashed neatly upon the screen.

CENTRAL FROM SARQUIST. CLEAR YOUR TANKS OF

ALL ORDINANCE DATA, EXCEPT ORDINANCES PERTAINING TO RECORDING OF INFORMATION IN YOUR TANKS. PREPARE TO RECORD NEW DATA.

He pressed the answer button, and the screen went blank, but the reply was slow to come.

'It won't work!' Marta snorted. 'It knows you aren't Sarquist. The subunits in the street have seen us.'

'What do you mean by "know", and what do you mean by "see"? Central isn't human.'

'It *knows* and it *sees*.'

He nodded. 'Provided you mean those words in a mechanical sense. Provided you don't imply that she *cares* what she knows and sees, except where she's required to "care" by enforced behavior-patterns—ordinances.'

Then the reply began crawling across the screen. SARQUIST FROM CENTRAL. INCONSISTENT INSTRUCTIONS. ORDINANCE 36-J, PERTAINING TO THE RECORDING OF INFORMATION, STATES THAT ORDINANCE-DATA MAY NOT BE TOTALLY VOIDED BY YOU, EXCEPT DURING RED ALERT AIR WARNING.

'See?' the girl hissed.

DEFINE THE LIMITS OF MY AUTHORITY IN PRESENT CONDITIONS, he typed. MAY I TEMPORARILY SUSPEND SPECIFIC ORDINANCES?

YOU MAY SUSPEND SPECIFIC ORDINANCES FOR CAUSE, BUT THE CAUSE MUST BE RECORDED WITH THE ORDER OF SUSPENSION.

Mitch put on a gloating grin. READ ME THE SERIES NUMBERS OF ALL LAWS IN CRIMINAL AND TRAFFIC CODES.

The reaction was immediate. Numbers began flashing on the screen in rapid sequence. 'Write these down!' he called to the girl.

A few moments later, the flashing numbers paused. WAIT, EMERGENCY INTERRUPTION, said the screen.

Mitch frowned. The girl glanced up from her notes. 'What's—'

Then it came. A dull booming roar that rattled the windows and shook the house.

'Not another raid!' she whimpered.

'It doesn't sound like—'

Letters began splashing across the screen. EMERGENCY ADVICE TO SARQUIST. MY CIVILIAN DEFENSE CO-

ORDINATOR HAS BEEN DESTROYED. MY ANTI-AIRCRAFT CO-ORDINATOR HAS BEEN DESTROYED. ADVISE, PLEASE.

'What happened?'

'Frank Ferris!' he barked suddenly. 'The Sugarton crowd —with their dynamite! They got into the city.'

CENTRAL FROM SARQUIST, he typed. WHERE ARE THE DAMAGED CO-ORDINATORS LOCATED?

UNDERGROUND VAULT AT MAP CO-ORDINATES K-81.

'Outside the city,' he breathed. 'They haven't got to the main tanks yet. We've got a little time.'

PROCEED WITH THE ORDINANCE LISTING, he commanded.

Half-an-hour later, they were finished. Then he began the long task of relisting each ordinance number and typing after it: REPEALED, CITY EVACUATED.

'I hear gunshots,' Marta interrupted. She went to the window to peer up and down the dimly lighted streets.

Mitch worked grimly. It would take them a couple of hours to get into the heart of the city, unless they knew how to capture a robot vehicle and make it serve them. But with enough men and enough guns, they would wreck subunits until Central withdrew. Then they could walk freely into the heart of the city and wreck the main co-ordinators, with a consequent cessation of all city services. Then they would be free to pillage, to make a mechanical graveyard of the city that awaited the return of Man.

'They're coming down this street, I think,' she called.

'Then turn out all the lights!' he snapped, 'and keep quiet.'

'They'll see all the cops out in the street. They'll wonder why.'

He worked frantically to get all the codes out of the machine before the Sugarton crowd came past. He was destroying its duties, its habit-patterns, its normal functions. When he was finished, it would stand helplessly by and let Ferris' gang wreak their havoc unless he could replace the voided ordinances with new, more practical ones.

'Aren't you finished yet?' she called. 'They're a couple of blocks away. The cops have quit fighting, but the men are still shooting them.'

'I'm finished now!' He began rattling the keyboard frantically.

SUPPLEMENTAL ORDINANCES: #1, THERE IS NO LIMIT OF SUBUNIT EXPENDITURE.

#2, YOU WILL NOT PHYSICALLY INJURE ANY HUMAN BEING, EXCEPT IN DEFENSE OF CENTRAL CO-ORDINATOR UNITS.

#3, ALL MECHANICAL TRAFFIC WILL BE CLEARED FROM THE STREETS IMMEDIATELY.

#4, YOU WILL DEFEND CENTRAL CO-ORDINATOR AT ALL COSTS.

#5, THE HUMAN LISTED IN YOUR MEMORY UNITS UNDER THE NAME 'WILLIE JESSER' WILL BE ALLOWED ACCESS TO CENTRAL DATA WITHOUT CHALLENGE.

#6, TO THE LIMIT OF YOUR ABILITY, YOU WILL SET YOUR OWN TASKS IN PURSUANCE OF THIS GOAL: TO KEEP THE CITY'S SERVICE INTACT AND IN GOOD REPAIR, READY FOR HUMAN USAGE.

#7, YOU WILL APPREHEND HUMANS ENGAGED IN ARSON, GRAND THEFT, OR PHYSICAL VIOLENCE, AND EJECT THEM SUMMARILY FROM THE CITY.

#8, YOU WILL OFFER YOUR SERVICE TO PROTECT THE PERSON OF WILLIE JESSER—

'They're here!' shouted the girl. 'They're coming up the walk!'

. . . AND WILL ASSIST HIM IN THE TASK OF RENOVATING THE CITY, TOGETHER WITH SUCH PERSONS WILLING TO HELP REBUILD.

The girl was shaking him. 'They're here, I tell you!'

Mitch punched a button labeled 'commit to data,' and the screen went blank. He leaned back and grinned at her. There was a sound of shouting in the street, and someone was beating at the door.

Then the skaters came rolling in a tide of sound two blocks away. The shouting died, and there were several bursts of gunfire. But the skaters came on, and the shouting grew frantic.

She muttered: 'Now we're in for it.'

But Mitch just grinned at her and lit a cigarette. Fifty men couldn't stand for long against a couple of thousand subunits who now had no expenditure limit.

He typed one last instruction into the unit. WHEN THE PLUNDERERS ARE TAKEN PRISONER, OFFER THEM THIS CHOICE: STAY AND HELP REBUILD, OR KEEP AWAY FROM THE CITY.

From now on, there weren't going to be any nonparticipators.

Mitch closed down the unit and went out to watch the waning fight.

A bigger job was ahead.

ANYBODY ELSE LIKE ME?

Quiet misery in a darkened room. The clock spoke nine times with a cold brass voice. She stood motionless, leaning against the drapes by the window, alone. The night was black, the house empty and silent.

'Come, Lisa!' she told herself. *'You're not dying!'*

She was thirty-four, still lovely, with a slender white body and a short, rich thatch of warm red hair. She had a good dependable husband, three children, and security. She had friends, hobbies, social activities. She painted mediocre pictures for her own amusement, played the piano rather well, and wrote fair poetry for the University's literary quarterly. She was well-read, well-rounded, well-informed. She loved and was loved.

Then why this quiet misery?

Wanting something, expecting nothing, she stared out into the darkness of the stone-walled garden. The night was too quiet. A distant street lamp played in the branches of the elm, and the elm threw its shadow across another wing of the house. She watched the shadow's wandering for a time. A lone car purred past in the street and was gone. A horn sounded raucously in the distance.

What was wrong? A thousand times since childhood she had felt this uneasy stirring, this crawling of the mind that called out for some unfound expression. It had been particularly strong in recent weeks.

She tried to analyze. What was different about recent weeks? Events: Frank's job had sent him on the road for a month; the children were at Mother's; the city council had recommended a bond issue; she had fired her maid; a drunk had strangled his wife; the University had opened its new psycho-physics lab; her art class had adjourned for the summer.

Nothing there. No clue to the unreasoning, goalless urge that called like a voice crying in mental wilderness: *'Come, share, satisfy, express it to the fullest!'*

Express what? Satisfy what? How?

A baby, deserted at birth and dying of starvation, would feel terrible hunger. But if it had never tasted milk, it could not know the meaning of the hunger nor how to ease it.

'I need to relate this thing to something else, to something in my own experience or in the experience of others.' She had tried to satisfy the urge with the goals of other hungers: her children, her husband's lovemaking, food, drink, art, friendship. But the craving was something else, crying for its pound of unknown flesh, and there was no fulfillment.

'How am I different from others?' she asked herself. But she was different only in the normal ways that every human being is different from the exact Average. Her intelligencc was high, short of genius, but superior. To a limited extent, she felt the call of creativity. Physically, she was delicately beautiful. The only peculiarities that she knew about seemed ridiculously irrelevant: a dark birthmark on her thigh, a soft fontanel in the top of her long narrow head, like the soft spot in an infant's cranium. Silly little differences!

One big difference: the quiet misery of the unfed hunger.

A scattering of big raindrops suddenly whispered on the walk and in the grass and through the foliage of the elm. A few drops splattered on the screen, spraying her face and arms with faint points of coolness. It had been oppressively hot. Now there was a chill breath in the night.

Reluctantly she closed the window. The oppression of the warm and empty house increased. She walked to the door opening into the walled garden.

Ready for a lonely bed, she was wearing a negligee over nothing. Vaguely, idly, her hand fumbled at the waist-knot, loosened it. The robe parted, and the fine spray of rain was delightfully cool on her skin.

The garden was dark, the shadows inky, the nearest neighbor a block away. The wall screened it from prying eyes. She brushed her hands over her shoulders; the sleeves slipped down her arms. Peeled clean, feeling like a freed animal, she pressed open the screen and stepped out under the eaves to stand on the warm stone walk.

The rain was rattling in the hedge and roaring softly all about her, splashing coldness about her slender calves. She hugged herself and stepped into it. The drench of icy fingers stroked her with pleasant lashes; she laughed and ran along the walk toward the elm. The drops stung her breasts, rivered her face, and coursed coldly down her sides and legs.

She exulted in the rain, tried to dance and laughed at herself. She ran. Then, tired, she threw herself down on the crisp wet lawn, stretching her arms and legs and rolling slowly on the grass. Eyes closed, drenched and languorous, she laughed softly and played imagining games with the rain.

The drops were steel-jacketed wasps, zipping down out of the blackness, but she melted them with her mind, made them soft and cool and caressing. The drops took impersonal liberties with her body, and she rolled demurely to lie face down in the rainsoft grass.

'I am still a pale beast,' she thought happily, *'still kin of my grandmother the ape who danced in the tree and chattered when it rained. How utterly barren life would be, if I were not a pale beast!'*

She dug her fingers into the sodden turf, bared her teeth, pressed her forehead against the ground, and growled a little animal growl. It amused her, and she laughed again. Crouching, she came up on her hands and knees, hunching low, teeth still bared. Like a cat, she hissed—and pounced upon a sleeping bird, caught it and shook it to death.

Again she lay laughing in the grass.

'If Frank were to see me like this,' she thought, *'he would put me to bed with a couple of sleeping pills, and call that smug Dr. Mensley to have a look at my mind. And Dr. Mensley would check my ambivalences and my repressions and my narcissistic, voyeuristic, masochistic impulses. He would tighten my screws and readjust me to reality, fit me into a comfortable groove, and take the pale beast out of me to make me a talking doll.'*

He had done it several times before. Thinking of Dr. Mensley, Lisa searched her vocabulary for the most savage word she could remember. She growled it aloud and felt better.

The rain was slowly subsiding. A siren was wailing in the distance. The police. She giggled and imagined a headline in tomorrow's paper: PROMINENT SOCIALITE JAILED FOR INDECENT EXPOSURE. And the story would go on: 'Mrs. Lisa Waverly was taken into custody by the police after neighbors reported that she was running around stark naked in her back yard. Said Mrs. Heinehoffer who called the law: "It was just terrible. Looked to me like she was having fits." Mr. Heinehoffer, when asked for comment, simply closed his eyes and smiled ecstatically.'

Lisa sighed wearily. The siren had gone away. The rain had stopped, except for drippings out of the elm. She was tired, emotionally spent, yet strangely melancholy. She sat up slowly in the grass and hugged her shins.

The feeling came over her gradually.

'Someone has been watching me!'

She stiffened slowly, but remained in place, letting her eyes probe about her in the shadows. If only the drippings would stop so she could listen! She peered along the hedge, and along the shadows by the garden wall, toward the dark windows of the house, up toward the low-hanging mist faintly illuminated from below by street lights. She saw nothing, heard nothing. There was no movement in the night. Yet the feeling lingered, even though she scoffed.

'If anyone is here,' she thought, *'I'll call them gently, and if anyone appears, I'll scream so loud that Mrs. Heinehoffer will hear me.'*

'Hey!' she said in a low voice, but loud enough to penetrate any of the nearby shadows.

There was no answer. She folded her arms behind her head and spoke again, quietly, sensually.

'Come and get me.'

No black monster slithered from behind the hedge to devour her. No panther sprang from the elm. No succubus congealed out of wet darkness. She giggled.

'Come have a bite.'

No bull-ape came to crush her in ravenous jaws.

She had only imagined the eyes upon her. She stretched lazily and picked herself up, pausing to brush off the leaves of grass pasted to her wet skin. It was over, the strange worship in the rain, and she was weary. She walked slowly toward the house.

Then she heard it—a faint crackling sound, intermittent, distant. She stood poised in the black shadow of the house, listening. The crackle of paper . . . then a small pop . . . then crisp fragments dropped in the street. It was repeated at short intervals.

Taking nervous, shallow breaths, she tiptoed quietly toward the stone wall of the garden. It was six feet high, but there was a concrete bench under the trellis. The sound was coming from over the wall. She stood crouching on the bench; then, hiding her face behind the vines, she lifted her head to peer.

The street lamp was half a block away, but she could see dimly. A man was standing across the street in the shadows, apparently waiting for a bus. He was eating peanuts out of a paper bag, tossing the shells in the street. That explained the crackling sound.

She glared at him balefully from behind the trellis.

'I'll claw your eyes out,' she thought, *'if you came and peeped over my wall.'*

'Hi!' the man said.

Lisa stiffened and remained motionless. It was impossible that he could see her. She was in shadow, against a dark background. Had he heard her foolish babbling a moment ago?

More likely, he had only cleared his throat.

'Hi!' he said again.

Her face was hidden in the dripping vines, and she could not move without rustling. She froze in place, staring. She could see little of him. Dark raincoat, dark hat, slender shadow. Was he looking toward her? She was desperately frightened.

Suddenly the man chucked the paper bag in the gutter, stepped off the curb, and came sauntering across the street toward the wall. He removed his hat, and crisp blond hair glinted in the distant streetlight. He stopped three yards away, smiling uncertainly at the vines.

Lisa stood trembling and frozen, staring at him in horror. Strange sensations, utterly alien, passed over her in waves. There was no describing them, no understanding them.

'I—I found you,' he stammered sheepishly. 'Do you know what it is?'

'I know you,' she thought. *'You have a small scar on the back of your neck, and a mole between your toes. Your eyes are blue, and you have an impacted wisdom tooth, and your feet are hurting you because you walked all the way out here from the University, and I'm almost old enough to be your mother. But I can't know you, because I've never seen you before!'*

'Strange, isn't it?' he said uncertainly. He was holding his hat in his hand and cocking his head politely.

'What?' she whispered.

He shuffled his feet and stared at them. 'It must be some sort of palpable biophysical energyform, analytically definable—if we had enough data. Lord knows, I'm no mystic. If it exists, it's got to be mathematically definable. But why us?'

Horrified curiosity made her step aside and lean her arms on the wall to stare down at him. He looked up bashfully, and his eyes widened slightly.

'Oh!'

'Oh what?' she demanded, putting on a terrible frown.

'You're beautiful!'

'What do you want?' she asked icily. 'Go away!'

'I—' He paused and closed his mouth slowly. He stared at her with narrowed eyes, and touched one hand to his temple as if concentrating.

For an instant, she was no longer herself. She was looking up at her own shadowy face from down in the street, looking through the eyes of a stranger who was not a stranger. She was feeling the fatigue in the weary ankles, and the nasal ache of a slight head cold, and the strange sadness in a curious heart—a sadness too akin to her own.

She rocked dizzily. It was like being in two places at once, like wearing someone else's body for a moment.

The feeling passed. *'It didn't happen!'* she told herself.

'No use denying it,' he said quietly. 'I tried to make it go away, too, but apparently we've got something unique. It would be interesting to study. Do you suppose we're related?'

'Who are you?' she choked, only half-hearing his question.

'You know my name,' he said, 'if you'll just take the trouble to think about it. Yours is Lisa—Lisa O'Brien, or Lisa Waverly—I'm never sure which. Sometimes it comes to me one way, sometimes the other.'

She swallowed hard. Her maiden name had been O'Brien.

'I don't know you,' she snapped.

His name was trying to form in her mind. She refused to allow it. The young man sighed.

'I'm Kenneth Grearly, if you really don't know.' He stepped back a pace and lifted his hat toward his head. 'I—I guess I better go. I see this disturbs you. I had hoped we could talk about it, but—well, good night, Mrs. Waverly.'

He turned and started away.

'Wait!' she called out against her will.

He stopped again. 'Yes?'

'Were—were you watching me—while it was raining?'

He opened his mouth and stared thoughtfully down the street

toward the light. 'You mean watching visually? You really are repressing this thing, aren't you? I thought you understood.' He looked at her sharply, forlornly. 'They say the failure to communicate is the basis of all tragedy. Do you suppose in our case . . . ?'

'What?'

'Nothing.' He shifted restlessly for a moment. 'Good night.'

'Good night,' she whispered many seconds after he was gone.

Her bedroom was hot and lonely, and she tossed in growing restlessness. If only Frank were home! But he would be gone for two more weeks. The children would be back on Monday, but that was three whole days away. Crazy! It was just stark raving crazy!

Had the man really existed—what was his name?—Kenneth Grearly? Or was he only a phantasm invented by a mind that was failing—her mind? Dancing naked in the rain! Calling out to shadow shapes in the brush! Talking to a specter in the street! Schizophrenic syndrome—dream-world stuff. It could not be otherwise, for unless she had invented Kenneth Grearly, how could she know he had sore feet, an impacted wisdom tooth, and a head cold. Not only did she know about those things, but she felt them!

She buried her face in the dusty pillow and sobbed. Tomorrow she would have to call Dr. Mensley.

But fearing the specter's return, she arose a few minutes later and locked all the doors in the house. When she returned to bed, she tried to pray but it was as if the prayer were being watched. Someone was listening, eavesdropping from outside.

Kenneth Grearly appeared in her dreams, stood half-shrouded in a slowly swirling fog. He stared at her with his head cocked aside, smiling slightly, holding his hat respectfully in his hands.

'Don't you realize, Mrs. Waverly, that we are mutants perhaps?' he asked politely.

'No!' she screamed. 'I'm happily married and I have three children and a place in society! Don't come near me!'

He melted slowly into the fog. But echoes came monotonously from invisible cliffs: *mutant mutant mutant mutant mutant* . . .

Dawn came, splashing pink paint across the eastern sky. The light woke her to a dry and empty consciousness, to a headachy awareness full of dull anxiety. She arose wearily and trudged to the kitchen for a pot of coffee.

Lord! Couldn't it all be only a bad dream?

In the cold light of early morning, the things of the past night looked somehow detached, unreal. She tried to analyze objectively.

That sense of sharing a mind, a consciousness, with the stranger who came out of the shadows—what crazy thing had he called it?—'*some sort of palpable biophysical energyform, analytically definable.*'

'If I invented the stranger,' she thought, *'I must have also invented the words.'*

But where had she heard such words before?

Lisa went to the telephone and thumbed through the directory. No Grearly was listed. If he existed at all, he probably lived in a rooming house. The University—last night she had thought that he had something to do with the University. She lifted the phone and dialed.

'University Station; number please,' the operator said.

'I—uh—don't know the extension number. Could you tell me if there is a Kenneth Grearly connected with the school?'

'Student or faculty, Madam?'

'I don't know.'

'Give me your number, please, and I'll call you back.'

'Lawrence 4750. Thanks, Operator.'

She sat down to wait. Almost immediately it rang again.

'Hello?'

'Mrs. Waverly, you were calling me?' A man's voice. His voice!

'The operator found you rather quickly.' It was the only thing she could think of saying.

'No, no. I knew you were calling. In fact, I hoped you into it.'

'Hoped me? Now look here, Mr. Grearly, I—'

'You were trying to explain our phenomenon in terms of insanity rather than telepathy. I didn't want you to do that, and so I hoped you into calling me.'

Lisa was coldly speechless.

'What phenomenon are you talking about?' she asked after a few dazed seconds.

'Still repressing it? Listen, I can share your mind any time I want to, now that I understand where and who you are. You might as well face the fact. And it can work both ways, if you let it. Up to now, you've been—well, keeping your mind's eye closed, so to speak.'

Her scalp was crawling. The whole thing had become intensely disgusting to her.

'I don't know what you're up to, Mr. Grearly, but I wish you'd stop it. I admit something strange is going on, but your explanation is ridiculous—offensive, even.'

He was silent for a long time, then 'I wonder if the first man-ape found his prehensile thumb ridiculous. I wonder if he thought using his hands for grasping was offensive.'

'What are you trying to say?'

'That I think we're mutants. We're not the first ones. I had this same experience when I was in Boston once. There must be one of us there, too, but suddenly I got the feeling that he had committed suicide. I never saw him. We're probably the first ones to discover each other.'

'Boston? If what you say is true, what would distance have to do with it?'

'Well, if telepathy exists, it certainly involves transfer of energy from one point to another. What *kind* of energy, I don't know. Possibly electromagnetic in character. But it seems likely that it would obey the inverse square law, like radiant energy-forms. I came to town about three weeks ago. I didn't feel you until I got close.'

'There is a connection,' she thought. She had been wondering about the increased anxiety of the past three weeks.

'I don't know what you're talking about,' she evaded icily, though. 'I'm no mutant. I don't believe in telepathy. I'm not insane. Now let me alone.'

She slammed the telephone in its cradle and started to walk away.

Evidently he was angry, for she was suddenly communicating with him again.

She reeled dizzily and clutched at the wall, because she was in two places at once, and the two settings merged in her mind to become a blur, like a double exposure. She was in her own hallway, and she was also in an office, looking at a calculator keyboard, hearing glassware rattling from across a corridor, aware of the smell of formaldehyde. There was a chart on the wall behind the desk and it was covered with strange tracery—schematics of some neural arcs. The office of the psychophysics lab. She closed her eyes, and her own hallway disappeared.

She felt anger—his anger.

'We've got to face this thing. If this is a new direction for

human evolution, then we'd better study it and see what to do about it. I knew I was different and I became a psychophysicist to find out why. I haven't been able to measure much, but now with Lisa's help . . .'

She tried to shut him out. She opened her eyes and summoned her strength and tried to force him away. She stared at the bright doorway, but the tracery of neural arcs still remained. She fought him, but his mind lingered in hers.

'. . . *perhaps we can get to the bottom of it. I know my encephalograph recordings are abnormal, and now I can check them against hers. A few correlations will help. I'm glad to know about her soft fontanel. I wondered about mine. Now I think that underneath that fontanel lies a pattern of specialized neural—*'

She sagged to the floor of the hall and babbled aloud 'Hickory Dickory Dock, the mouse ran up the clock. The clock struck one—'

Slowly he withdrew. The laboratory office faded from her vision. His thoughts left her. She lay there panting for a time.

Had she won?

No, there was no sense in claiming victory. She had not driven him away. He had withdrawn of his own volition when he felt her babbling. She knew his withdrawal was free, because she had felt his parting state of mind: sadness. He had stopped the forced contact because he pitied her, and there was a trace of contempt in the pity.

She climbed slowly to her feet, looking around wildly, touching the walls and the door-frame to reassure herself that she was still in her own home. She staggered into the parlor and sat shivering on the sofa.

Last night! That crazy running around in the rain! He was responsible for that. He had hoped her into doing it, or maybe he had just wondered what she looked like undressed, and she had subconsciously satisfied his curiosity. He had planted the suggestion—innocently, perhaps—and she had unknowingly taken the cue.

He could be with her whenever he wanted to! He had been with her while she frolicked insanely in the rain-sodden grass! Perhaps he was with her now.

Whom could she talk to? Where could she seek help? Dr. Mensley? He would immediately chalk it up as a delusion, and probably call for a sanity hearing if she wouldn't voluntarily enter a psycho-ward for observation.

The police? 'Sergeant, I want to report a telepathic prowler. A man is burglarizing my mind.'

A clergyman? He would shudder and refer her to a psychiatrist.

All roads led to the booby-hatch, it seemed. Frank wouldn't believe her. No one would believe her.

Lisa wandered through the day like a caged animal. She put on her brightest summer frock and a pert straw hat and went downtown. She wandered through the crowds in the business district, window-shopping. But she was alone. The herds of people about her brushed past and wandered on. A man whistled at her in front of a cigar store. A policeman waved her back to the curb when she started across an intersection.

'Wake up, lady!' he called irritably.

People all about her, but she could not tell them, explain to them, and so she was alone. She caught a taxi and went to visit a friend, the wife of an English teacher, and drank a glass of iced tea in the friend's parlor, and talked of small things, and admitted that she was tired when the friend suggested that she looked that way. When she went back home, the sun was sinking in the west.

She called long distance and talked to her mother, then spoke to her children, asked them if they were ready to come home, but they wanted to stay another week. They begged, and her mother begged, and she reluctantly consented. It had been a mistake to call. Now the kids would be gone even longer.

She tried to call Frank in St. Louis, but the hotel clerk reported that he had just checked out. Lisa knew this meant he was on the road again.

'Maybe I ought to go join the kids at Mother's,' she thought. But Frank had wanted her to stay home. He was expecting a registered letter from Chicago, and it was apparently important, and she had to take care of it.

'I'll invite somebody over,' she thought. But the wives were home with their husbands, and it was a social mistake to invite a couple when her husband was gone. It always wound up with two women yammering at each other while the lone male sat and glowered in uneasy isolation, occasionally disagreeing with his wife, just to let her know he was there and he was annoyed and bored and why didn't they go home? It was different if the business-widow called on a couple. Then the lone male could retire to some other part of the house to escape the yammering.

But she decided it wasn't company she wanted; she wanted help. And there was no place to get it.

When she allowed her thoughts to drift toward Kenneth Grearly, it was almost like tuning in a radio station. He was eating early dinner in the University cafeteria with a bedraggled, bespectacled brunette from the laboratory. Lisa closed her eyes and let herself sift gingerly into his thoughts. His attention was on the conversation and on the food, and he failed to realize Lisa's presence. That knowledge gave her courage.

He was eating Swiss steak and hashed brown potatoes, and the flavors formed perceptions in her mind. She heard the rattle of silverware, the low murmur of voices, and smelled the food. She marveled at it. The strange ability had apparently been brought into focus by learning what it was and how to use it.

'Our work has been too empirical,' he was saying. 'We've studied phenomena, gathered data, looked for correlations. But that method has limitations. We should try to find a way to approach psychology from below. Like the invariantive approach to physics.'

The girl shook her head. 'The nervous system is too complicated for writing theoretical equations about it. Empirical equations are the best we can do.'

'They aren't good enough, Sarah. You can predict results with them, inside the limits of their accuracy. But you can't extrapolate them very well, and they won't stack up together into a single integrated structure. And when you're investigating a new field, they no longer apply. We need a broad mathematical theory, covering all hypothetically possible neural arrangements. It would let us predict not only results, but also predict patterns of possible order.'

'Seems to me the possible patterns are infinite.'

'No, Sarah. They're limited by the nature of the building blocks—neurons, synaptic connections, and, so forth. With limited materials, you have structural limitations. You don't build skyscrapers out of modeling clay. And there is only a finite number of ways you can build atoms out of electrons, protons and neutrons. Similarly, brains are confined to the limitations of the things they're made of. We need a broad theory for defining the limits.'

'Why?'

'Because . . .' He paused. Lisa felt his urge to explain his urgency, felt him suppress it, felt for a moment his loneliness in the awareness of his uniqueness and the way it isolated him from humanity.

'You must be doing new work,' the girl offered, 'if you feel the lack of such a theoretical approach. I just can't imagine an invariantive approach to psychology—or an all-defining set of laws for it, either. Why do you need such a psychological "Relativity"?'

He hesitated, frowning down at his plate, watching a fly crawl around its rim. 'I'm interested in—in the quantitative aspects of nerve impulses. I—I suspect that there can be such a thing as neural resonance.'

She laughed politely and shook her head. 'I'll stick to my empirical data-gathering, thank you.'

Lisa felt him thinking:

'She could understand, if I could show her data. But my data are all subjective, experimental, personal. I share them with that Waverly woman, but she is only a social thinker, analytically shallow, refusing even to recognize facts. Why did it have to be her? She's flighty, emotional, and in a cultural rut. If she doesn't conform, she thinks she's nuts. But then at least she's a woman—and if this is really a mutation, we'll have to arrange for some children . . .'

Lisa gasped and sat bolt upright. Her shock revealed her presence to him, and he dropped his fork with a clatter.

'Lisa!'

She wrenched herself free of him abruptly. She angrily stalked about the house, slamming doors and muttering her rage. The nerve! The maddening, presumptuous, ill-mannered, self-centered, overly educated boor!

Arrange for some children indeed! An impossible situation!

As her anger gathered momentum, she contacted him again —like a snake striking. Thought was thunder out of a dark cloud.

'I'm decent and I'm respectable, Mr. Grearly! I have a husband and three fine children and I love them, and you can go to hell! I never want to see you again or have you prowling around my mind. Get out and STAY out. And if you ever bother me again—I'll—I'll kill you.'

He was outdoors, striding across the campus alone. She saw the gray buildings, immersed in twilight, felt the wind on his face, hated him. He was thinking nothing, letting himself follow her angry flow of thought. When she finished, his thoughts began like the passionate pleading of a poem.

He was imagining a human race with telepathic abilities, in near-perfect communication with one another. So many of the world's troubles could be traced to imperfect communication of ideas, to misunderstandings.

Then he thought briefly to Sarah—the nondescript laboratory girl he had taken to dinner—and Lisa realized he was in love with Sarah. There were sadness and resentment here. He couldn't have Sarah now, not if he were to be certain of perpetuating the mutant characteristic. The Waverly woman ought to be good for three or four children yet, before she reached middle age.

Lisa stood transfixed by shock. Then he was thinking directly to her.

'I'm sorry. You're a beautiful, intelligent woman—but I don't love you. We're not alike. But I'm stuck with you and you're stuck with me, because I've decided it's going to be that way. I can't convince you since your thinking habits are already fixed, so I won't even try. I'm sorry it has to be against your will, but in any event it has to be. And now that I know what you're like, I don't dare wait—for fear you'll do something to mess things up.'

'No!' she screamed, watching the scenery that moved past his field of vision.

He had left the campus and was walking up the street—toward her neighborhood. He was walking with the briskness of purpose. He was coming to her house.

'Call the police!' she thought, and tried to dissolve him out of her mind.

But this time he followed, clung to her thoughts, would not let her go. It was like two flashlight beams playing over a wall, one trying to escape, the other following its frantic circle of brightness.

She staggered, groped her way toward the hall, which was confused with a superimposed image of a sidewalk and a street. A phantom automobile came out of the hall wall, drove through her and vanished. Double exposures. He stared at a street light and it blinded her. At last she found the phone, but he was laughing at her.

'Eight seven six five twenty-one Mary had a little lamb seven seven sixty-seven yesterday was May March April . . .'

He was deliberately filling her mind with confusion. She

fumbled at the directory, trying to find the police, but he thought a confused jumble of numbers and symbols, and they scampered across the page, blurring the letters.

She whimpered and groped at the phone-dial, trying to get the operator, but he was doing something with his fingertips, and she couldn't get the feel of the dial.

On her third try, it finally worked.

'Information,' said a pleasant impersonal voice.

She had to get the police! She had to say—

'Pease porridge hot, pease porridge cold, pease porridge in the pot, nine days pretty polly parrot played peacefully plenti-wise pease porridge . . .'

He was jamming her speech centers with gibberish, and she blurted nonsense syllables into the mouthpiece.

'You'll have to speak more distinctly, madam. I can't understand you.'

'Poress, Policer . . .'

'The police? Just a moment.'

A series of jumbled sounds and visions clouded her mind. Then a masculine voice rumbled, 'Desk, Sergeant Harris.'

She found a clear path through the confusion and gasped, 'Three-oh-oh-three Willow Drive—'mergency—come quick—man going to—'

'Three-oh-oh-three Willow. Check. We'll have a car right over there.'

She hung up quickly—or tried to—but she couldn't find the cradle. Then her vision cleared, and she screamed. She wasn't in the hall at all!

The telephone was an eggbeater!

His voice came through her trapped panic.

'You might as well give in,' he told her with a note of sadness. *'I know how to mess you up like that, you see. And you haven't learned to retaliate yet. We're going to cooperate with this evolutionary trend, whether you like it or not—but it would be more pleasant if you agree to it.'*

'No!'

'All right, but I'm coming anyway. I hoped it wouldn't be like this. I wanted to convince you gradually. Now I know that it's impossible.'

He was still ten blocks away. She had a few minutes in which to escape. She bolted for the door. A black shadow-shape loomed up in the twilight, flung its arms wide, and emitted an apelike roar.

She yelped and darted back, fleeing frantically for the front. A boa constrictor lay coiled in the hall; it slithered toward her. She screamed again and raced toward the stairway.

She made it to the top and looked back. The living room was filling slowly with murky water. She rushed shrieking into the bedroom and bolted the door.

She smelled smoke. Her dress was on fire! The flames licked up, searing her skin.

She tore at it madly, and got it off, but her slip was afire. She ripped it away, scooped up the flaming clothing on a transom hook, opened the screen, and dropped them out the window. Flames still licked about her, and she rolled up in the bedclothing to snuff them out.

Quiet laughter.

'New syndrome,' he called to her pleasantly. *'The patient confuses someone else's fantasy with her own reality. Not schizophrenia—duophrenia, maybe?'*

She lay sobbing in hysterical desperation. He was just down the street now, coming rapidly up the walk. A car whisked slowly past. He felt her terrified despair and pitied her. The torment ceased.

She stayed there, panting for a moment, summoning spirit. He was nearing the intersection just two blocks south, and she could hear the rapid traffic with his ears.

Suddenly she clenched her eyes closed and gritted her teeth. He was stepping off the curb, walking across—

She imagined a fire engine thundering toward her like a juggernaut, rumbling and wailing. She imagined another car racing out into the intersection, with herself caught in the crossfire. She imagined a woman screaming, 'Look out, Mister!'

And then she was caught in his own responding fright, and it was easier to imagine. He was bolting for the other corner. She conjured a third car from another direction, brought it lunging at him to avoid the impending wreck. He staggered away from the phantom cars and screamed.

A real car confused the scene.

She echoed his scream. There was a moment of rending pain, and then the vision was gone. Brakes were still yowling two blocks away. Someone was running down the sidewalk. A part of her mind had heard the crashing thud. She was desperately sick.

And a sudden sense of complete aloneness told her that Grearly was dead. A siren was approaching out of the distance.

VOICES from the sidewalk: '. . . just threw a fit in the middle of the street . . . running around like crazy and hollering . . . it was a delivery truck . . . crushed his skull . . . nobody else hurt . . .'

After the street returned to normal, she arose and went to get a drink of water. But she stood staring at her sick white face in the mirror. There were crow's feet forming at the corners of her eyes, and her skin was growing tired, almost middle-aged.

It was funny that she should notice that now, at this strange moment. She had just killed a man in self-defense. And no one would believe it if she told the truth. There was no cause for guilt.

Was there?

Frank would be back soon, and everything would be the same again: peace, security, nice kids, nice home, nice husband. Just the way it always had been.

But something was already different. An emptiness. A loneliness of the mind that she had never before felt. She kept looking around to see if the lights hadn't gone dim, or the clock stopped ticking, or the faucet stopped dripping.

It was none of those things. The awful silence was within her.

Gingerly, she touched the soft spot in the top of her head and felt an utter aloneness. She closed her eyes and thought a hopeless plea to the Universe:

'Is there anybody else like me? Can anybody hear me?'

There was only complete silence, the silence of the voiceless void.

And for the first time in her life she felt the confinement of total isolation and knew it for what it was.

THE BIG HUNGER

I am blind, yet I know the road to the stars. Space is my harp, and I touch it lightly with fingers of steel. Space sings. Its music quivers in the flux patterns, comes creeping along the twitch of a positron stream, comes to whisper in glass ears. I hear. Aiee! Though I am without eyes, I see the stars tangled in their field-webs, tangled into One. I am the spider who runs over the web. I am the spider who spins, spinning a space where no stars are.

And I am Harpist to a pale, proud Master.

He builds me, and feeds me the fuel I eat, and leads me riding through the space I make, to the glare of another sun. And when he is done with me, I lie rusting in the rain. My metal rots with ages, and the sea comes washing over land to take me while I sleep. The Master forgets. The Master chips flint from a stone, leaving a stone-ax. He busies himself with drums and bloody altars; he dances with a writhing snake in his mouth, conjuring the rain.

Then—after a long time—he remembers. He builds another of me, and I am the same, for like the Soul of him who builds me, my principle lies beyond particular flesh. When my principle is clothed in steel, we go wandering again. I the minstrel, with Man the king.

Hear the song of his hunger, the song of his endless thirst.

There was a man named Abe Jolie, and he leaned against me idly with one hand in the gloom while he spoke quietly and laughed with a female of his species.

'It's finished, Junebug. We got it made,' he said.

And the girl looked her green eyes over me while the crickets sang beyond the wall, and while the shuffling of their feet echoed faintly in the great hangar.

'Finished,' she murmured. 'It's your success, Abe.'

'Mine, and a lot of others. And the government's money.'

She toyed with the lapel of his coveralls, grinned, and said, 'Let's steal it and run away.'

'*Ssshh!*' He looked around nervously, but there were no guards in sight. 'They can shoot you for less than that,' he warned. 'The S.P. doesn't have a sense of humor.'

'Abe—'

'What?'

'Kiss me.'

He kissed her.

'When is that going to be illegal, too?' she whispered.

He looked at her grimly, and she answered her own question.

'As soon as the eugenics laws are passed, Abe. Abe Jolie, who built the spacedrive, a genetic undesirable.'

'*Don't!*'

They stood there breathing quietly, and there was hate in their throats.

'Well?'

He looked around again, and whispered, 'Meet me here at eleven o'clock, Junebug.'

They parted to the sound of casual footsteps.

At eleven o'clock, a lion roared in the hangar. At eleven o'clock a steel juggernaut tore through the hangar wall and paused on a concrete ramp while bullets ricocheted off the hull. Then the first star-chariot burnt a vertical column of flame in the night. Thunder walked upward on fiery stilts, while men shouted angrily. When we were alone in the airless, star-stung, sun-torn blackness, I stroked the web of space, and listened to the muted notes. When the tune is memorized, I speak. I contradict. I refute the universe. We lived in a spaceless space beyond stars.

The man and the woman had gone. But the plan remained on Earth. My principle lingered on the drawing boards, and in the dreams of men—men who said they were sick of wars and politics and the braying of collectivist jackasses. Others were sick of petty peace and cheapness and Independence Day speeches and incorporated jackasses who blubbered disgustingly about various freedoms.

They wanted the one Big Freedom. They built me again, these pale, proud bipeds, these children of an Ape-Prince who walked like a god. They packed themselves in cylinders of steel and wandering, riding starward on a heart-tempest that had once sung them down from the trees to stalk the plains with club and torch. The pod of earth opened, scattered its seed spaceward. It was the time of the great bursting, the great birth-giving. Empires shivered in the storm.

Sky-chariots flung themselves upward to vanish beyond the fringes of the atmosphere. Prairie schooners of space bore the restless, the contemptuous, the hungry and the proud. And I led them along the self-road that runs around space. The world seethed, and empires toppled, and new empires arose whose purpose it was to build the sky-chariots.

Young men, young women, clamored at the gates of launching fields. Those who were chosen grinned expectantly at the stars. They climbed aboard in throngs and deserted Earth. They were hard laughers with red freckles and big fists. They wore slide rules at their belts like swords, and they spoke familiarly of Schwarzchild Line-Elements and Riemann-Christofel tensors. Their women were restless talkers, big women, with flashing white teeth. They teased the men, and their hands were strong and brown.

Poets came—and misfits, and saints, sinners, dirt-farmers. Engineers came and child-bearers, fighters, utopianists, and dreamers with the lights of God glowing in their starward eyes.

'Why were we taught to pray with *downcast* eyes?' they asked. 'When you pray, look starward, look to the God at the north end of the Universe.'

Man was a starward wind, a mustard seed, a wisp of Brahma's breath breathed across space.

They found two corpses in an orbit about Arcturus. The corpses were frozen and the ice was slowly sublimating into space-vapor. One of them had an Engineering Union card in his pocket. It gave his name as Abe Jolie. The other was a girl. And, because the corpse had given them the blueprints that led to space, they hauled him aboard with the girl. Somebody sang the '*Kyrie*' and somebody said, 'I am the Resurrection and the Life.' Then they cancelled out the orbital velocity and let the corpses go toppling toward Arcturus, toward a burning sun-grave where their light would shine forever.

There were those who remained behind. There were those who made Earth their business and stayed at home. Their tribes were numbered at two billion souls. And they were somehow different from the spacers. They liked to sit in their rocking chairs. They liked prettiness and a one-hundred-cent dollar. They voted for the Conservative Party. They abolished centralization. Eventually they abolished government. And for the first time in anyone's memory, there was peace on Earth, good will among men.

My Master was hungry for land. My Master sought new worlds. And we found them.

There was a yellow sun in Serpens called 27 Lambda, lying eight parsecs inward toward the galactic heartland and seven parsecs north toward the galactic pole. A lush green planet drifted at one hundred twenty megamiles from the friendly sun-star, and it awoke in the wandering biped nostalgic thoughts. We paused in space-black, we looked, we came down on tongues of lightning from the clear sky to set jet-fires in the grassy plain near a river and a forest.

Man was a seed replanted.

He wandered away from the sky-chariot and drank from a pool in the jungle. A behemoth with several legs and a parasite-rider came roaring his appetite at the pale biped. And his bones lay whitening in the sun, and his descendants learned that it was easier to stay alive by ignoring the biped from the sky.

I lay rusting in the rain. Houses of log and stone grew up on the hillsides. They crumbled slowly into ruin. A man wearing a fur robe came and built an altar at my feet. He burnt his eldest daughter on it while he sang a battle song and danced, danced a victory under strange sky.

The sons of men molded clay and chipped arrowheads and built fires. The old men told them stories of a space-going god, and the stories became their legends. They kidnaped the daughters of neighbors, knew wives, and multiplied.

A glacier came and ground me into dust. Millenniums passed, and each Prophet had his Hazar.

One of the prophets wrote an energy equation. Men crucified an Agitator on a telegraph pole. They purged a minority-group. They split a uranium atom into atoms of strontium and xenon. They wrote immortal lines deploring war while they invented better ways to wage it. They refashioned a body for my life-principle, for the tensor-transformers that constitute my soul. They mounted me again in a sky-borne prairie schooner because they were weary of sanctified braying.

There were growling columns of blue-white fire in the night, and growling voices of restless masses of men. Men darted along the road around space.

Men departed for other stars. But after a thousand years, many remained on the planet of their birth—homebodies and movie-idols and morticians, nembutal-addicts and advocates of world-government.

When the restless ones, the wild-eyed spacers were gone, the addicts got religion and the federalists became placid anarchists and the Parliaments voted themselves out of existence. There was peace of the third planet of 27 Lambda Serpentis, and good will among the inhabitants thereof. They made love and studied sociology under a friendly sun, under a pleasant blue sky forever.

On the road around space, my Master hungered for land.

And there was a yellow sun in the region of the Scorpion, and once it had been called 18 Scorpii, but now they named it Ba'Lagan. It was a little south of Serpens, a little nearer to the galactic nucleus. They named its planets Albrasa and Nynfi, and they were twins. Albrasa was already populated by a clan of hairy intellectuals with teeth and twittering voices. They liked the flavor of manflesh, digested it easily.

Man came down on sky-lightning. Man came down to walk on the land and own it. I lay quietly rusting in the rain.

Man taught his grandson to hammer virgin copper into a vicious battle-ax, and taught him the mystic recipe for roasting a hairy intellectual. It was forbidden to boil a young intellectual in the milk of its mother, but it was permissible to roast it alive and remind it that its fathers had dared to attack a two-legged god.

Man's grandson waxed strong and malicious. He committed genocide on the furry natives and used their skins for blankets. He shattered their braincases and erected his own altars in their temples. He butchered an octogenarian on one of the altars, because the old man had made the silly suggestion that they sacrifice a perfectly healthy young virgin to their god. The young virgin watched the ceremony with quietly triumphant eyes; then she married the chief priest and bore him many children.

The biped bludgeoned the planet into submission. He assured himself that he was the Chosen Child of the Most High. He built himself a throne and sat upon it—while he listened to a newscaster describe jet-battles over the North Pole. Centuries wandered by, decked in gaudy robes. And there was a war with Nynfi between the worlds.

And then another Abraham Jolie bent over his drawing board. Another crew of big-fisted men wrapped steel flesh around my principle. Another race of men spat contempt on the soil—the soil that had drunk the blood of their fathers, felt the fire of the suns as the rockets heaved skyward bearing my body and the bodies of my Master.

Men were steel-jacketed motes of flesh, scurrying among the stars. Men were as dust, rolling across the galactic prairie—bits of dandelion fluff whirling in a rising tempest that bore them along the arm of the galactic spiral and inward, ever inward. Their eyes were on Hercules and the fardistant globular clusters. He paused at Nu Lupi and 15 Sagittea and a nameless yellow sun in Ophiuchus where he met a native race who dared to be bipeds. He crushed them quickly.

There were always those who remained behind, lingered on the planets where their ancestors had fought. I watched them with my last eyes as the last ship hurtled into space. I watched, and saw the lust go out of them, saw them become as a cauldron removed from the fire. Their boiling waned to a simmer, and they cooled. They always found peace when the spacers were gone.

This I have never understood. I, the machine, the space-spider, cannot understand. But I have seen it—the exodus of the hungry, the settling of peace over those who chose to linger. The hungry drink of the emptiness of space, and their hunger grows. The placid eat of the earth, and find peace, yet somehow—they seem to die a little.

Even deeper pressed the starships, deeper into Sagittarius and Scorpius, and Lupus, Ophiuchus and Sagitta. Now and then they paused to colonize and conquer. A planet devoured a handful of men and tormented them with its biological devices. But the men grew and beat the savage planet into a slave after long ages, forced it to pay tribute to its king. Once more they coveted the stars. Once more they darted heavenward, leaving reluctant brothers in peace.

They wrote a song. They called it 'Ten Parsecs to Paradise.' They sang the song as if they believed it. This I have never understood.

It was always ten or twelve parsecs to another sun with a class G spectrum, with a planet chastely clad in green forests and white clouds. There he landed to rebuild, to furrow the fertile earth, to rock in a porch swing at twilight sucking his pipe, and to thoughtfully stare at the stars while his grandchildren romped like young chimpanzees on the cool lawn.

He had forgotten Earth—this old man—his race had forgotten its history. But he knew a little. He knew the star-going cycle

—the landing of the starships, the regression to savagery, the painful rebuilding, the cruelty, the re-learning, the proud exodus. He knew these things because Man had learned to keep a little of the past intact throughout a cycle. He no longer fell back to chipping arrowheads. Now he managed to begin again in an age of bronze or soft iron. And he knew in advance that he would carve mighty industries out of savage wilderness.

But the old man was sad as he sat on his porch. He knew so little of the Great Purpose. Why must his seed fling itself starward? He knew that it *must*—but he lacked a reason. His grandchildren played in the twilight, played space-games, although there was not yet a starship on the planet.

There was a small boy on the lawn who tried to tease the girls, but the girls put on masks of superior sophistication and ignored the little man. Disgruntled, he looked up and saw the old man dreaming on the porch.

'Gramp's got star-craze!' he shrieked. 'Look at Gramp menting! Nnyahh! Gramp's got star-craze.'

Musical laughter tittered over the lawn. Another voice took up the cry. The old man chuckled affectionately but wistfully. They were young, but they knew about the star-thirst. The planet was young, too young for star-ships, even though the priests preserved the records and scientific writings in the temples. The planet knew about space and coveted it. Yet, the children would all be dead before the first vessel was launched.

The laughter on the lawn subsided. The eldest child, a gawky and freckled girl of eight years, came trudging up the steps to sit against the post and stare at him quietly in the gloom. He felt a question lurking in her silence. He nudged her ribs affectionately with his toe.

'What weighty matter worries you, Nari?' he asked pleasantly.

'Why is star-craze, Gramp?'

He rocked thoughtfully for a moment. 'Why are there men to feel it?' he countered.

The child was silent.

'I know only what the priests say, Nari,' he told her gently. 'They say that man once owned a paradise planet, and that he ran away in search of a better one. They say he made the Lord Bion angry. And the lord hid the paradise, and condemned Man to forever wander, touched his heart with eternal hunger for the place he lost.'

'Will people find it again, Gramp?'

'Never—so the priests say. The hunger is on him, Nari.'

'It's not fair!' said the little girl.

'What isn't, my child?'

'Star-craze. Last night I saw a lady crying. She was just standing there crying at the sky.'

'Where?'

'On the street. Waiting for a motor bus.'

'How old was she?'

Nari scraped her heels and muttered doubtfully. 'It was kind of dark.'

Gramp chuckled reassuringly. 'I bet she wasn't over fourteen. I bet she was still a kid. Star-craze comes to little girls about the time they start being interested in little boys. Works the other way, too. But you grow out of it, Nari. By the time you're twenty, it won't make you miserable any more. It gives you a goal. Gives everyone a goal. Something to work for. Something to long for and fight for. The stars—you'll want to give them to your grandchildren.'

'Won't I get to go?'

'Not ever, Nari.'

They fell silent again, and the old man peered up into the deepening blackness with its countless array of suns sitting like hens on their nests of planets. He scarcely believed the legend of the lost paradise-planet, but it was a good story to tell little girls. It made him sad though, and revived a little of the forgotten restlessness of his youth. If only he could have lived two centuries later—

But then a gust of wind brought the sweet perfume of freshly cut hay from the field to the east of the farmhouse, and the odor made him smile. The field would have to be raked tomorrow, and the hay brought in to the barn. A lot of things like that needed to be done before the starships could rise again. And every straining muscle helped toward the ultimate goal. The hay fed the animals whose flesh fed the men who made the tools which built the factories which fashioned more complicated tools—and so the journey, down the long road to space again.

The old man didn't know why the road had to be traveled, nor did he really care. The road was there, and it beckoned, and it gave meaning to life, for surely the Lord Bion was less cruel a tempter than the priests sometimes proclaimed Him. Surely there was something more than despair at the end of the long, long road.

The old man grew older, and died peacefully, and his ashes

were scattered across the fields he had tilled since boyhood. His children, and his grandchildren, followed in his patient steps, and their ashes were mingled with his own before the first gleaming skycraft burst star fire in the night.

When the skycraft at last rumbled upward, the crowd thundered a triumphant roar, the crowd gathered to witness the culmination of their labors, and the labors of their ancestors. Men walked with shoulders erect and with pride glowing in their faces. Again they triumphed over forces that held them bound to a grain of sand in the sky. Again they slashed through the knot that held them in the web of the continuum, and shed the weights that dragged at their feet.

I noticed a subtle difference in those who lingered behind. They no longer lingered of their own choosing. They were no longer the peace-seekers and placid ones. They were those who could not go because they were old, or sick, or because the industries were half-deserted and there was no one left to build the ships. They still stared longingly upward on dark nights.

'We'll do it again,' they promised. 'We'll repopulate and do it again.'

But the bitterness of their plight was upon them, a sense of defeat and doom. They fought savagely among themselves. They fell in feudal wars, while the starward wave receded.

I am the acolyte of the space-priest, the server of the pale proud biped. I have taken him onward across the void, to the Hercules Cluster, and beyond it to the uncharted regions past the dust clouds of the Great Rift, into the star-pact heartland of the galactic nucleus where other races were testing their space wings and tasting of the great freedom. I have watched him, and have felt the life-aura of his longing. And I have wondered. What is his goal? Where is an answer to his hunger?

My neural circuits are not of flesh. My circuits are of glass and steel. My thought is a fanning electron stream. But I have prayed. I, the spider who builds around space, have prayed to the gods of the biped I serve. I have prayed to the God of the North End of Space. I have asked, 'Where is his peace?'

No answer came.

I have seen my Master change.

The biped was thunder across the galaxy. The biped was a swift and steel-clad spear hurtling ruthlessly onward. He made no friends; for he came as a being who owned the stars, and he took what he wanted along the way. He left his seed to grow anew. A creature of fierce pride! And fiercer longing. He trampled hatelessly such races as he encountered. He crushed them, or harnessed them to his plow, or borrowed their neural circuits for his bio-computers. Sometimes he fought against his own race, men who had traveled other routes to the galactic heartland. When man battled against man, they fought with hatred and cruelty and bitterness—but never with contempt. Man saw a rival king in man. Against other races, he waged only cool contempt and hot death.

Sometimes a thoughtful old man would say, 'Seems to me they've got as much right to live as we have. Seems to me all intelligent creatures have got a common denominator. God, maybe.' But he muttered it quietly, speculatively. Even if he believed it, he never objected to the swift ambush of the alien ship, nor to the razing of the alien city. For the biped stalked a new frontier. The ape-tribe stole across a field where danger lurked. He was fresh from the branches of the trees, not wise to the ways of the plains. How could he risk offering peace to the shaggy beast who crouched in the tall grass? He could only weigh the odds—then strike or run away.

He took the planets of the yellow suns—deep in the galactic heartland. He skipped from one to the next in jumps as long as his patience would last. He captured the globular clusters. He inhabited each planet for a few generations. He built ships, and battled with his brothers for the right to take them. Many were left behind. They repopulated after an exodus, rebuilt, launched a second flight, and a third—until those who finally remained at home were those who lacked the incentive of the big hunger.

Those who lacked incentive sought their peace. They molded a pleasant place to live in and infested it. Or else they scorned pleasantry and made themselves a battleground.

My Master is the Nomad, gaunt and tall. My Master grits his teeth in staring at the stars, and his eyes go narrow and moist. I have mirrored his hunger, have allowed his life-aura to seep into the cold steel and hot glass of me, have reflected his thoughts in my circuits. Sometimes he wonders if I am alive. But then he remembers that he built me. He built me to think, not to be alive. Perhaps I am not alive, but only a mirror that catches a little of my Master's life. I have seen him change.

The spearhead groups pushed relentlessly across the gleaming blackness, and each generation grew more restless than the one before it. The restless moved ahead. The contented remained at home. Each exodus was a separation, and a selection of the malcontent.

The biped came to believe his priests. He believed the legend of the lost home. He believed that Bion had touched him with the hunger curse. How else could they explain the pressing cry of the heart? How could they interpret the clamor of the young, the tears—except as a Divine Thirst.

The star-craze. The endless search.

There was a green planet beyond the heartland, and it was ripe for bursting its human star-seed. There was a launching field, and a ship, and teeming crowd, and a fence with guards to keep the others out. A man and a girl stood at the fence, and it was nearly dawn.

He touched her arm and gazed at the shadows on the launching site.

'We won't find it, Marka,' he said quietly. 'We'll never find it.'

'You believe the legend, Teris?' she whispered.

'The Planet of Heaven? It's up there. But we can never find it.'

'Then why must you look?'

'We are damned, Marka.'

There was a silence, then she breathed, 'It *can* be found. The Lord Bion promised—'

'Where is *that* written, Marka?' he scoffed coldly.

'In a woman's heart.'

Teris laughed loudly. 'What does the heart-writing say?'

She turned to stare at the dark shadow of the ship against the graying sky. 'It says: "When Man is content—without his lost paradise—when he reconciles himself—Bion will forgive, and show us the road home." '

He waved his hand fiercely at the fading stars in the west. '*Ours,* Marka. They're ours! We took them.'

'Do you want them?'

He stiffened angrily and glared at the shadow of her face. 'You . . . you make me sick. You're a hangbacker.'

'No!' She shook her head wildly. *'No!'* She caught at his arm as he retreated a step. 'I wish I could go! I want to go, do you hear?'

'I hear,' he snapped. 'But you can't, so there's no use talking about it. You're not well, Marka. The others wouldn't let you aboard.' He backed away another step.

'I love you,' she said frantically.

He turned and stumbled away toward the sky-chariot.

'I love you!'

He began to trot, then burst into a wild sprint. Afraid, she thought in triumph. Afraid of turning back. Of loving her too much.

'You'll never find it!' she screamed after him. *'You can't find it up there! It's here—right here!'*

But he was lost in the crowd that milled about the ship. The ship had opened its hatches. The ship was devouring the people, two at a time. The ship devoured Teris and the space crew. Then it closed its mouth and belched flame from its rockets.

She gasped and slumped against a fencepost. She hung there sobbing until a guard drove her away.

A rocket bellowed the space song. The girl tore off her wedding bracelet and flung it in the gutter. Then she went home to fix breakfast for the children.

I am the Weaver of space. I am a Merchant of new fabrics in flux patterns for five-space continua. I serve the biped who built me, though his heart be steeped in hell.

Once in space, a man looked at me and murmured softly, 'You are the cross on which we crucify ourselves.'

But the big hunger pushed him on—on toward the ends of space. And he encountered worlds where his ancestors had lived, and where his peaceful cousins still dwelt in symbiosis with their neighbors. Some of the worlds were civilized, some barbaric, and some were archaeological graveyards. My nomads, they wore haunted faces as they re-explored the fringes of the galaxy where Man had walked before, leaving his footprints and his peace-seeking children. The galaxy was filled.

Where could he go now?

I have seen the frantic despair in their faces when, upon landing, natives appeared and greeted them politely, or tried to kill them, or worshiped them, or just ran away to hide. The nomads lurked near their ships. A planet with teeming cities was no place for a wanderer. They watched the multifaceted civilizations with bitter, lonely eyes.

Where were new planets?

Across the great emptiness to the Andromeda galaxy? Too far for the ships to go. Out to the Magellanic clouds? Already visited.

Where then?

He groped blindly, this biped. He had forgotten the trail by which his ancestors had come, and he kept recrossing it, finding it winding everywhere. He could only plunge aimlessly on, and when he reached the last limit of his fuel—land. If the natives could not provide the fuel, he would have to stay, and try to pass another cycle of starward growth on the already inhabited world. But a cycle was seldom completed. The nomads intermarried with the local people; the children, the hybrid children, were less steeped in hunger than their fathers. Sometimes they built ships for economic purposes, for trade and commerce—but never for the hysterical starward sweep. They heard no music from the North End of Space, no Lorelei call from the void. The craving was slowly dying.

They came to a planet. The natives called it 'Earth.' They departed again in cold fright, and a space commander blew out his brains to banish the memory. Then they found another planet that called itself 'Earth'—and another and another. They smiled again, knowing that they would never know which was the true home of Man.

They sensed the nearness of the end.

They no longer sang the old songs of a forgotten paradise. And there were no priests among them. They looked back at the Milky Way, and it had been their royal road. They looked ahead, where only scattered stars separated them from the intergalactic wasteland—an ocean of emptiness and death. They could not consign themselves to its ultimate embrace. They had fought too long, labored too hard to surrender willingly to extinction.

But the cup of their life was broken.

And to the land's last limit they came.

They found a planet with a single moon, with green forests, with thin clouds draping her gold and blue body in the sunlight. The breath of the snowking was white on her ice caps, and her seas were placid green. They landed. They smiled when the natives called the planet 'Earth.' Lots of planets claimed the distinction of being Man's birthplace.

Among the natives there was a dumpy little professor—still human, though slightly evolved. On the night following the nomad's landing, he sat huddled in an easy-chair, staring at the gaunt nomadic giant whose bald head nearly touched the ceiling of the professor's library. The professor slowly shook his head and sighed.

'I can't understand you people.'

'Nor I you,' rumbled the nomad.

'Here is Earth—yet you won't believe it!'

The giant snorted contemptuously. 'Who cares? Is this crumb in space the fulfillment of a dream?'

'You dreamed of a lost Earthparadise.'

'So we thought. But who knows the real longing of a dream? Where is its end? Its goal?'

'We found ours here on Earth.'

The giant made a wry mouth. 'You've found nothing but your own smug existence. You're a snake swallowing its tail.'

'Are you sure you're not the same?' purred the scholar.

The giant put his fists on his hips and glowered at him. The professor whitened.

'That's untrue,' boomed the giant. 'We've found nothing. And we're through. At least we went searching. Now we're finished.'

'Not *you*. It's the *job* that's finished. You can live here. And be proud of a job well done.'

The giant frowned. 'Job? *What* job?'

'Why, fencing in the stars. Populating the galaxy.'

The big man stared at him in horrified amazement.

'Well,' the scholar insisted, 'you did it, you know. Who populates the galaxy now?'

'People like you.'

The impact of the searing words brought a sick gasp from the small professor. He was a long moment in realizing their full significance. He wilted. He sank lower in the chair.

The nomad's laughter suddenly rocked the room. He turned away from his victim and helped himself to a tumbler of liqueur. He downed it at a gulp and grinned at the professor. He tucked the professor's liqueur under his arm, waved a jaunty farewell, and lumbered out into the night.

'My decanter,' protested the professor in a whisper.

He went to bed and lay whimpering slightly in drowsiness. He was afraid of the tomorrows that lay ahead.

The nomads settled on the planet for lack of fuel. They complained of the climate and steadfastly refused to believe that it was Earth. They were a troublesome, boisterous lot, and frequently needed psychoanalysis for their various crimes. A provisional government was set up to deal with the problem. The natives had forgotten about governments, and they called it a 'welfare commission.'

The nomads who were single kidnaped native wives. Sometimes they kidnaped several, being a prolific lot. They begot many children, and a third-generation hybrid became the first dictator of a northern continent.

I am rusting in the rain. I shall never serve my priest here on Earth again. Nuclear fuels are scarce. They are needed for the atomic warheads now zipping back and forth across the North Pole. A poet—one of the hybrids—has written immortal lines deploring war; and the lines were inscribed on the posthumous medal they gave his widow.

Three dumpy idealists built a spaceship, but they were caught and hung for treason. The eight-foot lawyer who defended them was also hung.

The world wears a long face; and the stars twinkle invitingly. But few men look upward now. Things are probably just as bad on the next inhabited planet.

I am the spider who walked around space. I, Harpist for a pale proud Master, have seen the big hunger, have tasted its red glow reflected in my circuits. Still I cannot understand.

But I feel there are some who understand. I have seen the pride in their faces. They walk like kings.

EARTH ABIDES by GEORGE R. STEWART

Earth Abides is one of the few SF novels to break the barriers of SF readership and reach a huge and universal audience. Winner of the International Fantasy Award and First Choice of the Science Fiction Book Club, it tells of the death of civilisation and of the brave new race that emerges-stronger, self-reliant, primitive ... It is the story of Isherwood Williams and a small handful like him, who rise from the ashes of a destroyed world and begin again ...

0 552 11194 5 – £1.00

A CANTICLE FOR LEIBOWITZ by WALTER M. MILLER JR.

A Canticle For Leibowitz is one of the great legendary novels of SF. It begins twelve hundred years after the Fallout. The darkest of dark ages has passed and human intelligence has been reborn. And in a monastery cell the monks and novices of the Blessed Order of Leibowitz pore over the records left by the Saint – then, fearfully, tentatively, they begin to experiment with electric light . . .

TONGUES OF THE MOON by PHILIP JOSE FARMER

Man has colonized the planets, and lost his birthright. Civilization was a lonely chain of space stations linked by terror.

The Empire kept the pioneers enslaved with a weapon that shattered any protest into screaming insanity.

All they had left was the dream of someday returning home. Until their dream exploded in the holocaust that destroyed the Earth.

But the embers of their dead planet sparked a brain-blasting revolution that swept the galaxy. A revolution of exiles in an alien universe – with nothing left to lose ...

0 552 11821 4 – £1.00